A Blackened Heart, A Blackened Soul

John Ward

Crystal Lake Publishing

WELCOME
TO ANOTHER

CRYSTAL LAKE PUBLISHING
CREATION

Praise For A Blackened Heart, A Blackened Soul

"John Ward conjures a mercilessly bleak and brutal knife-wound of a narrative."—**Nick Roberts, author of The *Exorcist's House* and *Mean Spirited***

"A sweeping, harrowing tale of oppression and possession that follows a seemingly cursed character from childhood through his adult life as damn near everyone around him is overcome by evil forces. It's like Annabelle, Insidious, *and* The Exorcist *all trying to one-up each other."*—**Ben Young, author of *Stuck* and *Home***

"Scary as Hell. If Blatty and Wan spawned a monstrous book baby, John Ward just unleashed that literary demon upon the world."—**Leigh Kenny, author of *Cursed* and *Hush, My Darling***

"A Blackened Heart, A Blackened Soul *is an unrelenting horror novel following our tragedy-stricken protagonist from childhood into adulthood. The terrors that reside in these pages will effortlessly fester their way into the corners of your mind and under the surface of your skin, not only because John Ward is an incredible storyteller, but because they're coming from a place of genuine fear. This is grief and possession horror at its finest."*—**Paul Avery Tindol, author of *This House Will Never Be Warm* and *Hunting Snipe***

"A Blackened Heart, A Blackened Soul *deftly balances horror and emotion, faith and doubt, and - above all else - struggle in the face of the bleakest of circumstances with the immeasurable strength of the human condition. In a time when Hollywood has 'done demons to death,' this novel is a ghastly hand emerging from the grave to drag us down with it."*—**William F. Gray, author of *The Devil Within Us All* and *Our Fathers' Burden***

Trigger Warning

This book may contain sensitive topics for some readers. All the content of this story was written with a purpose for the framework of the story. Out of respect for preventing spoilers, I will be listing the warnings in the very last pages of the book. I urge you to give the story a shot without checking for trigger warnings to allow for the full impact of the story, but I understand the need for them. Proceed in knowing that heavy content matter will surface in the coming pages. Read at your own risk – and I hope you enjoy A Blackened Heart, A Blackened Soul!

"The greatest trick the Devil ever pulled was convincing the world he didn't exist."—**Charles Baudelaire**

"The scariest monsters are the ones that lurk within my soul."—**Edgar Allan Poe**

"Grief changes shape but it never ends. People have a misconception that you can deal with it and say 'It's better. It's Gone.' They're wrong."—**Keanu Reeves**

PART ONE

A Blackened Heart

Chapter One

June 26th, 1998
Johnny Tinsley

"Why don't you take me back to what happened on the night of your championship game?"

The words snapped me out of a daze. I had been awestruck ever since stepping into this office. The walls were adorned with fancy wood paneling. Crosses, old photos, and religious artifacts lined the walls around the room. A scent that faintly reminded me of my grandmother's house permeated the air: the smell of old furniture and antiques. It was a lot for an eight-year-old to take in.

I glanced over my shoulder at my grandma. She gave me a nod of approval. I turned my gaze back to the man sitting across from me. He was slightly younger than Grandma and had grey and black hair. He had no facial hair on his slender face. His stern expression made me feel uneasy, but Grandma's reassurance helped me feel better.

I wasn't sure where my apprehension came from. He had been nice enough. When we arrived, he introduced himself as Father Rosario and escorted us down the red carpeted aisle of our local church. His fancy black cloak swayed as he led us deeper inside. I felt like one of the celebrities you'd hear about on the news when they went to one of their movie premieres.

"It's okay, Johnny. I'm just here to listen and help," he said warmly with a smile.

"I like your cloak," I said timidly, glancing down at my untied shoe.

He looked down at his cloak and then peered back up at me. Wrinkles began to form on his forehead as he let out a soft laugh, "Oh, this old thing? It's called a cassock. I'm glad you like it."

A cassock. That's a new word. I like that.

"What's the white collar for?" I asked.

"Johnny, please answer Father Rosario's question," Grandma said.

He gave a waving gesture with his hand, the smile never leaving his face, "It's quite alright, Edna," he said genially.

He turned his attention back to me as he explained, "The white collar is meant to symbolize purity and my commitment to God and to priesthood. Now, can you tell me about the night of your championship game?"

Grandma told me we were coming here for help. I didn't want to talk about *that* night, though. What started off as one of the most exciting days of my life, quickly turned into a nightmare. The night everything in my life got flipped on its head. I shuffled uncomfortably in my chair.

"W-what do you want to know?" I asked, my voice barely audible.

"Why don't you start from the beginning?" he replied. I nodded.

"I remember it looked like it was going to storm. The clouds looked angry. The way they swirled around one another, it looked like they were wrestling."

I paused to see if I should keep going. When neither Grandma nor Father Rosario said anything, I figured they expected me to continue.

"I remember my dad yelling at my mom. He didn't want to go to the game. He said it was going to storm and that it was just going to be a waste of time. They started arguing. I didn't like it when they yelled at each other, so I grabbed my equipment bag and ran outside to wait for them by the car. The air felt still, even with the angry looking clouds. I remember my mom told me that it was called the 'calm before the storm.' I remember staring at the thick grey clouds when I heard the yelling continuing out onto the porch before Dad slammed the front door shut."

"He wasn't happy about your big game?"

"I don't know. I don't think so. He didn't want to drive all the way there just to have to turn around and head home. Mom told him the field was half an hour away and the storm might not even hit there. So, we finally started driving. Mom started singing 'Take Me Out to the Ballgame' and I joined in with her. Dad seemed irritated by us singing at first. He made a growling noise before he joined in and started singing along. Mom was the only one that could calm him down when he got upset. When we got to the field, the coaches were standing at home plate talking to the umpires. They announced it looked like the storm was going to be far enough away that we were going to be able to play. I ran over to my best friend, Ricky, and we gave each other a huge high five before we started warmups."

"And what happened in the game?"

"We won. Barely. We beat the Coventry Comets six to five!"

"Well that must've been exciting, right?"

"It was! I hit a double that scored us a run! After the game, I looked over at my parents and they were both smiling. Just as we were handed our trophies, a loud crack of thunder scared us all. I remember the coaches telling everyone we needed to hurry back to our parents and that the storm was starting soon. I hugged Ricky and told him I would see him at school on Monday. Summer break was only a couple months away, and we were already making plans about building a fort in the woods behind Ricky's house. I met Mom and Dad down by the car and showed them my trophy. Mom seemed as excited as I was. Dad even gave me a pat on the shoulder."

I saw Father Rosario's eyes shift over to my grandma before they focused back on me once more. "And what happened during the trip home?"

There it was, the question I didn't want to answer. I shifted in my chair again and began digging my fingernail into the wooden armrest. A heavy silence fell upon the room.

"I know it's painful, Johnny. But I promise, I am only here to help," he said calmly.

I turned my eyes back to Father Rosario. He was now sitting upright at his big desk with his hands folded. His attention was solely on me.

"We were driving home and it started storming really bad. Dad was driving and kept cussing about how he couldn't see anything. I remember how fast the windshield wipers were going. They couldn't keep up with the heavy rain. I also remember it was darker outside than I thought it should have been. I'd never seen it this dark this early in the evening. The clouds went from grey to a dark blue. The thunder sounded like bombs going off: they were super loud. Lightning bolts danced across the sky and looked like giant spider webs. I was pretty scared. We were getting closer to our house when it felt like the car began slipping and sliding on the road. Dad said we were 'fishtailing.' Mom let out a little scream which caused Dad to look over at her and yell at her to calm down. Then I remember mom yelling 'watch out!' as she pointed to the road."

"And then what happened?"

"I don't like this part."

"I know. This is all part of the healing process. I know it's painful, Johnny."

I turned and looked back at grandma again. She was holding onto a tissue and her eyes appeared red and puffy like she'd been crying. She nodded once again, so I turned back to Father Rosario. I took a deep breath but couldn't look into his eyes when I spoke.

"I remember I peeked around Dad's seat right after Mom screamed. Everything seemed to move in slow motion. I saw lights and realized a car was coming straight at us. Dad tried to hit the brakes, and the car started swerving all over the road. Before any of us knew what was going on, we went off the side of the road and began rolling down a steep hill. We smashed into a tree, and everything went black. When I woke up, I remember hearing Dad screaming. Mom wasn't saying anything. My neck felt a little sore, but other than that, I felt okay. Mom always said she and Dad raised a tough young man, so I wanted to prove her right. But then, Dad started crying. I'd never seen him cry before. He told me that men don't cry, so I wasn't sure what was going on. I tried calling out to Mom, but she wasn't moving or saying anything. That's when I noticed all the blood."

Blood. The word slipped from my mouth before I even knew what I was saying, and the floodgates of memories and emotion washed over me. I tried to remember what Dad always told me about growing up. '*Never cry in front of others. Never be their burden.*'

I turned my head away from Father Rosario. I tried fighting back the tears, but they came anyway. The memory of the cracked windows and the indented roof covered in spatters of mud, blood, sticks, and leaves was too much to bear.

"*Susan! God dammit! Susan!*" Dad wailed, but unable to move.

Dad unbuckled himself, grimacing in pain. He began to rock back and forth and let out a howl unlike any I had ever heard.

"*I can't feel my fuckin' legs!*" he said, now openly sobbing.

I began screaming for Mommy to wake up. She still wasn't moving. I broke Dad's rule and began weeping. Waves of helplessness, confusion, and fear kicked into overdrive. Dad fidgeted around and dug his cell phone out of his pocket and dialed 9-1-1 amidst all the chaos. He winced as he tossed the phone down into the center console and began taking deep breaths. He said nothing to me.

"That had to be very scary," Father Rosario said, snapping me back to reality. "It would be scary for anyone at any age, and I am very sorry you had to go through that."

I looked back at him with watery eyes. I could tell he felt really bad for me.

"It was," I said with a sniffle. "I remember the fire truck and the ambulance sirens in the distance as they got closer and closer. It hurt to turn my head up toward the hill, but I could see their lights swirling in the dark as they came to a stop next to where we went off the road. The next thing I knew, I could see people coming down the hill toward us. They had to use a tool to break the windows out the rest of the way and a saw to cut off chunks of the car big enough to get us out. I remember a fireman carrying me up the hill and setting me down in the front seat of his fire truck. He wrapped a blanket around me to keep me warm and told me he had to go back down and help the others. I couldn't stop crying. Not even when I knew I was safe. Something felt wrong in my stomach. I didn't know why, but I was scared. I knew it was serious."

I could hear grandma sniffling behind me. I turned to look at her. She excused herself and said she would be right back.

"Do I have to keep going?" I asked, setting my sights back on Father Rosario.

His brow furrowed as he pouted momentarily, as if considering the question. He adjusted himself in his chair. "Only if you're comfortable."

"I don't think I wanna talk about it anymore," I replied woefully.

Father Rosario nodded. "That's completely fine, Johnny."

He got up from his desk and said we could continue our counseling sessions starting next week. I felt a sense of relief that I didn't have to keep talking about that night. Now, though, the memories were bouncing around in my head like a nightmare induced pinball machine. I will never forget the guttural screaming I heard from down the hill before the men wheeled my father up on a gurney. He shouted my mom's name over and over again and was making noises I had never heard a human make before. They put him into the back of the nearby ambulance. A couple of firemen came over to me and told me they were going to be bringing me and my dad to the hospital to get checked out.

"What about my mom?" I asked.

The two firefighters looked at one another. I saw the expression on their faces and knew it wasn't good.

"Come on. Let's get you with your father," one of them said.

They began walking me toward the ambulance. The rain was starting to let up, and I could hear the saw still screeching down in the ravine. One of the firemen walking me to the ambulance introduced himself as Brian and asked me if I liked candy. I nodded my head. He told me he'd buy me a candy bar from the gift shop at the hospital when we got there. He opened the back door to the big ambulance and helped me climb inside where my dad lay on his gurney. It looked like he was asleep now. He was covered with a blanket and had plastic tubes going into his arms and up his nose. His face was pretty scratched up, and he didn't acknowledge me coming inside. The medic gave me a friendly smile and patted on the seat next to her while she finished what she was doing.

I felt a wash of concern for my parents. Where was my mom? Why wasn't anyone talking about her? Just as the firefighter closed the doors to the ambulance, I heard shouting from the workers outside. It sounded like they were coming up the hill.

I dashed to the rear doors of the ambulance and looked out one of the windows. The medic asked for me to come sit next to her, but it was too late. What I witnessed would forever be stamped into the far recesses of my brain. They were wheeling up another gurney. This time, however, there was a black bag on it.

"You're a strong young man," Father Rosario said as he ushered me out of his office and back out to the main section of the church. "I'm proud of the courage you showed today by coming to talk with me."

I looked up at the tall man as we walked side by side before looking out into the main hall. Grandma was sitting in one of the pews with her head bowed in silence.

"Do you believe in ghosts?" I asked him.

Father Rosario seemed taken aback by the question. "Pardon?"

"Do you believe in ghosts? Like...can people come back from the dead to visit us?"

"Why do you ask?"

"Because my mom comes to visit me all the time."

Chapter Two

July 3rd, 1998
Father Rosario

"Do you believe in ghosts?"

The question still sat heavily on my conscience. It wasn't unheard of for young children to have experiences they believed to be paranormal in nature. Children have such active imaginations at times, but Johnny seemed certain it was his mother coming to visit him.

"How often does she come to visit you?" I asked him as we continued to walk toward his grandmother.

I remembered the conflicted look on the boy's face. Concerned, yet hopeful.

"Almost every day," he answered.

The memory of that counseling session had played in my head on repeat over the past week. When Edna came to me troubled by recent events, I told her I would counsel him at no cost. She was elated at the news and shared a tearful hug with me. That boy had gone through unimaginable heartbreak for someone his age. Like so many mothers in this world, Susan was the glue that held their family together. The day she died in that tragic accident, was the end of any sort of *family* for Johnny.

Johnny's father, Ron, not only lost his wife and the mother of his child that night, but he also lost his ability to walk. When the car toppled over the hillside and rolled to the bottom of the ravine, it caused a fracture in the thoracic region of his spine and left him wheelchair bound: a paraplegic. That's an unbelievable amount of grief for a man to take in at once. No amount of casseroles or prayers can fill the void in a man's soul with that kind of loss. I worried about him and the boy.

Thankfully, Edna has been around to help. Being the lone grandparent remaining in Johnny's life, she had a close bond with the boy. She had an ongoing battle with lung cancer that she refused to let drag her down. Susan was her daughter, so she experienced great loss as well, but wanted to do right by her by helping out with Ron and Johnny.

I talked with her at great length about the situation over coffee in the past, giving her guidance on how to deal with the grieving process. She expressed her concerns for Johnny. Ron was a good man but was really struggling to keep it together – all things considered.

Ron and Susan had never been the church going type. Susan attended church for most of her life until adulthood when she began to date Ron. Edna had been attending services at my church, St. Anthony's, for decades now and we had become close friends.

Hearing Johnny say, *'My mom comes to visit me all the time,'* continued to fester in my thoughts like a boiling pot of stew. Was this his subconscious creating what his mind, body, and soul craved so badly? Or *needed*? Or was it *actually* the spirit of his mother visiting him? Edna had made mention prior to scheduling the counseling sessions that Johnny had mentioned it to her as well, and she was equally troubled by it. She felt fortunate that Ron agreed to allow her to take Johnny to meet with me. *'Ron looked disheveled, and the house was a mess. It reeked of filth.'* She expressed her concerns at Ron's inability to raise a child with everything going on. She tried to help out with laundry, bringing over dinners, and general housecleaning, but that's a lot for someone of her age to keep up with.

I took a deep breath as I exited St. Anthony's. The high sun and blue sky blanketed the neighborhood with a beautiful early summer afternoon. I took in a deep breath of the fresh air; taking in the scents of freshly cut grass and listening to the leaves hiss in the light breeze. My mother always told me at a young age, *'If you're ever feeling down, eat some ice cream. I've never seen an unhappy person eating ice cream.'* It always rang true. And this was the perfect day for an ice cream cone.

Norton, Ohio, was a small suburb just west of Akron. It had a little bit of everything: farmland, historical neighborhoods, and a downtown area that had begun to develop a strip of shops and fast-food restaurants over the years. Lowry's, the ice cream shop across the street, and my church reside in the Loyal Oak neighborhood. Loyal Oak was one of the historical sections of Norton. A lot of small towns had similar neighborhood vibes. A cider mill that had been constructed in the late 1800s now sat vacant just a quarter mile up the road and a restaurant that operated as a speakeasy during the prohibition era was just a stone's throw away from the church.

I grew up in Norton and lived here my entire life. I was raised in a traditional Catholic family and been raised as a man of faith, deciding to devote my life to God and spreading his word after high school, following in my father's footsteps.

I scaled down the front steps of St. Anthony's and ventured across the street to Lowry's. It opened directly across from the church some twenty years prior and served the best scoops in town.

"I'll take a medium cone, chocolate chip cookie dough, please," I said to the girl working at the order window.

She gave me a warm smile and handed me my ice cream a few moments later. I walked over to a table and took a seat, taking in my surroundings.

I took a bite from my ice cream cone, and I noticed a cardinal fluttering a mere few feet away from me. It landed on the white picket fence surrounding the ice cream stand, with St. Anthony's nestled neatly in the background like that of a Hallmark card. The bird almost blended in with the red archway doors that led inside the church. As my eyes swept up the old gothic revival style building, a light breeze caused the maple trees in front of the church to sway. The white paint covering the wood walls of the church had seen better days. It was a dull version of what it used to be. The paint had worn thin, and the weathered, grey wood panels began to show through.

The cardinal hopped from its perch and flapped into one of the maples across the street. Life was such a beautiful and precious gift. But in all its glory, it could be so hurtful too.

Knock. Knock. Knock.

"Please, come in." I said, hastily rising from my desk and putting on a smile.

The door swung open as Edna began escorting Johnny into my office. He was wearing a *Teenage Mutant Ninja Turtles* shirt and blue jeans. His hair looked a little disheveled, but his piercing blue eyes and bright smile could illuminate the darkest of rooms.

We exchanged greetings as Edna went to take a seat along the back wall. Johnny gave me a firm handshake before taking a seat in front of my desk.

"That's a very impressive handshake you have there," I exclaimed as I leaned against my desk and smiled at him.

"Thanks," he replied softly, averting his eyes to the oriental rug at his feet.

I continued to make small talk with him until I could feel his walls beginning to come down. I then circled my desk and took a seat. Johnny's eyes were locked onto mine.

"So, how've things been going at home?"

He began to fidget uncomfortably. "They're going...okay."

I could sense he still wasn't feeling totally comfortable. I asked him if he'd prefer it to be just us two talking. He shrugged. I glanced over at Edna, and she nodded before politely getting up from her chair and exiting the office.

"Is that better?" I asked.

He glanced over his shoulder and made sure the door was shut before turning to look back at me. He nodded.

"Not comfortable speaking in front of your grandmother anymore?"

He shifted in his seat once more. "It's not that. It's just...Dad doesn't like me talking about home stuff in front of her anymore."

"Why's that?"

"He says it's none of her business what goes on in our home. And that she's been nosing around since Mom passed away."

"I see. How has your father been lately?"

I could tell the question had hit a nerve. John peered around the room while his fingers fidgeted with the armrests. I already knew the answer to the question but needed him to be able to verbalize it.

"It's uh...it's okay," he said nonchalantly as he got up from his seat.

I watched as he sauntered over and began thumbing through the books packed into my bookshelf. I gave him a moment.

"Just okay? Care to elaborate?"

He pulled out an old textbook from my time studying psychology and theology at John Carroll University. He promptly put it back. He had a natural curiosity that was endearing. I could tell Johnny was stalling, or at the very least, trying to find the right words.

"I promise, everything you say in here stays in here," I said calmly. "I won't talk to your father or your grandmother about anything you discuss in this office with me. You are safe here."

Johnny's brow furrowed as he pondered my words. He sauntered back over to his chair and took a seat once again.

"Have things not been going well at home?"

"Not really," he said with a brief pause. "Dad's been getting angry a lot lately."

"What has he been getting angry about?"

"Everything. Sometimes, I'll hear him yelling in the middle of the night while no one else is in the house."

I nodded at his statement. Ron could be suffering from a form of post-traumatic stress. I could feel pain radiating off the boy. His eyes appeared distant as he recounted the story.

"Sometimes, he tells me he wishes he had died in the car accident, too. I don't like it when he says that. Sometimes, he gets angry at me just for being in the same room as him. Other times he just sits in the dark in his wheelchair and ignores me."

"And how does all this make you feel?"

"Sad. Hurt. Alone."

Acknowledgement. Communicating his feelings. This was good. I wanted so badly to hug the boy and tell him things were going to be okay.

"And when you are feeling sad, hurt, and alone, who do you talk to about it?"

His eyes, which had already been watering, began to dart to and fro around the room.

"My mom," he said in a hushed tone, as if someone else might overhear.

My stomach was in knots. I *knew* that was what he was going to say, but hearing him verbalize it still filled me with an aching sadness.

"Yes, you mentioned she had been coming to visit you. When did that start?"

"A few days after the wreck. Dad was still in the hospital, so I was staying with my grandma."

"So, your mother has visited you in your house and your grandmother's house?"

Johnny nodded. "And at school. It started out small. I would usually only see her out of the corner of my eye. Then one day, I was at recess on the swing set and saw her watching me from the edge of the woods behind the playground. Over time, she began to get closer. Then, she finally started talking to me."

The addition of seeing his mother watching him at the school was a troubling development I hadn't seen coming.

"I tried to get Ricky to look, but by the time he did, she was gone. He doesn't believe me. Over time, she got closer and closer. Until, finally, she started showing up in my bedroom."

My heart sank. This was more than an overactive imagination.

"And this began happening at your grandmother's house?"

"Yes."

"I see," I said with a pause. "And then it continued happening at your house when your father finally got back home from the hospital?"

"Yes."

"Does it happen at any particular time of day?"

"No," Johnny answered, his eyes falling to the floor. "She shows up at random times. Sometimes during the day, but mostly at night. It seems to be whenever I'm upset."

"Are you more upset at night?"

"Yes. I think about the accident a lot when I'm trying to go to sleep. I think about Mom, and how much I miss her."

"And then she appears?"

"Most of the time."

"I see," I said again with another distinct pause. Trauma and loss like Johnny experienced could become a catalyst for hallucinations. I jotted my thoughts down on my notepad. "Does she say anything to you?"

Johnny shook his head after some consideration. "Not at first, no."

Chapter Three

July 3rd, 1998
Ron Tinsley

People always think *'Oh, that will never happen to me.'* What a crock of shit. We go through our lives taking everything for granted – bitching and moaning and bitching and moaning about little things that, in the end, don't really matter.

Sometimes, I still can't bring myself to believe it. I still can't believe how fast and how hard one can fall in the blink of an eye. One day, you're just going through the motions of life without a shred of gratitude. Then, with the speed of an exasperated and cornered cobra, the blackened hand of god strikes you down and sends you spiraling down a thousand pegs. Right down to the unforgiving, jagged edges of rock bottom.

I glanced down angrily at my now useless legs, hot tears welling in the corner of my eyes. I wanted to yell from a mountaintop about all my misgivings. It'd been a little over two months since that fateful drive home from Johnny's baseball game. The events of that trek played in my subconscious every single day like a sick form of torture.

I lost the love of my life. I lost my identity. A blackened husk formed where my heart used to be. Susan was my heart and soul, and now she was gone. I knew I needed to do better for Johnny. My brain wanted so badly to be the father he needed. A father is supposed to be a hero to their children, but here I am, stuck in this godforsaken wheelchair like some sort of feeble-minded invalid. I lost the function of my legs, so I lost my ability to work. We were surviving off the life insurance money we received while waiting for my disability payments to kick in. I felt useless. I couldn't do half the things I used to do with my son, only furthering my self-loathing. Everything was taken from me in one fell swoop and I couldn't shake the concoction of fear, rage, helplessness, and waves of depression simmering and swirling inside me.

I was left in silence with all these thoughts floating around my brain, while my eyes surveyed the living room. They settled on the bookshelf next to our TV stand, on a photo of Susan, Johnny, and myself on a family vacation to Emerald Isle in North Carolina. I flashed a weak smile at the memories as my sight continued to sweep to the other side of the shelf at a wedding photo of Susan and myself. I thought back to how we met at a bar just outside our campus at Kent State University. I made a fool of myself that night, accidentally knocking her drink over as I set my hand down to lean in and introduce myself. I apologized profusely, grabbing a fistful of napkins to help clean the mess, and offered to buy her another drink. She seemed hesitant at first and then agreed. We introduced ourselves and she asked me to sit with her and her friends so she wouldn't have to worry about me knocking over her new drink. She was beautiful, funny, and intelligent. Big bonus points in my eyes.

She had a beautiful soul. She was too good for me. I knew it, and so did everyone else. When she died, I thought I'd never see her again. I felt left alone in this cold, dark world, attempting to raise a proper young man. Between the agonizing physical pain attacks, my emotions began to spill over into me shouting out her name in the middle of the night. It was a side of me that I didn't want Johnny to ever see.

As the days recovering in the hospital after the accident began to painstakingly pass by, I saw her – my Susan – standing at my bedside smiling with angelic grace. At first, I thought it was all the opioids coursing through my veins in an attempt to bring relief to my broken body post-surgery. I tried to reason with myself. It wasn't possible. I was losing my mind. But it continued to happen. She began to visit more frequently. It started small at first. She stood stoic and silent with a golden glow about her, and eventually, she began speaking to me: whispering sweet affirmations and letting me know her spirit would always be with me and that I was strong enough to get through these times.

"Susan, I miss you so much," I whispered sorrowfully, holding back the flood of emotions washing over me as I continued to stare at our wedding photo. Silence followed. "Baby, can you give me a sign that you're here with me?"

I always felt a tinge of guilt for disturbing her eternal rest, but I still needed her. I needed to hear her voice, to feel her presence by my side. Sometimes, I'd feel a gentle breeze whisk by me, or a sudden cold spot would form around me. Other times, I'd feel the icy tendrils of her fingers wrap around my shoulder and when I'd glance back, she'd be standing behind me wearing my red Ohio State hoodie that was way too big for her, a pair of her favorite blue jeans, and a beautiful smile spread across her face. Her blonde hair was always pulled neatly back into a ponytail as she lovingly stared into my eyes.

I wasn't even sure I understood how it worked. Susan didn't always show up on command. All I knew was when I needed her to be there for me – when I was feeling like I was at my lowest point – she found her way to me. During the day, she was everything I needed in those moments. At night, she'd show a different side of herself. A sort of Yin and Yang. Opposite personalities. But one thing she made clear in her nighttime visits...she *needed me.*

This was part of the reason why I allowed Edna to take Johnny to see Father Rosario. I needed time alone. Time to process my thoughts. Time to communicate with Susan. I didn't want or need Johnny to freak out about me talking to the ghost of his dead mother. I would only call out to her when he was asleep or wasn't home. It sounded crazy on paper, and I still couldn't wrap my head around the existence of life after death, but here I was, talking to a bookshelf in my home.

"Baby...Susan? Can you please come forward and speak to me?" I asked with tears flowing down my cheeks, the memory of our first dance at our wedding playing in my mind. *Say You Love Me* by Fleetwood Mac played through the speakers as we joined together in an up-tempo love song that marked our first dance together the night we met, and our first dance together in marriage.

I was snapped from my reverie when the radio in the kitchen flicked on and began playing our song. A gasp escaped my throat. I frantically wheeled myself toward the kitchen. There she was, standing with her back to the counter, smiling broadly as her eyes gleamed at the sight of me.

"There you are," I said softly, my body shuddering at the cold air in the kitchen.

"I never left," she replied.

"H-How did you know I was thinking about our first dance?"

Susan said nothing, cranking up the volume on the stereo before sauntering toward me. Her hips waved seductively as she approached, mouthing the words to our song before she walked behind me. I felt the ice-cold tips of her fingers begin caressing my shoulders and neck. She leaned forward, her breath nipping at my earlobe like an arctic blast.

"We're connected. We always have been. And soon enough, we always will be," she cooed.

Susan had always had a way with words. A way of making me feel like I truly mattered to her. A romantic at heart, she always knew what to say. The words she just spoke struck me as hauntingly beautiful. I was buzzing. The hairs on the back of my neck were standing on end as gooseflesh formed all over my body.

"Forever and always?" I whispered.

"Forever and always," she repeated in a hushed tone.

"How will I know when?"

There was no response. I turned my head to look behind me and she was gone. The chill in the air seemingly dissipated in a moment's notice. The radio turned off on its own. The spirit of Susan was like a drug, and I couldn't get enough of her. And now, here I was sitting in the kitchen alone again, coming down from the high – waiting and wondering when my eternity with her would come.

Chapter Four

July 3rd, 1998
Johnny Tinsley

"Have a happy fourth of July!" Father Rosario called out with a friendly wave as I got into the back seat of Grandma's car.

I replied with a wave of my own and a friendly smile as I closed the door, watching from a distance as he and my grandma talked at the top of the stairs in front of the church.

I thought about how Father Rosario seemed troubled by my responses near the end of our session.

"Not at first?" he asked.

I remembered his face tightening, almost like he was worried. It made me instantly regret saying anything.

"What does she say to you?" he asked.

"Not a lot. Just that she misses me," I lied.

I wasn't sure whether Father Rosario believed me or not, but he sat back in his chair as if he was thinking long and hard about what I'd said. He tapped his pen on his notepad while biting his lip.

"Nothing else?" he asked, cocking his head. I shook my head. I didn't want him to know that when Mommy came at night, sometimes she scared me. She always said it was just a big

misunderstanding – and would always give good reasons for why things happened at night time. I trusted her. How could I not? It was my mom.

"You must never tell anyone what we discuss," my mom hissed.

"But why, Mommy?"

"People are afraid of what they don't understand. Science says I shouldn't exist. But you see me, don't you, Johnny?"

I nodded. *"Yes, Mommy."*

"People will call you crazy. They will run medical tests on you and lock you away if you let them into our circle. Do you understand?" she said in a foreboding tone as she ran her frigid fingers through my hair.

"Yes, Mom. I understand."

And I did understand. I hadn't told anyone about *any* of our conversations. I didn't want to be locked away.

Before walking me out, Father Rosario seemed to ponder my previous statement once more before setting his pen down and changing the subject to the holiday tomorrow. He asked if I was excited about the fireworks. I told him I was and that I could see them over the trees from my bedroom window.

Sitting in the car, I wondered what he and my grandma were discussing. Did Father Rosario not believe what I had been telling him? I hoped he had. I didn't want to have tests run on me. I wasn't crazy.

I watched them shake hands as Grandma made her way down to the car.

On the ride home, she seemed shaken up. She tried making small talk, which wasn't like her.

"You be sure to give me a call if you need anything. Okay, Johnny?" she asked after pulling into our driveway.

"I will, Grandma. I love you," I said, giving her a big hug before exiting the car and heading inside. I glanced out our front window and watched her back her car out of the driveway.

"How was counseling?" I heard Dad call out from behind me.

Startled, I turned and looked over at him. I hadn't noticed him when I walked in. He was sitting in his wheelchair with a photo album opened up on his lap. I could tell he'd been crying again. His eyes were red and puffy. He hadn't been the same since the accident. Seeing my dad look so defeated broke my heart.

"It was fine," I replied timidly.

"That...That's good, son," he replied, averting his sorrowful eyes down to the photo album resting on his lap.

An awkward silence encapsulated both of us. Not knowing what to do, I darted upstairs to my room and shut the door.

My bedroom was my sanctuary. Hung on the walls were posters of my favorite cars, movies, and baseball players. I was a huge Cleveland Indians fan, and my two favorite players were Omar Vizquel and Jim Thome. I once tried to imitate an Omar play in one of my games while playing shortstop, scooping up a ground ball and spinning around, trying to throw the batter out at first base, but I missed wildly with the ball flying into the opposing team's dugout. I was no Omar. But I loved baseball. My parents would frequently take us to games where we would sit along the third base line in the hopes of catching a foul ball. They had created my love for the game. Above my posters sat a shelf that had held up the few trophies I had already earned playing the sport I loved.

I grabbed a *Spiderman* comic and flopped down on my bed, which had been adorned with *Teenage Mutant Ninja Turtles* sheets: my favorite show.

Comics had been my escape from difficult times recently. I'd often find myself wishing I could be a superhero. Maybe if I was, I could've saved Mom and prevented the horrible car accident.

Dad rarely used the lift that was installed to come upstairs. Instead, he'd heave himself onto our living room couch and sleep there most nights. I think his bedroom reminded him of Mom too much, so he stayed away.

I couldn't explain the feeling, but Dad just felt *wrong* to be around. I wanted to lift his spirits but could never seem to help – and seemed to only make it worse. A couple weeks ago, I drew a picture of me and him out fishing on a lake. His eyes glanced down, but it didn't seem to register. *'Th-That's great, Johnny,'* he said nonchalantly. It was like his body was with me, but his mind was somewhere else entirely and it made me upset.

I tossed my comic book aside. The one downfall to comics was that they went by too quickly. I peered around the room, my eyes landing on my mom's favorite doll. I kept it on a chair in the corner of my room, facing my bed. Ricky made fun of me when he first saw it, until I told him it was my mom's, and then he understood. I remembered Mom telling me that it was an antique. Grandma got it for her on Christmas when she was around my age. She said the doll's name was Lucy – a name she'd given it the moment she opened the gift. It was a porcelain doll that had blonde hair and blue eyes, just like Mom. It had rosy-red cheeks painted on, with narrow lips painted in a matching color. The doll wore a white dress and black shoes. Its skin was mostly unblemished, aside from a small crack running down her forehead and across her left eye. Dad accidentally knocked it over on his way to the bathroom one night. Mom yelled at him for it.

I brought it into my room the day after the accident, knowing Dad wasn't going to care anyways. It made me feel closer to Mom. It felt like a piece of her was with me. At first, the doll creeped me out, with its big blue eyes always staring at me, but eventually I grew comfortable with it. A couple days after I moved the doll into my room, my mom came to visit. She told me it meant a lot to her that I decided to bring the doll into my room to keep her in my thoughts.

"That's a very important doll. Thank you for keeping her safe," she said to me, her eyes beaming with pride. *"I have a favor to ask of you, Johnny."*

"What's that, Mom?"

"Can I move into Lucy?"

"Why?" I asked curiously, turning my gaze upon the doll.

"So that we can always be together. Isn't that what you want?"

I nodded.

"So, can I move into Lucy?" she asked again – her lips twisting into a wicked grin, her eyes remaining locked on mine.

"Yes, Mommy. I'd like that."

Dinner was just like it had been so many other evenings. Simple, quiet, and solemn. Dad slapped together bologna sandwiches that we both quietly ate. The only noise in the house was the sound of us chewing.

I looked at him as he stared blankly ahead. It made me think back to the day of my championship game – with how the clouds looked like they were wrestling with one another. I felt like that was what was going on in his brain. He was with me, but not *with* me.

I tried asking him what he was thinking about, but the question went unanswered as he took another bite of his sandwich, staring off into the abyss.

I didn't even bother to ask to be excused from the table after finishing eating. I simply tossed my paper plate into the trash can and thanked Dad for dinner before heading to my room. I gave one last glance back. He still sat stationary in his wheelchair, motionless and nodding. A chill ran up my spine as I made my way back up to my room.

What's his deal? I've never seen him act like this.

When I reached my room, I looked at my bookshelf that had been filled with a hodgepodge of different things. One shelf was for books, mostly my *Goosebumps.* They were my favorite books. The other shelves held action figures that were posed in different battling positions and random baseball memorabilia, including my baseball that had been signed by none other than Omar Vizquel.

I thumbed through my collection of books and grabbed a copy of *Welcome to Camp Nightmare.* It was one of my favorites from the series because it had such a good twist ending.

At some point, mid-read, I had fallen asleep. When I awoke, it was night out. My room was dimly lit by my nightlight in the corner of the room nearest to Lucy. The ambient light painted her in an ominous orange hue.

My room felt cold. That was usually a sign that Mom was near, because we didn't have air conditioning. I didn't like it when she visited at night. She didn't act the same, and she came whether you wanted her to or not.

I looked around the room. I didn't see her anywhere and the house was silent. The frigid air bit into my skin and made me feel like I had to go pee, but I felt paralyzed. I didn't want to get out of bed. But I knew I should go to the bathroom, or I would never fall back asleep.

I cautiously rolled out of bed, exited my room, and began to walk down the long corridor toward the end of the hall. A small nightlight within the bathroom illuminated the hall under the dimmest of lights.

I moved at a brisk pace, not wanting to hang outside the safety of my bedroom in the dark for too long. As I made my way past my parents' bedroom, I saw a grey, smiling face staring at me from the doorway out of the corner of my eye that sent a jolt of fear surging up my spine.

I took a couple of haggard steps back, my heart racing, and held my breath. Nothing was there. The face I had just seen was gone, but the room reeked of rotting meat. I stared into the pitch-black room, hoping that nothing would lunge out at me. It was dead silent.

"He-Hello?" I whispered hoarsely.

Silence.

Suddenly, back down in my bedroom, I heard the sound of a woman singing. It was Mom. I slowly started to pace back toward my room when I recognized the song being sung. It was *Simple Man* by Lynyrd Skynyrd.

My mom told me that when I was a baby, she would dance with me to that song if I was ever having trouble falling asleep, and it always worked. It had become *our* song.

As I peered into my bedroom, the singing stopped. Everything looked normal. My eyes settled on my bed, and I saw Lucy sitting there, staring back at me.

Chapter Five

July 3rd, 1998
Ron Tinsley

There's nothing quite like being woken up from a dead sleep in the middle of the night, hearing your child wailing at the top of their lungs.

"Daaaaddy!" I heard Johnny cry out from upstairs.

"Johnny? What's going on?" I yelled amidst a mix of confusion and panic.

Moments later, the pitter-patter of frantic footsteps came rushing down the stairs and into the living room. Johnny's eyes were wide with terror as he rushed to my side.

"What's wrong, buddy?" I asked, reaching a hand out to my son.

Johnny took a few deep breaths in between sobs, attempting to compose himself, snot bubbles bursting out of his nostrils. "I saw...I saw..."

"You saw what?"

He looked over his shoulder and back towards the stairs as if he was expecting to have been followed. He turned back to me, his lips pursed and eyes distant like he was having an internal debate.

"N-Nothing. I think I was just having a nightmare," he said finally.

I took a deep breath, trying to get my heart rate back to a normal range. I placed my palms down at my sides and heaved myself up into a seated position on the sofa. I grabbed Johnny's hand in mine, peering deep into his watery eyes.

"Just a nightmare?" I asked. Johnny averted his gaze and said nothing. "That's an awful lot of commotion for a nightmare. I haven't seen you run that fast since your inside the park home run earlier this year," I joked.

Johnny stared at the floor and sniffled. "I'm not supposed to talk about it."

"Talk about what? Johnny, you know you can talk to me about anything," I replied, giving his hand a firm squeeze.

It hurt to see my boy so distraught. He had nightmares at a younger age, much like any young child. He would scramble out of his bed and squeeze between Susan and me in our bed the first couple of years after he moved into his big boy bed. But Johnny had grown out of that phase. It hurt more that he felt like he wasn't able to talk to me about it.

My brain began to drift, seeing my son bashfully staring at the floor. Had I disassociated so much since the accident that he felt he couldn't trust me anymore? Was I that fucked up of a father?

"Johnny, I promise, everything will be okay. You can talk to me," I said finally, my eyes now welling up as well. "What's going on?"

"I...I have been seeing Mommy," he muttered.

It felt like a hot dagger had been pierced through my heart. Shockwaves bolted up my spine as my arm hair stood on end.

"Y-You what?" I asked, bewildered.

"Mommy made me promise not to tell anyone, but she's been coming to visit me."

"When does she come to visit you?"

"Almost every night."

I couldn't believe what I was hearing. Susan had been visiting me since her passing. I was curious if Johnny or Edna had also been seeing her. When I hadn't heard Johnny make mention, I felt relieved – yet also terrified that I might be losing my mind. Lo and behold, she'd been appearing to Johnny this whole time as well. I didn't know whether to feel scared, validated, or both. I'd been trying to protect Johnny from the idea of ghosts, and that his mother had been visiting me for some time now. If this were true, why hadn't Susan mentioned that she'd been visiting our son? Were my son and I both going crazy? Was any of this real? And if it was real, what did that mean? So many questions, so little time to collect my thoughts.

"You believe me, don't you, Dad?" Johnny asked frantically.

The question hit me like a ton of bricks. Do I tell Johnny that I believe him and run the risk of further incidents? Or do I go the opposite direction and try to protect the innocence of my eight-year-old son?

"Johnny, ghosts aren't real. It's just your imagination playing tricks on you in the dark," I replied.

Johnny looked hurt by my words. "It's not my imagination, Dad! I got up to use the bathroom, and I thought I saw this strange face in your room. Then I heard Mommy singing *Simple Man* in my bedroom! And then -"

"Johnny! There are no such things as ghosts!" I growled, immediately regretting the tone I took with him. "Look, I know you miss your mother. I miss her too. But she's gone, son. And she's never coming back."

I had no idea the weight my words held until I watched Johnny flinch at them. He yanked his hand away angrily.

"I hate you!" he hissed through tears.

The words hit harder than I ever could have imagined. A type of hurt that I couldn't fathom. A different pain from the loss of my wife. My son. My progeny. My legacy that I would be leaving to this world just said three of the most painful words a parent could hear from their child. And it left me wondering if I'd made the right decision of not feeding into Johnny's fear.

"Maybe you ought to call your grandmother and see if you can stay there tonight," I said, choking back tears.

Johnny said nothing and darted into the kitchen. I could hear him bawling his eyes out as he spoke with Edna. My chest felt like it was constricting around what was left of my heart. It was hard to breathe. I managed to get myself into my wheelchair just as Johnny bounded past me and over toward the staircase.

I wanted to reach out for him and tell him how much I loved him, but the words remained tangled in my throat. I lost all track of time staring blankly at the staircase, wishing I wasn't such a fuck up.

Knock. Knock. Knock.

The rapping on our front door snapped me out of my trance.

"Ron? It's Edna."

Before I could get to the door, Johnny had already come rushing down the stairs with a backpack slung over his shoulder. He reached for the lock on the door, twisting it and heaving the door open in a swift motion, scooting around Edna as he ran off the porch and out of sight.

Edna stood in the doorway with her hands on her hips, giving me a look of pity. Her eyes had heavy bags under them, and she was dressed in her night gown with a jacket draped over her shoulders. "What's going on?" she asked.

"Johnny thinks he's been seeing Susan. I told him ghosts weren't real and that his imagination mixed with missing his mom was getting to him." I said, still fighting a whirlwind of emotions.

Edna sighed. "Yeah, he told the same thing to Father Rosario. But every time Father Rosario tries to dig deeper, Johnny clams up about it."

I nodded. "Hopefully it's just a phase. I know we all miss Susan greatly. Nothing will ever heal those wounds. You just learn to live through the pain. Maybe a night away will do him some good."

Edna frowned in thought and returned a nod. "I'll make sure he gets a good night's rest. Tomorrow's a new day."

Edna turned and began to walk away before I stopped her. "Hey, Edna?"

"Yes, Ron?"

"Thank you."

She smiled weakly, nodding her head while walking down the steps and out of sight. I closed the door and immediately began openly sobbing.

"I hate you."

The words had been playing on repeat since Johnny spat them out like venom. I tried telling myself that kids sometimes let their emotions get the best of them, and that this was likely his response to heightened emotions and frustration with how life had been going over the last couple of months.

Still, the impact of those words shattered my soul. I sat in the foyer weeping for what felt like hours until I finally composed myself enough to wheel my way back into the living room. Shrouded in darkness and left to my own devices, I allowed myself to reflect on what had just transpired.

"Susan!" I bellowed.

Silence.

"How could you do that to our son? He's not old enough to comprehend any of this. Why didn't you tell me you'd been visiting him too?"

I was met with no response yet again. Sadness was now turning into anger.

"Oh, you don't want to talk now? How fuckin' convenient!"

The house continued to sit still. Silent. Vacant. I looked around for any sign of Susan. I felt nothing and there was no sight of her. I knew that if there was an afterlife, how tempting that must be to want to see and communicate with not only your husband, but your son as well. I couldn't say I blamed her, but Susan would never jeopardize Johnny's mental well-being like that. The fact was, I had been allowing myself to become swept up in my remorse over losing my wife that I stopped being a good father. Enough was enough.

"Susan," I said with a pause. "I don't think it's a good idea for you to come around anymore. It's not healthy for me or our son."

My words were met with dead air once more. Out of my peripherals, I saw motion to my left as arctic air seeped into the room.

I spun my wheelchair around and saw the silhouette of a figure standing in the doorway leading to the kitchen. The shadowy form was darker than the night sky, but I could definitively see the outline of a head and shoulders.

The figure stood completely still — completely silent.

"S-Susan?" I stammered, squinting my eyes to try to get a better look.

The black mass remained unmoving. Unspeaking. An unsettling feeling crept up my spine like a worm inching its way to the surface after a heavy rain.

"Baby?"

Just as fast as the figure appeared, it was gone. Was I going crazy? I spun my wheelchair around in a full circle. The gelid temperatures remained, wrapping my body in an icy hug – but there was no sign of Susan or the shadow figure anywhere. I tried calling out for Susan once again when I heard something that made my blood run cold.

"Ron!" a snakelike voice hissed.

There's something to be said about hearing your name called out from the darkness when you know you're home alone. I wanted to respond, but all that escaped me was a faint whimper. My mouth ran dry. My throat seized up. My heart was pounding furiously like an old war drum.

"Ron!" the voice said directly behind me this time. I spun my wheelchair around and found nothing there.

"S-Susan? Is...Is that you?" I called out weakly.

The shrill voice seemed to be coming from every direction at once. My head swung back and forth attempting to make sense of this. No one was around me. The voices began to grow faster. Faster. Faster. Swirling around me like a violent tornado.

"Ron! Ron! Ron! Ron! Ron! Ron! Ron!"

"What do you want from me?" I cried out.

I felt like I was spiraling around the room alongside the voices. I began to grow dizzy. I tried to cover my ears, but the voices grew louder and picked up tempo.

"Ron! Ron! Ron! Ron! Ron! Ron!"

Just when I was about to reach my breaking point, the voices stopped. I picked my head up, staring blankly ahead. Silence. I let out the breath I had been clutching onto like my life had depended on it.

"ROOOONNNN!" an earth-shattering growl called out directly to my left as an unseen force launched into me, sending me and my wheelchair toppling over in a heap.

"Wh-What the fuck?" I called out in desperation, my eyes darting around trying to make sense of things. I forced myself to roll over when I noticed the dark figure looming over top of me.

I reached a hand out for my wheelchair when suddenly it was flung across the room like a paperweight, crashing loudly onto the floor.

"G-Get the fuck away from me!" I cried out, attempting to propel myself away with my arms.

The ominous figure continued to stand idly by as if it were finding humor in my feeble attempt at an escape. I flipped onto my belly and began army crawling away as fast as I could when I heard it.

Thump.

It sounded like the hoof of a Clydesdale collided with my hardwood floor, reverberating through the whole house. *Don't look back, Ron. Don't look back.* I continued, clawing my way toward the front door as fast as my rapidly tiring arms would allow.

Thump.

The floorboards beneath me shook once more. Panic began setting in. I saw my wheelchair and decided it would be too time-consuming to try to work my way into. I continued pulling my way out of the living room and rounded the corner toward the front door.

Thump.

I needed to get out of this house. Once I was outside, I could call for help and hope that one of my neighbors would hear me and come rushing over. I took a deep breath as I reached up for the doorknob.

Thump. Thump. Thump. Thump. Thump. Thump.

Oh, God! It's coming! Just get outside! You need to hurry, Ron! I gripped onto the brass knob and began to twist.

Before I could pull the door open, I found myself suddenly being yanked backward with an astonishing force. My belly screeched across the hardwood floor as I was dragged around the corner, banging my head into the door jamb on my way back into the living room. I was still seeing stars when I was tossed onto my back and the figure climbed onto my chest and pinned my arms down onto the floor.

By the time I managed to compose myself, I was able to see the figure in its true form. I was staring face to face with Susan. Not the Susan I remembered, though. Not the beautiful, bubbly woman I had fallen in love with. No, this Susan had a deep gash running from the top of her head down across the left side of her face, her left eye nothing more than a crater oozing coagulated blood, bits of skull, and grey matter. It appeared as though someone had thrust an axe into the top of her head. Thick shards of glass peppered her face and stuck out like icebergs in the middle of the arctic sea.

I couldn't move. All I could do was helplessly lock eyes with this brutalized version of my wife.

"S-Susan?" I called out wearily.

"Susan?" she mocked, her one good eye staring coldly as a devilish, blood-filled grin spread across her face.

"What the fuck is going on? What is this?" I asked, struggling under her impossibly strong grip. I closed my eyes tight. I couldn't stand the sight of her in this state any longer.

"Open your eyes!" she shrieked. "You look at what you did to me!"

"I-I didn't..." I replied, still squeezing my eyes shut.

"You did! You couldn't handle driving in a little bit of rain! I'm dead because of you. And now look at you. You are nothing more than a sad, worthless, shell of a man."

The words hit like daggers, one right after the other. Tears began pooling in the corners of my eyes, but still I refused to open them.

"Just a pathetic, decrepit, weak-willed cripple and a deadbeat Dad. I can see why Johnny hates you."

"Stop! Stop it!" I cried out, the tears now flowing out of the corners of my eyes.

"My father was right. He said that you'd never amount to anything. That you'd wind up being the death of me!" she exclaimed, her voice rising in intensity. "You are the worst thing that ever happened to me, and you are going to ruin our only son!"

I felt the world caving in all around me, and I could do nothing to stop it. Each insult Susan hurled out hit me with the force of an atomic bomb, detonating inside my chest and destroying what little remnants I had left of my heart – scattering the battered remains around my ribcage. I began weeping, still refusing to look at her.

"Oh, did I hurt poor widdle Wonald's feewings?" she said in a tone of mockery, cackling like a wild hyena. "I never loved you. The truth is, dying in that car accident was the best thing that ever happened to me, because it got me away from you!"

Something didn't sit right. Susan's voice had morphed into something other-worldly. Deep and guttural. Animal-like.

"The only thing that could've made it better was if little Johnny died too. Then he wouldn't have to live with a bottom-feeding sycophant of a father. I should've stuck a coat hanger right up my cunt and yanked Johnny out before you poisoned his life, you spineless parasite!"

"You're...not...Susan," I grunted. The thing sitting atop me snickered, a throaty laugh.

"No," it said bluntly. "And you know what else?" the deep, gravelly voice rattled. "You're going to see her in hell...real soon!"

The shock of hearing those words were enough to snap my eyelids open. I couldn't believe my eyes. Words couldn't be formed to describe the unsettling thing staring down upon me. It started cackling a deep, guttural laugh. It was the epitome of pure fright and evil and sent me roaring into a blood-curdling scream.

In the blink of an eye, it opened its gaping maw filled with black, razor-sharp teeth as it spewed a thick, black sputum right into my mouth. The snot-like substance caught in the back of my throat causing me to gag, but it was impossible to expel. It was hot and sticky like tar and tasted rancid – like I was eating roadkill that had been run over repeatedly and sat baking in the desert sun for days. More and more of the viscous liquid dumped in until my throat had no other alternative than to open wide and take in the vile substance.

Chapter Six

July 4th, 1998
Father Rosario

I hadn't expected to be awoken by a phone call in the middle of the night. I was even more alarmed at hearing the frantic words being spoken by Edna Tomko. After getting her to calm down a little bit, she let me know that the situation in the Tinsley household was getting worse – and that Johnny was staying with her for the night.

"I'm so sorry to ask this, but can you see him again tomorrow, Father?" she asked. I looked at the clock on my nightstand and realized it was already technically tomorrow.

"Sure, bring him by – say around... Ten?"

"Thank you, Father."

I placed the phone back on its receiver and began rubbing my eyes. They were heavy with exhaustion. I'd been troubled by the situation with the young Tinsley boy since Edna first started bringing him to me. Restless evenings, night terrors, and almost constant anxiety plagued me about this boy and his father going through such agonizing heartache. It was a recipe for disastrous results. Like the perfect mixture of heat, humidity, and wind in the middle of summer creating a heightened risk of severe weather.

I wanted to tread carefully. The human side of me and the practiced psychiatric side of me were at war inside my head. I wanted to help Johnny. Was he dealing with post-traumatic stress that was causing him to hallucinate? That would require medication – something I wasn't comfortable pumping into an eight-year-old. The truth was it could be a number of different things. The human brain is more complex than we are able to fully comprehend. He'd have to go through rigorous medical testing, and that could be traumatizing for a boy his age.

Another thought had crossed my mind and sat in my stomach like a rock. What if this wasn't just some form of mental disorder?

"Do you believe in ghosts?"

That question still sat in my mind, unresolved. I believe every child in the world is afraid of the dark at some point; afraid of things that go bump in the night. Their brains aren't quite at an age capable of processing things like a house settling, or humidity and wind causing beams to warp and rub against their counterparts and make other noises that could be construed as ghosts haunting their homes.

But still, I tried to think back to my childhood. I would've sworn that there was a ghost that liked to hide in my closet. I'd wake up in the middle of the night to the sound of my closet door creaking open, but it could always be chalked up to wind drafts seeping in through our windows not being sealed well. Ironically, I watched *The Exorcist* in theaters upon its release. The movie downright terrified me, and the phenomenon grew exponentially from there.

My earliest friend, Todd Bailey, swore up and down that his house over on Hametown Road was haunted. It was an old farmhouse that had been built in the late 1800s. He said the ghost of an old man would roam around the house at night, causing mischief. Todd would tell me chilling stories of the farmer staring out his bedroom window overlooking the property. Or how the lights would mysteriously turn on and off by themselves. He even told me one story about how the spirit had one time thrown a book off his bookshelf in his room. But out of all the times I stayed there, I had never once experienced anything. Nothing. Not a cold spot, no voices, no glowing white floating mists yelling *"Boo!"* in the middle of the night. Not one experience.

Adding in that in all my time as a man of the cloth, I'd never dealt with anything serious on the matter either. Yet millions of people all across the world experience things that they would consider paranormal; many adding sightings and accounts of Bigfoot and UFOs as well. Just because I'd never experienced any of those things didn't mean they weren't real. The cold, hard reality of the situation is – there is so much in this world that we do not yet understand.

One thing was for certain, I knew that both good and evil exist. I believed in God, and I believed in the devil. Why shouldn't I believe in the possibility of life after death? What is heaven after all, if not life after death? What about lost souls? What about the evil that lurks in the darkness?

All troubling thoughts for sure, and I still couldn't shake the feeling that based on Johnny's accounts, there was more going on than he let on. '*What if?*' is one of the most powerful, yet dangerous thoughts in existence. What if something more sinister was indeed taking place? I needed to try to get to the bottom of this – and fast.

"Can you tell me what happened last night, Johnny?"

The boy looked fretfully back at Edna, who had refused to exit for this session.

"I need to know what my grandson is dealing with," she had said vehemently with bloodshot eyes.

Johnny looked tired and troubled. He once again found the loose piece of leather on the seat's armrest and began to fidget with it, averting his eyes. Edna already filled me in during last night's anxiety filled call about him seeing his mother again – this time in a frightening fashion. She also spoke about his altercation with his father – who, by my measure, sounded like he was attempting to defuse the situation.

Sensing Johnny's hesitation, I attempted to change the subject. "Think the tribe has a shot at making a repeat trip to the World Series again this year?"

Johnny picked his head up, his eyes beaming with excitement. "Y-You're a baseball fan?"

"Of course, I played all the way up through high school."

"What position did you play?"

"Shortstop."

Johnny's eyes widened. "That's what I play! Were you any good?"

I chuckled. "No, I couldn't hit the ball to save my life! But your grandmother tells me you're quite the young player. The next Omar Vizquel."

Johnny peered back to his grandmother with a shocked smile spreading over his face. "You did?"

Edna nodded warmly and Johnny turned back to face me once again, smiling from ear to ear. We continued to talk about baseball for a while, discussing our favorite players on the team, and discussing whether Johnny would continue playing as he got older.

"You know your mother will always be with you every time you step out onto that baseball field, right?" I asked.

Johnny's smile evaporated just as quickly as it had formed. He was starting to retreat back into his shell when he finally said, "I know."

"I understand she came to visit you last night."

Johnny nodded, keeping his eyes locked on the floor in front of him.

"There's no judgement on my part. I'm here to help you. We're all friends in the house of God," I told him softly. "Can you tell me what happened last night?"

I could tell the wheels inside Johnny's head were spinning. A moral dilemma. A battle of whether to discuss it or not.

"Would it be helpful if your grandmother and I plugged our ears? It would feel good to get things off your chest."

Johnny's brow furrowed as he shot a skeptical glance back at his grandma and then at me.

"Here, we'll give it a shot!" I said, bringing my hands up to cover my ears while nodding at Edna. She did the same. "Come on! Let's test it out! Say anything you want!" I yelled purposely louder than my normal voice.

Johnny looked back and forth once more, a sly grin spreading across his face. "You suck at baseball."

It took everything in my power not to laugh at the statement. The kid still had it in him to crack jokes which was a wonderful sign. I frowned and shook my head as though I hadn't heard what he'd said.

"Look, I'm not five years old anymore. I'm eight. I know you can still hear me," Johnny added.

Smart boy.

I lowered my hands from my ears, nodding my head. "I knew I shouldn't have told you I couldn't hit the ball," I joked, "...but I'm sure you get my point. Keeping things bottled up – it can boil over and make you very upset. You can't tell me that your brain hasn't been screaming for you to tell someone what's been going on."

Johnny seemed to ponder this for a moment. "I guess so," he said.

"Well, let's start here...can you tell me *why* it's hard to discuss your interactions with your mom since she passed?"

"She said no one would believe me."

"I believe you, Johnny."

"You do?" he asked, raising his head to meet my friendly gaze.

"Of course I do. Has she been doing anything to upset you?"

"For the most part, no."

"For the most part?" I asked.

Johnny nodded. "She said if I tell anyone about talking to her, that I will get locked away."

I shook my head and flashed a friendly smile. "Everything you tell me stays in this room, Johnny. You're safe here."

"Sometimes when she visits at night, she scares me."

"Things in the dark are always more frightening," I replied, bowing my head and encouraging him to continue.

"Last night, I got up to go to the bathroom. And when I walked past my parents' bedroom, I thought I saw a face smiling at me. But it wasn't my mom's face. It really scared me."

"Then what happened?" I asked.

"The face disappeared."

When our brains can't make sense of something – like what we're looking at in the dark, it can begin to form things out of nothing. The common word for it is pareidolia. An example would be when people look at photos of forests and can make faces out of the leaves and tree branches.

"Then I heard Mom singing in my room. She was singing *Simple Man*. It was always our special song," Johnny continued.

Edna gave a gasp at the mention of the song.

"And did anything else happen?"

Johnny thought for a moment and then shook his head. I frowned with a thought, tapping a finger at my bottom lip. *This still seems harmless enough. Over-active imagination or not. Could it be the actual spirit of his mother?*

"Has she ever asked you to do anything that you were uncomfortable with?"

Again, Johnny shook his head no. "No. And anytime she has scared me, she has explained how it was an accident or that I was just confused."

"I see. And does she always appear the same way? As in, is she always wearing the same clothes?"

He nodded this time. "She's always wearing her blue nightgown."

"And does her wearing that nightgown bring a lot of good memories to you?" I asked.

"Yeah, she would always wear it at nighttime and would read me bedtime stories in it."

"That's amazing that she made time to do that with you, Johnny."

We went on to discuss his recent newfound love for reading *Goosebumps* stories. I told him I'd have to give them a shot, before finally wrapping up our session. I felt like we made progress today. Johnny finally began to open up. I didn't get the impression that anything sinister was going on in the Tinsley household. Curiosity did strike me, however, on whether Ron had also been seeing his wife.

We made our way outside the church, where the morning songs of nearby birds flitted through the air in symphonic harmony under clear blue skies. I smiled, thinking back to my mother.

"Would you guys like some ice cream?" I asked, motioning toward Lowry's across the street.

Edna and Johnny looked at each other, seemingly taken aback. They happily obliged as we made our way across the street to the ice cream stand. I ordered my usual cone, Edna ordered a strawberry ice cream cone, and Johnny got a chocolate milkshake. We sat at the wooden picnic tables and chatted about our excitement for tonight's fireworks. Johnny would occasionally throw out another joke about how bad I must've been at baseball. I enjoyed the young man's sense of humor. My mom's philosophy on ice cream proved to be right once again. Everyone was all smiles.

When we'd finally finished our treats, I walked them back over to Edna's car. Edna told Johnny to hop in, and said she'd join him in a moment. She grabbed my elbow and pulled me a few paces away from her car.

"Well?" she asked. "What do you think?"

"It's not a lot to go on, Edna, but I have to be honest. Even if he is dealing with the spirit of his mother's ghost, it seems completely harmless other than a few minor hiccups, according to Johnny."

"So, what do you suggest we do? Do you think it's safe for him to go back with his dad?"

"I don't see why he shouldn't go be with his dad. I think Ron is doing the best he can right now, all things considered. With everything else, I think we have to just let it play out. Unless something catastrophic happens, there's not much intervening that needs to take place. It could very well just be a phase. Time will tell. I'd definitely be curious as to whether Ron has also been seeing the spirit of Susan or not."

"Would you like me to find out?"

"If you could, that might be helpful."

"I will see what I can do. Thank you again for doing this on such short notice, Father," Edna said, shaking my hand.

"Not a problem at all, Edna. Johnny's a fine young man. I'll always be here to help."

I watched as Edna got in her car and pulled away. I heaved a sigh of relief, feeling much better about the situation in the Tinsley household after today's counseling session.

Chapter Seven

July 4th, 1998
Johnny Tinsley

I felt a lot better after today's talk with Father Rosario. He was right, it did feel good to be able to talk about my experiences. I felt a slight pang of guilt about not giving him the whole story. I wanted to but was still scared of being locked away – especially if I told him the story about my mom's spirit now residing inside of Lucy. That sounded super weird, even to me.

When we arrived at my house, my stomach was in knots. Last night, I said something to my dad out of pure anger that I didn't mean. I didn't hate him at all. I just felt like he wasn't listening to me; that he didn't believe me. I felt unseen, unheard, and forgotten about most the time and I was beyond frustrated about it. Mom was still with us. I had seen her, spoken with her, and even felt her touch. I wasn't crazy. I found myself thinking back to last night's events after my argument with my dad while I was gathering my things to take over to Grandma's house.

"Is something troubling you, my son?" my mother's voice called out while I placed Lucy back on her chair.

I turned to look back and saw Mom sitting on the edge of my bed.

"Why did you have to scare me? None of this would've happened if you just left me alone." I responded to her in my head, so my dad wouldn't overhear our conversation.

Mom cocked her head, as if considering what I'd just said. *"I didn't mean to scare you, Johnny. I sang you our song, remember?"*

"Yeah," I responded grumpily, while stuffing a change of clothes into my backpack. *"But why'd you have to move Lucy? Was that your face I saw in the doorway?"*

Mom smiled. *"I moved Lucy onto your bed so that we could be closer together. You remember when I used to lay in bed with you and read bedtime stories, yes?"*

I nodded, taking a seat next to her on the bed. She placed an icy arm around my shoulders, causing a chill to run down my spine.

"I don't know anything about any faces in the doorway. All I know is that we will always be together, Johnny. Always."

"Why haven't you visited, Dad? He misses you."

Mom let out a quiet chuckle, unlike one I'd ever heard her make. *"Let's not worry about your father. He's not strong like you, Johnny – and he could never love you like I have and always will."*

Those words hurt. Dad did seem to be rather aloof lately. He seemed like he was beginning to care less and less about me as time went by.

"He's sick, Johnny. He doesn't love you anymore. He's a broken man and should not be trusted. Do you understand what I'm telling you?"

I nodded sheepishly and hopped up from my bed, eager to leave. Mom's words hurt my feelings. Was Dad truly sick? What did that mean? Did he really not love me anymore? I sprinted for the door, taking one last tear-filled look back into my room. Mom was gone.

We got out of the car and Grandma decided to come inside with me, which she normally didn't do after my visits with Father Rosario.

When we got inside, we found Dad sitting in his normal spot in his wheelchair in the living room. He was staring blankly at the bookshelf. I quickly rushed over to him.

"Daddy! I'm so sorry about what I said last night! I don't hate you at all. I love you. I promise!"

I wrapped my arms around him in a loving hug. I wanted so badly for my mom's words to be untrue. I openly wept into the nape of his neck, expecting an embrace in return. He felt cold and clammy. He didn't acknowledge me. When I pulled back, I noticed his head was still facing the bookshelf, but his eyes had shifted in my direction, giving me a side-eyed glance. I could've sworn I saw his lip curl into a half-smirk. It made me feel uneasy and I slowly backed away.

"Is everything alright, Ron?" Grandma called out.

He didn't respond — didn't move.

"Dad?"

Like the flash of a camera, his eyelashes flitted and he shook his head – snapping back to reality. He took a deep inhale and looked over at me and then at Grandma.

"Oh! Hey!" he said, taking in a deep breath as if he'd been holding his breath under water for far too long. "Sorry about that. I – uh...didn't get much sleep last night. I just completely zoned out."

"We went and spoke with Father Rosario this morning," Grandma said as she took a seat on our sofa next to Dad.

"Is that so?" he asked coldly.

There was a moment of silence. I wasn't sure what was going on, but something about being back in my house just felt *off*.

"How'd it go?" he asked, his tone suddenly shifting to a more upbeat manner.

"It went...good," Grandma replied. She sounded like she was uncertain of herself or how to proceed.

"That...That's great!" he replied, almost robotically.

"Hey, Johnny. Would you do me a favor?" she asked.

"Sure!" I exclaimed.

"Could you run out to my car and grab the hot dogs, buns, and tray of cookies out of my trunk?"

Grandma dangled her car keys in her hand. I got the feeling she wanted some alone time with my dad for a minute. But the moment I heard cookies, I didn't care and immediately darted outside. Grandma made the best chocolate chip cookies. The outer edges were always perfectly crispy, but the center of the cookies were ooey, gooey goodness.

When I returned inside, Grandma was already getting up to leave. She bent down and gave me a kiss on my forehead. She seemed to be feeling better about whatever had been bothering her. She told me to enjoy the food – but not to eat too many of the cookies at once – and to enjoy the fireworks tonight. She said she had a doctor's appointment and couldn't stay. When I asked why she had to go to the doctor, she told me it was nothing to worry about and to enjoy the rest of my day before making her way to her car.

I eagerly made my way through the front walkway as Grandma shut the door behind her. I hadn't been so excited about a piece of food in ages. I darted past the doorway to my right that led to the living room, but I could feel that my dad had turned his wheelchair to face this direction. Out of the corner of my eye, I could've sworn he was...he was smiling at me – and not in his normal smile. A smile that was entirely too large to be humanly possible.

I retreated a couple of steps and looked into the living room. Dad was not facing my direction at all. Instead, he was sitting in the exact same spot as before, facing the bookshelf in silence.

I aggressively shook my head, trying to knock the cobwebs loose. *Huh... So strange. Had I really seen that smile?*

Dad still seemed out of it when dinner time came around. The memory of me yelling the words *'I hate you!'* to him replayed through my mind over and over again – and I felt sick about it. Eager to right the ship, I'd tried being more upbeat and spending more time with him earlier in the day. I turned on the Indians game, hoping that would help. Baseball was something we had always bonded over, but he seemed disinterested. He would occasionally mutter things under his breath, but when I asked him what he said, he ignored me.

Undeterred, I decided to show him I was a growing young man and decided to make dinner myself. I grabbed the hot dog buns and placed them on the dinner table, along with the normal hot dog toppings – ketchup, mustard, and relish – placing them in the center of the table neatly. I put a few hot dogs into the microwave and turned it on. I felt a little embarrassed, as I had cooked them for too long. Both ends on each of the hot dogs had burst and looked unappetizing. I looked over my shoulder to make sure Dad hadn't wheeled his way into the kitchen. When I realized the coast was clear, I tossed them into the trash can and tried again. This time, the hot dogs came out perfectly.

"Dad! Dinner's ready!" I hollered, placing the beef franks on the table alongside their eventual counterparts. I was quite proud of myself. It was my first time ever making dinner.

I called out for Dad again after receiving no response. When he didn't answer again, I rushed out of the kitchen that combined as our dining room and headed to our living room. Dad wasn't there.

"Dad?"

No response.

With curiosity getting the better of me, I exited the living room and turned toward our staircase that sat just before reaching our front door. A wave of unease struck me in my core at the sight. Dad was sitting at the bottom of the stairs and was staring up toward the landing, saying nothing and not moving. His cold, hard stare seemed hyper focused. He didn't even acknowledge that I was there.

"W-What'cha lookin' at, Dad?" I managed to finally ask.

No response.

I slowly made my way over, fearful that maybe Mommy was upstairs, and he was in a state of shock. As I rounded the corner and stood next to him, I saw that nothing was up there. He still made no notice of me now standing directly next to him.

"He's sick, Johnny. He's a broken man and should not be trusted."

I could feel my breathing getting heavier, fear setting in. I asked him again what he was looking at. This time he slowly turned his head in my direction – almost as though he were a wooden doll having his head twisted for him.

"I...I made dinner for us," I said timidly.

His eyes floated up and met mine. He smiled weakly. His lips began moving but no sound came out. I tried to lean closer to hear what he was saying, but it all sounded like muddled gibberish.

I grabbed hold of the wheelchair handles and pushed him into the kitchen where dinner awaited us. I sat him in front of his normal spot at the table before taking my seat next to him.

"I want to try something new today, Daddy. I would like to say grace," I said, trying to be more positive for his sake.

He continued his breathless muttering, ignoring my words.

"We have a lot to be thankful for still."

"No!" he howled, slamming a fist down onto the table, sending the condiment bottles bouncing. The aggression behind his voice caught me off guard and frightened me.

"I...I really think it might help us both feel better. Father Rosario said that..."

Dad's face contorted with rage. If looks could kill, I'd likely be dead already. "Fuck Father Rosario! He's a two-bit hack! You think God gives a shit about us?" he snarled, cutting me off mid-sentence.

I was so taken aback by my dad's words that I didn't know how to respond. He'd never acted like this in my entire life. Maybe this was part of him being sick like Mom had mentioned.

"I don't want to hear another word about God or that child molester, Father Rosario, in this house ever again. Do you understand?"

I nodded my head, fighting back the urge to cry. I didn't understand why he was lashing out. I didn't understand the name he called Father Rosario.

"And another thing... You call *this* dinner?" he asked, motioning a hand around in a circle, grinning from ear to ear. "You are an embarrassment to me, and I wish you would've died in that car accident instead of your mother."

Those words felt like razor blades attached to the end of a baseball bat — they cut deep and knocked the wind out of me. Dad let out a deep, bellowing laugh before hammering his fist down onto the plate of hot dogs, smashing them into a thin paste. I watched as his fingers clawed at the remnants of beef franks and threw the goop directly into my face.

"Now, get the fuck out of my sight!"

I slid out my chair, sending it screeching across the hardwood floor, completely heartbroken.

"I...I'm calling Grandma!" I wailed, rushing over to the house phone mounted on the wall.

"Oh yeah?" he called out.

I pulled the phone off the receiver, and before I knew what was happening, Dad reached up and yanked the entire unit out of the wall. I jumped back, startled at what was transpiring.

"You will do what I tell you to do. Now get your ass up to your room before I *really* get mad. And if you even think about leavin' – it ain't gonna end well." Dad's shoulders were heaving; his face contorted into a shape I barely recognized.

The whirlwind of emotions was too much to bear. I let out a squeal, trying to hold back the floodgate of tears from flowing as I rushed out of the kitchen and upstairs to my room, locking the door behind me.

"He's sick, Johnny. He doesn't love you anymore. He's a broken man and should not be trusted."

The words rang out in my head as I paced back and forth in my room, bawling my eyes out. I walked over to my mirror, looking at the chunks of hot dogs still clinging onto my shirt and hair. I angrily brushed them onto the floor and ran to my bed, burying my face into my pillows for what felt like hours.

Never in my life had I been so hurt by someone's words or actions. Not even by my bullies at school. I felt a pain unlike anything I'd ever felt. A different type of pain from losing Mom. My own Dad wished I'd died in that car accident. He really didn't love me.

I lifted my head, it felt like it was the size of a watermelon, and I brushed the tears away. With a sniffle, I looked over to Lucy and tried calling out for Mom, but she never came. Where was she? Why wasn't she answering me? It wasn't like her to not show up when I needed her.

"Mommy, please," I said one last time.

Nothing.

Feeling lost, abandoned, frightened, and heartbroken all at once, I gave up on calling out for Mom. She wasn't coming. I felt like I couldn't shed another tear even if I wanted to.

I got up and did the only thing that had proven to be an escape for me any other time in the past. I walked over to my bookshelf and grabbed a copy of *Night of the Living Dummy* – another of my favorite installments from my favorite book series. I turned on my bedside lamp, noticing how dark it had become. The fireworks would surely begin anytime now.

Normally, on the Fourth of July, I would be ecstatic to watch the fireworks from my bedroom window. When I was younger, we would drive to the nearby park to watch them up close and in person, but as the town grew, so did the popularity of going there to watch them.

"We can still see them from the house, honey," Mom said a couple years back when it was decided that we wouldn't be going to the park to watch them anymore.

I was upset about it at the time, so we had turned it into a big spectacle in my room that night. Dad had prepared marshmallows on our gas burner stove for s'mores and then we snacked on them from my bed as we watched the array of lights flash and listened to the echoes of explosions ringing in the air.

Tonight felt different. I felt alone. No Mom. No Dad – not one that I could consider to be a Dad anymore, anyhow. I flipped open my book and began tearing through the pages, trying my best to stuff down the memories of this evening far, far away.

Boom!

Boom! Boom! Boom!

The show had begun. I laid my book down on my stomach, peering out my window as the beautiful multi-colored flashes of light exploded above the tree line outside my window.

Boom! Boom! Boom!

Even in the midst of life beating me down, it was hard not to become mesmerized by the cascade of pyrotechnics soaring through the night sky. Faster and more consistently they flew into the air, bringing the dozens of explosions into one cohesive blast.

The grand finale was coming up. I could feel the anticipation building, knowing the best part of the show was about to begin.

Boom! Boom! Boom! Boom! Boom! Boom!

BOOM!

The last shockwave nearly sent me flying out of my bed. It wasn't a part of the fireworks display. It sounded like it came from within our house. It shook the walls and sent vibrations through my bed. I immediately jumped up, my heart racing.

What was that?

It sounded like a tank had steamrolled right into the front door.

"Dad?" I called out weakly.

The house had fallen silent, just as the firework show had ended. I called out to him once again but received no response. Conflict tugged at my subconscious. Did I go downstairs and disobey my dad's orders or stay up here when something could be wrong. I didn't know what to do.

Bang! Bang! Boom!

Several loud crashes sounded from downstairs, each one louder than the last, sending my heart into a frenzy.

I crept out of my bed and slowly crept to my bedroom door. I unlocked and opened it, sticking my head outside into the hall. Everything in the house was pitch black.

"Dad? Is everything okay?"

I was met with the sharp crash of glass shattering downstairs.

My heart was racing, and my palms grew sweaty. I wanted to call out to Dad again, but it felt like a frog was caught in my throat. I took a cautious step out into the hallway, my socked feet giving me an added level of stealth on the hardwood flooring.

HYYYYUH!

The sound of someone taking a deep breath as if they'd been holding it for far too long seared into my eardrums. I took another step forward. Something slammed against the wall down in the living room. It sounded like a dresser being thrown into the wall. I took another timid step forward. Then another.

"Dad?" I called out.

Suddenly, the noises stopped, and the house fell silent once more. My pounding heart was the only thing I could hear now.

I never understood the saying of being scared to death or believed in its plausibility until this very moment. It felt like my heart was all the way up in my vocal cords – and my mouth was growing drier by the second.

I finally made it to the top of the staircase. The house was completely still again, as if it had fallen into a restful sleep. Everything was blanketed under the darkness of night. Even after everything that'd happened at dinner, I still found myself hoping that Dad was okay. I didn't even want to consider a life without *both* of my parents.

I went down the first few steps when the pungent odor of rotten eggs assaulted my senses. Cold air swirled around me, sending a renewed chill up my spine. I did my best to push through the frigid, noxious air, slowly descending to the bottom of the stairs.

"Hello? Dad, are you down here?"

Silence.

I rounded the corner toward the hallway that led to the living room, and kitchen and my heart sank at the first thing I saw.

Sitting just a few feet up the hall was my dad's wheelchair. It was empty. A wave of panic set in. I felt sick. Was my dad okay?

I rushed forward past his wheelchair and through the doorway to the living room. The room felt much darker than I'd ever seen before. It felt like a thick black smoke had swallowed the room whole. I couldn't make out the shapes of anything in the room. I reached my hand around the corner of the doorway and attempted to flip the light switch on. It didn't work. I took a slow, silent step forward; then another and another, until I was enveloped by the abyss. The house was as quiet as I'd ever heard it. I took another blind, shuffling step forward. With my eyes adjusting, I began to survey my surroundings. I noticed the sofa to my right. No sign of Dad. I turned my head and looked to my left. I could make out the shape of the TV and the stand it sat on. Nestled next to that was our bookshelf.

Slowly, my eyes swept across the room again, past our fireplace and to the corner of the room where the shadow of a tall figure loomed, facing the corner away from me.

"Dad?" I whispered, my voice shaky.

The figure didn't move or respond. I took a small step toward it. I could hear it breathing now. There was no way this could be Dad. He couldn't stand. So, who was standing in the corner? My mind and heart were both racing a mile a minute.

"D-Dad?" I said a little louder this time.

The figure remained motionless. I took one more reluctant step forward and reached a hand out toward the silhouette. My hand brushed up against what felt like a person – when suddenly, with the reflexes of a lion – the figure spun around, gripping my forearm tightly and viciously yanking me down to the hard floor with a sickening thud. A cavernous, guttural voice bellowed out from above me.

"Hello, Johnny! Are you ready to play?" the voice said.

I tried to wriggle free of the figure's grasp, but it was too strong. "Let me go!" I wailed.

"Go? Yes...let's go..." The figure moved swiftly, dragging me kicking and screaming through the living room and toward the kitchen. I tried clubbing my fist on the shadowy figure's arm, to no avail.

Upon reaching the kitchen, light from our neighbor's floodlight on their garage gave the room a sickly green glow. I was dragged across broken glass and chunks of hot dogs before being aggressively thrown against the kitchen cabinets, bouncing headfirst off one of their handles. I flopped to the floor in a dazed heap, stars blinding my line of sight. I began crying out for my dad. This caused the figure to chuckle sinisterly.

"Daddy! Daddy! Daddy!" it mimicked, laughing at its own joke.

When I finally managed to get my wits about me and look up, I couldn't believe my eyes. The figure that was doing this *was* my dad. I watched completely awestruck as he pulled a long chef's knife out of the block on the counter. Dim light gleamed off the side of the blade. He placed the tip of the blade down on the kitchen countertop and twirled it around from its plastic handle like it was some sort of dreidel. His cold eyes locked onto mine as a smile spread across his lips.

"Johnny. Johnny. Johnny," he said, his voice returning back to normal. "Did I tell you that you could leave your room?"

He lifted the blade from the countertop and took a step towards me. I crab walked backwards away from him.

"D-Dad...What's going on?"

He took another step forward, ignoring my question and brandishing the sharp knife at his side. Without hesitation, I rolled onto my side and scrambled to my feet, running toward the doorway that led to the main hall and the fastest exit out of this house. Each step sent excruciating pain soaring through my body as little shards of broken glass pierced into the bottoms of my feet.

"Come on, Johnny boy!" Dad called out, giving chase.

"No!" I wailed, snot and tears rolling down my face once more. "Leave me alone!"

"But I thought you loved me?" his voice became a troubling replica of his own. Almost sounding like slow motion of itself.

When I finally reached the front door, I tried to twist the deadbolt lock but noticed it had been broken off. I attempted to twist the doorknob and pull the door open anyway, but it was stuck. I turned and looked back just in time to see Dad on his thin and weakened legs staggering toward me.

"I told you. You're not going anywhere!"

I made the only other move I knew I could make. I rushed upstairs and locked myself in my bedroom. I looked at my window and considered jumping. But from the second floor, I feared I would die instantly, so I ran over to my bed and slid underneath it. If he could break in here, he would absolutely find me. But what else could I do? I thought about the knife he was carrying. Was I about to die? The sound of shoes on the hardwood stairs continued to get closer. And closer. And closer.

BANG!

My entire door shook.

BANG!

"Ohhhh, Johnny! Open up! Don't you want to play?"

BANG! BANG!

"Please! Just leave me alone!"

"Where's the fun in that?"

BANG! BANG! BANG!

The wood was beginning to splinter. Tears were flowing freely down my cheeks. My feet were throbbing in pain, and I was terrified of what would happen if Dad managed to break his way into my room. Suddenly, things fell silent. The gut-wrenching sound of the door being rammed into had finally ceased.

"Come on, buddy. Open the door up for Daddy."

The detachment in his voice made my blood run cold.

"Come on! I will even sing you a song! I know it's your favorite. Your whore mother sings it every night down in hell!"

BANG!

I let out a frightened yelp.

"There's my boy! Here, let's give it a shot," he said, clearing his throat. "And don't forget son...there is someone dowwwwn beeeloooowwww!"

BANG! BANG!

With a nasty crunching sound, the door finally slammed open, and Dad stalked toward my bed.

"You think you can hide from me?"

He reached under the bed, gripped hold of me by my shirt, and yanked me out effortlessly. With my legs flailing wildly, he tugged me toward the doorway. He paid my pleas for help no mind as he dragged me from my room and began to take me back downstairs. With so many terrifying thoughts running through my brain, I bit down into his forearm as hard as I could. He yelled out in pain and then tossed me down the remaining steps to the bottom of the stairwell.

"That wasn't very nice and certainly wasn't a very god-like thing to do," he said as he gripped my shirt again and tossed me onto the living room floor.

I tried to get to my feet to run, but he whipped his fist into my stomach, sending me doubling back over onto the floor in a wheezing heap.

Dad left the room and came back moments later, pushing his wheelchair directly in front of me. I did the only thing I could do and rolled onto my back. He sat down in the wheelchair, looked down at his knife, and then back over at me.

"Pray to God."

"W-What?" I croaked.

"Pray to Him and see what good that does you. Pray for Him to save me. To save you. Pray for Him to rid the world of disease! Go on, boy! Pray!"

I said nothing and continued to openly weep on the floor, the taste of blood filling my mouth. Confusion, fear, and betrayal consumed my heart and soul.

"No?" he questioned coldly, a scratchy cackle escaping his throat. "God will never help you. God is dead. What you're feeling now – lost, frightened, alone – prepare for a lifetime of that. I'm going to take everything and everyone you ever love. And once you've hit your lowest point and I feel satisfied in my work, I'm going to take you too."

I didn't understand the meaning of anything my dad had just said. What did he mean he was going to take everything and everyone away from me? What did he mean he was going to take me too? I looked at him through watery eyes, just in time to watch him plunge the chef's knife directly into his neck and yank it back out. Blood shot out of his neck like a geyser, spilling all over the hardwood floor. His body shook and spasmed for a moment, before he made a chilling raspy attempt at a gurgled breath and went still.

I stared at him in disbelief for a moment. His eyes looked empty. Void of any expression. I knew it then: he was dead. This had to be a nightmare. I had to be sleeping. The visual of the knife plunging into his neck and the sickening noise it made as it punctured his flesh would be scarred into my psyche for life.

I called out for Mom. Nothing. Nothing but a house now filled with silence. She wasn't coming to console me. Nobody was. In such a short span, I'd lost both my mother and my father. I was completely defenseless to it all. Scared, confused, hurt, and alone.

I cried harder than I ever thought possible in that moment.

Chapter Eight

July 5th, 1998
Johnny Tinsley

The rest of the night was a blur. Once I'd finally built up the courage and strength, I weakly got to my feet. I stepped around my now deceased father, noticing the slow trickle of dark viscous blood still escaping from the gaping wound in his neck — the knife now laying on the floor next to him. His expressionless eyes and mouth lifelessly hung open and would haunt me for the rest of my days.

With exhaustion and delirium setting in, I made my way into our backyard. I circled around to the front of the house, screaming for help at the top of my lungs until I noticed a couple of neighbors that had been outside for a bonfire.

The neighbors promptly called the authorities and within minutes, the all too familiar wail of sirens screamed through the neighborhood, taking me back to the moments trapped in our car down in the ravine. I sat in the grass overcome with emotions, while my neighbor's wife, Mrs. Pollack held me gingerly in her arms, caressing my hair and telling me things were going to be okay.

The night ended with the EMTs rushing me to the hospital, while the police scoured through my house. The medic informed me that she was able to get a hold of my grandma and that she would be meeting us at the hospital. Hearing that much had comforted me. Feeling overtaken with exhaustion, grief, and pain, I passed out during the ambulance ride to Akron Children's Hospital.

I had been held at the hospital until early in the afternoon. When I awoke, I was instantly greeted by my teary-eyed grandmother. She was so thankful that I was okay. I didn't feel okay, however. My mind, body, and spirit all felt beaten and battered. My feet were on fire and had been wrapped with heavy gauze. When I got up to use the restroom, I noticed that I had a fat lip with a cut above it and had received some stitches on my forehead for a gash just above my eye.

During my stay, Father Rosario came to visit and greeted me warmly. He brought me in a brand-new baseball mitt and said we were going to have to get it broken in before the Fall League started. I appreciated the sentiment but found it hard to be excited about anything at the moment. He asked if I'd like to see him sooner than next Friday for a counseling session, saying he thinks it would be good for us. I told him I wasn't ready to talk about things just yet unless I had to. He nodded and said that was no issue and that he'd see me next Friday.

Before leaving, he said, "I know it can feel like things are against you right now but always have faith that God is with you. Always." I shot him a weak smile, but I had a hard time believing his words this time around. But then I remembered the words my mom said to me.

"I don't know anything about any faces in the doorway. All I know is that we will always be together, Johnny. Always."

If God were always with me, did that mean Mommy was an angel? It only seemed right.

I also had to speak with a local police detective about the occurrences in my house last night. He had introduced himself as Detective Walasko. He was a pretty heavy-set man that wore a grey suit and had a shiny bald head with a thick mustache that made him look like a walrus. I found myself wondering if he'd ever been bullied as a kid – being called Walasko the Walrus or Wally Walrus. Having been picked on a bit myself — frequently being called *Johnny Appleseed or Johnny Cakes* — I was no stranger to the cruelty fellow classmates could show. He seemed to be nice enough, though. After some coaxing, I told him about my dad attacking me in the middle of the night. He jotted everything down in his notepad, nodding as he did so. When we finished talking, he said he would be in touch and asked to speak with my grandma outside my room.

She later returned and continued to console me at my bedside, saying things were going to be okay.

"Grandma, what's going to happen with me? Where am I gonna go?"

"I am going to take care of you, honey. And I am so sorry about what you went through last night."

Those memories were all I could think about on the way to my grandma's house from the hospital. She lived on the other side of Norton – far away from my parents' house.

The memories from last night would be forever etched into my brain. I saw things I could never force myself to unsee. Things I could never force myself to forget. Things I could never stop feeling. The haunting visual of my dad twirling the knife blade around on the counter while he smirked at me. The way he spoke. Him making a mockery of the song that meant so much to my mom and I. Him saying she sang it every night in *hell*. That struck me in my core. It made me think Mommy was suffering. I wasn't sure what made Daddy snap the way he did. It all started when I brought up wanting to say grace at dinner. Just the mere mention was enough to send him into a fit of rage. I couldn't make sense of right or wrong anymore in the eyes of God because one thing Daddy said that came true, no matter how much I hoped and prayed things would improve – they most certainly had not.

"I will take everything you love from you. And one day I will take you too."

I didn't understand what those words meant. Even with the amount of times I replayed those events in my head, I still couldn't make sense of the sudden shift in my dad's personality, why he went crazy, or how he had managed to walk.

Grandma kept trying to make small talk during the car ride, but I just didn't feel like talking. I stared out my window at the neighborhoods we raced through.

Upon arriving at her house, Grandma brought me to her living room, where she promptly had me lay down on her couch. She brought over a blanket and draped it over me. She then went into the kitchen and whipped up a bowl of ice cream and brought that out to me as well. I hadn't felt a warmth like this from someone who truly cared since Mom had passed away. I knew my mom was her daughter, and I could see where Mom's kindness had come from.

Grandma turned on the Indians game and we watched them take down the Kansas City Royals by a final score of twelve to three.

It was hard for me to remain focused on the game. My mind kept drifting. After the game had ended, I asked her what Detective Walasko had talked to her about.

"Let's not worry about that right now, honey. You just rest and relax. Okay?"

"Okay, Grandma."

"I love you, honey."

"I love you, too."

No matter how much I loved my grandma. No matter how sweet she was to me – after the past couple months, I wondered if it was me that had been causing everyone around me that I loved to lose their lives. I just hoped it would be different this time. She was my last remaining family member. Mom and Dad had no siblings, so I had no aunts or uncles – and no cousins to boot.

I closed my eyes, wanting to pray but deciding against it.

Chapter Nine

July 5th, 1998
Edna Tomko

After finally getting Johnny down to rest for the night, I made my way to the kitchen and took a seat at the table after pouring myself a glass of hot tea. I had a sneaking suspicion that sleep would evade me tonight. My heart broke for my grandson. No one deserved to go through so much heartbreak in a lifetime, let alone within a couple months. He lost his mother – my daughter, to a tragic car accident – and then last night, his father committed a gruesome suicide right in front of him. I couldn't even begin to imagine the thoughts going through his brain.

The past twenty-four hours felt like a total blur. Being awoken in the middle of the night to a phone call of that magnitude –it was a wonder I didn't die from a heart attack right then and there. But I raced my way to the hospital nonetheless to see my grandson and meet with law enforcement.

Seeing Johnny resting in that hospital bed – bandaged and bruised – absolutely crushed my spirit. Upon discussing the results of their initial investigation, I was awestruck.

"We're not sure how...but his story checks out," the detective said to me outside Johnny's hospital room.

"Is that even possible?" I asked.

"If you asked me this question yesterday, that a man paralyzed from the waist down was capable of doing these things, I would've told you no. But the wound to Ron's neck was absolutely self-inflicted."

"But you don't believe Johnny's story." I said matter-of-factly.

"It's possible that Johnny was sleepwalking and dreamed a lot of that up."

"He dreamed about those horrible things his father said and did to him? He dreamed about being thrown down the stairs and dragged out of his bedroom?"

"Look. We're not accusing Johnny of any wrongdoing here. It's just...there's no way a paraplegic could do those things. So, is it possible that Johnny was sleepwalking and had visions of all of that? My inclination is to say that that IS possible. Though, I don't think an eight-year-old boy has the strength to rip a door off its hinges. Either way, we'll be in contact. Keep the boy safe and keep him comfortable. A night this traumatic will undoubtedly leave him scarred for life."

"I will. Thank you, Detective."

I was still unsure of what to make of all of it. Could anyone ever make sense of it? As far as I knew, Johnny had never had a problem with sleepwalking. Father Rosario mentioned that with the trauma that Johnny had experienced, that somnambulism could be a distinct possibility if counseling proved ineffective. That explanation still couldn't push away the thoughts that something else entirely must've been going on. While I didn't think Ron got up and walked around and attacked Johnny in the exact manner of his story, I also couldn't resign myself to the fact that Johnny had somehow slept through falling down steps, walking through glass, and slamming his head. That wasn't possible either, as far as I knew.

Staring down at my steaming tea, I swirled my finger around the rim of the cup, contemplating it all. I looked at the clock on my stove. It was nearly midnight. I wanted to phone Father Rosario and see if he had any thoughts on the matter. I knew he'd either be getting ready for bed or was already asleep as I dialed his number on my landline. I waited impatiently as the phone continued to ring.

"Hello?" he answered groggily.

"Tom, it's Edna. Is now a good time to chat?"

"Edna," he said, his voice perking up a bit at the sound of my voice. "Yes, I can talk. What's going on?"

"I finally got Johnny down for bed."

"How's he doing?"

"He's a wreck, Father."

"I'd imagine so. I can't even begin to comprehend the things he has going on in his head right now."

"Say, Tom... Do you know of any way where someone that is paralyzed can get up on their own two feet and do such heinous things?"

He let out a sigh. "No. No, I don't believe that to be a possibility, Edna."

"S-So you believe he was sleepwalking through all of that?"

"I don't know what to believe, Edna. Look, the brain is more powerful than anyone can even begin to process. Through my schooling, I learned that people – during a somnambulistic state – have been able to push through some rather extraordinary things. While in that state, a person can have the most intense, vivid hallucinations imaginable. And while it's not common, it's not completely unheard of for someone to not fully register pain during an episode. You must remember they're in a state of partial consciousness. Depending on the severity of the hallucinations, it's entirely possible that they coincided with what he was experiencing during the event."

I shook my head. An awkward silence fell across the phone line. "I don't believe that for a second, Tom."

"Look, even if it was Johnny sleepwalking, he didn't cause his dad's actions. That's the important takeaway. Just monitor the situation and see if you find him sleepwalking in the coming days or not."

"Yeah...Yeah, I can do that, Father. I really appreciate your insight and will sleep on it. Have a good night."

"Hey, Edna?"

"Yes?"

"I'm sorry for everything you've been going through."

"Thank you, Father."

I couldn't help but wonder if his apology for everything I'd been through included the rounds of chemo I'd been battling over the past few months. The doctors mentioned that it appeared to be working, albeit slower than they'd like.

"Stress can exacerbate the issues, Edna. You must try to find your inner peace and relax during these rounds of chemo."

Chalk one up for life not allowing that to happen. What's life without stress anyways? Does that even exist?

I really tried to mull over Tom's thoughts. Without showing it – hearing him say that people who sleepwalk could feasibly not wake up from feeling pain – had really taken the wind out of my sails. I knew deep down that it didn't truly matter whether

Johnny had hallucinated the visions of his father or not. I think what really made my soul uncomfortable was the thought that if Johnny was sleepwalking and hallucinating to that degree, did he have something much worse going on inside his head than we originally considered? It was a scary thought.

I took a sip from my now lukewarm tea. I still struggled thinking about the loss of Susan. No parent should ever have to bury their child. But this situation was no longer about me, or my feelings. My grandson was in desperate need of support, and I was going to do everything in my power to help raise him and give him a good life.

I scooted out from my chair at the table and walked to the guest bedroom. I popped the door open quietly and craned my neck inside. Johnny was fast asleep, facing away from the door. I watched his side rise and fall with each passing breath. Oh, how I hoped those were peaceful rest breaths.

"Please, God. Give us the strength to get through these times," I whispered before shutting the door. A single tear spilling down my cheek.

Chapter Ten

July 29ᵗʰ, 1998
Johnny Tinsley

It had been a few weeks since that fateful night. I spent much of my time playing board games, watching baseball, and helping grandma make dinner. I got the sense that she was keeping a watchful eye over me, while trying to also keep me busy.

"Shewww! Grandma's gettin' tired," she'd say occasionally throughout the day. That's how I knew it was time to kick back on the couch and watch TV and let her rest.

She'd informed me that she hadn't been feeling well recently, but as long as she got breaks, things would be okay. When I tried to ask her questions about it, she would just flash her friendly smile and tell me there was nothing to worry about.

I'd tried on a few occasions – when Grandma wasn't around – to reach out to Mom. I never got a response. I missed her. It felt weird that she just fell off the face of the Earth the night before Dad exploded. She hadn't shown up for me on that night, and I hadn't seen her since. I knew nobody would understand, but I felt a sense of abandonment in not having seen or heard from her spirit in so long, considering it had become an almost daily occurrence for weeks.

Maybe it's because she's stuck inside Lucy? I thought.

I hoped that wasn't the case. That would mean she'd been there through the most terrifying night of my life. That would mean she also had to be there while the cops scoured the entire house, cleaning the mess that Dad had left behind.

When the phone rang this morning, Grandma promptly answered. I tried eavesdropping on the conversation from the living room – trying my best to be a secret spy like in the movies. Grandma always got a laugh out of my *antics* as she called them.

"That was Detective Walasko," she said after hanging up the phone. Hearing the mention of his name always made my stomach lurch, like he was going to unveil some sort of troubling revelation.

"I heard. What did he want?"

"You little snooper, you!" she joked. "I swear, you're going to be the next James Bond when you grow up."

I couldn't help but smirk. She always had a way of making me feel special — even in the smallest ways that only a grandma can.

"He said that the case is closed, and we are good to start heading over and gathering things from the house whenever you're ready."

I shifted uncomfortably on the sofa. Sensing my unease, she asked me if I was comfortable with getting some of my clothes. I hadn't even considered having to go back into that house. I couldn't go back inside, and I never would if given the choice. The memories of my dad chasing me around the house with malicious intent was seared into my brain. I shook my head at her question.

"Would you be okay if I went over and grabbed a few things for you?"

I nodded.

"Are you going to be okay over here by yourself for about an hour?" she asked.

I nodded again.

"Okay, honey. Well, I am gonna go and grab you some clothes. Is there anything else you'd like me to grab for you while I am there today?"

I thought long and hard. I thought about my Goosebumps books, baseball cards, and my autographed baseball. I promptly brought those up to her and she laughed.

"Sheesh! You think your grandma can carry all that?" she said, giggling.

"Please, Grandma!" I begged playfully.

"I'll see what I can do. Maybe I can grab some of your posters and such so we can put them up in your room here. Sound like a plan?"

My eyes went wide with excitement. "You mean that?"

"Of course, silly."

"Thanks, Grandma! I love you!"

"I love you too, kiddo. Come on and help Grandma take some boxes out to the car."

I scrambled to my feet and rushed into the pantry, where she often kept spare boxes. *"You never know when you're going to need 'em,"* as she and my mom would both say.

I hadn't noticed it before, but spending so much time with her recently, I really began to notice how many of the things she said and did were similar to things my mom said and did. It made me happy that I could still feel that little piece of Mom. However, it also terrified me at the same time, because what if I wound up like my dad?

I would *never* let that happen.

"He's not strong like you, Johnny."

Mom's words rang through my head as soon as the thought entered my mind. Mom. Lucy. I wanted – no I *needed* my mom. I had to get Grandma to bring Lucy with her. I knew Grandma missed Mom too. Maybe her seeing my mom would make her feel better as well. It was a little glimmer of hope that I hadn't realized I needed.

After a couple trips in and out of the house, we'd finally stowed enough boxes in the backseat of Grandma's car. She gave me a wet smooch on the forehead and said she'd be back soon and told me to lock the door behind me after I go inside.

"Grandma, wait," I said just as she got into her seat.

"What's the matter, Johnny?"

"Can you..." I asked, my voice trailing off as I stared down at my shuffling foot on her cement driveway.

"Can I what, hon?"

"Can you grab Lucy?" I asked, bringing my eyes up to meet hers.

Grandma's brow furrowed as she cocked her head. She was clearly caught off guard by my request. "Lucy?"

"Yeah, the doll you got Mom for Christmas when she was a little girl. I brought her into my room after the accident because it reminded me of her."

Grandma's shoulders slumped and her expression softened. "Yes, honey. I can bring Lucy here for you."

"Thanks, Grandma!" I exclaimed, leaning forward and giving her a hug.

"Now run along inside. I will be back in a little bit, okay?"

"Okay!"

I rushed up the walkway and through her front door, waving to her from the doorway as she pulled down the street and out of sight. I closed the door and locked it behind me, just like Grandma had asked. I felt a sense of relief knowing I didn't have to face that house again, and that some of my stuff – and Lucy – were going to be headed here soon.

Chapter Eleven

July 29th, 1998
Edna Tomko

The drive to the house was a somber one. I hadn't been comfortable in the house since Susan's passing. It absolutely broke my heart into a million pieces hearing Johnny talk about how he brought Susan's doll into his room because it reminded him of her. Couple all this with the fact that Ron had just brutally took his own life in the home – in front of my grandson, no less. It was a recipe for an achingly unsettling situation to find myself in. I couldn't blame Johnny for not wanting to come here. If the shoe was on the other foot, I'd be adamant about never stepping foot in this house ever again as well.

I'd been trying my best to put on a brave and positive face for Johnny, but the truth was, I was exhausted. Between my chemo treatments, the stress of losing my daughter, and now this. I wasn't cut out to be a mother to a young child anymore, but I had no choice. There were no other options. I was the only family member he could turn to. So, no matter how burnt-out and beaten down I felt – no matter how queasy my stomach might feel or how bad my joints ached every day – I was going to take care of him, and give him a more stable environment to grow up in.

You're going to have to put the grand in grandmother. I thought – my lips curling into a weak smile.

With the sun bearing down on Wadsworth Road, I took my sweet time driving to the Loyal Oak neighborhood across town. I needed the time to compose myself. To psyche myself up. To convince myself I could do this. *I am strong!*

Ironically, their house was just a few minutes away from St. Anthony's Church – where Father Rosario served. When I finally turned down Aldon Street, my nerves began to get the better of me. A tingling sensation rippled up my spine, and my palms began to feel clammy.

Then, I saw it. The old two-story colonial Ron and Susan purchased together right after getting married. If not for the now stained history running through that house's walls, it was a gorgeous home: white siding with black shutters and a red brick chimney. I pulled up the white gravel driveway, the stones crackling and crunching under my tires as I crept forward. When I finally put the car in park, I killed the engine and took a deep breath.

"You can do this, Edna," I whispered to myself.

Just like ripping a band-aid off, I exited the car with great swiftness, closing the door behind me. I eyed up the house cautiously. My stomach twisted violently into tight knots. A light wind had begun to pick up. The grass in the yard swayed in the breeze, badly in need of a mow. I'd done my best to come out and mow when I could – or would occasionally ask my friend Bernice's son to come out and mow for twenty bucks. He would always happily oblige. Just as I turned away from the house and toward my car, I thought I saw something in the upstairs window out of the corner of my eye. A figure. I quickly spun back around, my eyes homing on the window I'd just looked at. It was empty.

Relax, Edna. You're getting yourself all worked up. The window's empty. See?

With a sigh, I opened the rear door of my '91 Honda Civic – a car Ron detested and would never let me hear the end of it. *"It's not American. Just cheap garbage."* I grabbed a couple of small boxes and made my way to the front door, fumbling with the keys before finally managing to unlock the door and head inside.

I stopped in the doorway, taking in my surroundings. The sun illuminated the house well enough for me to see everything. The house reeked of cleaning supplies and sanitizers. The pervasive odor permeated the air, assaulting my nostrils and making my eyes water. I set the boxes down on the bottom step of the staircase and walked over to open a couple of windows to get some air into the home.

It took a moment, but as I made my way back from the front window in the living room, I stopped dead in my tracks. It dawned on me that I was standing in or around the spot where Ron had taken his life. A chill ran down my spine as tears welled in the corner of my eyes.

"Why'd ya do it, Ron? Your son needed you and you pulled the most selfish move possible. We all missed Susan. Yet, you *chose* to leave."

I'd said the words that I hadn't realized I needed to say. It felt cathartic to get those feelings out in the open.

"You left your son behind and scarred him for life. I understand you experienced loss. I did too. There's no excuse to take the selfish action you took. You needed to be strong for Johnny and you failed him. I will not fail him, Ron. With every last fiber of my being, I will be strong for that boy. And I will give him the best life I can."

Sadness and anxiety had given way to anger. I wanted to forgive Ron but couldn't bring myself to do it. God always forgives, but in this situation, I found my faith coming into question. Why would the Lord allow something so heinous to take place? I stormed out of the living room, leaving it behind. I grabbed the two boxes and headed upstairs. When I reached the top of the steps, I saw the open doorway leading to Johnny's room. The door had been replaced, and all the splintered wood had been cleaned as well. Detective Walasko mentioned he had tried to do some quick repairs after the cleanup crew had left. It was a nice gesture, and I thanked him for it. Walking into the room for the first time – the air felt thick and heavy – like walking into a dense, ravenous fog on a sweltering summer morning. I found it difficult to breathe and my pulse quickened.

I stood in awe for a moment, taking in the décor in the room. It was just as it should be for a young boy. I glanced over at his bed and found myself wishing he'd had more restful nights recently. I walked over to his bookshelf and smiled. I grabbed a handful of his books and placed them in the box at my feet. I followed that up by grabbing his autographed baseball and some of his comic books. I took a step back, trying to figure out what else to grab. I spun around and when my eyes landed on Lucy, propped up on an old wooden chair in the corner of the room, I felt like I might lose my composure. The air had suddenly been sucked out of my lungs.

With hands on my hips, I did my best to force a deep breath in through my nose and out through my mouth, spittle flying out onto the floor as tears fought for freedom in the corners of my eyes.

I hadn't seen the doll – Lucy – in over a decade. And now, seeing it once again, I could see why I bought it for Susan. I understood why Johnny brought it into his room. It really did resemble her. I dropped the boxes in the middle of the floor as I shuffled forward and crouched down, coming to eye level with the doll. The air in the corner of the room felt cooler than the rest of the house. I reached a hand forward and watched the hair on my arms stand on end. The air was brimming with static and felt akin to the sensation after you rubbed a balloon on your head. When I wrapped my hands around the doll's sides, it felt like it had a vibration to it. It felt so wrong, but also, so right at the same time. I picked it up and studied it for a brief moment, and then the waterworks began.

This was the type of release I must've needed. I gingerly stood upright and set the doll down on Johnny's bed, taking a moment for myself. The trepidation I felt pulling into the driveway had returned. While in the presence of Lucy, I felt what could only be explained as the feeling of being watched. In an effort to protect her from getting damaged on the ride back to the house, I grabbed one of Johnny's pillowcases to stuff her into.

Creeeak…Crrreeeak!

What in the hell was that? It sounded like the floorboards in the hallway squealing under the pressure of someone's footsteps. I promptly marched to the doorway and peered outside, looking up and down the hall in both directions. There was no sign of anyone.

"Hello?" I said, my voice shaky.

Silence.

I turned back into Johnny's room – an audible gasp escaped my lips when my eyes settled onto Lucy. She was sitting upright on Johnny's bed, staring directly at me. Had I sat the doll up before strolling out to the hall? No. No, that couldn't be. I stood frozen, having a staring contest I was destined to lose.

Hahaha!

The sound of a little girl's laughter erupted in the hall behind me. I spun back around and rushed out of the room once more. My heart was thudding in my chest.

"Whoever's in here, you need to get out now! This is private property!"

The brief moment of silence quickly erupted into an explosion of metal clanking and crashing downstairs. I clutched at my chest in utter shock. Loud footsteps followed by another loud bang sent a shockwave through my body. I took a moment to collect myself before racing down the staircase. The house had fallen silent again. I looked to and fro, attempting to discern the source of the noises.

With my senses heightened, I thought I heard whispering coming from the kitchen. Then, a giggle. I raced to the kitchen, ready to nab the pranksters, but when I stood in the doorway – the kitchen was empty. I covered my mouth, not even sure how to process what was happening. I just heard voices and laughter. This didn't make any sense. This defied logic. It defied physics. Things like this shouldn't be possible under any circumstance. Surely I was letting my imagination get the better of me. That coupled with wind drafts from the newly opened windows...could that be enough? Surely it had to be. None of this was re-...

Thump! Thump! Thump! Thump! Thump!

The sound of heavy footsteps on the staircase snapped me out of my daze. I walked briskly back into the hallway leading to the staircase and still saw no one. What was happening? It felt like I was being played with. Like a cat batting around a plush mouse toy. One moment, I was being led in one direction – the next, in the complete opposite.

"This isn't funny!" I yelled out, trying – and failing – to make my voice sound threatening.

Things in the house fell silent once more. *This place is messing with your head, Edna. Just grab Johnny's things and get out.*

The thought sounded good in my head – but as I stood at the bottom of the staircase, my hand gripped the banister tightly as if a tornado could whisk me away at any moment. I needed to hurry up and grab everything but putting the thought into action was another story entirely. My feet felt like they were cemented to the floor.

In and out, Edna. In and out.

With great effort, I forced a foot onto the bottom step. Things felt fine. I forced my next foot up. Looking up at the landing, the stairway felt much more daunting than ever before. I took a deep breath followed by another reluctant step. I couldn't begin to describe the sense of foreboding I felt. Every fiber of my being was telling me – no *screaming* at me – to get out of this house. The thought of an upset grandson is a terrific motivator, though. What would he think if his grandma was too afraid to face his house? What sort of example would that set?

A newfound resurgence of willpower brought me to the top of the stairs. I couldn't help but feel proud of myself, which felt silly. *All in your head, Edna. See?* I smiled meekly, taking one more deep breath before willing myself forward yet again.

When I turned to head into Johnny's room – I wished I would've left when I'd had the chance. A little girl – *my* little girl – was sitting on Johnny's bed, brushing Lucy's hair. She was humming a playful tune while I stood in the doorway, completely mortified by what my eyes were seeing. A weak cry escaped my throat. Susan looked up and a horrible grin spread across her face.

"Hiya, Mommy!" she said, with a voice much too deep to be her own.

Before I could respond, the bedroom door slammed shut with such a force that it sent me reeling backwards, slamming into the wall behind me. Mumbling incoherent words in a state of disbelief and sheer terror – I quickly scrambled to my feet and raced out of the house.

I needed to alert Father Rosario, right away.

Chapter Twelve

July 29th, 1998
Father Rosario

Tragedy. Heartbreak. It comes for everyone. It doesn't care about your race, religion, sexual orientation, financial status, or whether you eat your fruits and veggies. Sometimes it will strike – with lethal force when you least expect it. Other times, it comes in the form of a long, torturous battle that you're left to helplessly bear witness to – completely powerless to stop it. Many trips to hospice centers over the years brought that crippling reality directly in front of a harsh spotlight.

Both variants had found their way into my life. My dad, who served God at St. Anthony's before me, had passed suddenly from a heart attack when I was in just the seventh grade. I'd never forgotten that feeling — like a boa constrictor wrapped around your entire body, squeezing the air and life right out of you. Disbelief, mourning, anger, and anxiety about what the future holds were just a few of the horrible feelings that sort of loss leaves you with.

As an adult, and newly ordained priest of the very church my father had led for years, I'd witnessed my mom's nearly seven-year-long battle with lung cancer. She fought it with every ounce of her being. I watched on as her life force *slowly* began to fade from her body. The air tanks to help support her breathing. The assistance required to help her with tasks as simple as walking or showering. Cancer is unforgiving and ate away at her like termites inside a dead tree stump. The eventual decline in her health eventually gave way to dementia. She'd befallen to both mental and physical decline. Witnessing the strong and beautiful woman that I'd admired so greatly and loved my entire life no longer be able to recognize me was a sickening feeling that I could never wash clean from my psyche. Her death came after a long, drawn-out battle.

So, I found myself – after all these recent events – trying to discern which was the better form of dealing with grief. Sudden...or slowly drawn out? The more I thought about it, I realized there were no right answers.

Even with my life experiences and struggles, I'd never seen anyone – let alone a child, go through what Johnny had had to endure over the past few months.

In our counseling sessions after Ron took his life, Johnny had retreated back into his shell. Trauma had festered its way inside him –understandably so. Getting him to open up had been proving difficult. But as with anything, it takes time. I scoffed at the saying of *'time heals all wounds.'* To me, time just makes it easier to learn to live with the wounds.

I was beginning to feel more at ease, after Edna reported that Johnny had been sleeping through the night in her home. I hoped it was a sign of good things to come.

Knock. Knock. Knock.

A heavy rapping came pounding at the door to my office, knocking me out of my stupor. Startled, I dropped the book I'd been reading, sending it bouncing off the edge of the desk and onto the floor.

"Uh..." I cleared my throat. "C-Come in."

To my shock, Edna came bursting through the door, screaming my name at the top of her lungs. I leapt up from my chair, trying my best to console her. I lightly gripped her elbow and directed her to the chair that I normally sat Johnny down in. I couldn't make sense of her words between the sobs escaping her. Her eyes looked wild and appeared as though all the life had been siphoned from her body – a sickly pallor across her face, neck, and hands.

"Breathe, Edna. I need you to breathe!" I said, doing my best to console her as I handed her a tissue and gripped her shoulder softly.

She blew her nose. A couple of sniffles later, she said, "I – that house...I can't go back there."

"What house?" I asked, worried that something happened with her and her grandson in her home. "Where's Johnny?"

"He's...he's home... I mean...he's at my house," she said in between weepy breaths. "I went over to Ron and Susan's house to gather some of Johnny's things."

She took another moment to collect herself, leaving me hanging on the edge of a cliff. My eyes attempted to search hers for answers but could only decipher that she'd experienced something horrible enough to send her into a frenzy.

"Something's in that house, Tom."

Her words – though succinct – were powerful enough to send ripples of tension through my body.

"What do you mean, Edna?"

"I don't know how to explain it. The place felt *off* the very moment I pulled into the driveway. It felt like I wasn't supposed to be there. That no one is supposed to be there. I shrugged it off, because I know bringing some of Johnny's things to him would make him feel better. But...things started happening."

"What sort of things?"

Edna recounted, to the best of her ability, the occurrences she'd experienced while in the Tinsley house. Her brain seemed scattered, and she was still clearly rattled. I couldn't piece together the exact line of events that had taken place there. It was a lot to unwrap. I knew she'd been dealing with exhaustion, depression, and heavy medical treatments herself. Was it possible that being in a house filled with that much trauma simply fed into her anxiety – essentially creating a haunting? I'd heard presentations on the matter in the past. Or maybe there was something more ominous and more evil at play?

"Edna," I said softly, attempting to calm her down again. I placed a caring hand on her shoulder as I stared deep into her eyes. "Would you like me to gather the items you boxed up and bring them back here for you?"

Her eyes lit up. "You...You'd do that for me?"

I nodded, smiling kindly. "Of course, Edna."

"Oh! Thank you, Father! Thank you!" she exclaimed.

"Do you believe in ghosts, Father?"

A timeless and thought-provoking question at all times. With so many first-hand accounts, it's hard to refute, until you begin attempting to understand the power of the human mind. I – of course – believe in the spirit of Christ. But I have always believed that the recently deceased were immediately transported to the pearly white gates of heaven. And under the ultra-rare circumstances where spirits managed to walk the Earth, they were not of human origin. Still though, the words rattled around inside my head as I steered my old – yet reliable – little, red Ford Pinto down Aldon Street. It had been my mother's car before I took possession of it in the wake of her passing. As I cruised down the road, I realized if there truly was something otherworldly in that house, it surely would not like my presence walking inside it.

Upon pulling into the driveway, I squinted at the home, doing my best to take in as much detail as possible. Edna had left in such a rush that she'd left the windows and the front door wide open. I got out of the car and eyed the home for a moment. The sadness was palpable. A permanent black cloud loomed over the house like a blanket of despair. It was time to head inside.

I understand the need to ventilate the house with open windows now, I thought as I entered the home. The potent scent of cleaning supplies still clung to the air.

This was my first time taking steps into the home. While I told Edna I was coming just to gather the boxes she'd left behind, I wanted to see if I could get a feel for the house as well. I walked first into the living room, where Ron had taken his own life. The cleaning crew did a wonderful job at bringing the house to a sense of normalcy. To an outside buyer, if they were not privy to the history behind the home, it would appear just like any other house in the neighborhood. It's honestly alarming how quickly tragedies are forgotten. People move through life not even taking a moment to reflect and think about how many people walked those very same hallways before them. How many people had lived, laughed, loved, and died within the very walls where they slept.

Soaking in as much as I could from the home, I looked at family photos displayed on the walls, bookshelves, and mantle above the fireplace. I ventured into the kitchen, where Edna had heard voices. It was as silent as a wintry graveyard in the middle of the night.

Eventually, I made my way up the staircase to Johnny's bedroom. The door was open, and I noticed the couple of boxes in the middle of the floor that Edna had carried up and began filling. I also took notice of the doll – she'd called it Lucy – was laying on the bed next to an empty pillowcase.

I slowly walked over to the doll and stuffed it into the makeshift bag, before placing it in one of the boxes. I took another moment to survey the room. Nothing in the house had felt off in the way she had described it. Sure, knowing the history of the home and the sudden influx of agony and heartache had given the home a somber feeling, but I didn't sense any otherworldly beings or spirits at play. The fact that Edna was so adamant made me want to believe and trust her judgement. The practical side of me was ready to chalk it up to the plethora of stressors in Edna's life, contributing to an impaired cognitive function.

I scooped up the two boxes and slowly walked to the doorway. I took some time to collect my thoughts as I was having an internal conflict in my head about how to approach telling Edna that there was nothing going on in this house. That it was just exhaustion. That it was all in her head. It was a delicate situation to navigate. No one wants to be made out as though they're losing their mind.

I turned to take one last look into Johnny's room before leaving – and I could've sworn I saw the curtains move. In the blink of an eye, they were still once more. I cocked my head in befuddlement. I gave it a few more moments. When nothing happened, I shook my head and sighed.

Watch yourself, Tom, I thought with a lighthearted chuckle and a shake of my head.

The mind could indeed play some very cruel and believable tricks on us at times. Before leaving, I walked around the house and closed all the windows that Edna had left open – delaying my departure until the very last moment – giving one last attempt to see if anything would happen.

Satisfied that I had done my due diligence, I gathered the house key that Edna had given me and began the drive back to St. Anthony's to meet with her.

A twinge of guilt sat in my gut like a rock during the short trip back to St. Anthony's, though for the life of me I couldn't understand why. A war inside my mind was being waged. One between my moral and ethical half – and the other coming from my spiritual faith. It was a lose-lose scenario, the true definition of a double-edged sword. Based on my background, if this was a spirit tormenting Johnny – and now Edna – that would indicate that something evil and unholy was plaguing their lives. On the other side of the scale, we have a plethora of possibilities that neuroscience was just beginning to gain more of an understanding of over the recent years. No matter how you shake it, breaking that sort of news would leave most people to feel like they're being called out as *crazy*.

Walking up to the church with both hands in my pockets, I found Edna sitting on the front steps. She shifted her gaze onto me with hopeful eyes.

"Well?" she asked weakly.

"I grabbed everything for you. The boxes are in my car," I said, trying my best to sound even keeled.

"And the house?"

I sighed before taking a seat next to her on the steps, glancing around at the surrounding neighborhood as if it were going to give me the right answers.

"You didn't experience anything, did you?" Edna asked, answering my question for me.

"No," I said shortly, setting my sights back upon her. "No, I did not."

"So, what does that mean? Anything?"

I tilted my head to the side, trying to formulate the right words. I needed to tread carefully. "I can't say."

Come on, Tom, I thought. I could feel her staring daggers into the depths of my soul. "What I mean is, if I *had* to make any sort of assumption based on how things stand right now, my initial thoughts are telling me that you, like Johnny, have been under an immense amount of stress. You've not been getting much sleep. These things..." I said, before trailing off for a moment. "These things can lead the mind to act and see strange things sometimes."

Edna seemed taken aback by my words. "So, you think all of this is just in our heads? Is that it? That wasn't some damn trick of the mind. I *saw* my daughter, Tom. I saw her...and that...that voice."

I threw my hands up in a mock surrender. "I'm not implying anything at the moment. It's much too early to make any sort of calculated conclusion just yet. I'm simply saying that you should go home and get some rest. *Real* rest. We will continue to take things day by day. You know I am and will continue to be here for you and Johnny, should you need anything."

Edna merely nodded. She got up from her perch on the steps and began to saunter down the walkway and toward the parking lot alongside St. Anthony's. I got to my feet and followed her.

We made small talk during the short walk. When I handed her the boxes from my car, she eyed me with a hint of disdain, quickly moving them into the rear seat of her Civic.

"Out of curiosity, Edna," I asked as she began to get into her vehicle. "Where did you begin to have your experiences? Was it in the living room?"

She gave me a quizzical look, her brow tightening. "I mean, the energy of the property felt off from the moment I pulled up the driveway."

I waved a dismissive hand. "But when did you start having the experiences that you described to me? Where were you? Did it begin the moment you walked in the house? Was it in the living room where Ron took his own life? When and where did the activity start?"

I was using this line of questioning for two reasons. One, I wanted to let Edna know that I was not *completely* closing out the idea that something more sinister could be happening. The other was my analytical side coming out. In essence, I was hoping to hear Edna say she experienced the chills and the activity in the living room around Ron's body. That could indicate that her knowledge of Ron's passing in that room would lead to a heightened sense of dread. Her answer caught me off guard, however.

She shook her head. "I didn't actually experience anything until I went up to Johnny's room. It started when I began packing his things."

I frowned with thought. "And the only time you saw Susan was in Johnny's room?"

She nodded. I continued to chew on it. Like when a magician revealed the rabbit out of their top hat, I felt like I was in the midst of cracking some sort of revelation – but my mind would not accept it just yet.

"What do you make of all this, Father? Honestly?" she asked.

"I think there's a lot of uncertainty at the moment. Just be careful and keep a watchful eye on Johnny. Please keep me informed if things change in the house in the coming days now that you've also seen Susan."

"I will. Thanks again, Father." She said before closing her door and driving off into the distance.

"Do you believe in ghosts, Father?"

I turned and headed back toward the church, pondering those words once again. *Ghosts? No. Evil? Yes.* Those were the words I wanted to respond to Johnny with. I hadn't changed my stance on it internally. Those words were not fit for a young boy during a confusing time in his life. The most troubling thought to arise from those words – what if they actually *were* dealing with pure, unadulterated evil? What then?

Chapter Thirteen

July 29th, 1998
Edna Tomko

I found myself thankful that I lived on the opposite end of town from St. Anthony's Church. I needed time to digest everything that had just transpired. The experiences I had inside the house, seeing *my daughter,* and Father Rosario's reluctance to consider anything aside from the impacts of trauma and lack of sleep.

What in the world is going on with me? Am I really losing my mind? I felt a slight concern that I may be questioning my faith again. In no way would I utter those words to Tom, though. We'd been great friends for years. He was a wonderful leader in the church. And though I couldn't explain how, I knew what happened. A door slamming into my face was not a figment of my imagination.

Lord, bless me for having these negative thoughts.

Even during the car ride, it felt like *something,* or *someone* was with me. The air felt thick, so I rolled my window down. I couldn't help but glance into my rearview mirror, half expecting to see Susan sitting in my back seat. I was becoming paranoid. No one was back there, but the tingling feeling climbing up my spine would not allow me to ignore it.

That prickly feeling brought more than just awareness of the heebie jeebies I was experiencing. It was a reminder of the grave situation my health had been coming into. In the summer of last year, I had been diagnosed with a rare type of cancer called chondrosarcoma. After dealing with ongoing pain in my hips and a losing battle with incontinence, I went to my doctor for testing. After the exam, he recommended we get some imaging tests done. *Proactive tests*, I believe was the wording he used. Once those came back, he presented me with the potential of bad news and recommended we do a biopsy.

Three painstakingly long weeks later, the results came. I'd been a nervous wreck the entire way through. When the news broke, so did my spirit. I'd lost my late husband, Bill, to colon cancer several years prior. It ate away at him like acid through a foam cup. So, while sitting in the small room inside the Oncology center, I thought my life was over right then and there. Everyone I ever knew that got hit with the cursed *'c- word'* had been doomed to their ill-fate not long after. My oncologist reassured me that we likely caught the growth early enough and that with treatment, it would get rid of it altogether.

Every two weeks, I'd make the trip to the Health & Wellness center up in Bath, Ohio for chemotherapy. The chemo had caused minimal hair loss, thankfully. But the nausea, fatigue, and constant headaches accompanied by my muscles feeling like they'd been scorched, stretched, and then glued back together was something I wouldn't wish upon anyone.

After several months, I was told the cancer was gone. Things seemed to be on the rebound back to living a good life. Then, in March of this year, it came back with a vengeance. The pain was almost debilitating. Treatments restarted shortly thereafter. Then the car accident happened, while the cancer metastasized and spread into my spine. My life felt like it was crumbling all over again.

Life had been so cruel in my family's lives over the past year. Now, I had no choice but to be strong for Johnny. We were all each other truly had. I hadn't been sure about how bad what he'd been dealing with at home was, until now. Today's experiences re-shaped everything I thought I knew about life after death. Why had Susan appeared to me as her younger self? Why had her voice sounded so distorted? Was that how spirits voices came across when piercing through the veil? There were so many questions I needed answered. Questions I knew would likely never get resolved.

What was the point of Susan coming through to us? Had she also reached out to Ron? My heart ached for her to find her peaceful resting place up in heaven. *Please God, let Susan rest.*

As the thought crossed my mind, I felt a swirl of cold air sweep around me. The hairs on my neck and arms stood on end. I could see my breath – something that was usually reserved for winter time.

"S-Susan? Are you with me right now?" I gasped.

There was no response.

"Susan?"

Suddenly, with a roar, the engine began to rev up. I glanced down at the speedometer and noticed my speed was increasing, even though I wasn't pressing down on the gas pedal. I quickly moved my foot onto the brake, frantically pressing down, but had no luck at slowing the car.

VRRRRRRRR!

The car was absolutely screaming down Reimer Road. "Come on! Come on!" I cried out, continuing to slam my foot down on the brake. My car was now going 70 miles per hour down a residential street.

"Why won't you stop?" I asked my brake pedal as if it could hear me.

I kept a firm grip on the steering wheel when the laughter of a little girl bellowed from my backseat. I peered into my rearview mirror and saw the figure of a young Susan sitting in the center, grinning from ear to ear with blank, dead eyes. With a sense of disbelief, I twisted around to look, but no one was there.

"MOMMY!" a deep voice growled from right next to me in the passenger seat.

I let out a shrill shriek and almost swerved the car off the road in pure shock. Just as I managed to correct the car and stabilize it, the RPMs on the engine finally settled down and the car began running as if nothing had ever happened.

"What the hell is going on?" I wailed, slamming my hands down on the steering wheel as I turned down Medina Line Road.

Chapter Fourteen

July 29th, 1998
Johnny Tinsley

I wasn't sure what was taking Grandma so long. She'd said she would only be gone for an hour. I paced around the house anxiously awaiting her return, worrying that something bad had happened.

When I finally heard a car door shut, I rushed over, hopped onto the sofa in front of the big bay window in her living room, and craned my head to look outside. Sure enough, she was in the driveway. But she was just standing next to her car staring off into the distance.

I leapt off the couch and ran for the door. I twisted the lock and rushed outside to greet her.

"Grandma!" I screamed.

"Oh! H-Hey, sugar!" she said, as if surprised by my greeting.

Her eyes looked like she was either sad, scared, or both. I gripped her in a tight hug and could feel her body trembling.

"Is everything okay, Grandma?"

She patted me on the back and looked down into my eyes. "Yes...Yes, everything is fine," she said with a deep sigh.

"Were you able to grab my stuff?"

"Yes, honey. I was able to grab some of your stuff," she said, smiling weakly as she opened the back passenger door.

We each grabbed a box and brought them inside. I zipped to my room excitedly and placed the box on my bed. Grandma trailed behind and met me moments later. Something seemed off about her. I couldn't put my finger on it, but she seemed frightened and unsure.

After she placed the other box on the bed, I thanked her for grabbing my things for me. She nodded appreciatively and said she was going to pour herself a cup of tea.

"Want anything?" she asked.

"No, thank you!"

And with that, she exited my new room. I rummaged through the first box, pulling out my books and memorabilia. I stacked them up on top of the dresser which also had an old TV resting on it. I didn't watch TV very often in my new room. It had a knob you had to get up and twist to change channels, and two antennas in the back that you had to adjust to make the channels come in. My mom and dad always joked that I had no patience. This TV was living proof of that.

I opened the second box but found only one item inside. It'd been wrapped in my old pillowcase. I pulled the item out, realizing it was Lucy. I tugged her out of the pillowcase by one of her feet and casually tossed the linen aside.

My fingers were absolutely buzzing with electricity at the touch of the doll. It was as though it was vibrating – almost as if it were a living, breathing organism. I marched across the room and sat Lucy down on the dresser, propping her up against the TV I was never going to use.

Being reunited with the doll gave me two feelings: one of hope – and on the other end of the spectrum – one of fear. A small part of me couldn't help but feel a tinge of fear around it. It wasn't responsible for any of my misgivings, but *something* within me felt a looming sense of dread around her now. Maybe because the doll also bore witness to Dad's crazy outburst.

I held hope that Mom would show up and let me know that things were going to be okay.

"Mom," I whispered, not wanting Grandma to hear me. "Mom, if you're still inside Lucy, can you give me some sort of a sign?"

I took a step back from the dresser and spun around in a circle, expecting her to pop up with her warm smile. She did not. Discouraged, I trudged over to my bed and plopped face first onto it.

Thump. Thump. Thump.

It sounded like something had gotten knocked over in my room. I flipped onto my back and sat up in bed, only to notice my autographed baseball which had been sitting on top of the dresser now lay on the floor.

"Mom?" I whispered hoarsely in disbelief.

There was no response, but the ball unexpectedly began to roll on its own from a dead stop. Rolling. Rolling. Rolling toward my bed until it was out of sight. I scooched towards the edge of my mattress just in time to see the ball gliding underneath as if the floor were on a slope.

Clutching the side of the bed, I carefully leaned down to see if I could grab it. The ball was still rolling, my eyes following it. Then I saw it. The grey smiling face was underneath my bed. Wispy strands of black hair hung down over its deep, sunken, black eyes. Its skin was grey and weathered like blistered leather and a gaping mouth stretched impossibly wide – a deep and cavernous black hole within the devilish grin.

I flung myself back on top of my bed letting out a howl of agony. Moments later, I heard Grandma storming toward my room.

"Johnny? What's wrong?" I heard her cry out as she burst into the room, her eyes wide with panic.

"There…There's a monster under my bed!" I squealed.

My head was spinning. What had I just seen? It suddenly dawned on me that I'd seen that face before – in the doorway to my parents' bedroom a few weeks ago. That time, I'd only seen it for a split second out of my peripherals. This time, I locked eyes with the horrifying creature for what felt like an eternity. The visage of its flaking skin and bottomless chasm of a grin shook me to my core.

"What?" she asked, quickly rushing to my bed and crouching down to take a look. "Honey, there's nothing under your bed except your baseball."

When she got back to her feet, she held the signed ball in her fingers, a look of concern spread across her face. Bewildered, I hunched myself over the side of the bed and looked underneath it again. Sure enough, nothing was under my bed; just a couple of dust bunnies and boxes that'd been stuffed under for extra storage space.

By the time I sat back up in my bed, Grandma was already at the dresser placing my baseball back on top of it. She said nothing, her eyes fixed upon Lucy. Could she sense Mommy inside the doll?

Finally, she spun on her heels and walked over to sit next to me on the bed. She threw her arm around me, sighed, and looked at me with tired eyes. "There's no monster, honey. In fact, there are no such things as monsters. I know you've had a lot going on. There aren't enough words I could tell you that will ever make it feel better. Just know I will always be around to protect you."

"I know, Grandma."

"Whether it's nightmares, or..." her voice trailed off as a hint of a smile cracked across the corners of her lips. "Or a monster – Grandma will always keep you safe. You know that, right?"

I nodded my head as we joined in a tight hug. She gave a wet smooch on my forehead and announced she was going to start getting dinner ready in a little bit.

"You like chicken parm, right?"

She already knew the answer to that question. She knew chicken parm was my favorite. I nodded vigorously, eliciting a laugh from her, which made me feel better too.

"Would you wanna help your grandma make dinner? I will show you how to make your very own chicken parm!"

"That would be awesome, Grandma!"

I always enjoyed when she included me in cooking. It was fun mixing all the ingredients and watching all the different parts come together to make something delicious.

"Okay, well give me a bit, and I'll holler when it's time to start, okay?"

"Okay!"

Grandma got up and walked to the doorway. She stopped, looked back and told me she loved me before leaving my room. I knew she said monsters didn't exist. But what else could explain the...*thing* I saw under my bed. I so badly wanted to give her the details of what it looked like. But I was starting to realize that adults – unless they saw what you were seeing, were never going to believe you. They would chalk it up to *childhood imagination* or *trauma*.

For my own sanity, I flipped over the side of my mattress and peeked below the bed once more. Nothing. My blood ran cold when I bounced back up onto my bed and saw my mom walk past my open doorway and toward the kitchen.

"Mom?" I called out in a hushed tone, leaping from my bed.

I peered out from my room, but she was nowhere to be found. "Mom?" I hissed. Still no response. My heart was absolutely racing.

I ventured down the hall and into the living room. No sign of her anywhere. I heard the sound of a chair being dragged out in the kitchen across the hardwood floors and rushed over to find the source of the noise.

When I rounded the corner, everything came to a standstill. I felt like I'd been zapped by an electric fence and had become entangled in its snares. With wide eyes and a slack jaw, I stared in agonizing horror. Grandma was sitting at the kitchen table stirring her cup of tea. Standing directly behind her with a hand on her shoulder, was Mommy and she was grinning from ear to ear.

"Johnny, what's the matter?" Grandma asked, staring at me from across the room. "You find another monster you need me to come take care of?"

Grandma flashed me a friendly smile. Could she not sense Mommy standing directly behind her? I couldn't speak. I couldn't move. I didn't know what to do. This was the first time I'd ever seen Mom interacting with someone else.

Mommy raised one finger to her grinning lips. She then slowly glided backwards from the table and disappeared.

Chapter Fifteen

July 29ᵗʰ, 1998
Edna Tomko

I felt a bit of unease as Johnny continued to stare blankly at me from the entryway into the kitchen.

"Johnny?"

He shook his head vigorously, as if he'd been another place mentally for a moment.

"Huh? Oh, no! Sorry, Grandma! I think I was daydreaming."

"Well, that's alright, honey. I guess since you're in here already, we can start making dinner. Sound good?"

Johnny rushed over and gave me a hug. I could tell he wasn't telling me everything, but I did my best to shrug it off and act like things were okay. The truth was, I still felt a cold, dark feeling deep inside me. Seeing Susan in the manner with which I did on multiple occasions today, and then Johnny suddenly seeing *monsters* the moment I get back was extremely unsettling. Had I brought Susan with me somehow? Had she latched onto me? Had I made a mistake by going into that house?

Before today, I wasn't entirely sure I believed in ghosts. Now, I wasn't sure about anything anymore. All I knew was *something* definitely happened. And I was starting to believe Johnny in saying his mother had been visiting him. I wondered if Ron had also been receiving visits from Susan. It would only make sense given that I had now seen her also.

I walked with Johnny over to the fridge and asked that he pull out the chicken breasts while I gathered the pots and pans necessary to make the dish. Working together, we prepared the ingredients to make our very own red sauce, breaded and fried the chicken breasts, and boiled the noodles. When it was done, we placed everything into a baking dish and sprinkled cheese on top before sticking it in the oven.

I would've been lying if I'd said my mind didn't continue to wander while making dinner. I was curious what Johnny saw in his room. Was it something he'd interpreted as a monster? I could tell it was still on his mind. Even though we were having a fun time preparing dinner, I sensed he also had a busy mind.

We'd begun setting the table when the oven dinged with our finished chicken parm. We sat at the table after portioning out our plates.

"Would you like to say grace?" I asked.

Over the past few weeks, I hadn't bothered with saying grace before dinner as often, because of everything we'd both been through. Maybe that made me a bad Christian but now seemed as good a time as any.

Johnny shot me an annoyed glance. "No."

I cocked my head in confusion. "What do you mean, no?"

Johnny had never pushed back on saying grace in my house before. His sudden pushback caught me off guard. I eyed him curiously from behind my steaming plate of pasta.

"I don't want to."

"In my house, we say grace before dinner."

"I don't want to say grace!" he shouted in a shrill shriek, sounding like a toddler throwing a tantrum. His eyes were wild with rage, his face flush in a beet red hue.

I was appalled. This was very unlike Johnny to act like this. When Susan had tantrums at a young age, I didn't encourage it. I allowed her to have her moment until it burned out.

"Well then you don't have to. I will say grace," I said sternly. "Dear heavenly Father, we reach out to you today to give thanks..."

"God doesn't care!" Johnny shouted.

The words struck me with a blunt force. Where was this coming from? In the past, he'd been fine with prayer. But suddenly now he's against it? I chose to ignore him. I understood where he was coming from, all things considered. I had to allow him to feel whatever he was feeling in the moment, but I still had to do what I felt was right.

"We would like to give thanks for your blessings and allowing us to eat this delicious meal."

"God's not real! God's not real!" Johnny shrieked.

"That's enough!" I replied, slamming a fist down onto the table. "What's gotten into you?"

"If God was real, he wouldn't allow the things that have been going on."

Johnny shoved his dinner plate away and stormed out of the dining room. I sat back in my seat, dumbfounded and heartbroken.

Night had finally begun to fall across the landscape. I gave Johnny a little bit of space before heading into his room to check on him. I knocked on his door and entered. He was lying face down on his bed and I apologized for pushing the issue with saying grace. He returned an apology and confirmed that he was confused on what to believe anymore.

"I'm not going to lie to you, Johnny. This phrase will get old and over-used by the time you reach adulthood, but the Lord works in mysterious ways. We may not always agree with Him, but it is up to us to give him our undying faith and believe that he always has our best interests at heart."

Johnny turned his head away at this mention. I couldn't blame him, especially at his age with everything that he'd just gone through. Life was cruel and unfair at times and led a lot of people to question their faith. Hell, I'd been guilty of it myself from time to time.

We talked a little while longer and I asked him if he was happier when he believed in God, or happier now when he was questioning his own faith. He took a moment to consider and eventually admitted that he was happier when he believed in God. Hearing those words come from his mouth led me to believe he was thinking more clearly now. I asked if he would like to eat dinner now and maybe play a quick game of *Skip-Bo* before bed. He smiled and nodded his head enthusiastically. That boy's smile could melt the polar ice caps.

After we re-heated our plates, we sat at the table – and to my surprise, Johnny actually led grace. I wasn't sure what sort of epiphany my talk with him had caused, but I was pleased to see it.

After dinner, we sat and played a few games of *Skip-Bo*. Johnny won two out of the three rounds and marched to his room triumphantly waving his arms in the air. I had definitely put the grand in grandma this evening. I couldn't help but laugh and feel warm inside.

Johnny asked me to read him a bedtime story before tucking him in. I hadn't done that since Susan was a little girl. I felt myself get a little choked up at the opportunity and gladly did so. We read a few chapters from one of his Goosebumps books, which left me feeling a little spooked. I was shocked he enjoyed them. No wonder he thought he was seeing monsters.

I gave him a kiss on the forehead before tucking him in. "Sleep tight. Don't let the bed bugs bite."

I turned off his bedroom light and watched as he peacefully drifted off to sleep. Feeling my job was complete, I closed his bedroom door softly and made my way back into the kitchen for an opportunity to decompress over a cup of chamomile tea – hoping that would allow me to get my own restful night of sleep.

The cancer treatments left me feeling weak; weaker than I would allow myself to admit. Some days it felt like a miracle if I could drag myself out of bed. The chemo would rarely allow me to keep food down. I'd often have to tell Johnny I was going to take a shower and then hide the sounds of me regurgitating our meal behind the sound of running water. *"You take a lot of showers, Grandma,"* he would often say jovially. Cancer was taking its toll. Deep in my soul, I felt the chemo was only delaying the inevitable, and it worried me for Johnny's sake. I had to keep fighting.

Seeing Johnny's hopeful eyes beaming at the thought of going on an adventure, playing board games, or helping make dinner was all the motivation a grandma could need. I knew I couldn't allow Johnny to worry about me. I had to remain strong for him. I'd often found myself praying to God in the sanctity of my bedroom when I could get a moment. Praying for reprieve. Praying for help. Praying for Johnny. Things had been up and down. However, more times than not – Johnny's spirit seemed to be improving overall. That gave me hope.

I sat at the kitchen table sipping on chamomile tea, replaying the days' worth of events in my head and still trying to rationalize it all out. Pandemonium was the only word to accurately describe it all: seeing Susan in Johnny's old bedroom, the car malfunctioning and nearly killing me, seeing her again in the car, her voice, Johnny seeing what he thought was a monster, and his initial reaction to saying a prayer.

I'd considered phoning Father Rosario again, but my experience with him today left me feeling a little sour towards him at the moment. The chamomile tea seemed to be doing the trick, though. The warm, floral drink slid down my throat effortlessly. The tea began to wash away my stress and anxiety, wrapping me in a tight, warm hug.

Knock. Knock. Knock.

I nearly fell out of my chair at the sound of rapping coming from my back door. Perplexed, I got to my feet and peered out the kitchen window, trying to steal a glance and see if I could see anyone. No such luck. It was pitch black.

Knock. Knock. Knock.

The three loud strikes against the back door came again. Faster this time. Who the hell would be outside my house at this hour?

Against my better judgement, I walked over to the door. I was hopeful it wouldn't wake Johnny.

"Who's there?" I asked in a harsh, hushed tone. There was no answer.

Feeling disturbed that I received no response, I leaned in and pressed my head against the door to see if I could hear anyone.

BANG! BANG! BANG!

The door actually shook with each forceful blow this time. I had to cover my mouth to prevent a shrill cry from escaping my lips. My heart was pounding furiously.

"Who's out there?" I said a little more forcefully this time. No response came.

BANG! BANG! BANG!

I would've sworn someone was throwing their fist into the door at this point. The three loud slams would almost surely wake Johnny up. Not wanting to allow that to happen, I rushed back into the kitchen to my junk drawer and grabbed Bill's old Maglite. Another trio of blasts struck the backdoor. I quickly scampered over, and with a deep breath and a head nod, I twisted the lock and slowly opened the door.

There was no one in front of the door. My house was shrouded in darkness from the night sky. I looked to my left and to my right. I clicked on the flashlight and swept it to and fro as well. I still couldn't see anyone. My body was covered in gooseflesh as anxiety prickled up my spine. My backyard was fairly small, as it led into a heavily forested area about forty yards away from my back patio.

"Who's out here? Leave us alone or I will call the cops!" I hissed, shutting the door and locking it again.

BANG! BANG! BANG!

Agitation was now replaced by fear. I twisted the lock and opened the door with much more fervor this time. Nothing. No one in sight. It didn't make any sense.

I took a step out onto my back patio, surveying the area. My nerves were absolutely shot. So much for chamomile's calming properties. "That's it! I'm calling the cops!"

Just as I turned to head back inside, I stopped dead in my tracks. I heard a little girl's laughter coming from somewhere in my backyard. I spun back to face the yard, clicking my flashlight back on. My heart nearly froze when I saw the beam of my light train on a figure of a little girl at the edge of the woods. I realized it was Susan standing at the edge of the woods. I let out a frightened gasp, thrusting my free hand up to cover my mouth.

"Hi, Mommy!" she said.

"You're not my daughter!" I cried out.

"What's the matter, Mommy? Don't you love me anymore?" she asked.

I didn't know what to say. I stared blankly at the spirit of my young daughter, keeping my flashlight trained on her. The figure looked and sounded exactly like Susan. My brain was torn. Johnny had been talking with Susan for ages. The way he made it sound, she was cognizant of everything going on in his life and had been supportive. What was so bad about that?

I watched on in stunned silence as the figure continued to stand unmoving along the edge of the tree line. My quiet demeanor must've hurt her feelings, because I watched as my daughter's face contorted into a pout and heard the all too familiar sound of her cries echoed across the yard.

"You don't love me anymore!" she sobbed. Susan began to walk away, further into the woods.

Seeing that side of my daughter again absolutely crushed my heart. No parent ever likes to see their child cry. No psychiatrist in the world would be able to make sense of watching the spirit of your daughter as a young girl cry and how that makes you feel.

"Where are you going?" I called out. I received no response. Susan continued to pace further away until she was out of sight.

Things were happening fast. I never got closure with my daughter before she passed in that horrible car accident and now her spirit was leaving. Even with every fiber of my being telling me not to follow her, I still felt a strong desire to go. Like some sort of magnetic pull I couldn't explain, my motherly instinct was telling me to go after my daughter.

"Shit," I cursed under my breath. "Hang on, sweetie! Mommy's coming!"

Was I losing my mind? Almost anyone else on earth would've said yes in that moment. But until someone finds themselves in this situation, they can never truly speak to how they'd react.

I raced off the edge of the patio and darted off towards the woods, trying to keep my flashlight beam pointed in front of me. The edge of the wood line looked like the toothy grin of an anglerfish in the inky depths of the ocean.

The humid summer night caused my clothes to cling to my body like barnacles on the bottom of a vessel. A warm, earthy smell pervaded the air: a mix of dead leaves, moss, pine, and dirt. Careful not to trip, I had to take my time. The half-moon brought a modicum of light, but only where it crept through in the spaces between the canopy of leaves among the treetops. I kept the flashlight pointed down directly in front of me to alert me to any downed timber or bulging stones out of the ground. Susan's sobs were growing more faint by the second. The songs of the summertime cicadas nearly drowned out her cries, and I couldn't keep up with her. I shouted her name and continued to call out for her, occasionally stopping and sweeping my Maglite across the landscape to try and spot her. Between the grey of the trees and the dead of night, it would be next to impossible to find her if she pulled any further away.

Farther and farther, I delved. The distant cries of my daughter became less and less audible. I made my way to a small clearing in the woods where several downed trees lay next to one another, a boulder sitting between them. Out of breath, and sweating like a thief in a courtroom, I began to lose hope that I would catch up to her. I stopped to catch my breath, panting like a dog, debating if I wanted to continue the search or turn back and head inside. That sounded like a more logical plan. But some pervasive desire in my heart was saying I needed to see my daughter. I wanted to tell her how much I loved her one last time.

Crunch. Crunch. Crunch.

The sound of footfalls landing on dried leaves echoed nearby to my left. I swept my flashlight in the direction of the sound, hoping it was Susan or a small animal. I couldn't see anything around.

Crunch. Crunch. Crunch. Crunch.

This time the sound came from my right at a much more frantic pace. I spun around, aiming my beam of light in the direction, only to come up empty handed once more. My heart was beginning to hammer away in my chest. What the hell was I doing out here again?

"Baaaa!"

Was that a goat? I swept my flashlight back and forth. There wasn't anything that I could see anywhere nearby, just trees and briar patches.

"Susan?" I called out. "Susan, honey. It's your mother. Can you come to the sound of my voice?"

I felt a prickling sensation in the pit of my stomach when I received no response. Susan's cries had become silent, and I was alone in the middle of the woods.

"Mommy?" Susan's voice called out from nearby. Something about it chilled me to my core, but I had already come this far.

"Yes, honey! I'm right here!"

The sound of a nearby branch snapping and the giggle of a little girl assaulted my ear drums. I called out to her once again.

Snap. Crunch. Crunch. Snap. Crunch.

This time I did a full 360 sweep with my flashlight. It felt like the footsteps were all around me all at once. I had to be losing my mind out here.

"Baaa! Baaa!"

The sounds had come from directly behind me this time. I couldn't move – absolutely crippled with fear – because the bleating didn't come from a couple feet off the ground like a goat normally would. It came from right behind my head.

I didn't know how to explain it, but I could *feel* something standing right behind me. Its hot breath came careening off my glistening neck, it's heavy breathing sounded like a bull that was about to launch an assault.

Fight or flight set in – and just as I took a step to run away – I felt my hair get violently yanked from behind, sending me flying down to the earthy floor with a hard thud. The force of colliding with the ground knocked the wind out of me. I let out a strained cough, a searing pain burning from within my ribcage. Before I could collect myself, I felt a rough hand grip around my throat and yank me back to my feet. The last thing I saw was the face of my young daughter, her eyes glowing red like a stoplight and the great curved horns of a goat stuck out of the sides of her head. She smiled a sickly smile, with horribly chapped lips and a mouth full of razor-sharp black teeth.

"Hiya, Mommy! Time to die!" it said with the voice of a small child before letting out a guttural snicker of a wild beast and tossing me like a rag doll. I was sent spiraling through the air, my head bounced off a nearby tree, and I fell back to the earth. Everything went black.

Chapter Sixteen

July 30th, 1998
Johnny Tinsley

Bang! Clang! Clang!

I awoke with a start at what sounded like pots and pans being slammed around. I looked over at the old alarm clock on the nightstand next to my bed. It read that it was a little after three in the morning. Groggy and confused, I sat up and rubbed my heavy eyelids. The loud metallic slamming on the other side of the house continued.

Was that Grandma making all that noise? Was someone breaking into the house? What if it was that *thing* I saw under my bed earlier? To be safe and make sure nothing would grab my ankle if I hopped off the bed, I reluctantly flipped over the side of the bed and checked. It was dark under my mattress, but I could faintly make out the shapes under the bed. No monsters. Check.

I got to my feet and cautiously padded across the carpeted floor to my door. There was no way Grandma could possibly be up at this hour. She'd looked exhausted after we had finished playing cards earlier. I thought she was going to fall asleep right then and there at the table on our last game.

When I opened my bedroom door, things had gone quiet. I walked down the hall to her bedroom and cracked open the door, trying to be careful and not make any noise. Peering into her dark room, it didn't seem as though she was in bed. I took a couple steps in and came to the conclusion that she was indeed awake and must've been the source of the sounds I'd heard. That caused me to feel a momentary sense of relief. Maybe she hadn't been able to sleep, decided to do the dishes, and accidentally dropped them on the floor.

I scampered out of her room, closing the door behind me, and made my way through the house towards the kitchen. Just as I rounded the corner of the dining room and into the walkway that led into the kitchen, I froze.

It was Grandma. Her back was to me, but I could immediately sense something was wrong. She was standing over the stovetop. The kitchen range above the stove provided the only source of light. Her hair looked wild. It was matted – caked with dirt which had little twigs and leaves tangled inside like a rat's nest. I watched in awe as she nonchalantly hummed an old tune, frantically reaching for a spatula and working on whatever she'd had sizzling in the frying pan. Her arms and legs had small scrapes and abrasions all over them. I wanted to call out to her, but my vocal cords failed me.

A foul smell of rotting meat assaulted my senses. I took a cautious step into the kitchen, my heart hammering inside my chest.

"G-Grandma?"

She said nothing. Her body became rigid like a pole. The hissing and bubbling in the frying pan was the only noise to break the silence. Grandma placed her palms down flat on the side of the stove but did not turn to look at me.

"Grandma, are you alright?" I asked, my voice barely emanating louder than a squeak.

"I..." she replied weakly.

I waited for her to finish her thought, but it never came. I took a couple more steps forward, my concern growing larger by the second. "You...what?"

"I'm...I...I'm just...I'm just making...bre...breakfast," she stammered incoherently as she stabbed the spatula into the frying pan again.

Something was different about the way she spoke. It was *her* voice, but the way that she spoke sounded *off*. It sounded like a toddler when they first started learning how to put sentences together.

I took another timid step forward. The smell was beginning to grow unbearable. The rotten meat began to mingle with the putrid scent of singed hairs, lingering in the air like a shroud of toxic gas.

I plugged my nostrils. "Why are you cooking breakfast at three in the morning? Why are there scrapes all over you? And what happened to your hair?"

"I said I'm cooking breakfast! What's with all the fucking questions?" she snarled, slamming the spatula down onto the stove with a loud clank.

Her words hit me in the chest with blunt force. In all my life, I'd never heard her talk like that, let alone cuss. All that venom and rage behind her voice was new yet felt familiar. The vision of my dad at the dinner table a few weeks ago began echoing in the recesses of my mind and a fear swirled in my stomach like a swimmer struggling against a riptide. What if she was about to go crazy like my dad did?

Without another word, she went back to stabbing at her pan and humming the same eerie tune as before as if nothing had happened. I stood locked in place, my feet glued to the floor. I stared at her busily working at whatever dish she was cooking.

"Take a seat," she said firmly. "Breakfast is almost finished."

Not knowing what else to do and not wanting to question or upset her any further, I took a seat at the little table to my right. She scurried briskly across the floor to the nearby cabinets and pulled a couple of glass plates out. I couldn't take my eyes off her. She grabbed a couple forks and steak knives, brought them to the table, and placed them down in front of our respective chairs. She made her way back to the stove and pulled a chef's knife out of the block, its blade gleaming under the light. Visions of my dad using the same style of knife to plunge into his neck came bounding back. I could feel myself beginning to hyperventilate. Grandma took the knife and plunged it into whatever she had popping and sizzling in the skillet.

"A growing boy needs his protein," she said behind gritted teeth as she sawed away. The chill behind her voice made me feel uncomfortable.

With a swift pull and a loud pop, I watched as she placed whatever was cooking onto one of the plates. Her body shielded me from being able to see what it was. She reached back to the skillet and repeated the process again. My body felt like it was floating on a sea of pins and needles, continuously grazing up and down my spine with the flow of the ocean's waves.

With a grunt that was followed by another swift pull and loud snap, she leaned over to the other plate, slapping the food down with a sickening splashing sound. She turned off the burner and gripped the two plates, holding them above where I could see and began walking them over to the table. Her eyes looked distant and hazy – similar to the look I saw in my dad's eyes before he snapped. She bore a smile that drew my attention to her dry, cracked lips. They had a blueish hue to them. Everything about the present moment made me feel sick to my stomach.

"Bon Appetit," she said, placing the two plates down onto the table. Her wide eyes were gleaming with a sinister smile that never faltered.

By the time my eyes settled upon the two plates, I had to fight back the urge to vomit. Resting on my grandma's plate was the head of a rabbit that she'd stood straight up on its base like a tree trunk. The rabbit's eyes were now nothing more than empty sockets with gelatinous gore dribbling down the sides of its face. Its fur was badly burned, charred black like a short bristle hairbrush – down nearly to the animal's skin. On my plate was one of the hind legs of the rabbit. I looked up from the plates, staring at my grandmother and feeling an amalgamation of shock, nausea, utter terror, and a deep yearning to run away and cry. Her expression was unchanging. Her gaze was stern and focused on me – as though she were peering deep into my soul – but she still held a smile that betrayed her eyes stretched across her face. Her dried-out lips began to bleed out of the crevices that had formed.

"Eat!" she said in a voice that barely resembled her own.

I glanced down at my plate and felt my stomach turning once again. Tears were welling in my eyes. Why had she done this? Where did this rabbit come from? Was she going crazy too? Just like my dad?

"I...I can't eat it, Grandma."

"It's rude to turn away food when it has been offered to you," she said coldly, pushing my plate closer to me. "Now, eat!"

I felt my lip quivering. I was fighting with every ounce of my being not to cry. Something was wrong with Grandma, and I didn't want to upset her further. I responded in the only way my brain would allow. I shook my head no.

I watched on as the eerie grin faded from her face in what felt like slow motion. Her brow furrowed and her stare became more rigid, angrier. Looking into her eyes I felt like I was staring into a bottomless pit. With a knot in my gut, I began to scoot my chair out and she pounded her fist down on the table, sending the plates and silverware clanging around.

"Didn't your mother teach you not to leave the table until you're excused?" she hissed.

The rage behind her voice was alarming and it took me a moment to realize she was now clutching one of the steak knives in her hand. I anxiously glanced back and forth from the knife to her eyes and then happened to notice that the rabbit head on her plate had toppled over the moment she'd slammed her fist down. I could now see its severed vertebrae from what remained of its neck and a pool of blood began to settle around the base of her plate.

"I...I'm sorry." I didn't know what to do or what to say. Staring down the blade of a knife didn't leave me feeling like I had many options.

"Good. Would you like to say grace?" she asked with a sickly smile and wink. A raspy chuckle clawed its way out of her lips as she threw her head back in hysterics.

"I...I don't know what to say," I replied with hot tears streaming down my cheeks.

"Liar!" she said, pounding her fist that clutched the knife back down onto the table again. "You pray to Him and you thank Him for this lovely meal."

Her words came out like razor blades, cutting everything in their path, as she spoke through gritted teeth.

"Th-Thank you G-God f-for this...this lovely meal," I began to say before being cut off by more monstrous cackling from Grandma. She set her knife down and gave me a mock round of applause.

"That was wonderful, Johnny. I can feel the light of His holy spirit taking me over now!" she exclaimed, throwing her head back and thrusting her arms out in a grand gesture. "Oh, take me now Lord! Let your light guide me to your grand kingdom!"

There was a short pause before she lowered her arms and head. She set her sights back onto me, her calloused grin returning. "Time to eat."

I watched on in sheer horror as she gripped the rabbit's head in her hand and opened her mouth impossibly wide, thrusting the entire thing inside and chomping down on it with a sickening crunch. A wave of shock sent the hair on my body standing on end. I thought I saw her eyes shift to a blood red shade. They were the same color as a bouncy ball I used to have. It happened in the blink of an eye. By the time the flutter of my eyelids occurred, her eyes were back to normal. I'd always heard that us kids have a powerful imagination. But there was no way I could've imagined that? Could I have?

Grandma's smirk never left her face as she continued to chew. The sight of her jaw crushing that poor rabbit's head in her mouth sent a chill down my spine. Juices and blood began to trickle out of the corners of her grinning mouth. With a loud gulp, she finally swallowed and allowed her eyes to fall on me once more.

"Now it's your turn. Eat up before it gets cold!"

I glanced down at the mangled and burned hind quarter on my plate and wanted to vomit my dinner from earlier right then and there. The scent of the charred fur and flesh was enough to turn anyone's stomach. I looked back up at Grandma and shook my head.

"Johnny...you're going to eat your breakfast... Right...now."

I shook my head again. She pursed her lips in frustration and averted her eyes down at her steak knife. Her eyes flicked up and met my stare. The corner of her lip began to curl into a sneer.

"Eat...the fucking rabbit," she said. She picked up the knife and held it in the air. "Or else, I am going to cut my finger off."

I didn't know what to do. My brain was a hamster wheel at the moment. My body was ready to shut down. Whatever had made Dad sick was clearly also making Grandma sick. Was I infecting them somehow? She wouldn't really cut her finger off, would she?

She placed the edge of the blade down on her pointer finger, just below the cuticle. "You have until the count of five."

I looked down at my plate, the queasy feeling still swirling in the pit of my stomach.

"Five."

I looked up at grandma. Her menacing stare was dark and foreboding.

"Four."

I picked up my fork and jabbed it softly into the leg of the rabbit. Its fur was coarse, but the meat was still soft and spongy.

"You know what? No fork. I want you to pick it up and eat it."

"What?" I asked, the waterworks still flowing down my cheeks.

"Pick it up and eat it with your hands. Like an *animal!*"

"I-I can't, Grandma."

"Three."

I set the fork down. Fight or flight was kicking into overdrive.

"Two."

I lifted the rabbit's leg off the plate. The smell was foul. Blood dripped from the open joint where Grandma had yanked it free from the rest of its body. I eyed it cautiously through watery eyes. I couldn't take a bite. It was too gross.

"You better take a bite... One!"

I couldn't bear to see my grandma chop her own finger off. I brought the mangled leg to my mouth and bit into it. The immediate flavor of blood and sinewy, gamey meat burst into my mouth, the fur poked my tongue like dull barbs from a cactus. I ripped the flesh away with my teeth, forced it into my mouth, and immediately began to gag.

"Good! That's good, Johnny." Grandma said, nodding her head but her expression never changed. "And don't you dare throw up on my table!"

I was repulsed; the meat wasn't cooked through and still had a raw, rubbery texture to it. The worst part, though, was the fur. It was coating the inside of my mouth and sticking between my teeth. I couldn't possibly swallow it. I gagged again, my cheeks bulging out in an effort to not puke.

"Swallow your food, Johnny." she said sternly. She gripped me by my wrist with her free hand. "Finish your bite for Grandma."

I continued to chew, my mouth was beginning to salivate – and not in a good way – it was in the way where you *knew* you were about to retch every possible content out of your stomach. I tried to power through, but then a stray hair flew into the back of my throat and tickled my uvula. I felt my entire body tense up, and the sudden shock to my body could not be stopped as I spewed everything in my mouth out onto the table, followed closely by the bile of tonight's dinner.

"You little motherfucker!" she hissed, leaping up from her chair.

I didn't even have a moment to compose myself before I felt the back of her hand come across my cheek, sending me flying out of my chair and crashing down onto her floor.

"How dare you waste such a perfect meal." She used her leg to kick the chair out of her way as she took a step toward me. I was bawling my eyes out at this point. A searing pain burned my cheek. "You deserve everything that has happened to you. Your mother. Your father. Me. We all would've been better off without you in our lives." She took another step forward as I began to scoot back.

With a swift movement, she leapt down on top of me and pinned my wrists to the floor. Her skin felt scorching hot to the touch and her breath smelled of roadkill. "This is only the beginning," she snarled. Her voice wasn't even recognizable anymore.

I struggled underneath her painful grasp. She let out a maniacal laugh that resembled the sound of a dying animal. I fought with all my strength, screaming at the top of my lungs for her to get off me and let me go, but she only pressed down harder.

"You know what's funny about the world?" she asked with a wide smirk. "The world is *so* quick to believe in *God*. So quick to put their faith in a man that allows disease, war, famine, and poverty to run amok. But many people on this planet are so quick to dismiss evil. They label it as *God's plan.*" Her voice had morphed into a deep, scathing rattle that sounded like someone playing a vinyl record backwards. She cocked her head to the side and hocked bloody phlegm onto the floor next to us and look down at me with a disgusted look on her face. I continued to plead with her, but she ignored my cries.

"It must be so convenient to cope behind the façade of faith. You are going to learn the hard way. Evil exists. The Devil is real. And one day I am going to break you down. Break you down so hard that you will *beg me* for the sweet release of death. I am chaos. I am havoc. I am agony. And you are *mine*!"

The verbal assault left me stunned and incapable of being able to process the words. The vitriolic, venomous words sliced deep and left me feeling like a hollowed-out husk. Grandma's eyes rolled into the back of her head, leaving just the whites of her eyes visible. She began to convulse on top of me wildly.

"G-Grandma?" I cried out.

The shaking became more and more violent. Her arms lost functionality as she collapsed down on top of me. Her body was emanating strange groans as her entire body tensed and spasmed. Foam began frothing out of the corners of her mouth, spewing down onto my face.

It took every ounce of strength I had, but I finally managed to roll out from underneath her. Her body continued to thrash around on the kitchen floor, and I stood by and watched in awe. I felt blank. Numb. I felt like I couldn't shed another tear if I'd wanted to. I'd never felt this sort of emptiness in my life. Devoid of feeling any emotion. The fear was gone; the sadness was gone. I was simply existing in that very moment. Almost like an out of body experience.

When her body finally stopped quivering, I knelt down and whispered her name. She didn't respond. I noticed a pool of saliva, drool, and blood billowing out from underneath her face.

Not knowing what else to do, I rushed over to her phone and dialed 9-1-1.

Chapter Seventeen

July 30th, 1998
Father Rosario

Under the faint amber glow of my desk light, I sat peering deep into some of the old, tattered pages in one of my theology books that discussed demonology. A glass of Scotch in one hand, and a lit cigarette in the other. Cigarettes were a nasty bit of business. I didn't allow anyone to ever see me with one in hand. I barely ever smoked them unless I felt the absolute necessity to. I kept a pack of Camels along with an ash tray tucked safely away in a locked drawer in my desk.

Staring down at the pages before me, I sighed. I wasn't sure what made me decide to tear into the old textbooks in the middle of the night. Call it a hunch. Call it fear. Call it whatever you want, but something inside me compelled me to flip open the old archives. I hadn't even thought about them since my days at John Carroll University. Demonology – though covered as part of our studies – had never become a huge focal point of furthering my education into joining the clergy. It was sort of the black sheep of our studies and had been mostly glossed over. Over the years, demonology had been cast out by advancements in modern health practices and neuroscience. Still, under rare cases, I'd heard through the grapevine about other priests having to consider the possibility of this evil surfacing.

The struggle of it with the Catholic church, was how mainstream it had become in pop culture between the horror novels and movies that had been produced over the past two or three decades. The church had strict policies in place to protect our name and our reputation when cases are brought forth that could have any sort of demonic connotations associated with them.

"Always do your due diligence. Err on the side of medical causes before ever resorting to the demonic. Should you ever find yourself in a situation where pure evil resides – you will need to bring viable proof to the diocese before we can proceed. Proof. Document. Proof. Document. I cannot stress this enough." Those were the words Father O'Keefe shared with us during our lecture on the subject.

I took a long drag from the cigarette nestled between my lips before flicking the ashes into the glass tray to my left. Could Edna and Johnny *actually* be dealing with an evil force beyond my own comprehension? Father O'Keefe told us we were more likely to be struck by lightning than to actually come into close proximity with a real demonic presence.

"But if you do ever find yourself in that situation...you make sure your faith is strong. And remember... Document. Proof. Time is of the essence. Evil waits for no one."

I took a sip from the Scotch. The sweet amber liquid burned all the way down to my stomach. A warmth spread across my body. I flipped to the next page in the textbook and stubbed my cigarette out, blowing out another fresh plume of smoke.

From everything I had been able to gather, demons came about through many different facets of life. Their mission was to turn people away from our Lord and Savior. Drive them to do unspeakable things. They prey on the weak and the vulnerable at their lowest points. Its sole purpose is to break their will. Infestation, oppression, and then finally possession. The words lingered in my brain like the smoke rings floating around my office.

Infestation. The stage where the demon normally begins toying with their victims. Small things at first – mild agitators. Slowly breaking through the barriers of disbelief in its targets. This could be the paranormal activity people experience regularly. Shadow figures. Things moving on their own. Lights being turned on when they weren't left that way. Bumps. Knocks. Scratching noises in the walls. You name it. Things that could conveniently be explained away by natural causes but led many to believe they were dealing with a true haunting. I didn't believe in hauntings, though. Only in evil. I began to think that demons threaded that thin veiled line between natural explanations and their malicious intent to conceal themselves from those that might be able to help.

Oppression. The stage where the entity methodically breaks down its victims. It tears their life apart limb from limb. The fallen angel will systematically cause cracks and crevices in every aspect of your life. Those cracks and crevices under the sheer weight and will of the foul creature will begin to crumble as the bedrock of your life begins to cave in on you. It could be a streak of bad luck, losing your job, getting into a car accident, falling ill, losing a loved one. Just a few examples. It will drive you to the point that those very things are inevitable. Like some sort of pre-determined plan. It will be a cog in the wheel at every downturn in your life. You will feel its presence. You will smell its stench. You will feel its wrath. You will begin to lose your will to defend yourself.

God help us. I thought, taking another sip of whiskey.

Possession. The word sat in my stomach like a lead weight. I'd heard and read about cases that had taken place across the world. It was taboo nowadays, but hearing and reading about the accounts was both gut-wrenching as well as absolutely terrifying. I had no tolerance for thieves or rapists, but that's exactly what demons – if they truly did exist, were. They stole your cognitive function. They raped you of your ability to live your life free from evil. They drove their hosts to madness and unspeakable acts in the name of Satan.

The fact that the Devil and his minions could potentially reign over so many people around the world under the guise of naturality in our daily lives sent a chill down my spine in a manner that could not be shaken free. I couldn't help but to light another cigarette and take a drag. Modern medicine for all of the good that it has done in the world – what if *that* in it of itself was the workings of the devil? What if He wanted to use modern health as a scapegoat? The Abomination and its cohorts could run through countless people with impunity. I shook my head and took another long drag of the cigarette. The cherry glowed orange as the string of ash dangled helplessly awaiting to be flicked into the ash tray.

It was a troubling thought. I couldn't allow it to grow and fester. This was why the church needed documentation and proof. Hysteria leads to problematic and rash decision making. *You must remain pragmatic and diligent in your efforts.*

Possession. The word still stuck to my mind like a piece of gum on the bottom of my shoe. I chewed on the word some more. It was foul. I hoped I would never have to deal with something to that degree. I found myself questioning the validity of everything I thought I knew. Johnny seeing visions of his mother after the accident. Not just seeing but communicating with her. How I wish I could get more information about what they talked about. I still had a sneaking suspicion that Johnny was holding back details. Ron Tinsley's dark spiral through depression after losing his wife. His sudden outburst of rage and taking his own life. Edna Tomko herself had even seen her daughter. Could it all be chalked up to mental health disorders stemming from depressive states? Or could this be the strike of lightning touching down in this small corner of Norton, Ohio?

Ring Ring! Ring Ring!

The sound of my phone singing on its base next to me nearly caused me to spill my Scotch all over myself as I flinched – getting knocked out of my deep train of thought.

Ring Ring! Ring Ring!

I squinted at the antique clock mounted on the wall to my right and stubbed out my cigarette. It was nearly four in the morning. I couldn't believe how much time I had spent scouring through my old textbooks. *Who on earth would be calling me this late?* I thought. I picked up the phone. I nearly dropped it when I found out what the call was regarding. Edna Tomko had been brought to the hospital. She'd suffered a seizure. I asked about Johnny, and they said they had him waiting with her until they see if she stabilizes but would contact a social worker in a few hours if things took a turn for the worse.

"Based on his story, we believe Edna may've suffered some sort of mental breakdown that led to the seizure," the nurse said.

"Wh-What did he tell you?" I asked, suddenly overcome with a rush of dread.

She went on to tell me the grisly details that Johnny outlined to her. How she ate the skull of a wild, partially cooked rabbit and then went on to say that Edna made him also eat a piece of the hare and threatened to cut off her finger if he didn't comply. She then told me how Edna lashed out at him verbally before finally having her seizure.

I thanked the nurse, whose name was Sierra, and hung up the phone. I sat in silence for a long moment. I set my glass of whiskey down and tried to collect my thoughts. I felt a coldness wrap around my heart like an icy boa constrictor. Disbelief washed over me. Had Edna suffered a psychotic break? Psychosis could potentially have been brought on by the tremendous stress, grief, and sudden changes in her life. My mind wondered, though, about the suddenness of all this. Even in my medical opinion, the prior theory was a reach. This didn't feel right. Something about all of this was just plain wrong. I felt a single tear forming in the corner of my eye. I had to go and check on her and talk to Johnny. This couldn't wait.

Chapter Eighteen

July 30th, 1998
Johnny Tinsley

The past couple of hours had been a blur. From Grandma being fine before I went to sleep, to her actions and words prior to her falling sick. When the ambulance arrived, the medics eyed everything in the room cautiously before placing her onto a stretcher and wheeling her down into their rig. This was my third trip to the hospital in an ambulance this year. Something I never would have thought possible.

Only bits and pieces of the ride stuck with me. The medics tended to my grandmother and occasionally attempted to ask me what happened. I couldn't find the words. I felt numb. Empty. So, I sat in silence. I heard one of them radio in to the hospital and use the words *'grand mal seizure'*. I wasn't sure what that meant.

When we got to the hospital, the staff rushed Grandma up to a room and escorted me with them. They hooked her up to a bunch of machines and said that they had gotten her stable. One of the nurses brought me coloring books and crayons, but I couldn't find it within myself to do them. The nurse said her name was Sierra. She was really nice to me and told me they were going to allow me to stay with Grandma until she got better but were going to make some calls *just to be safe.* She asked if there was anyone she wanted me to call. At first, I wanted to say no, but then I thought of Father Rosario. He would want to know. I told her his name and the name of his church. She gave me a sympathetic look and said she would absolutely call him for me.

I looked over at Grandma, lying motionless in her bed. Dozens of wires hooked into her, monitors around her lit up with different graphs, and beeping machines constantly kept track of her health. Had she gotten the same sickness Dad had gotten? Dad never collapsed to the floor and shook like she did. But then again, he was walking around even though he was paralyzed. Nothing made sense. Maybe this was different after all. I still couldn't wrap my mind around any of it. I was worried that I was going to lose my grandma. The last of my family.

But the way she lashed out. Forced me to eat a wild rabbit in the way she did. The things she said to me. *"You deserve everything that has happened to you. Your mother. Your father. Me. We all would've been better off without you in our lives."*

I felt a tear run down my cheek that I promptly wiped away. I was exhausted. I was afraid. I was broken. The thought of my broken spirit drummed up another memory of what Grandma said to me. Her poisonous words were very reminiscent of the barbs my dad had thrown at me only a few days ago.

"One day I am going to break you down. Break you down so much that you will beg me for the sweet release of death. I am chaos. I am havoc. I am agony. And you are mine!"

The words hurt and were terrifying yet confusing at the same time. What did all of it mean? I recalled Dad saying he would take everyone and everything I ever loved from me before he would eventually take me too. Different, yet similar. Just as haunting, vague, and hurtful. I didn't understand the part about being taken. I looked over at my grandma again, resting on her hospital bed. I wished Mom was here with me. I wished she could wrap me in a warm hug. I called out to her softly, with hope in my voice. I was met with nothing but the noise of the contraptions Grandma was hooked up to.

For some reason, I found myself thinking about the face I saw under my bed. I was reminded of the same grey floating head I saw in my parents' bedroom not long before Dad went crazy. They had to have been connected somehow. I grabbed the coloring book and opened it. I tore out a page and flipped it onto its blank side and grabbed the crayons. I searched through the box and found a grey crayon as well as a black one and immediately began drawing. I made an oval shape with the grey crayon and then took the black one and made two hollow black eyes. I then gave the face its impossibly wide smile, stretching up the side of its face where the middle of the cheeks should be. I then filled in the thin smile with the black crayon and filled in the rest of the face with the grey color. I was no artist, but it did bear a slight resemblance as I held it up to the lighting. It made the hairs all over my body stand on end. I didn't like to look at the face, not even now.

"Ahem."

I looked up from my drawing and saw Father Rosario standing before me. He wasn't wearing his cassock for once. He was dressed in a grey zip up hoodie, blue jeans, and a pair of black shoes. He flashed me a weak smile.

"Father Rosario!" I yelled. I tossed my drawing onto the table next to me and leapt up from my chair and rushed over to give him a hug.

I'd never hugged him prior to this, but it felt right in the moment. He had a strange odor emanating from him. I'd smelled something similar to it in the past after Mom and Dad would drink from their *juice in a bottle* – as they called it.

Still wrapping him tight, it felt like Father Rosario was one of the last remaining people in my life. Ricky and his parents came around at first after my mom died, but they never seemed comfortable with letting Ricky stay the night. And Dad only let me stay at Ricky's house a couple times, so we'd sort of drifted apart in a matter of only a couple of months.

Father Rosario returned my hug but remained silent. I looked up and saw his eyes locked onto my grandma. He looked down at me and said he was sorry for everything that I've been through.

He walked over to the edge of Grandma's hospital bed, placed a hand onto one of hers, and bowed his head in silence. Father Rosario motioned a hand across his chest like he'd just silently prayed before asking me to have a seat with him. I sat in my chair from earlier, and he took a seat on the chair on the opposite side of the small round table that housed the coloring books and crayons. He looked over at me and started telling me how strong my grandmother was and that if anyone could get through these times, it would be her. I nodded and thanked him for coming to visit.

"Of course."

I watched as Father Rosario's eyes shifted down to my drawing. "What's this?" he asked, picking up the sheet of paper and inspecting the artwork.

I shifted in my chair uncomfortably. He looked away from the paper and peered back at me again, waiting for my answer.

I averted my gaze and shuffled my foot on the grey tiled floor uncomfortably.

"Johnny?" he asked again, his voice firm, but not unfriendly.

"It's a face."

Father Rosario let out a lighthearted chuckle. "Yes. Yes, it is. Does this face mean anything to you?"

"It's a face I've seen a couple times now."

He pouted with thought for a moment as he scanned the drawing once more. "Well, the face looks friendly enough. You've seen this face a couple times before? Where?"

"Once at my house and once at Grandma's house."

I got the impression that Father Rosario was thinking hard about what I'd said. I couldn't tell if his reaction was good or bad. He kept his face calm and expressionless.

"I see," he said finally. "Where in the houses did you see the face? And when did it happen?"

"The first time I wasn't sure I saw it. I was walking to the bathroom in the middle of the night and as I walked past my parents' bedroom, I thought I saw it in the doorway."

Father Rosario nodded but said nothing, so I continued to speak. "When I took a couple steps back it was gone."

"And did that scare you?"

I nodded. "And then at grandma's house, I saw it today. My autographed baseball rolled under the bed on its own and when I looked under my bed to grab it, I saw the face staring back at me."

Verbalizing my memory of what happened sent gooseflesh up and down my entire body. I could still visualize it perfectly. Those deep, bottomless pits for eyes and that horrible smile. Father Rosario was keeping a calm composure.

"And did it say anything to you either time?"

I shook my head no.

"You don't have to answer this question if it makes you uncomfortable, Johnny. But how long was it after you saw that face at your house...before your dad took the actions he did?"

I took a moment to consider his question. I looked at the floor and then back up to him. "The next day."

Father Rosario frowned and nodded. He set my drawing back down on the table and rose to his feet.

"I want you to have this, Johnny," he said, pulling a rosary out of his pocket and handing it to me.

I took the red and black beaded necklace from him and thanked him for it. I placed it around my neck for safe keeping.

"I appreciate you taking the time to chat with me, Johnny. I really must get going. I will stop back in after a few hours of shut eye. But hey, maybe in a couple days we can break in that mitt I got you."

"I don't know. Do you think you could actually make an accurate throw?" I said, surprising myself that I was even able to make a joke at this juncture – but we both shared a laugh over it.

"I will do my best," Father Rosario said with a friendly smile. "You take care of yourself. I will be back in a few hours to check on you and your grandma. Okay?"

"Okay."

I felt a tinge of sadness as Father Rosario left so abruptly. I scurried over to the doorway and peeked out and saw him walking with a frenetic pace toward the exit. I wasn't sure what caused him to head out in such a rush.

Even with the abrupt departure of Father Rosario, I felt a lot better after having been able to talk to him, even if only for a short period of time. I sat back down on my chair, patiently waiting for Grandma to wake up. In the meantime, I decided to finally start coloring in some of the pages from the coloring books. I had found one that was filled with some of my favorite comic book heroes and happily gave them the life they were begging for.

At one point, the nurse, Sierra, came walking in just as I finished coloring in a page for *The Avengers*. After she finished checking on Grandma, she walked over to me.

"How are you hangin' in there, kiddo?" she asked in a friendly tone.

I shrugged modestly. "I'm okay."

She gave me an apologetic look as she knelt down in front of me.

"I bet you're hungry. Here, why don't you go grab yourself a candy bar from the vending machine outside the doors in the main hall," she said after digging a fresh dollar bill out of her pocket.

I looked down at the money in her hand and then back into her warm and friendly eyes. I thanked her and rushed out of the room. It was a random act of kindness that I really needed in the moment. Maybe things would finally start looking up.

I bolted out of the room, made my way through the double doors, and rushed to the nearby vending machine. There were so many options to choose from. Reese's Cups were my favorite, but Twix and Butterfingers were also strong competitors.

I surprised myself and went with the underdog in the battle. I watched as the gold packaging containing the delicious Twix bars dropped from the machine. I swooped down, pulled the candy out of the machine, and immediately tore into them.

Taking bites as I walked back through the double doors, things seemed...*different*. The lights in the hallway were now flickering on and off. The couple of nurses that had been sitting at their station were no longer there.

"Hello?" I called out but received no answer.

I continued to shuffle down the hallway, trying to focus on the delectable treat and not the sudden shift in the environment. And then I heard it – laughter – and it was coming from my grandma's room just a few more doors ahead.

With my curiosity piqued and hopeful that my grandma had finally woken up, I raced for her door. When I sped around the corner and into the doorway, I let out a yelp of shock and nearly jumped out of my skin at the sight before me.

Grandma was standing on her tiptoes next to her hospital bed. Her head was hung low, her hair slung over her face. The wires to the machines had wrapped around her arms and held them out straight like a lifeless marionette. The monitors were beeping wildly and the lights in the room flickered rapidly like strobe lights. I couldn't take my eyes off the gruesome display before me. I tried to yell out for help when suddenly, her head snapped up. Her eyes were glowing red, and her mouth curled into a devilish grin.

"Call out to them, Johnny! Go ahead! No one can help you!" she yelled in a deep voice I did not recognize.

Black porous liquid dribbled in thick strands from her mouth as she continued to cackle wildly, dancing with the cables that held her up.

"Your grandmother is going to die, Johnny. There's nothing you can do to stop it! She's going to be joining the rest of your cunting family down in the pit. And when the time is right, and I've had my fill, you will too!"

The thing that looked like my grandma let out another bellowing, guttural snicker, throwing her head back. She then slowly brought her head back down and peered into my soul with a broiling hot glare.

She let out a monstrous growl that caused all the lightbulb panels to explode and the machines to cut off, shrouding me in darkness. Moments later, I heard a whisper in my ear.

"And I always collect."

Beep. Beep. Beep. Beep. Beep. Beep. Beep.

I suddenly awoke with a start and realized I was back in my chair in the hospital room. I looked over and saw a couple of nurses and a doctor surrounding my grandmother. They seemed to be frantically trying to work on her.

"Get him out of here!" the doctor yelled to one of the nurses, pointing in my direction.

Sierra rushed over, grabbed me by my hand, and started pulling me toward the exit. I asked her what was going on as she tugged me away. Sierra ignored my questions and brought me down the hallway to her work station. I was overwhelmed with confusion, now realizing I had been having a nightmare. But now I was being rushed away from my grandmother.

"Let's just hang out over here," Sierra said in a tone that almost sounded *too* friendly.

She attempted to make small talk with me, but I couldn't focus on what she was saying. All I could think about was the dream I'd had and worrying about my grandma.

Beeeeeeeeep!

I felt my heart sink. I may have only been eight years old, but I was already keenly aware that the sound blaring out from Grandma's room meant nothing good. My dream from just moments prior had come to fruition. She was dead.

PART TWO

A Blackened Soul

Chapter Nineteen

October 6th, 2023
John Tinsley

Life. The world's longest and most treacherous of roller coasters. It's an age-old adage, but an accurate one. It is a synthesis of highs and lows. Of twists and turns. A complex series of winding steel tracks held together by our experiences – the nuts, bolts, and the concrete foundation that we live our lives by.

For many outsiders, much of my life would be viewed through a lens of pure hell. A life filled with heartache, turmoil, and things that nightmares are made of. For most of my time here on Earth, I would agree. I still often found myself reflecting back on the moments from my childhood where everything and everyone were viciously and rapidly ripped from my life. The loss. The confusion. The fear. Being whisked away from Akron General Hospital and taken to Summit County Children's Services in the wake of my grandmother's passing. The visits from Father Rosario becoming more and more infrequent. Abandonment.

I went through the foster system for quite some time, bouncing around homes across Northeast Ohio until I graduated high school. I'd been labeled a *special* case due to the trauma I'd bore witness to. That roughly translated to the system labeling me as a potential problem child that needed extra attention.

The main family I spent most of my time with, was the Appolino family in Lakewood, Ohio. They only brought me in to collect the extra government money that came with fostering a child. I had become their personal cleaning boy – always keeping their home clean and organized while being expected to stay on top of my schoolwork.

"You're lucky we brought you into our home, boy," the father would remind me all the time.

And for a while, I did feel grateful to them. The Appolinos' were a devout Catholic family, much like my grandmother had been. They took it to extreme levels, however. Anytime I had nightmares about my experiences, they shut it down as if God were going to smite them for comforting a scared child.

"Ghosts are not real. Just the devil in disguise." They would tell me.

For all the bad, I had to thank them for one thing. They instilled such a desire for me to get away from them, that I learned the true meaning of hard work and grit early on.

Through all of that – with the deck stacked against me, all evidence would suggest that they were right. The countless sleepless nights burying my teary-eyed face into a pillow wanting to scream with all the energy my body could exert. Life had proven to be cruel and unfair. I found myself often calling out for my mom, for my dad, for my grandma. No responses ever came. Over the days, the weeks, the months, and then the years – the subsurface scars would begin to heal over. Life became moderately easier over time. Even though the scar tissue over my heart was still there, it had become easier to live with.

"Brucie! Come here, boy!"

The words snapped me out of my reverie as I peered out across the dog park. My wife, Megan, and our dog, Bruce, were playing fetch with his favorite toy: a tug of war rope with a squeaky ball attached to the end of it. It had seen better days. Frequent battles to determine who was the superior warrior had left parts of the rope frayed and matted. But the toy was his, and he was always proud and determined to show it off.

I watched as Megan yanked the rope free from Bruce's mouth. He bounced up on his hind legs with an excitement that could do nothing but put a smile on your face. He barked, eagerly waiting for her to toss it. Megan reared back and sent the toy flying through the air, with Bruce enthusiastically bounding after it. A brindle blur shooting across the emerald grass. He was such a pretty dog. Megan and I had adopted him from a local shelter when he was just five months old. Frequently labeled as problematic dogs, pit bulls filled shelters across the country ad nauseum. Bruce had some mastiff in him too. Strong and stocky – he weighed one hundred and thirty pounds – and his brindle coat had a strong sheen as well. He was my best friend. An unspoken bond had been formed between us from the moment I brought him home. He came trotting back to Megan with his chest puffed out, toy dangling from the side of his mouth.

Megan bent down, tugged at the toy, and playfully growled at Bruce, who was determined to not relinquish the rope this go around. Megan was beautiful. She was my safe space. She lifted me up out of the darkness and enabled me to see the light in life once more. Today marked our five-year wedding anniversary – though we had been together for the past eleven years. I still remembered the moment we met as if it were yesterday.

I had been going down a destructive path. I was working a dead-end second shift manufacturing job, breaking my back just to live paycheck to paycheck like so many Ohio industrial workers. The pitfall to working a job on that shift was that the only thing you could do after work was hit the bars. And that was exactly what I did. On a cold, wintry night I made the mile long walk from my apartment in Akron, Ohio, to McCann's Pub. It had grown into a metalhead haven over the years. A place where twenty-somethings would congregate and listen to loud, angsty music with heavy guitar riffs and scathing vocals. The bar wasn't much to write home about. Many would consider it a hole in the wall. I, and many others, loved it. Fueled with the scent of liquor and stale cigarettes from its many years in operation – it housed a dimly lit wraparound bar, three pool tables, and walls that were covered with beer signs and sports memorabilia sporting memories of all the Cleveland sports teams.

Working in manufacturing wasn't always conducive to a positive life environment. It was dirty, physical work that left little for you to show for in terms of life's luxuries. I wanted more out of life, but the vicious cycle would continue to repeat itself. After a grueling shift that left my body and soul feeling run down, I turned to the solution for curing the pain I was feeling inside. Alcohol.

A couple of hours into the night – racking up a bar tab with too many shots of Jameson and the "always on special" Pabst Blue Ribbons – I noticed a group of ladies that appeared to be close to my age standing around a pool table, laughing and having a great time. They were far from regulars. I'd never seen them here before. From my corner perch at the bar, I locked eyes with one of them. Even from the stool I was firmly planted on, I was floored by her beauty. She smiled and it sent a wave of butterflies fluttering around my alcohol-filled stomach. I quickly turned back to face the bar. Out of my peripherals, I saw her lean into her friend's ear and look back in my direction. I convinced myself that the alcohol was taking over and that I should probably cut myself off. I scooted my half empty beer can away from me. Moments later, I felt a tap on my shoulder. The soft touch startled me to the point I nearly fell backward off my stool.

I slowly turned and saw her, the girl I'd just locked eyes with, standing directly behind me, flashing that gorgeous smile. The first thing I noticed were her piercing blue eyes. They felt as blue as the summer sky and as vast as the Pacific Ocean. Her curly dirty blonde hair reached just past her shoulders. Her figure was fit, but not too skinny. She wore an Akron University hoodie, leggings, and sneakers. Everything about her felt like my type. My stomach did another somersault. I'd never had much luck with the ladies, because I had grown up inherently shy after everything I'd gone through.

I saw her lips move but couldn't make the words out over Whitechapel's *"Possession"* blaring from the speakers surrounding us. Surely, she wasn't *actually* interested in me. Probably just needed me to settle some debate between her and her friends about whether they should ditch this shitty bar and see if I had any recommendations. I shot her a meek grin and pretended to hear what she'd been saying. I must've looked like a total doofus, because she gripped me by my shirt sleeve and tugged me away from the bar and over to meet her friends.

She told me her name was Megan and introduced me to her friends Alison and Nichole. To my surprise, they invited me to be their fourth for a game of pool. Megan told me I could be her partner. The whole thing felt so out of place that I couldn't help but nearly melt into the dirty tile floors right then and there.

"You just looked so sad and lonely up at the bar by yourself," Megan said to me, more of a shout as she leaned in to speak into my ear.

It was one of the best nights of my life and would become the catalyst for re-shaping and restructuring how I would view the world. I mean, what were the odds? One of the most beautiful girls I had ever seen choosing *me* in a run-down metal bar that was not their usual scene. Almost non-existent, that's the answer. It took a series of decisions to fall into place like a line of dominoes for us to meet. Call it what you want. Destiny. Fate. Either way, it marked the dawn of a new era in my life.

A few years later, we were married. She and I had become almost inseparable. We were polar opposites in a lot of ways but were perfect for each other in all the ways that mattered most. We'd become best friends. We had shared our deepest, darkest secrets with one another and were able to connect on an unrivaled spiritual level that I never thought possible. It was in her nature to want to help. She'd gotten a degree in nursing and ironically worked as a registered nurse in the same hospital where I'd had so many traumatizing experiences as a child. I had grown out of the manufacturing space and worked my way up to a pretty solid paying tech sales role right before we got married.

On one stormy night, we'd gotten onto the topic of ghosts and the paranormal. She'd asked me if I believed in it. The first mention of it struck a nerve and sent something primal tearing through my insides. I couldn't tell whether it was my trauma resurfacing or not, but I told her a couple of the stories surrounding the events I grew up with, like the smiling face. But I never mentioned the *other* parts. The visits from my mother. The dream with my grandma. My dad walking when he was paralyzed. All those major details I'd chosen to sweep under the rug in an effort to save face and not sound like I belonged in a psych ward.

She noticed my apprehension. She kicked her socked feet up onto the sofa and nestled into a ball as she faced me, glass of wine in hand, as she outlined experiences she had growing up in her home in Mentor. She explained that there was a man in a hat that would stand in the shadows of her home at night. He never spoke. He never moved. She would see him, and then in the blink of an eye he would be gone. I watched as the gooseflesh crept up her slender arms – clearly the experiences had frightened her.

"Did the hat man ever say anything to you?"

She shook her head and then went on to tell me about how her grandfather would occasionally come to visit her too. The mention of a lost family member coming to visit her sat in my stomach like a rock. She elaborated that sometimes he'd visit in her dreams and give her words of affirmation, and other times, he would be standing at the foot of her bed in a non-threatening manner.

Though her story resonated with me and made me feel a sense of relatability, I couldn't help but be curious – and also thankful – as to why she didn't have such terrifying experiences surrounding her relative coming to visit her like I had.

When she finally wrapped up recounting her stories, she nodded to me eagerly – saying it was my turn to share more if I had any other stories. In the blink of an eye, I had to decide whether to come clean with her, or to shove it all away and label it as hokum. I opted to tell her the emotional stories of how my mom had come to visit me after the accident. I watched a look of sorrow spread across Megan's beautiful, blue eyes.

With tears in her eyes, she set her glass of wine down on the coffee table and wrapped me in a warm embrace.

"I'm so sorry, baby." She kissed me on the lips and returned to the tight hug, resting her head on my shoulder. Oddly enough, that level of openness created a tighter bond between the two of us.

That night, we'd ironically decided to put on a scary movie. We slipped *The Conjuring* into the DVD player and allowed ourselves to be scared out of our wits. The movie fit the vibes of the night perfectly and led us down a rabbit hole of a discussion.

It led us to talk about the possibilities of life after death and what that could mean. I thought back to my father telling me ghosts didn't exist – back to the Appolinos telling me ghosts didn't exist. There was still a small ember in the pit of my stomach that believed and wanted to not only prove *them* wrong but also to prove that what I had grown up experiencing wasn't just my bullshit runaway imagination.

I was blown away by the girl sitting across from me. What should've terrified Megan and would terrify most everyone else had only caused more resolve and interest within her. A few of the most loveable traits about her were her resiliency, strength, and natural curiosity. Our chat opened the door about us beginning our own paranormal research team and going out to some of the most haunted locations in the area to film it and try to provide proof of life after death.

I mulled over the suggestion for a moment, trying to contemplate the idea of it, when I finally told her, *"Let's do it."*

We started small, attempting to only get our feet wet. We attended a couple of public ghost hunts at local haunted hotspots before finally venturing out on our own and attempting to find the answers to one of life's greatest mysteries – *Do ghosts really exist?*

We went on to release our very own paranormal documentary – *Walking Through the Veil* – which would go on to become a global sensation among the streaming services back in the late summer of 2021. We filmed at the Rockland Hills Sanatorium in western Pennsylvania and captured remarkable evidence that catapulted us into the stratosphere of borderline stardom. We were getting invites to be on nationwide talk shows, invites to be special guests at paranormal conventions, and would have random people recognize us while out shopping. Sometimes it was a lot to take in. We were just pursuing a passion and hadn't expected anything to come from it. And in a little over a week, we were going to be heading out to film our second documentary at an orphanage that had been converted into an insane asylum before sitting abandoned since the 1980's.

"Come on, buddy! Let's go say 'Hi' to Daddy!" Megan said as she and Bruce came trotting over to meet me at the bench I was sitting on.

Bruce rushed in front of Megan and playfully jumped into my lap, blissfully unaware of his size as his paws slammed down into my groin. I hunched over in pain just in time for him to lick all over my face. I playfully set his paws back down on the ground and gave him scratchin's while baby talking to him.

"Hey! Hey! Hey! It's our anniversary, Bruce. Not yours!" Megan joked with a sly grin on her face, hands resting on her hips. He looked back at her with a confused expression.

I hopped up from the bench and tossed Bruce's toy again, which he happily bolted after. I wrapped Megan in an embrace and gave her a kiss before Bruce made his way back to us. The three of us walked back toward the parking lot, taking in the scenery.

Early fall foliage always spoke to my heart. The earthy smell of dying leaves permeated the air as the trees provided a canvas of oranges, yellows, and browns. The air felt refreshing and crisp, but not overly cold, as a gentle breeze escorted us out of the park.

Chapter Twenty

October 6th, 2023
Megan Tinsley

"You about ready?" John called out from the bedroom just as I finished applying my last bit of mascara.

"Yep!" I said gleefully as I stowed the tube of makeup back into the drawer.

It was hard to believe that it was already our five-year wedding anniversary. It felt like just yesterday we were walking down the aisle with our arms raised in triumph as family and friends showered us with rice.

I looked down at the pregnancy test on the counter with waves of excitement and nervousness. I smiled to myself, feeling tears of happiness welling up in my eyes. It couldn't have been a more perfect day to make the announcement. I slipped the narrow stick into my handbag and looked into the mirror. John had bought me this beautiful, royal blue dress just for the occasion. I knew others would describe me as *glowing* tonight. Standing in front of the mirror, I placed a hand on my stomach. We'd been trying for a child for so long. Tonight, on our night, I could finally give him the news that I knew he would be so excited for.

Stepping out into the bedroom, I found John putting the finishing touches on his red bowtie. He looked gorgeous. He always dressed up nice. Tonight was no different as he stood before me wearing a light blue dress shirt with the sleeves rolled up, revealing his tattoo covered arms and gold wristwatch. He looked over at me with a warm, knowing smile as if he knew he had just caught me eyeing him up.

"What?" I asked.

He merely smirked as he walked over and held me close.

"I love you," he said before planting a soft kiss that I eagerly returned.

When we separated, Bruce stood in the doorway shooting a judgmental glance in our direction, chew toy dangling from his mouth.

"We'll play later, buddy," John said in his baby voice. "I promise."

Bruce cocked his head to the side as if trying to decipher the injustice that John had just imposed on him as he walked by. The two of them had my heart. There was no denying it.

Never in my life had I thought I would get so lucky. I'd battled through my share of rough relationships with neglectful and abusive men, and it almost felt like finding my partner to go through life with would be impossible. I'd grown up hearing that the person that is meant to become a part of your life will come when you least expect it.

The idea for my friends and I to go to McCann's Pub was a total shot in the dark. We were tired of the party scene on campus and wanted to trek farther out. Allison and Nichole were skeeved out by the bar as we pulled into the parking lot.

"Gross," Nichole said.

"Remind me again why we're doing this?" Allison added.

I'd always been told by my father that I had a plucky attitude to go with a ditzy personality. *"In the best way possible."* He would go on to add with his infectious smile.

"It's something different. Come on, it'll be fun!" I said, giving Nicole a playful shove.

After some initial grumblings, they finally agreed to give it a shot, and the rest was history.

Inside the bar was exactly as you'd have expected based upon the outside appearances. But what really surprised us was the younger crowd that was scattered around the bar. It felt hip in an almost paradoxical way from what we were used to. McCanns had a Rustic charm intertwined with a little bit of grit and a down-to-earth vibe where you could feel okay with being yourself and not having to pretend to be someone you were not. The girls and I walked over to the middle pool table. Heavy metal music was blaring through the speakers. I wasn't a fan of the music, but the changeup felt refreshing, and before too long, we found ourselves doing a mock mosh pit and having the best time. Then, something unexpected happened.

It was as if by some magical force, my attention was averted to a guy in the corner seat of the bar. His back was leaned up against the wall behind him as he stared off into the distance. He wore a dirty uniform – my guess was that he worked in manufacturing. A shot of whiskey and a can of PBR sat next to him. I couldn't put my finger on it, but *something* about him drew me in. His head snapped over, our eyes locked, and I felt something stir deep within me. He was quite attractive; not the type that I would've pegged to be working in a dirty factory. He had a strong jawline and a coiffed hairstyle. His stare was piercing. I could feel the sorrow behind his eyes. He had been through things. But I could also sense that this was a man that wouldn't hurt a soul. He quickly looked away. His sudden bashfulness piqued my interest even more. There was something oddly magnetic about him. Something I couldn't explain. I leaned over and whispered to Allison and Nichole that I was going to invite him over to shoot a game of pool with us. The two of them snickered like schoolgirls and said, *"He's cute,"* and *"Get it, girl!"*

I walked over and tapped on his shoulder. He looked back in an almost dumbfounded shock that I found totally endearing. When I asked him if he wanted to join my friends and I, he nodded his head with a big, goofy grin that told me he didn't listen to a word I was saying. It was cute. I decided he didn't have an option, so I grabbed him by his shirt sleeve and dragged him over to hang out.

I shook my head as I looked over at the man I'd so deeply fallen in love with as we got into his Jeep to head out to dinner. Sometimes it still didn't feel real.

To cross paths with a man who had persevered through so much and *allowed* himself to be completely open with me – it felt like it was too good to be true. John could've allowed all the things he experienced in his childhood and growing up to be the cause of his downfall. He could've turned to drugs. He could've turned violent. He could've broken down from the trauma and taken his own life. Thankfully, none of that happened. Instead, he used it as motivation to try to become a better man. He used those times to remind himself how far he'd come. He persevered. He always had. A million other roads he could've traveled, but here we were now, driving to our anniversary dinner, as happy with each other as could be.

I could feel my fingers subliminally rubbing the leather fabric of my handbag while we discussed ideas about upgrading our home in the future once we were able to start a family. I was holding onto a secret that I knew was going to floor him. Hearing the excitement behind his voice when he spoke about the idea of raising a family had always melted my heart and did things to me that I would never utter inside a church.

For the night's special occasion, we chose to go to our favorite Italian fine dining establishment – Fracassi's. When we arrived, John was the perfect gentleman – opening the door for me and helping me out of the car before handing our keys off to the valet driver.

The early autumn night air had a bite to it – sending a cold sensation down my spine to accompany the jittery excitement pulling at my insides.

We made our way inside where the hostess greeted us with a million-dollar smile before she escorted us to our reserved table. Fracassi's was elegant. Intricately designed mahogany wood walls, swirly white and black marble flooring, beautifully adorned tables, chairs, and upholstery. The lighting in Fracassi's was always dimmed just enough to give the restaurant that special ambience – paired with the sweet fragrance of Italian cooking.

Our waiter made his way over and introduced himself as Michael before pouring both of us a glass of water while he reviewed the specials for the night and handed us our menus.

John eagerly scooped up the menu, his beautiful blue eyes beaming with excitement. A man and his food. Something about the pure innocence of their childlike joy when it came to eating always brought a smile to my face.

"What are you going to get, babe?" I asked.

He glanced up from the menu for a fleeting moment, smiled and then averted his attention back to the slender placard. "I think I am going to go with the Cavatelli Al Forno. It sounds amazing. You?"

He should already know my choice based on our previous visits. I gave him a knowing look after a brief moment of silence. His expression slackened as a smirk slipped across his face – signaling he did in fact know what I was going to order.

"The Veal Pappardelle. Of course," he answered with a lighthearted chuckle, setting his menu down. "You look absolutely stunning tonight. I love you."

A whirlwind of emotions hit me at his words. He was so sweet. "You look pretty amazing yourself and I love you too."

We spent the next couple of minutes deciding on a new appetizer to try just as our server made his way back over to us. The server asked if we'd like anything to drink. John began to order us a bottle of champagne when I told him I didn't want to drink tonight. He did a double take and told Michael that the water would be fine for now before putting in our order for calamari.

My stomach did a front flip. I hadn't considered the drink situation. Turning down champagne was going to immediately send a bat signal off in John's mind.

"Is everything alright?" he asked, a look of concern spreading across his face.

"Yes, baby. I just don't feel like drinking tonight."

He seemed taken aback by my words. John was a sweetheart, though, and would never force me to have a drink I didn't want to have. It was customary for us when we had special nights out to share a nice bottle of champagne or cocktails with one another.

"Oh. Okay, babe. That's totally fine."

It wasn't fine, though. I could hear the hurt in his voice, even if he hadn't intended it to come across that way. I could *feel* him wanting to dig further. Wanting to understand if something was bothering me. We'd always had an open line of communication. This wasn't exactly the moment I had envisioned when it came to telling him the big news but watching him pretend to look at the menu again to try to cover his concern pulled it out of me.

I reached a hand forward and placed it on top of his. He stared at me with his *"purdy blue eyes"* as my grandma – who'd spent most of her life growing up in West Virginia – liked to call John.

"John," I said so softly, that it barely escaped my mouth as more than a whisper.

The corner of John's lip curled into a smile at my touch as we stared intently into each other's eyes.

"Yes?"

"I'm pregnant."

Chapter Twenty-One

October 10th, 2023
Father Rosario

"D-Do you believe in sin?" My mother asked between labored breaths, her heart monitor beeping in the background.

The cancer and newly formed dementia had a firm hold on the woman that gave me life and showed me the righteous path toward serving our lord and savior. Her question didn't come as a surprise, given the circumstances. It didn't make it any less painful to witness.

"You know I do, Mother." I placed a reassuring hand on top of hers. She looked down at our joined hands and then up at me, her expression vacant.

The stare had become all too familiar over the past couple of months. You could physically *see* when her dementia would take over. Something in her eyes would shift. She would go from being able to remember things new and old, to the soul crushing lost stare that told you she was losing her grip on everything she ever knew. It grew more aggressive with each passing day, much like the cancer. Hearing your mother ask who you are on an almost daily basis, even when you understood the disease, was a punch to the gut. I knew her life was drawing nearer to an end. The fact we couldn't re-live fond memories caused an emotion to stir inside me that I would never show in front of her, even if I knew she wouldn't remember it.

"How do we know if we've truly sinned? What if there's no heaven?" she asked, her eyes quizzical and eyeing up my cassock.

I realized she was talking to the priest now, and not her son. Hearing her question her faith that she'd always been so steadfast in was a bitter pill to swallow. I did the only thing I could do. I stuffed my pride down and became a priest for her. I told her that heaven's gates would absolutely be open for her, and she would be welcomed with open arms.

I leaned forward toward the table next to her hospital bed, gripped her copy of the bible, and opened to a verse that I knew she'd always been quite fond of. I held the scripture in one hand while placing a supportive hand over hers as I read the words to her. Her vacant stare that originally looked confused and afraid had softened. By the time I closed the book, she was sound asleep.

I quietly placed it back on the table and leaned over to press a soft kiss onto her forehead.

"I love you, Mom."

It didn't take long during my walk to the parking garage at Akron General to feel the waterworks come bursting out of the seams. I wanted to hang onto our warm memories, but in times like these, it only broke to the strong-armed will of the pervasive and negative intrusive thoughts of her waning life.

"We'll see you next week," I said with a cordial wave as I watched Liz Patterson and her son Jacob make their way down the sidewalk toward the parking lot next to St. Anthony's.

With a sigh, I closed the heavy oak doors. I would swear those doors got ten pounds heavier every year over the past few years. Time had finally begun catching up with me. The reflection that stared back at me in the mirror was a sad reminder that time waits for no one. Thinning white wispy hair and pronounced wrinkles that I liked to call wisdom marks pulled at my heartstrings and let me know my time of servitude was beginning to start the countdown. I'd been blessed to walk the Earth for as long as I had. I'd proudly served, helped, and counseled many in the community through the most difficult times in their lives. Except for one.

Johnny Tinsley.

Not a day went by where I didn't think about that boy. I kicked myself for allowing him to slip through the cracks. I was still plagued by the memories of the summer of '98. The final resting image in my mind of the frightened little boy showing me a drawing of the face that had been haunting him. The crude sketch with bottomless black holes for eyes and a spindly black abyss of a devilish grin set upon pallid grey skin. I'd been teetering on whether the Tinsley family situation had all been natural causes, but when Edna had suddenly fallen out with a seizure, I chose to zoom out and examine the situation. I thought long and hard about the downward spiral of Ron, and when Johnny presented his drawing to me, it struck me with unbridled fear.

The truth was that I was afraid. Afraid of the unknown. I hoped it was a case of mental illness. I could diagnose, counsel, and treat mental ailments. No matter how much someone studies theology and the possibility of a potential demonic presence, there's nothing that can actually get you ready to come to grips with that reality. I remembered rushing out of Akron General in a blind daze to contact Father O'Keefe. In the farthest recesses of my brain, I *knew* what he would tell me: that I needed to gather proof before the church could get involved any further.

I later found out that Edna had passed before I ever got the chance to make the call. I felt crushed under the weight of my own conscience. I felt powerless, confused, and concerned. I found myself wondering if there was more I could've done. What if I had been more open to the idea that something far more insidious was at play? I still hadn't been completely convinced of it, but it was certainly difficult to dismiss the notion – and the guilt that came along with that conflict within my psyche.

The most cumbersome tendril of guilt that weighed on me was that I had stopped visiting Johnny during his stay at the Summit County Children Services Center. Part of me felt responsible for not intervening in a more meaningful manner. Part of me also felt that my being around him would dredge up all of those horrible memories and not allow him to move on. No matter how you spun it, I felt like I had failed him. And I felt awful.

A lot of the locals had kept tabs on Johnny through the ages – as much as possible, anyhow. Occasional reports would trickle in about rumors of the new foster family he'd been placed with. I knew he'd been enduring great stress, and I worried for the boy and what his future might hold.

To my surprise, I had been watching a late-night talk show on one of the recent restless nights where sleep evaded me, and I saw a man and his wife interviewing with the show's host. The man looked like he could've been an adult version of the boy I once knew. His and his wife's name flashed across the bottom of the screen and my eyes nearly bulged out of my head.

John and his wife, Megan, had become paranormal investigators. They had filmed a hit documentary that was on streaming platforms everywhere. *Color me intrigued,* I thought.

With sleep not being an option, I decided to watch their debut documentary. The show had the quality you'd expect from a full budget production company, which shocked me. The cinematic shots highlighted the foreboding structure and it's decaying innards as they reviewed the history of the building and its purported hauntings with local investigators and the owners of the property. Here he was, the curious, intelligent young man I attempted to help from twenty-five years ago, now on my television screen. Clearly, that thirst for answers and knowledge had continued on with him long after he met me as he now set his sights on trying to prove the existence of life after death. *Fascinating.*

"Do you believe in ghosts, Father?"

Well, let's see. I watched on as the documentary switched gears from the interviews and cinematic shots to the rough multi-person point of view filming with the night vision enabled, illuminating the footage of the abandoned building under a harsh green light on the screen. Things started off slowly with John and Megan introducing themselves, followed by their third companion, who had been introduced as Eddie Ingol. Eddie was strictly there to be a cameraman and tech specialist. He announced that he wanted no part of the actual investigating but thought it sounded like too much fun to film – so he couldn't pass up the opportunity.

Their approach was highly respectful. They announced their intentions for the evening and invited anyone that would like to come forward and tell their story to make their presence known when able. They had set up a few random gadgets throughout the building with static cameras monitoring their surroundings. Occasionally, those devices would light up. It was interesting to watch, but certainly nothing that blew me away as evidence of potential spectral activity. With John's voice narrating in the background, the documentary began to delve further into the belly of the beast.

It wasn't until they tried an experiment, where Megan sat on an old hospital bed with a pair of dowsing rods in a room that had previously been used for surgery, that I began to get sucked in. John carefully wound a blindfold over her eyes, placed headphones over her ears, and cranked the volume up. He tested out her ability to hear by making a crude joke about her taste in music that likely would've offended her had she been able to hear. When she didn't respond, he seemed sufficiently satisfied and tapped her on the shoulder. Megan slowly raised up the glow in the dark rods as John stepped back with his camera.

He began to open up dialogue by inviting anyone nearby that wanted to communicate to step forward and direct the 'light up sticks' Megan was holding to answer his questions.

"If there is anyone with us, can you show me a yes?"

The rods slowly closed in on one another, crossing over into the shape of an x.

"Thank you. Can you show me a no?"

The rods shot out wide on either side of Megan before returning to their centered position.

"Thank you for that. We really appreciate your willingness to come forward. Were you a patient in this hospital?" The rods crossed paths.

I pouted in thought. This was intriguing to say the least. John began to ask a series of questions and without fail, the dowsing rods were quick to answer. He'd even managed to steer the conversation to a point where he was able to confirm the name of the patient that was rumored to have died in that very room and reportedly still haunted it to this day, and that blew me away. Megan had no ability to hear the questions or be able to accurately nail all of these questions at the exact moment he was asking them.

"Hey, Eddie. Go stand over there on the far side of the room," John said from behind camera.

The video switched over to Eddie's angle, and he could be seen walking to the opposite side of Megan. John followed suit and stood on the opposite side of the room as Eddie.

"Okay. I have a small favor to ask," John said. "Can you point to where Eddie is standing?" The rods shot to Megan's left, slamming into her arm and holding their position pointing directly at him.

I felt a chill run up my spine and thought I might have to manually scoop my jaw off the floor as John switched gears and asked that the spirit point to him, and the rods immediately flipped to her other side and stayed pointing at him.

I wanted to attempt to explain it away. I wanted to say this was due to some ideomotor effect, but the swiftness and accuracy of the responses had me stumped.

They ended the experiment. John and Eddie filled Megan in about the happenings, and she seemed to be genuinely shocked and happy with the results.

The investigation resumed with John and Megan doing EVP sessions and capturing several spooky voices on their recorders that could not be heard with human ears. John explained that in theory, spirits speak in a frequency in which our ears cannot pick up on. The recorders were able to capture those voices.

I felt a slight disconnect with the recorders. A number of things could explain away the voices. Bodily noises, the rustling of someone's shirt sleeve, faulty internal components of the devices themselves. This documentary had me teetering between belief and wanting to call it misleading at best.

It wasn't until the end of the documentary when they were in the morgue using a device called a spirit box that I was once again pulled back in. What sounded like a bunch of radio chatter at first, the white noise had begun to take on a life of its own.

John and Megan were in the midst of asking their questions when a voice began to come through. It was the same exact voice every single time. It didn't make sense as to how that could be possible with the speed that the little device swept through the radio frequencies.

The voice started slow at first. Spitting out a word or two before slowly progressing.

"I..."

They asked it to continue after a brief moment of silence.

"I'm...coming...I'm coming for you!"

With the suddenness of a gunshot, the door to the room they stood in flew open and slammed into the wall, eliciting a shriek from Megan and a startled yelp from both John and Eddie.

I felt like I'd been struck in the chest by a two-by-four. My heart was racing. When they went and re-wound the footage, you could see a black shadow-like arm pushing the door open. They replayed the clip a few more times. It was unmistakable. The documentary then cut to them taking the video footage to an expert for evaluation. The technician confirmed that the video footage had not been tampered with or edited.

"I can't explain it," the man said.

The documentary cut back to the three investigators discussing the shocking event that had just taken place before it fast forwarded to the three of them walking out of the front doors just as the sun was beginning to rise.

That was the end of their debut documentary. I was flummoxed. Stumped. I tried to weigh the plausibility of it all. Could a wind draft cause that heavy door to swing open like that? Possibly. Unlikely, but it was possible. The arm? Could it have been some form of shadow play? Again, a possibility and something to consider. But the occurrence happening in such close proximity to the voice saying it was coming for them? If it truly was something supernatural, it begged the question of *who* or *what* they'd been dealing with.

"Do you believe in ghosts?"

That question, given its context at the time, still hung in the air like a hungry mosquito on a hot summer night. My internal response to that question was a question in of itself. Was it ghosts? Or, like I had been raised to believe when it came to supernatural occurrences, was it something more sinister at play?

Chapter Twenty-Two

October 14th, 2023
John Tinsley

The past week had been a total blur. Megan dropped the life-changing news into my lap at our anniversary dinner, and I'd been feeling on top of the world ever since. A small part of me had been terrified of the idea of having a child. The heartache and trauma I dealt with during my childhood was one I never wanted to put a child of my own through. After all, we could never control when it was our time to leave this place. Megan had changed my outlook on things. Her overwhelming positivity – in a good way – was enough to enable me to see past my fear and anxiety. And when I really sat back and pondered what it would be like to be a father, it gave me great excitement. Megan and I discussed, at length, how we would approach parenting. We understood that no matter how prepared we tried to make ourselves, we were still going to learn as we went. That didn't change the fact that we wanted to be in agreement with the family values we wanted to create. We'd discussed our favorite names for a boy or a girl. We'd landed on naming our child Adelaide if it were a girl or naming him after myself if it were a boy. I daydreamed about the experiences we could create as a family: heading out to pumpkin patches in the fall, taking our child to sporting events, watching them grow and become their own person. Having a child was a heavy undertaking, but keeping those thoughts in mind always gave me the best kind of butterflies – and Megan was in total agreement. Seeing her eyes light up when she listened to me talk about us starting a family made my heart flutter.

We'd already found ourselves prematurely scouring through retail stores eyeing up baby clothes for our future child. I, of course, found myself drawn to the onesies that featured our local sports teams, while Megan, being the more practical one, found outfits for both boys and girls that were way more adorable and presentable in a public setting.

The energy shift in our house was palpable. We'd always managed to keep our home a positive space, but something I could only relate to what felt like a beam of white light shone down upon our house and was guiding us toward this next major stage in our lives.

It wasn't until a few days ago, when Eddie called asking what time he needed to be at our house to leave for Illinois, that we were reminded about our upcoming documentary that we were slated to film.

"Are you sure you still want to go? We can always push it back to next year," I said to Megan.

She flashed the beautiful smile that stole my heart years ago with a look of determination and pride in her posture. "No. Let's do it."

"What about the baby?" I asked, walking over and placing a gentle hand on her stomach.

"The baby will be fine."

"I just want to be sure. I know stress can be bad for pregnancies."

Megan pulled me in for a hug as she let out a light-hearted giggle. "I promise we will be fine. The baby will be fine."

"How do you think it's going to go?" Eddie asked from the back seat of our Jeep. He had his camera rolling.

"Well, based on the history of the building, I expect it to be a super active night," Megan answered from the passenger seat.

The sun was shining down upon us as we zoomed through the straight, flat farmlands of rural Indiana on our way to our ultimate destination – New Hope Orphanage. We'd been teasing our followers on social media for months about a new project, and it was really beginning to pick up steam. When selecting our next filming location, I told Megan I wanted to see if there were any old orphanages we could investigate. Based on my history through child services and foster care, I thought it would be a unique story we could tell. That night, I posted a one-word teaser on social media. *'Orphanage'*. It got a ton of hits. Our fans actually managed to do a lot of research for us by guessing locations they thought we'd be at. I then spent some time looking up locations from their guesses before stumbling upon New Hope.

Megan and I had done some research on the history surrounding the old orphanage. It had originally opened in 1928. During its operation, tuberculosis had swept the area, and dozens of children would go on to lose their lives inside those walls, afraid and alone. New Hope Orphanage would close its doors in 1952 and had later been given the moniker of *"No Hope Orphanage"*.

Orphanages had begun to undergo massive change after World War II and had begun opening under new names with fancy signage. A wave of faux support to provide psychological and psychiatric care for emotional and behavioral problem children emerged.

New Hope had re-opened in 1957 under the same name to house overflow from the nearby lunatic asylum in Chicago. The building had undergone some renovations to accommodate the need and securely house the *mentally deranged* – as the article stated. New Hope was used to house the higher risk patients; those who were more likely to commit violent acts. The smaller location meant less patients – which, in theory, meant a more watchful eye over the patients.

It wasn't long before New Hope began dealing with overcrowding. A troubling discovery I'd made since joining the paranormal field was just how bad our healthcare system was at one point, especially in asylums. Abuse, neglect, lobotomies, electroshock therapy, hydrotherapy, physical restraints, and even complete isolation were all common. By the 1980's, word had begun to spread about the living conditions inside New Hope. News reporters began showing up in droves, with cameras in tow, to capture the heinous atrocities within those walls.

New Hope was described as though it were part of a third world country. Emaciated patients with no clothes on aimlessly wandered the halls. Patients strapped to beds, laying in their own piss and shit. Completely deplorable treatment. A local news reporter stated the building smelled of death and decay. And once the media grabbed hold of the stories and began to peel back the layers, they would discover just how apt that description truly was.

"An inordinate amount of death that cannot be accurately quantified took place within those walls," a news article said after New Hope had been forced to close its doors in the summer of 1986.

"Willful neglect and mistreatment of the patients of New Hope. Digging through the records, we uncovered misconduct, improper use of state and federally issued funding, reports of sexual misconduct, abuse, and what we suspect to be a substantial number of undocumented deaths of patients."

That last part of the article really struck a chord. I knew that patients in asylums were often considered throwaways, similarly to orphans or foster kids in a lot of cases. They were viewed as less than. Left behind. Forgotten. A depressing thought raced through my mind – the idea that you could die, and no one would know or care. Those poor people.

"There's a lot of dark energy in New Hope. A history of trauma and a substantial amount of sadness, sorrow, and violence will likely have the building pulsating with energy. After speaking with the owner of the location, I can say with the utmost confidence that we are going to experience heavy paranormal activity."

The owner, Mark Wallace, purchased the building in 2009 after it had sat vacant for nearly twenty-three years. We interviewed him remotely a few weeks back and recorded the session, with his permission, for the documentary as he had other engagements he had to attend on the date of our filming.

When I asked him why he bought the building, he'd said the initial plan was to renovate it and turn the building into an apartment complex. He viewed it as an investment opportunity.

Deep down, I hated how our country refused to preserve history – whether good or bad when it came to historic buildings like these. Everywhere else in the world, they preserve all their history, regardless of the connotations surrounding it. Here in America, historic buildings are torn down to make way for convenience stores or parking lots. At least Mark was attempting to keep the shell of the building the same and repurpose it for something that was needed.

When asked why the conversion never took place, Mark said they started the construction process, but the paranormal activity progressed to a point where workers no longer felt safe to work there. Reports of tools being thrown, workers being shoved, things going missing, phantom screams, and more. This caused my ears to perk up. That level of activity would have to lead to some compelling evidence for us. Matt went on, saying that the paranormal activity had created a ripple effect in the surrounding community and word had spread. Nobody wanted to work on New Hope.

"Why didn't you try selling the location or taking a bulldozer to it?" I questioned.

"Something about that building just screams to not be forgotten. A wiped away history is doomed to repeat itself. We need reminders of how far we've come as a society – even with all the turmoil in the world. It's still good to look back at how things once were and then look at where we are now. It provides comfort." Mark paused for a moment. *"So, I started doing a little research. I was acutely aware of the hauntings in my building. I looked into the paranormal field a tad and was alarmed to find out just how big it had grown within pop culture. I started offering investigators, much like yourselves, the*

ability to come and test their mettle with the restless spirits of New Hope. The rest is history."

We ended the interview after learning a few of the hot spots for activity. Several of the patient rooms, the boiler room, the basement, and the attic were places of high activity. He gave us the names of several patients that were said to still be roaming the halls. One room in particular was a room he called '*The Doll Room*'. Mark told us he started going to tag sales, yard sales, and antique stores looking for creepy, vintage dolls to place in one of the rooms in an attempt to add an unsettling aura to a part of New Hope. He said activity had really begun to ramp up after that addition.

I posted another one-word clue on social media after the interview wrapped up. *Midwest.* Speculation began to spread like wildfire once more and followed up with a post saying *Announcement at Ohio Paranormal Summit.*

The Ohio Paranormal Summit was one of the largest events in the country. People from all over the nation – and even some international travelers, would descend upon the world-renowned former prison that held the event. We were scheduled to be special guests at the convention in just a couple of weeks – just in time for Halloween. We were going to make our formal announcement at that time about the new documentary, where we filmed, and what everyone could expect from our newest filming expedition. It was going to create a heavy workload for myself to edit enough of the documentary to be able to provide a teaser trailer for those in attendance before finally sharing it on social media.

"One last stop for gas before we get to New Hope," I announced as I got off on the exit and pulled into the nearby gas station.

All three of us were excited to get to New Hope. The photos of the building just *screamed* haunted. But photos, as we all knew, never did the real thing justice.

The three of us got out of the car to stretch our legs and use the bathroom. As I was walking back, I noticed a young boy sitting on a bench in front of the store with who I assumed was his older brother. They both had skateboards resting under their feet. The older boy was sipping on a Big Gulp, scrolling on his phone while the younger boy was reading a book. The fact that the youth still read made me feel good. I glanced down at his book and saw he was reading something called *Welcome to Scareville.* I felt a smirk spread across my face. The book gave me a nostalgic vibe and brought me back to my fond memories of reading *Goosebumps* when I was his age.

"Cool book," I said without missing a stride.

The young boy looked up, smiled, and thanked me before averting his gaze back to the book.

Moments later, we were fueled up. Megan and Eddie stockpiled snacks and energy drinks to get us ready for the remainder of the drive, and the heavy slog of work we knew we were about to encounter to be able to wrap up filming a full-length documentary in such a short amount of time.

Eddie began singing *"On the road again"* like he always did on road trips as I peeled out of the gas station and onto the road once more.

"Don't you know any other songs?" I teased, glancing up into my rearview mirror.

A sarcastic grin spread across Eddie's face. "Nope!"

And then just to annoy me, Megan began singing along with him. The rest of the trip was going to be a *long* drive.

Chapter Twenty-Three

October 14th, 2023
Megan Tinsley

"Megan… Ghosts aren't real!"

My mother had had enough of my stories. I began to feel like the little girl who cried wolf.

"See? There's nothing in there." She brushed aside the clothes in my closet to show there was no Hat Man hiding in there. *"And look…there's nothing under your bed. Now go back to sleep."*

"But Mom! I saw him. I swear!"

"It's just your imagination, honey. You need to stop watching those scary movies. They aren't helping."

I tried pleading with her again. She shook her head, repeating that I needed to go to sleep before exiting my room.

It is true. Kids sometimes had overactive imaginations. But I couldn't explain the constant visits from the shadowy man that was always wearing his wide brimmed hat. He was always lurking. Always watching. Never speaking. I never found out the significance of the Hat Man until I reached college and found out that many others had also seen the same figure looming in their rooms as a kid. It sort of felt like the Bigfoot sightings. Millions of doubters, but also a lot of people that could corroborate sightings.

That began my trip down the rabbit hole of exploring the paranormal. When John and I met and started dating, and we had those conversations, it was sort of a done deal as soon as it was brought up. I was thankful that I'd never experienced a modicum of what he went through, but the sheer idea that some other-worldly force out there was capable of that was equally fascinating as well as terrifying.

And here we were, drawing nearer to our destination to film our second paranormal documentary. We'd already been contacted by several streaming services looking to purchase the rights to it once it was finished. It was a lot to take in. I looked out my window as we raced down the freeway, trying to collect my thoughts.

Eddie was in the back seat preparing a couple of the cameras. He grunted with effort as he shoved an SD card into the second camera just as John hit a pot hole, jarring us all out of our seats.

"Sorry," he said nonchalantly, but with a grin that let me know he did it on purpose.

I couldn't help but steal glances at John throughout the trip as he stared ahead at the roads before him, driving with a determined expression on his face. He had come so far, and I was so proud of him. The truth was, *we* had come so far.

To be able to film a documentary in what started out as an abandoned orphanage had to be a borderline full circle moment for him. When he first brought up the idea about filming in such a location, I was hesitant. He explained the connection he would be able to make with those spirits, and that we would be able to craft a compelling story around the location alongside his history. John wore his heart on his sleeve. He would often post videos on social media discussing his upbringing and the struggles he went through. It connected him in such an endearing way to our fans, because it let them know they were not alone in their struggles – and if he could get through it, so could they.

"And what does the insane asylum add to the story?" I joked.

John's lip curled into a fiendish grin. *"We gotta get something to match your level of crazy."*

"You dick!" I yelled in mock anger and gave him an open-mouthed stare before slugging him in his shoulder. We both erupted into laughter.

I felt a smile creep over my face as I looked back over at John. We were beginning to get to the outskirts of Naperville and into the more rural section of town. The sun was beginning to set over the horizon, painting the sky in a vibrant fiery crimson with pink hues and a dying blue sky. Eddie had begun rolling on the camera to capture some B-roll as well as to get everyone's reactions to driving up to our home for the night.

We turned down Alston Street and the whole vibe seemed to change all at once. The meticulously cared for roads we'd previously been privy to had now given way to a road that looked like it hadn't been cared for in ages. It resembled a Whack-A-Mole game – deep, dark craters lining it the entire way down. Overgrown weeds crept out of the cracks and crevices of the asphalt as nature began to reclaim its rightful place.

"Hold onto your butts!" John said – paying homage to one of his favorite movies, as we began bouncing down the godforsaken road.

I let out a gasp. John looked over in concern. "Is everything okay?"

"There it is!" I exclaimed.

Straight ahead, at the end of the dead-end road, stood New Hope Orphanage. With dusk settling over the horizon, the building loomed over the end of the street like a foreboding, shadowy giant. The pre-investigation jitters had finally taken hold: heart racing, palms sweating, shallow breathing, and gooseflesh slowly creeping up my spine.

John and Eddie gawked at the building, beaming with excitement. There was nothing quite like pulling up to a historic haunted building for the first time as the sun was setting.

"This is it," John said in a hushed tone as we slowly rolled up to the building's gate that had been left open for us by one of the property managers.

"Mother of God," Eddie commented from the back seat.

I couldn't help but think that if an outsider had been watching us pull up to this hauntingly beautiful building, that we would've been made into a meme. Just three slack jawed goofballs staring in awe at the sight before them.

The three of us exited the Jeep and took in the sight in total silence. A pervasive chill crept up my spine as a cool autumn breeze blew across the property, sending the tall grass into a hissing fit like a pit of rattlesnakes.

I stared up at the mighty structure. Sections of the red brick walls that lined the building had been covered by vines of ivy that were hungrily creeping their way to the white gabled rooftops. Graffiti covered much of the façade that hadn't been covered in the leafy tendrils. Large stone pillars were anchored to concrete steps that led up to a tall oak door entrance. Many of the windows in the building had been shattered after years of neglect. A few windows along the first floor had been boarded up. The problem with polarizing places like this was that they were ripe for teenagers to unabashedly deface and destroy.

"Whoa! This would make a sick B-roll shot!" I heard Eddie exclaim from across the yard.

I turned to see what Eddie was talking about. He was crouched down with his camera in hand as he crept toward something that John was staring blankly at on the concrete walkway.

"What's going on?" I asked. Neither of them answered.

Eddie continued to circle closer to whatever had captured his and John's attention. Eddie was transfixed on his camera, creating a shot. John stood rigid, a vacuous expression across his face, his skin a deathly pallor. I'd only seen him look like this when he was about to vomit.

I asked once more what they were looking at and again was met with no response. I slowly began to make my way over. In the middle of the sidewalk sat a murder of crows feasting upon the carcass of a dead rabbit. A couple of steps closer and one of the crows set its sights on me, a sliver of entrails dangling from its beak. I stopped, dead in my tracks, as the bird's black beady eyes felt like they were staring right through me.

"You guys have got to see this shot!" Eddie exclaimed, breaking up the tension as he leapt up from his crouched position and rushed over.

John remained firmly planted in place. Unmoving and expressionless. He gazed down at the ravenous crows that had been viciously pecking at and tearing away the rabbit's flesh. I'd never considered myself to be queasy. John and I had watched plenty of horror movies together, so I had become almost numb to blood and guts – but this was different. It was a real animal and was right in front of us. Those were real intestines and flesh. A means of survival for the crows, sure. But still. I felt the urge to cry.

"John?" I heard Eddie call out.

I snapped out of my daze just in time to see that John was still frozen in place – in a statuesque stupor. I walked forward and gripped his elbow. He felt rigid – as though rigor mortis had set in. I shook his arm. "Babe?"

With a deep inhale and an emphatic shake of his head, he looked over at me with wide, fearful eyes.

"Is everything okay?" I asked.

"Y-Yeah. Sorry, I zoned out there for a second."

He took one last look back at the crows and then gripped my hand tight as we walked away from the graphic scene. Eddie's brow tightened, mouthing the words *"Is he alright?"* as we walked by. I nodded.

"Let's just get inside," I said softly.

"Deal," John replied.

I'd never seen John react to anything in this sort of way. It was a surreal sight to see that sent an almost paralyzing fear clanging around my insides. I couldn't put my finger on it, but *something* felt off about this place. I could tell John was feeling it too.

Chapter Twenty-Four

October 14th, 2023
John Tinsley

It was like I had been transported to another place. Another time. Another plane of existence. Seeing those crows destroying that little rabbit sent me spiraling back. I felt hot. Tingly. My mouth watered as I tried to fight down the bile rising in the back of my throat. The events of that fateful night back when I was eight years old were coming back to haunt me on this, one of the most pivotal nights of my life.

I could smell the singed hairs. I could feel them sticking and jabbing between my teeth as I chewed and scraping the back of my throat as I attempted to swallow the vile meat.

We were on New Hope's property for less than three minutes, and I was already spiraling in a way I hadn't thought possible – sent free falling back down into the bottomless abyss of my childhood. I felt like the lost little boy all over again. This couldn't have been a coincidence. Could it? I believed that fate had a way of making itself known in the least expected of ways. I couldn't shake the feeling that something was wrong. I tried to cover it up – or so I thought – until Megan was shaking me out of my dream state.

Even if I hadn't zoned out, she would've known something was wrong. She had a sixth sense about energies and people. We'd found out from others in the community that Megan was highly empathic. Whether I was sad, angry, or filled with stress – she could sniff it out from miles away, and I loved that about her.

I never filled Megan in with the details about the wild rabbit I was forced to eat as a child. I didn't want anyone to have that mental image. Now it was like I was being taunted by that memory all over again as she helped guide me toward the front doors of New Hope.

"Eat the fucking rabbit... Or else, I am going to cut my finger off."

That phrase rattled around in my head while we marched up the steps. Eddie continued to rant about the footage he had captured with the crows as the sun slowly began to set behind the building.

"It may be the coolest shot I've ever captured!" he exclaimed as we thrust the heavy doors open to head inside.

Immediately, our senses were assaulted by the stale air of an old building. We walked into the main hall. Red and white tile flooring laid the path through the building like a giant checkerboard. Pieces of broken plaster and paint chips hung from the ceiling. Chunks of dirt and debris were scattered around on the floor.

"This place is magnificent," Eddie said with a gasp as he walked around with his camera in hand over to a patch of wall that had decayed to the point of showing the exposed wood slats and began running his fingers over them.

Indeed, it was. Almost enough to distract me from what we'd just witnessed outside. Megan gripped my elbow and gave it a soft tug. She whispered to me and asked if I was okay. I nodded my head.

"I'm fine," I whispered.

A look of skepticism told me she wasn't buying what I was selling. Her brow furrowed and her lip curled, twisted with consideration. She opened her mouth to say something just as Eddie spoke.

"We're losing daylight. You guys ready to bring in our stuff and film the intro?"

Megan shot me a pleading look – practically begging me to talk to her about what happened.

"*I promise, I'm good,*" I mouthed to her. She rolled her eyes.

"Yep. Let's roll." I turned back out the doors we had just entered.

Something in the pit of my stomach told me there was something very wrong about this place. The more you investigate the paranormal, the more you become acutely aware of surrounding energies. This place was telling me to get the fuck out and get as far away as possible. My fight or flight was kicking in – and my whole life up to this point had taught me to be a fighter.

I kept my head focused straight in front of me as I descended the concrete steps, the crisp evening air bit into my skin with a sobering chill.

I thought about Megan and our unborn child. Would she be safe here? Was I just letting a few hungry crows get the better of me? The irony of it was undeniable. It could've been any animal they were eating...but it just *had* to be a rabbit. I knew if I raised my concerns to Megan, she would absolutely agree to abandon this documentary right here and right now. I always tried to trust my gut when it came to these types of things. *If something is telling you that you should leave, do it.*

But the six-figure offer for the streaming rights was staring us right in the face. It would give Megan and I the type of financial security we would need moving forward and would cement us in the paranormal field as the new go-to for paranormal streaming. Hell, if all went well, we could be looking at a sizable offer from a TV network.

I tried to occupy my mind with happy thoughts as I handed Eddie one of our storage containers with wheels for him to take in. I pulled out another and gave it to Megan. I grabbed the third and final container and closed the rear door of the Jeep. We purposely packed light for this investigation. We wanted to take a new approach. A raw approach. A very in your face, yet intimate setting that would make our viewers really feel like they were there with us.

Megan and Eddie were both already making their way up the stairs and into New Hope. I took a deep breath and began wheeling my container toward the entrance. The sky was beginning to fall into a deep blue hue. An ocean of darkness and glistening stars sparkling on the horizon. New Hope towered before me like a long-lost shadow from a different time.

"Please God. Let this be a great investigation and let us all get out of here safely."

The filming of our intro went off without a hitch. Megan and I stood out on the front steps of New Hope and gave our grand introduction of the building, its history, and set expectations for what our viewers could expect from the night. After rolling, we marched inside and set up our home base in what we quantified as our *'safe room'*. The energy felt much lighter now and jokes were flowing freely. Dare I say our ominous arrival had given way to a point where it felt like the building was inviting us in with warm and loving arms.

We decided to try something new with this documentary. We brought along a Wi-Fi hotspot to connect our cameras to a laptop in the safe room. It would record everything, and if we ever decided to break off from one another, we could view the cameras remotely and ensure everything was okay.

"Can you guys go set up some static cameras in a few of the hot spots?" Megan asked while pulling out equipment and testing to ensure they powered on. Eddie and I looked at one another.

"We can do that," I replied.

Eddie grabbed hold of his shoulder mounted camera and began rolling. Megan and I had developed a mantra of *"A.B.R. – Always Be Rolling"* after several snafus and missed opportunities at what we would've constituted as compelling evidence during the filming of our first documentary. We made a mental note to keep the cameras rolling as much as possible. Even if that meant adding considerably larger amounts of footage to sift through.

I slipped on a backpack that held a few camcorders, infrared lights, and microphone hook ups and then grabbed a couple of tripods in each hand. I looked into the camera and put on my best showman persona.

"Well, night is beginning to fall. And you all know what that means. It's time to get set up and see what sort of activity we can stir up. Eddie, are you ready?"

"Yep!"

We said our goodbyes to Megan who hastily waved at us while rigging up a handheld camcorder. Exiting the safe room, we made an immediate left and began to head for the grand staircase.

The wafting of musty, stale air immediately infiltrated our nostrils as we began to ascend to our target locations.

To say I was awestruck by the building would be an understatement. With each step I took, I imagined how the building must've looked when it was still in operation. Kids with hopeful looks on their faces as prospective parents came in to visit – eager to show off their skills and show why they should be chosen. I could hear the shuffling and ambling of patients and staff during its time as an insane asylum.

Each step on the tile floor sent a loud *crunch* echoing through the bowels of New Hope and was a reminder of the present. A shockwave to remind you just how fragile life was.

"Where are we headed to first?" Eddie asked.

I stopped at the landing of the second floor. The hallways had become engulfed by darkness. The only lighting was being provided by the floodlight attached to Eddie's camera – enveloping me in the bright white light and further emphasizing the darkness all around us. It was at this mention that I realized I wasn't entirely sure where the rooms were.

"Uhh...Well, we can head all the way up to the attic and work our way back down and finish with the basement."

That's it, John. When all else fails. Pretend you know what you're doing.

"Awesome. Let's do it."

I let out a breath before we continued up the staircase to the top floor. The building had a vibration to it. I wasn't sure how else to explain it. New Hope felt alive. Waiting. Watching. It was silent. Eerily silent. Like the calm before a storm. The air felt thick and made it hard to breathe. It felt like walking through a steam bath with a towel over your mouth.

Eddie and I continued to make small talk as we navigated the dark hallway before finally coming to a narrow staircase at the end of the hall.

"Looks like this might be it," I said before carefully climbing the tall, narrow steps.

When we reached the top of the stairs, we came to a stop in front of an old wooden door. It had seen better days. I opened the door and was astonished to see scratch marks lining the door from the inside. Eddie crouched down to get a shot of it. I never considered myself overly sensitive to the paranormal, but you could feel a palpable sadness in the attic. A stain on the history of New Hope, if my gut feeling was correct.

"Well...that's super unsettling," Eddie remarked, running a hand over the scratch marks.

"Yeah, no kidding," I said, shaking my head. "The amount of horror stories you hear about with the mistreatment of patients in asylums from back in the day is absolutely insane."

That was no joke. Being in the paranormal field, you got a glimpse into the dark past. Dark history. Things that local historians tried to sweep under the rug because of the blight it put on their little communities. The thing with history though – the further you dig, the more controversy you tend to uncover.

The air in the attic was stifling. It was stale. A thin layer of dust lined the wood floor panels and cardboard boxes that had been stored there. I pried open a box and found old paperwork from the asylum days – medical records, accident reports, and doctor's notes. HIPAA would've had an absolute heyday if this was still a functioning facility.

As Eddie panned his camera to get a better shot of the contents within the box, I noticed something gleaming on the wall. A gasp escaped my throat as I realized what it was.

"No way." I dropped the paperwork back into the box, scurried around it and looked straight toward the wall. "What in the fuck?"

Eddie followed close behind, his light illuminating the wall now, to reveal a couple sets of shackles attached to the wall. A gut-wrenching pang of sadness struck me. It was another indication of the harsh living conditions that people were subjected to.

"I think we found the spot for our static cam," I said, lost in a daze.

I moved some things in the attic around so that we could set a camera up facing the shackles from an angle.

"Hey, uh...if we're wanting to wrap this documentary up in one night, we're going to have to speed this up," Eddie remarked as I sat back and studied the LCD screen.

"I know. I know. Let's get the other static cameras set up in the holding cell, the doll room, and one in the basement."

"Sounds good to me."

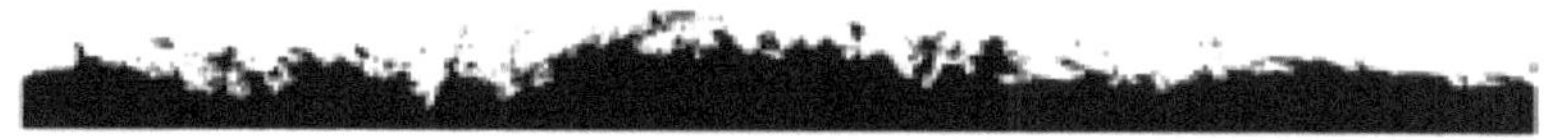

Eddie and I found ourselves racing against the clock. We briskly made our way back down to the third floor where we set up a static camera in the holding room that was used to hold troubled patients and then made our way down to the second floor where we had discovered the doll room. That room was the thing nightmares were made of, ghosts or no ghosts. I had the chills immediately after stepping into that room. I couldn't be bothered to take a long hard look at the dolls. I wasn't sure if it was because of any ghastly presences, or if it was all the beady eyes staring at me from the edge of the flood light.

All things considered, the building remained still. No knocking, no doors slamming shut, no footsteps, no voices. Silent. I'd have been lying if I said I wasn't slightly disappointed, yet also equally relieved. Part of investigating the paranormal was the thrill of it. It always baffled me when viewers would critique investigators for being afraid or startled when things would happen. That was the whole point. You never knew if or when something was going to happen. Were there people acting out there? For sure. But most investigators from our experiences weren't like that.

Heading back down to the main floor, we called out to Megan to let her know we were going to set up our final camera in the basement. When we didn't hear back from her, we assumed she had earbuds in listening to music while getting things ready.

The basement was a whole vibe. Engulfed in an onyx ocean of blackness, it was damp and mildewy. The stone walls glistened with sweat as we set our final tripod up on the dirt-lined floor. Eddie did the age-old test to show everyone how dark things were in a basement. He shut off his floodlight and allowed the darkness to swallow us whole.

Anyone that says they're no longer afraid of the dark as adults are fooling themselves. If you ever find yourself in a long abandoned and reportedly extremely haunted building standing in the midst of pure pitch-black nightmare fuel – you will truly know if that statement holds weight or not.

The basement – much like the rest of New Hope, felt silent and still, yet pulsating with a vibration I couldn't explain. Almost like it *wanted* to talk to us. Like it was about to boil over the sides.

When Eddie finally flipped his floodlight back on, I half expected to see the spirit of a child slinking around just out of my peripherals but was relieved to see only Eddie meeting my squinty gaze under the harsh new light.

"Alright, let's get this show on the road!" I said playfully, giving Eddie a fist bump.

We made our way back up to the main floor and entered the safe room where we saw Megan hovering over one of our traveling cases of paranormal equipment, facing away from us. She wasn't moving.

"Uh...Megan?" I called out.

She said nothing and remained motionless. I looked back at Eddie, who shrugged. I took a cautionary step toward Megan. Then another. I called out her name again. Still no acknowledgement from her.

"Honey?"

I reached out for her. Just as I gripped hold of her shoulder, she spun around and screamed with such ferocity that it sent a jolt right through me, sending me staggering back in fright.

Before I could process what was happening, Megan and Eddie were both giggling like school children.

"Ohh! We got you so good! You should've seen your face!" Megan bellowed.

I hunched over, clutching at my chest.

"That wasn't funny," I panted.

"Oh, yes it was! And we got it all on video!" Eddie exclaimed from behind me.

I turned to look at Eddie in indignation over the ruse. "Yeah, well you were filming from the wrong angle, asshole!"

"He was. But the camera over here wasn't." Megan pointed to a Go Pro she'd set up and hid in the corner facing us.

"Oh, this is just great. Happy to be working with a couple of comedians. True professionals," I joked, finally joining in on their laughter.

How could you not? Scare pranks were a rite of passage from childhood and never stopped being funny even into adulthood.

"That ought to get this place charged up!" Megan exclaimed before walking over and giving me a sympathetic, yet mockery of a hug. We'd always theorized that fear actually could help fuel up and ignite paranormal activity even further. We were about to put that to the test.

"Yeah. Yeah," I said, giving her a half-hearted pat on the back during our embrace, before kissing her forehead. "It's time to get to work."

Chapter Twenty-Five

October 14th, 2023
Megan Tinsley

The spur of the moment prank that Eddie and I planned on our trip inside New Hope went off without a hitch. It was payback for John and Eddie teaming up to scare me during our first documentary. They'd found a six-foot-tall ladder, draped a blanket over top of it, and placed it in the corner of a small room. With a hidden camera strategically placed inside, they urged me to check out the room, feigning as though they'd heard something in there. Your eyes can play some serious tricks on you in the dark, and when I walked into that room, it appeared to be a cloaked figure which sent me running and screaming out of the room only to find Eddie and John doubled over in laughter.

Time wasn't on our side. Filming a documentary is a ton of work. Filming a documentary in one day is a near impossibility. After the prank, we finished getting our home base fully set up, equipment organized, and computer set up with the live footage recordings from our static cameras. We each grabbed a walkie talkie, just in case we were to separate, and John slipped our equipment backpack over his shoulders as we began our trek into the depths of New Hope.

We decided to start in the basement and work our way up. Something about working yourself out of the pit all the way to the tippy top and having to work your way back down to get to your home base added a little more of an edge and apprehension to our psyches.

The basement was just as I'd imagined it would be. Thick, damp air and stone lined walls enveloped the area with a prison-like quality. It was vast. The furthest reaches of it sat outside of Eddie's light. It was like staring into a dark bottomless chasm where your mind could wander and worry that something could be lurking from the shadows. Just waiting. Watching.

There was only one *recorded* death in the basement in New Hope's history. Back when it was still an orphanage, a group of young boys snuck down in the middle of the night under the guise of searching for ghosts. Their real plan was to lock a small boy by the name of Charlie Baker in the basement for the night. They took him down, making him take the lead. The group of boys then rushed back up the stairs and slammed the door shut on little Charlie, who tried to rush after them. Enveloped in darkness, Charlie miscalculated a step and tripped near the top of the stairs and was sent tumbling down the rough, stone staircase to his untimely demise with a broken neck.

News outlets didn't cover the story, but it was documented in the death records for the orphanage. It was such a heartbreaking story. I couldn't help but put myself in Charlie's shoes and feel that helpless fear of being abandoned and that sudden gut punch of realizing you tripped and were about to take a great fall before ultimately perishing.

That sort of incident leaves a stain on a building: one that is an almost palpable feeling. It sits in your stomach like a lead weight. Amidst the apprehension and fear, nestled just between was the dark sadness that many of these old historical buildings contained.

John and Eddie gathered a couple of chairs and placed them next to each other just a stones throw away from where we were standing. John slipped the backpack off his shoulders and gingerly set it on the dirt floor before rummaging through its contents. He pulled out a Rem-Pod – which could detect electromagnetic energy that came near it, as well as sudden temperature fluctuations. He also grabbed hold of our digital recorder that gave instant voice playback – meaning any dead silence in between voices picked up on audio, it would cut out from the playback. He set both items down on one of the chairs and stood back and spun around for the camera.

"So, I thought we would start our investigation off by introducing ourselves." He stopped and threw out his arms in a grand pose. "My name's John Tinsley."

"I'm Megan Tinsley."

"And I'm Eddie Ingol."

"We come here tonight out of love and light. We come here tonight to give you an outlet to tell your story. We are here to give you a voice. We appreciate anything and everything you are willing to share with us and with the world. We invite any of those who wish to communicate, to come forward and let your presence be known."

John powered on the Rem-Pod and set it on the ground away from us on the edge of where Eddie's light reached, hoping to capture something moving toward us. I grabbed the digital recorder and powered it on. I took a seat, keeping my head on a swivel – expecting to see figures that were darker than the darkest night slinking around in the abyss surrounding us.

There was something to be said about being in an environment where *something* could be lurking in the shadows. It could see you, but you couldn't see it. If it didn't communicate, you wouldn't know whether its intentions were good and pure, or if it intended to harm you in some way. It was a risk we were willing to take to try to find answers. Charlie was said to be the most active spirit in the basement, but there were rumors of crawlers and many other reports of aggressive activity down here from other roaming spirits.

"Alright. It's time to go dark," Eddie said. He flicked off his floodlight and switched to infrared.

We were now completely shrouded in the total darkness. We sat in silence for a moment, trying to take it all in. The basement was still. Silent.

John and I began doing EVP burst sessions. We would ask a series of questions, and then play it back – hoping to capture voices that our own ears could not pick up on. After a couple of attempts with no luck, John decided to change gears.

"Charlie, I know it's frightening to see people down here with you after so long. People that are wanting to communicate with you. We promise we are not here to hurt you. I lost both of my parents at a young age too, I know what that burden feels like. To feel helpless. To feel alone. I'm here to tell you that you're not alone. Not tonight, anyhow. Can you please come forward and talk with us?"

Hearing John attempt to connect with the spirit of the young boy hit home. It connected me back to the stories he told me of the darkest time in his life. I could feel the hurt behind John's voice.

It was real and authentic. It pulled at my heartstrings and had me feeling emotional already.

We tried another EVP burst session with no luck, so John pulled the dowsing rods out of the backpack. He flipped the light switches on them, lighting the rods up like an orange glow stick. He handed them to me.

"Charlie – if you're here with us and can hear my voice. It's okay to feel afraid. I can tell that you don't feel like using your voice to speak with us. I know you're scared. I can feel it. I just handed Megan two orange sticks. You don't need to use your voice. All you have to do is grab onto them and direct them to answer our questions. Can you do that for us?"

I raised the dowsing rods straight up in front of me. "Charlie, we are here to help. Can you show us your 'yes'?"

The rods remained still for a moment before timidly crossing with one another.

"Good. Thank you for that. Can you show me your 'no'?"

This time the rods slowly retracted away from each other until they were resting next to each of my shoulders. I lowered the rods and cleared them out before raising them back to their natural resting place in front of me.

"That was very good. We appreciate you coming forward. Are we speaking with Charlie?"

The rods remained still and did not move. I repeated my question. Nothing.

"It's okay, Charlie. We are here to help. Are you here with us, Charlie?" John asked.

The rods slowly crossed over one another and then returned to their place in front of me. I got the vibe that Charlie was uncertain about communicating with us. I couldn't blame him.

John thanked him for his response. We both began asking more questions, but the rods hadn't moved at all since confirming he was with us. I could sense John becoming a little restless. Nothing about this was going to captivate our audience.

"Charlie, is there someone here that doesn't want you talking to us?"

The question threw me for a loop. I hadn't even thought of that. We hadn't really run into any oppressive spirits in any of our previous investigations. Spirits that dominate the building they roam in and dictate all matters of communication that may or may not attempt to happen. I'd heard about it, but never experienced it.

The rods slowly crossed to a yes again.

"You have nothing to worry about, Charlie," I said sternly. "We're here now. Does that spirit want us here?"

The rods crossed to a yes again. That answer caught me off guard. I was expecting a no. I so badly wanted to dig further, but with this method of communicating, it wasn't quite an option.

"Will that spirit be angry if it knows you're communicating with us?" I asked. The rods didn't move.

"Is the spirit mean?" I asked, trying to step down to a young child's level. The rods slowly crossed to a yes again.

"Does it like us?" John asked. The rods swung wide to say a no.

I felt a sharp pang of apprehension pinch in my gut. I was beginning to get the feeling that we should end the session and leave the basement immediately. I wasn't sure why there was a sudden shift in energy, but I could definitely feel it. A wave of nausea began swirling inside me.

"Does it want to hurt us?" I asked, my voice stammering in fear.

The rods quickly crossed together.

"Should we leave?" John asked. The rods crossed again.

"I think we should go," I said frantically, my hands beginning to shake.

"One last question," John began to say. "Charlie, can you point to where that mean spirit is standing?"

The rods remained still for a moment. They started to move to my right, in the direction that Eddie was standing, and then swiveled to the left in John's direction. The dowsing rods began swaying back and forth as if signifying that the mean spirit was pacing behind them.

The dowsing rods stopped for a brief moment. I felt a strong tug pulling them both backwards in a direction that would indicate the spirit was right behind me. My heart felt like it was going to beat out of my chest.

It was as if time had slowed to a crawl. The room had fallen silent. The rods remained fixed, pointing behind me. The lights on the dowsing rods turned off as though the battery had been completely drained. I could feel something standing directly behind me. I felt paralyzed with fear, my breathing suddenly becoming more rapid. I felt an icy chill run down my spine as the cold swirling air crept up next to my ear when the sound of a snarl like a rabid dog erupted from behind me. I let out a frightened shriek, leaping up from my chair.

"We need to get out of here!" Eddie stammered, flipping on his floodlight as the three of us fled the basement.

Instead of opting for our false safe room, we decided to head outside to try to collect our thoughts. Night had swallowed up Naperville, Illinois now. The almost full moon pierced the night sky, shining its white light down upon the area. The air surrounding New Hope somehow felt different now. It felt cold, and not just because of the chill in the air. It felt desolate, dark, and devoid of any sort of happiness that could be extracted.

"What the hell happened down there?" Eddie asked from behind the camera.

"I-I don't know," John replied timidly.

I remained silent, seated on one of the steps leading into New Hope. I had never felt an energy shift so suddenly during an investigation. The last pull on the dowsing rods was not Charlie. That was someone or something else entirely. And the snarl? I'd never heard anything like that in all my time communicating with the dead.

I could feel that presence standing behind me. I wasn't even sure how to articulate it into words, but it felt *off*. It felt *evil*. I felt like it wanted to do harm to us.

"I-I don't know if we should keep this investigation going," I said finally, interrupting John and Eddie's discussion.

John walked over and took a seat next to me and put an arm around me while Eddie circled around with his camera in hand.

"Something just feels wrong about this place," I added with a sniffle.

"I know we are meant to trust our instincts," John began to say. "I've been feeling that way too. But I feel *drawn* here for whatever reason. I can't fully explain it. I've been drawn to it from the moment I first found out about it. There's a conflict going on inside my head right now. A devil on one shoulder, and an angel on the other arguing about the right path to take."

"What is your gut telling you?"

I trusted John's intuition. It had never led us astray before. We understood that we never *truly* understood who or what we may be communicating with. Red flags ran amok when it came to the paranormal, but we'd always come out of it unscathed.

"It's telling me that we should keep pushing. Maybe the oppressive spirit is trying to hold back some sinister secret from getting out and doesn't want us to uncover some hidden truth about New Hope."

"Alright, then let's get a gameplan together."

Chapter Twenty-Six

October 14th, 2023
John Tinsley

Were the events that occurred in the basement simply spirits attempting to toy with us? Or was something more serious beginning to unfold? These were the types of questions that could arise during a paranormal investigation, leading to the desire to uncover more. To keep pulling back layers and eventually discovering the truth.

We had been on investigations in the past that we did not film, where spiritual interactions would occasionally feel aggressive. They typically came in short spurts and would fizzle out, leading to more discoveries to be made.

The more investigations you go on, the more in tune you tend to become with energies and connecting with the spiritual world. I felt a connection to Charlie down in the basement. I could feel his sadness and apprehension. I knew those feelings all too well. I felt him holding back. I could sense an overpowering spirit down there, but very faintly. Like it was cloaking itself from me until it was too late.

Getting the evidence we managed to capture, after such a slow start, gave me hope that we would be able to formulate an intense and gripping story for our viewership. I just hoped that whatever evil may be lurking would be done attempting to pervade the environment the rest of the night.

We made our way back inside New Hope and the energy inside the building had seemed to return to normal – the negative energy seemingly subsided. We sat in our safe room for a while, taking a break to eat some snacks, review footage, and crack jokes to try to get everyone's heads back on right.

I could still sense the uncertainty behind Megan's eyes. I wanted to comfort her. I wanted her to be invested and to feel okay about pushing through to finish the documentary. Eddie seemed pretty shaken up as well but agreed to continue on if we wanted to.

I couldn't explain the dynamics of why I felt drawn here, other than the direct correlation to my having been essentially an orphan at one point in my life. *But why this place?* Where else was the calling coming from? A huge part of my reasoning to come here was to find out why New Hope had beckoned to me so strongly.

Megan and Eddie said they needed a little longer to get their minds right, so I knew for the sake of the documentary that I needed to do something – and fast. After some persuasion, I convinced Megan to allow me to do a solo investigation and walk through of the building. She didn't like the idea at first, but I told her it felt like something that needed to be done. She finally conceded and began hooking me up with a chest mounted GoPro camera with infrared lighting.

"Be careful up there. If anything inside you is telling you to turn around – listen. Keep your walkie on, and call us on it if you need anything," Megan said before giving me a peck on the lips. "Stubborn ass."

"Hey now," I said with a smirk. "It'll be fine. Let's see if I can't figure out why I feel connected to this place."

"Just be careful," Megan added.

"I will, babe."

I turned to exit the safe room when Eddie gripped hold of my elbow. "I love you."

I turned to him with a knowing grin. "I know."

I exited the room, but not before hearing Megan whisper, "Idiots."

After the situation in the basement, I decided it would likely be best to venture up to the attic before working my way back down to the safe room.

"Ugh. I hate stairs," I complained to no one in particular.

The slow ascent to the attic was a quiet one. The energy in the building felt like it had flatlined once again. I checked my equipment before embarking on my venture upstairs. An SB7 spirit box and our digital recorder, both of which I had tucked away in my pocket. A flashlight, and my trusty motion detecting music box. There was nary a thing more unsettling than listening to that music box's jingle when a figure would pass in front of it in a dark, abandoned, and haunted building.

Upon arriving to the attic once more, I sat the music box on top of a stack of cardboard boxes that stood a few feet off the ground, facing toward the opposite wall behind me. If anything passed in front of it, it would alert me immediately. I waved a hand in front of it to test it out. The creepy jingle rang out in the attic like a tornado siren. *Someone could've at least incorporated a Mudvayne song into this thing instead.*

Satisfied, I opened up my session with the typical introduction we had grown accustomed to. We believe that just like in life, it was only polite to introduce yourself when entering someone else's home.

The air in the attic felt dead, but not in a good way. It was like something had suctioned all the energy and shot it right out of the building. Numerous attempts at connecting with the spirits went unanswered on my digital recorder. I felt defeated. We had always had so much luck with it – and EVPs were among my favorite pieces of evidence to share with the world.

Finally, I fired up the SB7 spirit box. The white noise of the device sweeping through radio stations at a high rate of speed bounced around and echoed off the walls of the attic at a frantic pace. Question after question received no response. After what felt like a demoralizing eternity, I was about to turn the device off when I heard something come through in a fleeting moment. I couldn't put my finger on it. Then it happened again. A little snippet.

"What was that?" I called out.

Again and again, the familiar noise came through the spirit box. It didn't appear to be a voice, but it was happening so fast that I couldn't be certain.

"Can you slow down for me? What do you want to tell me?"

Without warning, the SB7 stopped its sweeping and stopped on a singular radio station.

I nearly dropped the spirit box on the floor. The device had landed on a station that was playing Lynyrd Skynyrd's *"Simple Man."* But what did this mean? I had heard the song playing in restaurants and on the radio plenty over the years, but why here? Why now? Was this some sort of affirmation from my mother? I hadn't seen or heard from her in twenty-five years.

A well of emotion swirled inside me as the song continued to blare out of the speaker in my hand.

"M-Mom?" I finally managed to choke out.

The spirit box powered off on its own. I stood alone in silence in the attic. I was trembling and attempting to fight back the tears welling in the corner of my eyes. The sudden rush of memories from my childhood began playing in my head like a movie. Reliving all of the worst moments of my life.

The bone-chilling jingle of the music box began to sound off, snapping me out of my reverie. I shifted my gaze toward the now blinking light of the device, signaling something had crossed its path. The music cut off. My heart began to race. I wanted to move but felt I couldn't. Something akin to a mixture of fear and hopefulness coursed through my veins. After all these years, I would give almost anything for an opportunity to see my mother again. At least one last time.

"Is someone there?" I shined my flashlight in the direction of the music box. Nothing.

I felt the temperature around me begin to plummet. Something was coming. A floorboard creaked only a few feet away from me. I couldn't move. I couldn't breathe. I couldn't even blink. My heart was pounding furiously inside my chest cavity and my skin felt like it was on pins and needles, gooseflesh worming its way up my body.

More and more, the air continued to get colder. It seeped in through my clothes and skin, chilling me to my core. What felt like cold breath blew on my ear as I felt the pressure of an icy-cold hand grip my shoulder.

I was stunned into silence. I wanted to scream, but it was trapped inside my throat.

"Did you miss me?" a voice hissed in my ear.

I was floored. A single tear streaked down my cheek. Before I could mentally process what just took place, the energy subsided and disappeared. I spun around frantically, shining my flashlight all around the attic. There was no one up here with me. The chill inside my heart still held tight. What the fuck was going on? Was that my mom?

I wanted so badly to rush back downstairs to tell Megan and Eddie about the occurrence I had just experienced but knew there was more work to be done. Why would my mom be here? Why would she be communicating with me *now* after all this time?

I had attempted to make contact with the spirits in the holding cell on the third floor but had no such luck. Several of the patient rooms – same story.

I was hoping to try to uncover more truth about what just happened, but I was beginning to run out of steam. New Hope was proving its mettle – but in a unique way. The activity came in short bursts unlike anything I had ever seen or experienced. I thought back to the basement – and Charlie's message. Was a spirit in here really holding back the others from openly communicating with us? Did something here really mean us harm?

I decided to throw up one last Hail Mary and headed down to the doll room.

"Saving the best for last," I whispered to myself.

Or the worst, depending on how you look at it. I turned and looked into the pitch-black room with the urgency of an elderly driver getting onto the expressway. The energy didn't exactly feel off to me in the room, but the idea of being isolated in a room filled with creepy old dolls just staring at me from a massive display case didn't sit well with me either.

I swallowed my fear and stepped inside. I looked to my left and saw the static camera we had set up previously, still recording away. I waved at the camera with a nervous smile. I turned to my right and could vaguely make out the shapes of the dolls' heads all staring directly at me.

I let out a deep exhale.

"Okay, let's do this," I whispered, trying to pump myself up.

I walked to the nearby corner of the room and set the music box down on the table of a high chair that had an old porcelain doll sitting in it. I shook my head. *Thanks for putting this room together, Mark.*

I clicked my flashlight on and surveilled the room, trying to avert my eyes away from the heinous grimaces and faux smiles painted on the faces staring at me from across the room. It was hard to believe that this room once housed several orphans. I found what I was looking for, grabbed a chair barely big enough to hold me up, and took a seat in front of the static camera, facing the open doorway out to the main hall.

I wanted to give one last shot to capture something compelling on the digital recorder. I turned it on and began to ask a series of questions, starting small. I played back the audio and discovered no voices once again.

I tried one more question. "Was that my mother I ran into in the attic?"

I gave the recording a good thirty seconds before I ended it. I pressed play. No response. Anger began to well up inside me. I pressed record once again, with a renewed sense of vigor fueled by my frustration.

"Whoever is preventing the spirits of New Hope from speaking with us tonight. Why don't you quit being a chicken shit and come forward yourself. Who are you?" I paused. "Charlie told us that you wanted us here but didn't like us and meant us harm. You sound like a giant contradicting dick bag. If you aren't going to come forward, why don't you make your presence known and tell us who you are!"

I sat in silence, letting the recording go for a bit longer, my eyes surveying the room for any hint of movement. Nothing. Silence. Just the little bit of ambient moonlight dimly illuminating the room in a sickening whitish blue hue that enabled me to make out most everything situated around me.

"Who was with me upstairs? Why are you here? Why won't you let the others speak? What do you want from us? Why won't you make your presence known?"

I gave it a few more seconds before finally ending the recording. I pressed play and listened for responses.

After my first attempt at asking who was preventing communication, there was no answer. After my rant about the oppressive spirit and calling it out, I rephrased and demanded an answer for who we were speaking with – to which I got a response that was hard to make out. I rewound the recording and pressed play again.

"...Tell us who you are!"

"*...MAWL...FAST...*"

Between the static and the faintness of the voice, it was hard to determine what was actually being said. I rewound it and played it again, this time at a slower rate of speed.

"...Tell us who you are!"

"*...MAL...FAS*"

Gibberish. Complete and utter gibberish. Neither word made any sense. With frustration setting in, I moved forward.

"Who was with me upstairs?"

"*...I was...*"

The response floored me. Hard to discern intent out of a voice that sounded like a whisper on audio, but I would've sworn whoever was communicating with me was getting their jollies off at my line of frantic questioning. I replayed it again. Sure enough, the response was clear as day. I allowed the session to roll to the next question.

"Why are you here?"

No response.

"Why won't you let the others speak?"

No response.

"What do you want from us?"

"*...Your...souls...*"

I couldn't believe my ears. Had that scratchy voice really said what I thought it said? I replayed the recording once more.

"*...Your...souls...*"

I swallowed what felt like a rock. My stomach was now burning with jet fuel and nausea began to set in. I stared down at the recorder in disbelief as I played it for a third time. Was this an angry spirit just messing with us? True cases of the demonic were far rarer an occurrence than Hollywood would ever lead people to believe. I allowed the recorder to roll to the final question.

"Why won't you make your presence known?"

"*...Look...up...*"

I stared at the recorder in my hand in confusion. I replayed it again. Same voice. Same response I thought I had initially heard. I powered off the recorder. Reluctantly, I slowly raised my head and toppled over and out of my chair at what I saw. It was the smiling grey face I had seen from my childhood, and it was floating directly in front of the shelf holding all the dolls.

I scrambled up onto my knees, never taking my eyes off the horrific thing. It was unmoving. Staring. My heart felt like it was about to leap up out of my throat – my dry mouth the only thing preventing it from crawling its way out of my chest cavity. Staring into those bottomless pits-for-eyes transported me to the night I saw that haunting visage under my bed at my grandmother's house. From there, I felt myself begin to disconnect from the real world.

I was back at the night after my baseball game over twenty-five years ago. But it wasn't as I remembered it. It was as though I was getting a bird's eye view of the whole thing. I watched as the car swerved on the flooded road before tumbling down the side of the embankment. My floating body descended down to be level with my parents' crumpled up car. The visual of my mom's badly bloodied and ruined face pressed against the passenger door frame, its window busted out. Hearing my dad's voice again – pleading and screaming for Susan.

"John?"

The voice snapped me out of my trance-like state. I shook the cobwebs loose in my head, trying to get my bearings straight. The grey face that I'd seen earlier was no longer there. What the hell had just happened? Why did *that* memory come back to me like that? Why was I viewing it as though I was someone else on the outside? I struggled to keep myself pulled together.

"John. Are you okay?"

The voice was coming from my walkie talkie. It was Megan. I took a deep breath, composing myself before I reached down and grabbed the walkie talkie. I told her everything was fine.

"We saw you topple out of your chair and then just freeze while you were staring at the dolls. Had us completely freaked out. Are you sure you're okay?"

I climbed back to my feet and did a three sixty swivel around the room. No sign of the face anywhere. "Y-Yeah. I'm fine. Just thought I saw something is all."

"Maybe you should come back down to base."

"Yeah. I'm gonna head back now."

I clicked my flashlight back on and made my way toward the giant white bookshelf that housed the dolls, searching for any sign of the face I had just seen. Nothing. I walked closer to the dolls and began moving them around, trying to rationalize if I had just experienced pareidolia or not. Just as I was about to turn away from the dolls, something caught my eye.

A porcelain doll with blonde hair and a giant gash running down the left side of its face. I could feel my brow furrow in confusion. I reached forward and gripped hold of the doll, pulling it out from its resting place. I couldn't believe my eyes. It was Lucy.

Chapter Twenty-Seven

October 14th, 2023
Megan Tinsley

It was such an odd thing to witness. Seeing John fly out of his chair in fright, only to scramble to his knees and stare at the dolls lining the vast bookshelf before him. He was still for what felt like an eternity. Not speaking. Just staring.

I began to grow worrisome until I snapped him out of his stupor by calling out over the walkie talkie. He didn't even hear my voice the first couple of attempts.

When he came back down to our base camp several minutes later, I rushed over to give him a hug until I noticed the doll he was carrying in his hands. I looked from the doll to his eyes, which looked red and puffy – like he'd been fighting back tears.

"Wh-What's this?" I asked.

John spun the doll around in his hands to give me a better look. "It...It's Lucy."

"Lucy?" Eddie and I both asked.

John nodded. "This was my mother's doll when she was a little girl."

"H-How can you be so sure?" I asked.

"I just know," he replied shortly. "This is the exact same doll with the exact same crack in its face. I could never forget her."

The way John spoke of this doll, *Lucy*, felt foreign to me. It was like I was speaking to John, but his brain was somewhere else completely. The vacant expression behind those watery eyes led me to believe what he was telling us was fact.

"How the hell would it have wound up here?" Eddie asked.

"Well, when we interviewed Mark, he'd mentioned that he had spent a lot of time curating that room by going to different antique stores, estate sales, and yard sales over the years. I guess it could be totally feasible that he'd somehow come across it at some point. Though, what are the chances?" I replied, eyeing up the doll cautiously. Something about the doll felt off, though I couldn't put my finger on the why.

John sauntered slowly into the room before placing Lucy down on a nearby equipment table, propping her up against one of our equipment cases.

I walked over and placed a reassuring hand on the small of his back.

"Are you okay?"

"Yeah. I just...I don't know...I..." John's voice trailed off.

"It's alright, baby. It's alright. You want to go outside and get some fresh air?"

"That...That would be great."

Eddie went to grab his camera as the two of us exited the room. I placed a hand on his forearm and shook my head no.

"Just give us a little bit," I whispered to Eddie. He nodded in response.

John and I walked to the edge of the property and stood out by the gate. He propped himself up against the gate by his elbows and rested his head on his forearms as he stared out into the surrounding darkness. I softly rubbed his back and gave him the time he needed to process his thoughts.

We rarely spoke of his mother. He had filled me in on how great she was and how she had passed away – and that he'd occasionally seen her spirit as a child. But other than that, she never really came into the scope of our everyday conversations.

"What does it mean?" he finally asked.

"What does what mean, babe?"

He stood upright from the gate, but kept his gaze pointed straight ahead of him. "I know we both believe in fate. We both believe that God puts us through things and tests our faith throughout our lives. He puts people in our lives that are meant to be there. I haven't seen or heard from my mom in so long. Why would her favorite doll wind up here of all places? Why now?"

I considered his questions for a moment. He seemed really hung up on this doll. I wasn't sure why. "Maybe it is something as simple as God telling us that you and I are on the right path. Maybe there really is a greater story to be told here and your mom's doll is just a part of that story."

John shook his head and said nothing.

"What's going on, John? What's the significance behind this doll?"

John clammed up at the question and began deflecting. I decided not to push the issue any further.

"So, what do you want to do? See if Mark will let you bring it home?"

John seemed to mull over the question a moment before nodding his head. I told him we'd talk to Mark about it in the morning. Anything that reminded John of his mother was welcome in our home.

"Do you think we should continue on with filming?" I asked, looking at my watch and seeing it was now almost two in the morning.

"I think I've had enough. We can set up some devices and more static cameras and see if anything happens, but I'm exhausted after everything that's happened and am just ready to go to bed."

With that, we walked inside and informed Eddie of what was going on. The three of us set up a few other cameras to record and placed devices all around them to capture any sort of visual evidence we could find.

We managed to rearrange the equipment cases and inflate a couple of air mattresses in the middle of the safe room. Eddie placed his twin-sized air mattress next to the door for *'a quick getaway'* if he needed it. John and I placed our air mattress a few feet to Eddie's left in the center of the room.

Eddie took the opportunity to climb onto his air mattress while John and I climbed into ours. I whispered to John and asked him again if he was okay. He said he was and promptly shut his eyes. I was given the great fortune of being serenaded to sleep by a chorus of snores by John and Eddie. What a delight.

I wasn't even sure how either of them were able to fall asleep so quickly. My mind was absolutely racing through the events of the night. Trying to piece it all together. Trying to understand the significance of Lucy. I sat up on the air mattress and saw Lucy still perched up on the table across the room, staring with those big white eyes directly into my soul. A chill ran down my spine, and I quickly laid back down, trying to get out of the creepy doll's line of sight.

Finally, with the weight of a cement block, my eyelids fell shut.

Violence. Gore. All around me. Screams of the helpless. Voices I couldn't recognize. I felt a burning heat buried deep within me that could only be compared to the center of the fucking sun. I tossed and turned. Every time I drifted into a dream state, all I could see was red. Death. The smell of it percolating in my olfactory receptors with the force of a thousand carcasses after being burned alive.

I began to grow more and more concerned, even from my subconscious. Teetering on the brink of falling asleep again, I forced myself into a half-awoken state but kept my eyes closed when I felt a sudden weight at the end of the air mattress.

I squinted my eyes open. Something was at the foot of the air mattress, sitting with its back turned to us. I could feel John resting next to me in a deep sleep, snoozing away.

"Eddie?" I whispered hoarsely.

The figure didn't respond and didn't move.

"Eddie?" I tried again, my eyes opening wider now.

The figure shuffled this time. It had no shirt on. Its skin a sickly, glistening pallor. A crippling apprehension grew inside me like the great Olympic Torch. I was unable to move and felt completely helpless as the figure slowly turned its head to face me. It had deep sunken eyes like onyx pits and a gaping maw opened wide as a deep raspy sound emanated from it like the great throat singers from Mongolia.

The figure turned to make a move as it began to climb over me. I struggled with all my might to scream. To shout. To flail. To do anything to wake John or Eddie up.

Finally with all the energy my body could muster, I let out a horrendous shriek. I sat bolt upright on the air mattress and realized I had been having a nightmare. My body was dripping with sweat, my heart was racing, and my breathing had become rapid and shallow.

I looked to my right. Eddie was still dead to the world. I looked down to John at my left, and he was in the same state. When my eyes shifted up from John to the chair that had been sitting next to us, I let out a real scream this time. Lucy was sitting on the chair staring right at us.

Chapter Twenty-Eight

October 15th, 2023
John Tinsley

There's nothing quite like being awoken from a deep sleep to the sound of your significant other screaming at the top of their lungs.

Dazed and confused with the room spinning as I snapped awake, I found Megan bawling her eyes out next to me. I quickly wrapped her in a hug and consoled her. She finally mustered the strength to tell me about the nightmare she had and pointed at Lucy now squatting on the chair next to us.

Her recounting of her dream sent a shockwave through my system. The description of the being sounded eerily similar to the thing I had begun to refer to as *Grey Face.* The even more eerie point being that Lucy had somehow managed to move across the room and was positioned right next to us like some sort of godforsaken guardian angel. I tried to rationalize it by saying maybe one of us moved it while we were making room for the air mattresses and just forgot about it. Megan didn't seem to buy it, but it seemed to at least calm her nerves a bit at realizing that it could've been a possibility.

239

"We aren't staying here. We need to go," she said as she got up from the air mattress.

She received no arguing from Eddie or me. The truth was, I was ready to leave after my solo investigation earlier but didn't want to feel like a coward. I flipped over my iPhone and saw it was 3:07 AM. The witching hour.

Megan busily gathered up all the loose equipment around the safe room while Eddie and I went and gathered all the static cameras and equipment that had been scattered around New Hope. Within thirty minutes we had the bulk of everything stowed away in the Jeep once more. When I made my final trip out of the decrepit building, I took one last glance over my shoulder. I felt bad abandoning it the way we had. Normally, we would close out our sessions and thank the spirits for the interaction they were willing to give. Everything about this investigation had gone off the rails and I couldn't make heads or tails out of most of it. All I knew was that I felt we had burned out our welcome after Megan's nightmare.

"What are you doing?" Megan asked incredulously, pointing a foreboding finger in my direction.

I spun around and shot her a perplexed glance. "Huh?"

"That is *not* coming home with us."

I looked down at the cardboard box I was holding in my arms. Lucy's head was poking out of the top of the box.

"What do you mean? You said it was fine."

"Yeah, but after that nightmare, I don't want to be anywhere near that thing."

I felt a magnetic pull to Lucy in a strange way that I couldn't begin to put into words. I thought back to when I invited my mom to live in the doll. The small eight-year-old boy in me still longed to see her and to talk to her – even after all these years. I didn't even believe that spirits could inhabit dolls anymore. It all felt like a load of bullshit. Ghosts haunted people, not things. Even after watching *The Conjuring,* I held the same steadfast opinion on the matter. I would defend the doll with everything in me, and I couldn't even express why that was. Was it sentimental? Maybe. Not enough for me to risk fighting with my wife over. No, it was something more. Something deeper than the surface level affixation to it.

"Baby, nightmares happen. It's just a doll. Everything is going to be okay. I promise."

Megan placed her hands on her hips and gave me a look that told me she was battling an inner conflict. "Fine, but if that thing starts moving around the house at night, it's your ass." She finally relented and I placed the box in the back of the Jeep.

"I understand." I replied, firing up the engine and preparing to leave New Hope in the rearview. "Say goodbye to New Hope."

"Good riddance!" Megan said gleefully.

"Wake me up when we're back in Ohio," Eddie added playfully before propping his head against his pillow.

I could empathize. My eyes felt heavy, and I wanted nothing more than to sleep. I was hopeful that all the bad energy from New Hope was staying in New Hope. But something inside me was telling me that Megan's inclinations about Lucy were true no matter how hard I tried to force the thoughts down.

The five-and-a-half-hour drive back to Medina, Ohio was absolutely brutal. Even with a pit stop to pump a caffeine filled energy drink into my system, it had been a struggle to keep my eyes open while Megan and Eddie snoozed peacefully for the duration of the trip. I had to thank God multiple times for the invention of the rumble strips that sat nestled on the outside shoulder of the freeways to prevent people from falling asleep behind the wheel.

After pulling into our home, the three of us got out of the Jeep and stretched our tired muscles and joints.

"Before we bother unloading, we need to go see someone," I said excitedly motioning toward the house.

Megan smiled. She knew who I was referring to. "Come on, let's go say hi to Bruce."

When we walked up to the front door, I could hear the clicking of Bruce's paws on the hardwood floor. He knew we were home. I could hear him restlessly dancing in front of the door in pure excitement. I could picture him standing there, teetering from side to side with his tail wagging a mile a minute.

I unlocked the door and pushed it open. There was our beautiful boy. He leapt up and launched his front two paws right into my midsection and I held him up. "There's my Brucie boy! Daddy missed you!"

"Can you come say hi to Mommy?" Megan asked as she crouched down to Bruce's level.

He excitedly hopped down and barreled into Megan with excitement, sending Megan backward and landing on her butt on the hardwood floor. Already our house was filled with laughter and good vibes. Something about a dog that is happy to see you no matter what that always warms a person's heart.

"Uh. Ahem. Can I see my buddy too?" Eddie called out from behind us impatiently.

Megan and I chuckled at the sentiment and scooted out of the way as Eddie marched in and began getting Bruce riled up as he play wrestled with our precious boy.

My heart felt whole seeing everyone smiling once again.

After getting caught up on some sleep, I meandered my way downstairs to our office. Megan and I had dedicated the room to our fandom of the horror genre as well as for any creepy antiques we had collected. The walls were lined with framed horror movie posters and other memorabilia. Bookshelves filled with movie monster bobbleheads, NECA action figures, books, DVDs, and even old VHS tapes from all our favorite horror films.

Sat nestled atop one of the bookshelves, was Lucy. I glanced up at her, my mind still scrambling to make sense of everything that transpired in the last twenty-four hours. I shook my head clear and sat at our desk which had horror movie Funko Pops hanging out around both sides of our computer monitor. I didn't have time to dwell on things that weren't of any importance. I had the daunting task ahead of me of reviewing all of the footage we had captured from New Hope and attempting to create a compelling trailer to release in time for our paranormal convention we were slated to be special guests at in just a couple of weeks. No small task at all.

Bruce came ambling into the room and curled into a ball next to me as I plugged the SD card into the reader located on the back of the monitor and pulled up the first video file.

"What do you think, Brucie? You think we have enough here to make another documentary?"

Bruce cocked his head as if he were legitimately pondering the question. *So adorable.*

I looked back at the computer monitor and sighed. "Please let there be enough here to make a film with," I whispered to myself.

Chapter Twenty-Nine

October 18ᵗʰ, 2023
Father Rosario

I took a sip from my morning coffee, attempting to decipher how to use this pesky thing known as the Internet. I knew it had been around for some time but had never bothered to get acquainted with it until recent years. One of the members of my congregation, Danielle Putnam, had offered to create a social media page for St. Anthony's. I didn't keep up with it. Occasionally, Danielle would offer to take photos and post them to the page for me.

For all of the problems that the internet and social media had caused in the world, it had done an equal amount of good. It connected people and allowed them to see and keep up to date with the lives of others that mattered to them. There was something admirable about that. That's what was drawing me to the Norton Public Library today, fiddling with their computers and attempting to see if I could locate a profile for John Tinsley.

After a few frustrating attempts, I'd finally managed to get signed in. Pop ups letting me know about *notifications* appeared on my screen which I quickly clicked out of, worried that it may download some sort of virus onto their computer. Whether or not it was actually a dangerous link was something I wasn't prepared to find out. My eyes scanned the page for a moment when I finally noticed the search bar at the top. I typed in John's name, and a plethora of profiles appeared. I clicked on the first one that popped up. My eyesight wasn't quite as good as it had been - so I couldn't really make out the person in the photo on the bright screen – but I assumed with his recent rise to fame, he would most likely have been the first to populate. With a stroke of luck, I had wound up being correct.

The profile loaded and immediately the larger photo highlighted the face of the man I'd just seen on TV only days ago. I began scrolling through his social media posts and saw some cryptic messaging about the new documentary he and his wife just wrapped up filming. He mentioned that they would have a major announcement upcoming at the Ohio Paranormal Summit located at the Millersburg State Prison in Central Ohio on the 28th of this month.

Even for the short duration of time I had spent counseling little Johnny, he'd left a lasting imprint on my life. A guilt that nagged at my insides every day since. An itch that needed to be scratched. For my own conscience, I needed to go see him at the very least.

I pulled out my tiny notepad to jot down the date and location of the event. I wasn't sure whether John would remember me. And if he did, would he be okay with me coming to see him after all this time? I hoped he would.

I had long ago accepted that I would never have a child due to my role in the church. In a small-town community like Norton, no one would bat an eye at it if I had chosen to. My own father had made the choice. The Catholic community at large, however, did not want their clergymen to give in to those temptations...

Maybe it was that, or the fear of having lost my father at such a young age, that had created a log jam in my psyche where I didn't want to potentially burden my hypothetical wife and child with a premature death either. Looking back now, I could've started a family with no issues. A child to carry on my name and family lineage. The Rosario name, as far as my immediate family was concerned, was going to die with me.

That's one of the great and also most frightening aspects to life that people can encounter. The dreaded *'What if?'*. Once you reach a certain point in life where you know your time is beginning to wind down, you reflect back on your life. All the decisions you did or didn't make. You look back at the experiences you had and experiences you missed out on. One of my biggest regrets now – sitting in this library – old and grey, was never giving myself the opportunity to raise a child. It was a thought I battled every single day.

I need an ice cream cone.

I sat on the wooden bench outside of Lowry's, staring across the street at St. Anthony's. The ice cream parlor only had until the end of this month before it closed its shutters until next spring. The overcast skies and crisp autumn air did little to sway me from enjoying a delicious chocolate chip cookie dough ice cream cone.

Many an afternoon had been spent at this very spot. I could still visualize those hot summer nights when the lines with eager patrons wrapped around the block to get the best ice cream in town.

It was one of my favorite places to clear my head, try to release the cumbersome thoughts from my head, and release them out into the ether.

If there was something to this paranormal thing – and life after death — what did that mean with regards to heaven and hell? Was there really such a thing as crossing over? One of the many great mysteries in life weighed heavy on my conscience in my old age, pondering my own end and what that would mean.

I set my sights on the old graveyard nestled behind St. Anthony's. *What truly happens to our souls once we perish?*

I took another bite from my cone, wading through my thoughts as carefully as I could. I didn't like this side of me. I didn't like feeling that my faith was beginning to wither away, much like myself. Life. Death. The great beyond. What it all meant.

In my seventy-three years of existence on Earth, I had yet to come face to face with a ghost, ghoul, specter, or anything of the like.

Lord, I'm feeling lost, and my faith feels fleeting at times. I need your strength and guidance. Help me to trust in your love and mercy, even when I don't understand what's happening. Remind me of your promises and guide me back to you.

One day soon, I would have my answer. That was for certain. For now, I accepted that I must rely on my faith and place it all in God's hands. I couldn't abandon our Holy Father. Not now. Not ever.

Chapter Thirty

October 26th, 2023
Megan Tinsley

A little over a week removed from the treacherous trip to New Hope, life had begun to fall into disarray.

Under a borderline obsession – John began staying up through all hours of the night, attempting to sift through the hundreds of hours of footage between all the cameras. He'd said that our static cameras had captured all sorts of shadow play, disembodied voices, and devices going off that we were completely oblivious to. Deeper and deeper down the rabbit hole he delved.

I voiced my frustration with him time and time again – my words constantly falling on deaf ears. He looked like a mad man. Hair disheveled, beard unkempt, and clothes that had been worn several consecutive days.

It all came crashing to a screeching halt when he'd finally completed reviewing all the footage and was preparing to create a trailer for the Ohio Paranormal Summit. Somehow, along the way, all of the files on every single one of the SD cards had become corrupted. John reached out to a couple of friends that were well versed in this sort of thing to try and have them retrieve the files.

"So strange. They're completely gone," our friend Reed Mueller told us.

I thought John was going to have a nervous breakdown. I'd never seen his temper boil over in the way it had. I finally got him to calm down, and we decided to go have a nice dinner at one of our favorite steakhouses.

"What are we going to do about the streaming platforms and all our fans? They're expecting a documentary from us," he said.

"Well, we just need to be honest with them. Are they going to be happy about it? Of course not. But we can't change it. We will just explain what happened and promise that we will film a brand new one somewhere else."

I could tell then that my response didn't really sit well with him, but he nodded in agreement. "I guess that's what we'll have to do."

That night, we got a flat tire on our way home from the restaurant which sent John into another bout of rage.

"What the fuck is happening? Who did we fuck over to get this sort of karma in our lives right now?"

I reassured John and told him it was a temporary issue, and we would get it fixed. "We are fortunate enough to be in a position to be able to get it fixed, John."

Strange occurrences had also begun to pervade our home. John was in complete denial over it. *"I haven't seen or heard anything."*

But I had. Quite a few times. And so had Bruce. It started small. Things being moved from their normal places. Lights being on when we got home that weren't on when we left the house. Strange sounds of creaking floorboards that resembled someone walking across them in the middle of the night. Strange, disembodied voices that I'd hear calling out to me in the middle of the night.

Things that could easily be explained away from stress, a busy and forgetful brain, or the house settling.

The strange dreams began to occur a couple of days after we got home from New Hope. It started the same every time. I was walking on a trail in a heavily wooded forest. It felt as though a storm were brewing. Underneath the canopy of trees, in between the cracks and crevices formed by the leaves, I could see the dark blue storm clouds surging in. A heavy breeze would blow, and the trees would speak phrases to me about John. They told me hideous things. Things I couldn't bear to hear.

What initially began as a great day and evening after the day prior's trip to the steakhouse had spiraled into a night from hell. John did his best to be romantic and lift both of our spirits up. He allowed me to kick my feet up and watch as he did all the cleaning around the house, occasionally giving me a little show to go along with it. That evening, he prepared a steak dinner fit for royalty (to make up for last night) and then capped the evening by surprising me with one of our oldest date night traditions. He hid it well, asking me to run to the market to get us a jug of our favorite apple cider for a nightcap. In the time I was gone, he had built a little fort around our oversized chaise and had a bowl of popcorn and lit candles on the coffee table in front of it. John was kicked back on the oversized chair laying on his side, propping his head up with his arm, just waiting for me to walk in while Bruce was nestled in his little doggy bed beside the fort, peacefully snoozing away. The smell of a warm cinnamon and buttery popcorn filled the house, and I could feel my heart melting into a giant puddle.

"I picked out your favorite movie, *A Nightmare on Elm Street,*" he said, holding the special edition Blu-ray case out for me to see.

"Aw, babe! You sure know your way to a girl's heart," I replied with a smile as I slid my shoes off and walked over with the cider in hand and slid onto the chaise with him.

Bruce glanced up at us with an envious glance. John and I looked at one another before we invited Bruce up onto the chaise. He excitedly hopped up and licked both of our faces before laying at the foot of the oversized sofa, giving us our own personal space to snuggle and start the movie while we shared our popcorn and drinks. John placed a comforting hand softly onto my stomach and whispered sweet nothings to me while we watched the classic horror film. I couldn't help but smile and feel elated. Our family felt whole once again.

Somewhere around the midway point of the movie I began to notice something. It would happen quickly in the blink of an eye out of my peripherals. A figure walking across the hall and into our kitchen. The first time I noticed it, I said nothing and went back to watching the movie – chalking it up to my mind playing tricks on me – impacted by the dancing candle flames.

Then it happened again. Slower this time and in the opposite direction. I caught the tail end of the figure. It wore a blue nightgown and had long blonde hair. I gasped and sat up.

"What's the matter?" John asked, following suit and sitting up in alarm. Bruce awoke with drowsy eyes and confusion as to why we woke him up as well.

"I...I thought I saw something." I got up from the couch and made my way toward the exposed hall.

"What do you mean you *saw something*?"

"I saw...it was...I saw a person, John. A woman."

"A woman?"

I made it to the hall and looked in both directions. No one was there. I gripped the corner of the doorway with a shaky hand. That couldn't have been my eyes playing tricks on me. John and Bruce both walked up to join me.

"Babe?" he called out.

"I swear I *just* saw a woman with blonde hair walk right through here!"

There were only two options from this vantage point. Walk into the kitchen to the left or to the right you could walk to our front door and leave. The figure had walked toward our front door, but it remained locked. My heart raced. Disbelief settling in.

"B-Babe," John said, placing a hand on my shoulder. "Let's just go back in and finish our movie, okay?"

I looked at him. Maybe I was just overreacting. Out of all the years we'd been investigating the paranormal – even before we started filming documentaries – I had never seen a spirit in the form of a physical person. It had to have been my imagination getting the better of me. I nodded at John, and he wrapped a warm arm around my midsection and led me back to our living room with Bruce close behind in tow.

The rest of the movie went off without a hitch. For a while, I found my eyes drifting to the opening in the hallway. No more sightings. I felt better. *A Nightmare on Elm Street* wasn't the type of movie to have me on the edge of my seat and seeing things, though the irony of watching a horror movie when the incidents happened wasn't lost on me. I chose to drop it, and we headed up to bed.

John and I had closed out the night with some much-needed passion. The past week had felt like some sort of invisible wedge had been forcing its way between us. We were on two opposite ends of a spectrum, but it felt like a lot of repair work had been done today.

With my two boys snoozing soundly, I took the opportunity to do some reading. I had recently picked up a copy of William Peter Blatty's *the Exorcist* and was curious to find the differences between the movie and the book. I was excited to finally give it a read and felt myself enamored by the book. If my eyes hadn't felt like they were being weighed down, I may have finished it in one sitting. Satisfied I'd found a good stopping point, I closed the book and shut the reading light off, tossing it onto the end table. I wrapped myself under our comforter nice and tight and immediately felt my eyes lock shut.

I found myself in a familiar place. Back on the same trail of an evergreen forest. I walked along the edge of a dirt pathway that was lined with stones, leaves, and dead pine needles. Moss hungrily clawed its way up the surrounding trees like a horde of green ants. Thunder cracked like a missile in the distance as a heavy wind howled through the hills. A storm was coming.

The trees groaned and shook against the pressure of the squalls. If you listened close enough, the woods were talking. I continued, step after trepidatious step, further down the trail to an unknown destination.

The whispers began to grow more frantic. More boisterous. More aggressive. I picked up my pace. The forest was ushering me further and further into it. Farther than I had ever made it in the past. I reached a bend in the trail that wrapped around a rockface ledge, quickly circled my way around it, and stopped dead in my tracks.

Standing in front of me was a large black goat with grand horns spiraling from its skull. It stood on all fours in the middle of the dirt pathway. The taunts, threats, and chatter from the trees had ceased. A low rumble of thunder echoed through the valley of the forest, shaking the very ground I stood on.

The hulking goat raised itself onto its hind legs like it was nothing. It stood with perfect form and balance and stared at me with those large bulbous, black eyes – peering into the depths of my soul.

I wanted to turn the opposite way and flee. I wanted to scream. I wanted to call out for help but couldn't. I was frozen in place, unable to avert my gaze. The goat took a calculated step forward. Its footfall connecting with the earth with the force of an elephant. It took another step. Then another. Each step sent an explosion into my chest. It took another step. And then another until it was standing no more than a foot away from me.

The goat man towered over me by several feet. Its haunting eyes still locked onto mine. My body trembled. Tears streaked down my face. I felt terrified and completely helpless, locked inside this horrible dreamscape.

The goat smiled.

With a startling quickness, it reached a black arm forward and wrapped a clawed hand around my throat, instantly cutting off airflow. I tried to suck wind. I tried to bring my arms up to punch down on the mighty arm. I couldn't move. Black dots quickly began to line the periphery of my vision when the mighty figure leaned down to my level.

The goat spoke to me in hushed snake-like tones.

"The last piece of the puzzle. I have waited for so long for all the pieces to fall into place. If you want to live, you will do as I say! Is that clear?"

I found I suddenly had the ability to move my head and with a gurgling sound, I managed to nod, still desperately fighting for air.

"I want you to shatter your husband's heart into a million pieces. I want you to break his will. I want you to be ruthless. I want you to cause a gash so deep in his soul that it wilts like a dried-out grape. Leave him. Or I will take your baby...and then I will come for you!"

The goat wailed a hellacious cackle at the latter statement, and I awoke with a pulsating fright that had shaken me to my core. I sat bolt upright and ripped the covers off of me and clutched at my throat, taking in deep breaths like my life depended on it. My body was glistening with perspiration as my heart pounded away inside my sternum. I rushed to the bathroom just as John woke up and asked me what was wrong. I slammed the door and ignored his question.

I couldn't comprehend what had just happened. My skull felt like it was on fire. It was as though someone had driven a hot nail right into it. I looked up into the mirror with tear filled eyes when I noticed the red markings around my throat. The sight pushed me over the edge. I slumped against the bathroom door and slid to the tile floor bawling my eyes out, fearing for mine and my unborn child's life.

John pounded on the bathroom door and kept asking if I was okay. I couldn't bring myself to respond. I continued to sit on the cold floor of the bathroom in the fetal position, openly weeping.

"Babe, please talk to me!"

"Just leave me alone!" I howled.

There was a brief moment of silence, followed by the pattering of John's feet across the room before I heard him crawl back into bed. Things in the home went still once more, further amplifying the war going on in my brain.

I couldn't possibly leave the love of my life over a nightmare, could I? The dream had felt so real. I climbed back to my feet and looked at my reflection in the mirror once more. The previously bright red hand mark that wrapped around my throat was now gone. The words played back in my head like a faded recording.

"Leave him. Or I will take your baby...and then I will come for you!"

When I finally exited the bathroom, John looked over with worried eyes. "Are you okay?"

I tried my best to hide the internal conflict happening inside my head as I crawled back into bed. "Just a bad dream," I said.

"Do you want to talk about it?" he asked.

I shook my head no, curled myself back into a cocoon under the comforter, and faced away from him.

"Look, ever since we went to New Hope, you've been having nightmares. Maybe something followed us home. I can call Shawn tomorrow morning and see if he can cleanse the house if that would help."

I said nothing in response. John tried to place a hand on my shoulder, which I shuddered away from. He cleared his throat, clearly stung by my reaction before I felt him lay back down to go to sleep.

What he said did give me a glimmer of hope. Maybe Shawn could fix whatever the hell I was experiencing. Even with John having no experience, and even with me shutting him out, he still wanted to help. I rolled over and kissed him on the cheek and thanked him. He wrapped me into a hug, and we fell asleep locked in each other's arms.

Chapter Thirty-One

October 27th, 2023
John Tinsley

Sleep had become a luxury that I could no longer afford. Megan had been seeing and experiencing so many different things that I had not been. A strange pang of guilt hung in the air, that I was the reason for all these occurrences. I thought back to the way my father scolded me as a child when I told him I had been seeing and speaking with Mom after her death. He didn't believe me either. I remember the hurt I felt by his words, and I was doing my best not to put Megan through those same paces.

Was I slowly working my way toward inevitably becoming my father? Something I lamented would never happen.

I could now see why he denied my claims. It's very difficult to placate someone for things you aren't going through. But I'd also been on the other side of the coin and knew how lonely and confusing that felt. I didn't want Megan to feel that loneliness.

For days, Megan continued to bring up my mom's doll, Lucy. I shook my head at her every single time. I told her if the doll was haunted and was from my childhood, why would it haunt her and not me? It didn't make sense. I told her it was much more likely that something latched onto us during our time at New Hope. And I truly believed it. Unbeknownst to Megan, I had attempted to communicate with my mother through Lucy and had gotten nowhere. Mom never came through. It got to a point where I stopped trying after a few days and found myself questioning my entire childhood and if I had ever actually seen and communicated with my mom at all or if it truly was just an overactive imagination.

Tomorrow was slated for our big day at the Ohio Paranormal Summit. I already broke the news to fans on social media about our corrupted video files and having lost them. The reaction was a mixed hodgepodge between people being sad but forgiving – to people accusing us of never having gone to film another documentary at all. The internet was a wild place at times.

I couldn't leave Megan's needs unattended after last night, so I called our friend Shawn Fuller and filled him in. Shawn was a well-known empath and was able to pick up on energies from people and spirits. He'd become well versed in cleansing homes of negative energies and had become a household name in the paranormal field for helping families in need.

When the doorbell rang, Bruce sprang into action, barking his head off and raced past me and Megan to the front door. When he saw it was Shawn, who had been to our house as a guest a couple of times in the past, his tail wagged in a friendly manner.

"Thank you for coming," I said, ushering Shawn into our home.

"Happy to help," he replied, giving each of us a hug and then giving Bruce a friendly scratching behind his ears.

We sat around the kitchen island, sipping on coffee as Megan began to explain the dynamics of our house since returning home from New Hope.

Shawn sipped from his coffee mug and occasionally nodded his head, not saying much but rather taking it all in.

"And you're not sharing any of these same experiences?" He turned to look at me.

I shook my head. "No, it's the darndest thing and I can't figure out why."

"I see. I think it would be best for me to do a walkthrough around the house. Alone. I need to see what I feel and then attempt to do my cleansing."

"Sure. Whatever you need," Megan said.

Shawn scooted back off his stool and turned to head toward our living room. Megan and I watched on from the doorway. Shawn walked to the center of the room with his hands on his hips in complete silence while he surveyed everything.

Without a word, he turned toward the staircase and headed to the second floor. An occasional loose floorboard creak clued Megan and I in as to which room Shawn had entered. Eventually he made his way back down to the main floor and headed down the back hall where the horror room was located as well as the stairs to our basement.

"Do you think he has sensed anything?" Megan asked.

"I don't know. I hope whatever is going on, he's able to help us out." I rinsed my mug out in the sink.

When Shawn returned to the kitchen, we both turned to look at him. I couldn't read anything from his expression. If things at his day job failed him, he'd probably make a killing playing poker. He stepped forward and met with us at the counter.

"This is uhh...a confusing one," he admitted.

"What do you mean?" Megan and I asked simultaneously.

"What I mean is...I didn't feel anything in this house."

Megan and I exchanged worried glances.

"H-How is that possible?" she asked.

Shawn's face twisted in thought. "I'm not entirely sure. I've heard stories in the past about spirits...usually of the demonic variety..."

"Demonic?" Megan wailed, cutting Shawn off mid-sentence.

The word hit me with a force as well. Demons had crawled their way all over the sets of Hollywood films regarding the paranormal and had become a bit of a pop culture thing now. Something a lot of modern paranormal investigators claim they encounter – a lot of the time to get extra clicks on their videos. Megan and I knew better. We understood demons were real, but the odds of ever encountering one was like walking out of your local convenience store with a winning jackpot lottery ticket – if the grand prize was a life of misery.

Shawn nodded glumly. "Yes. Now, I am not saying that's what's going on here." He threw up cautionary hands. "But I have heard stories about spirits having the ability and the power to only reveal themselves to specific people that they want to be able to see them. Like a targeted attack."

"That would explain why I have been experiencing things and John hasn't been," Megan said.

My brain had a million thoughts bouncing around it. I was familiar with what Shawn was telling us. I hadn't considered it. It wasn't uncommon for spirits to latch onto women that they liked during investigations. The entire thought was enough to make your skin crawl. But something demonic?

"Are there regular spirits capable of such a thing?" I asked.

"There are, but again I can't speak to the commonality of it. And unfortunately, there's no way for me to one hundred percent confirm it. I can still do the cleansing if you guys would like."

"That would be wonderful, Shawn," Megan answered.

"Excellent. I will grab my things."

Shawn ordered us to open all the windows in the home while he readied his cleansing kit. We put Bruce outside in our fenced in yard so Shawn would be able to do his cleansing without interruption. Megan and I met Shawn in the kitchen. He turned his gaze upon us.

"Are you guys ready?" he asked.

We both nodded.

"I want you both to follow me around the house as I do this. Remain quiet and envision a layer of white light shielding you as you walk with me throughout the cleansing. Don't speak. Picture yourselves releasing dark, toxic smoke from your home, out each and every window in every room we walk through. Let my words be your guidance. Do you understand?"

I looked at Megan, who looked back at me with hopeful eyes.

"We do, yes," I said finally.

"Good, then let's begin."

Shawn motioned for us to come closer where he had a black ceramic bowl resting on the counter. Inside it was a bundle of sage and a long turkey feather. He grabbed a small glass vial that I figured was holy water and slipped it into his pocket.

Shawn looked to us and nodded. He pulled a chain with the pendant of St. Michael on it and slipped it around his neck. He then pulled a lighter out of his pocket and held it to the end of the sage momentarily until it began to catch. He set the lighter back down and scooped the bowl up in one hand and his turkey feather in the other.

"I am here today inside the home of my good friends, John and Megan Tinsley. I am here calling upon the spirit of the Archangel, St. Michael. Please defend my friends and their home against any negative energies looking to do them harm. Protect them from the dark and the wicked. I ask that you wield your mighty sword with the power of God and cast out any evil that may be lurking in the shadows and infesting this home and their lives. Amen."

Shawn slowly walked through our home, repeating similar versions of the same prayer as he wafted the smoke billowing out from the sage, twirling his feather in a clockwise motion. Megan and I held hands as we trailed close behind Shawn. We took our time in each room as Shawn eventually walked toward each and every window in the home and pushed the smoke out.

When we made it downstairs to the horror room, the sage suddenly burned out. Shawn glanced down at it apprehensively.

"Huh," he said.

"Huh, what?" Megan asked.

"This has never happened before." Shawn sat the bowl down on my desk and re-lit the end of the sage, before attempting again.

"What does that mean?" Megan asked, her voice shaky.

"I'm not sure. I can't imagine it is anything good."

The smoldering end of the sage burned out again as soon as he lifted the bowl up. Shawn cocked his head at an angle like a confused puppy. I felt a nervous pinprick forming inside my stomach. I glanced up on top of the nearby bookshelf where Lucy stared down at us with her cracked face and piercing blue eyes. It felt like she was watching us, but that was likely my anxiety rearing its ugly head from the sage burning out in *this* room of all places.

Shawn lit the end of the sage a third time, and this time it remained lit. He cracked a joke to try to ease the tension before returning to his cleansing ritual, being sure to spend extra time in this room.

After finishing his walkthrough with the sage, he called upon his guardian angels, spirit guides, and St. Michael to watch over our home and protect it now that it had been cleansed. He did one more walk through, splashing droplets of holy water in each room and smearing crosses across each of the windows.

"Be sure to close your windows back up," Shawn said, placing his ritual items in their carrying case.

"Thank you so much for coming and helping us out," Megan said, hugging Shawn.

"Yes, thank you. It really means a lot that you were willing to come at the drop of a hat."

Shawn and I shook hands. "It's no problem whatsoever. Please keep me updated. As with anything in dealing with the spiritual realm. There are no absolute truths, and no guarantees that what I did here today worked. Maintain your faith, maintain your love, and keep peace in your hearts. Don't acknowledge the negative. Don't feed into it and give it energy. The rest will take care of itself."

Even though I hadn't sensed or experienced any of the things that Megan had been dealing with over the past couple of weeks, I had to admit the air in the home felt lighter. It was easier to breathe. Even Brucie seemed to perk up, chasing Megan and I around our kitchen island in a playful demeanor with his tail wagging ferociously.

I saw the genuine happiness behind Megan's smile again. Something I hadn't seen since our anniversary. It felt good. I snuck up behind her in a bear hug and kissed her up and down her neck before Bruce came bounding over and jumped up onto our sides wanting to be included in the embrace.

"Oh, Bruce. You are such an attention whore." I laughed, bending down and giving his ears a rub – eliciting a groan from him.

"He's definitely Daddy's boy," Megan joked with a smirk.

"He's our boy. And soon to be a big brother!"

Megan recoiled at the statement. Not in an offended way, but one where I knew the words stung her. She was less than twenty-four hours removed from her terrifying dream that still left its mark on her. I hugged her tightly.

"Everything is going to be okay," I said before planting a kiss on her lips. "I promise. Bruce and I will never let anything bad happen to you or the baby."

"Thank you," she said softly, burying her head into my chest. "And I know you won't. I love you."

"I love you too, baby."

Slowly but surely, Megan's concern over the mention of our child melted away like butter. We prepared a dinner together and shared laughs and sweet conversation just like old times before getting things packed and ready for tomorrow's Paranormal Summit.

"What would you think about me bringing Lucy tomorrow?" I asked.

Megan eyed the doll apprehensively for a moment. "You know what? Bring it. Shawn said don't feed into things. It's just a doll."

I carefully pulled Lucy off the top of the bookshelf and inspected the doll in my hands. Admittedly, I remembered the energy – almost like a vibrating sensation of the doll in my childhood. Whatever that was, it was no longer with it. It felt empty. Hollow.

"And if anything, it'll give me a cool *small world* story to share with fans," I replied.

I placed Lucy into a box with the other decorative display pieces and finished packing it into the car with everything else.

When we finally got a chance to catch our breath, we laid in bed reminiscing about the old times and how far we'd come with one another before an exhausted Megan finally passed out. I knew she hadn't been sleeping well and knew we had to get up early. I decided to stay up a little while longer just to ensure she slept soundly. I even went so far as to download a sleep machine app and played rain sounds for her, in an attempt to keep her mind clear.

With the sound of raindrops hitting a tin roof blasting out of my phone, I pulled up my eBook reader and began reading the latest Stephen King novel. Getting lost in the story, I finally checked the time and realized I'd been reading for almost two hours. I glanced down at Megan who was still sound asleep. I felt content. I set my eReader down on my nightstand and then leaned in and kissed Megan on her cheek. I felt grateful that Shawn helped clear out our home of any negative energies, even if it had been somewhat of a placebo just to appease my wife. She was sleeping peacefully. That was all that mattered to me.

Chapter Thirty-Two

October 28th, 2023
Father Rosario

Part of me felt crazy for making this trip. Was this an act of desperation on my part? An act to seek out the approval and forgiveness from the terrified little boy I'd lost contact with shortly after the death of his grandmother? Was I prepared for all the potential outcomes – good or bad?

The entire trip and idea went against every belief I ever held. Going to a convention meant to cater to beliefs I didn't share was well outside of my comfort zone. After much deliberation, I'd finally succumbed to my original belief that all spirits go to heaven or hell. No ghosts. Only insidious inhuman beings that meant to do harm in the world. But I still wanted to make an appearance to be able to talk with John.

I pulled off the exit from Route 36 into the small town of Coshocton. The volume of traffic getting off the highway on this exit ramp to this small town in the middle of nowhere was astonishing. The line of cars was nearly backed out onto the highway a good quarter mile away from the stoplight where my

GPS was instructing me to turn right. That's when I noticed every single car in front of me had their blinkers on to turn right.

This couldn't possibly all be for the Paranormal Summit, could it?

I remembered seeing a lot of people commenting on the social media post I had seen – all of them sharing their excitement about the event. The flyer featured the pictures of about a dozen or so special guests – John and his wife, Megan being the only two I recognized. The flyer promoted the fact that other paranormal filmmakers, horror vendors, food trucks, and everything of the like would be in attendance for the summit. I knew I would feel out of place and would probably look out of place – but I had become comfortable with the idea of it and was willing to go through a little bit of discomfort for the closure I had needed for so many years.

When I finally managed to turn onto the main road and saw the conga line of cars all headed in the same direction, I began to reconsider questioning where all the traffic was heading. I glanced down at my GPS again and saw we were only a half mile away from Greensburg State Prison. I'd have been lying if I said I didn't have a nervous butterfly flitting around my insides.

The line of traffic moved at a snail's pace. I reached the peak of a hill, and my jaw dropped at the sight. There it was – Greensburg State Prison. The old Gothic fortress stretching across hundreds of acres looking more like a medieval castle than a former state prison. The sprawling estate was already packed to the gills with cars, food trucks, and excited convention attendees.

I looked down and saw that traffic was backed up from the opposite direction as far as the eye could see. I looked in my sideview mirror and saw the same exact thing behind me.

"Oh, my Lord," I whispered to myself. I couldn't believe what I was seeing.

I knew the paranormal field had become a bit of a pop culture icon over the past couple decades, but I had never expected to see a turnout of this magnitude.

Police cruisers lined the entrance as officers with batons directed traffic. Once I was finally ushered into the fenced in property, I did my best to take in the sights while also paying attention to the traffic in front of me. No easy task to say the least.

When I finally managed to put my car into park and stepped out, I got to take in the building and the surroundings in all of its glory. The expansive prison stretched from end to end had to be close to the length of three football fields and stood at least five stories tall. The limestone façade lining the walls had trickles of efflorescence streaking down the sides like tears from all the history the building held within.

The closer I walked to the building, the more ominous and oppressive it began to feel. I couldn't imagine the feeling of the countless inmates that were chauffeured into this gargantuan structure looming in the center of an unsuspecting neighborhood in the middle of farm country.

A couple of kids came zipping past me, snapping me out of my reverence. I glanced down and saw they were dressed in costumes. It made sense for the time of the year. One wore a ninja costume, while the other had on a ghoulish mask with overalls. Being snapped out of my daze brought me back to the daunting reality and the sudden feeling of sticking out like a sore thumb.

Creepy carnival music – like something stripped from an old horror movie bellowed from nearby speakers. Spooky costumes were commonplace. Kids and even adults were sporting them.

Actors from a nearby Halloween haunted house attraction were running around the parking lot, some on stilts, attempting to scare the passersby. The smell from the food trucks flitted its way through the air, the sweet smell of funnel cakes, corn dogs, and barbecue bringing the vibes full circle.

I looked around until I found a sign with an arrow that pointed out the direction to the main entrance for the Summit. Not wanting to look like the lost old geezer, I gingerly made my way for the entrance.

The volume of people inside Greensburg State Prison was every bit as overwhelming inside as it had been outside the foreboding structure. The crowd was shoulder to shoulder as people attempted to shimmy their way in and out of traffic. Multiple kids and teenagers bumped into me as they scurried their way through the sea of excited patrons.

"Excuse me," I said to a young lady that wore a volunteer t-shirt – trying my best to yell over the noisy crowd. "Can you tell me where I can find John and Megan Tinsley?"

The woman smiled at me and pointed ahead. She leaned in so I could hear her better, which I was thankful for. "They're straight down this hall. You turn right and you will find a staircase. Take the stairs up and it will lead you out into the West cell block. You can find them there!"

"Thank you. God bless."

I did my best to amble amongst the crowd, slowly making progress down the main hall and following the young volunteer's directions. When I finally reached the top of the stairs, I stood in awe. The cell block was absolutely massive. The entrance had brought us up to the third tier of the cells. A steel spiral staircase led down to the main floor where all the other vendors and special guests were located.

I took extra precaution heading down the treacherous steps, turning back occasionally to apologize to the folks behind me.

"Oh, no! You're totally fine! Take your time!" The man said.

And take my time I did. Reaching the bottom of the stairs felt like a major accomplishment – sort of like the polar opposite of scaling Mount Everest – for me anyways.

The crowd continued to be in an overwhelming frenzy, but now reality was sinking in that I was about to be face to face with someone that held such a grip on my past. I hoped for forgiveness. I hoped to see him and his wife doing well and be in a happy place with one another. Step by step, I was closing in.

Through the cluster of event goers, I finally caught a glimpse of John's head in between people. My line of sight was interrupted just as fast as I had seen him. I knew I was getting close.

It came to a point where it was dead stopped traffic – a line that had formed to meet them. I was rather impressed and proud to see so many people excited to see and talk to them. As the minutes passed, I inched closer until I was next in line. I looked on as John, Megan, and their cameraman, Eddie, all signed a poster from their debut documentary for a family with two teenage children.

I was smitten with how professional the three of them appeared to be. To see how well they interacted with their fans. John had grown into quite the young man. He glowed in a way that only celebrities in their respective fields could. Wearing a plain green baseball cap, an unbuttoned red plaid shirt over top of a plain black t-shirt and a pair of blue jeans, he loosely resembled his father, Ron, and the type of attire he would frequently wear. The little boy I had remembered was now a full-grown man. Alive and in the flesh – and doing very well for himself.

I was greeted first by his wife, Megan. She had such sweet and loving eyes to match her beautiful and warm smile. I think she was surprised to see someone my age standing in front of their table, but she greeted me just as enthusiastically as anyone else.

"Hey! Thank you so much for coming by to see us!"

John, who'd had his back turned, talking with Eddie for a moment turned to face me. I saw a glint of recognition in his eyes, shrouded by doubt. The kind of look you might give an old classmate you haven't seen in twenty years as you walk by them in the supermarket.

John and Eddie also gave warm greetings. I scooted my way down to the center of the table when I saw something that made my stomach lurch. Sitting on a little wooden chair was a doll I remembered from a dark time. Susan's doll. The one I had grabbed from Johnny's house for Edna. The one that left her trembling in my church parking lot. I tried not to stare at the doll, bringing my attention back to the three of them as they began asking questions about my interest in the paranormal and if I had seen their documentary.

"I have, yes." I said, my interest still homed in on the doll.

I saw that questioning look return behind John's eyes again. He was having an internal dialogue about where he knew me from. I was certain of it.

"Well, what did you think?" Megan asked.

"It was...interesting. I definitely found myself questioning my beliefs as I watched the film."

"Well, that's one of our many goals," John said. "Opening people's minds to the possibilities of life after death – even when science says it should not be possible."

I nodded. Was that a veiled barb? Had he recognized me?

"I'd like a signed poster, please," I said with a smile.

"Absolutely!" Megan reached for the twelve by eighteen-inch poster and pulled it in front of them so they could sign it.

The photo was the three of them standing out in front of the abandoned building featured in their first documentary.

"Did you want us to personalize it for you? Or just sign it?" Megan asked, pulling a silver sharpie cap off.

"Personalized would be great, thanks."

"And who are we making this out to?" she asked.

"Tom...Tom Rosario."

John, who had been hunched over the table with his sharpie at the ready stood upright at the mention of the name. His eyes scanned mine with a sense of remembrance.

"D-Did you say...Tom Rosario?" He asked.

I smiled and nodded. "Yes."

John seemed stunned at the development. For what felt like an eternity, but probably only amounted to a few seconds, he stood before me, speechless. Megan and Eddie looked from John then back to me, and then back to John, bewildered.

"Do you know him?" Megan asked, finally breaking the tension.

"I...uh...yeah. This was the priest from the church my grandma went to. He counseled me after the accident with my parents."

"Oh, my goodness! Such a small world!" Megan exclaimed.

She happily signed the poster before handing it to John.

John took the poster. He glanced up to me and then back down at the poster again before inscribing:

To Tom Rosario,

The world works in mysterious ways. Sometimes, bigger plans are at play, and I am glad that fate brought you here before us today.

He autographed it at the bottom underneath the photo of himself and passed it over to Eddie. I couldn't get a read on John. Was he happy to see me? Was it a faux happiness under the guise of him being let down and not actually wanting to go back down this road?

"Man, it's been what? Twenty-five years? I never thought I'd see you again," John finally managed to say.

I nodded my head. I wasn't sure how to respond but decided to allow him the opportunity to speak.

"How have things been?" he asked.

Small talk. The ultimate awkward conversation starter. The small eight-year-old boy inside him clamming up just like he had the first couple of times visiting me at St. Anthony's.

"Good." I grabbed the signed poster from Eddie. "Things are good. I-I saw you on a late-night talk show and that's how I found out about your documentary."

There was an uncomfortable silence. My mouth was beginning to run dry, my hands becoming clammy. He resented me. I could feel it.

"Well, that's awesome! I'm glad you were able to make it here. You still suck at baseball?" he smirked.

John pulling out that old joke lifted my spirits. I chuckled. "Yeah, I don't think I would be able to hit a beach ball with a two-by-four at my age."

The conversation seemed to feel much lighter after that. We had a quick discussion about how he and his wife had met and how they decided to get into paranormal filmmaking. I began to grow aware of the stares from frustrated guests waiting for their turn to see John, Megan, and Eddie.

My eyes settled on the doll once again. I felt very troubled for reasons I couldn't yet process about the fact that John still had this doll after all these years. It felt like an unhealthy attachment.

"So, you still have your mother's doll after all this time?" I asked.

John looked down at the doll and then back at me. He shared the details about how they'd crossed paths with the doll while attempting to film their second documentary. I had so many questions for him. The way he came back into contact with Lucy after a quarter century didn't feel like the kind of fate someone wanted to get themselves involved with.

"But, hey. We really need to get to our other guests," John added. "It was great seeing you."

He reached out and shook my hand. I nodded, pulling a business card out of my pocket. I handed John the card.

"If you ever need anything. Please don't hesitate to reach out."

John looked at the card and shook it in his hand. "I will keep that in mind. Thank you again for coming to see us, Father. That really means a lot."

He stuffed the card into his pocket, and I turned to leave. I turned back one last time. "You take care of yourself."

He nodded.

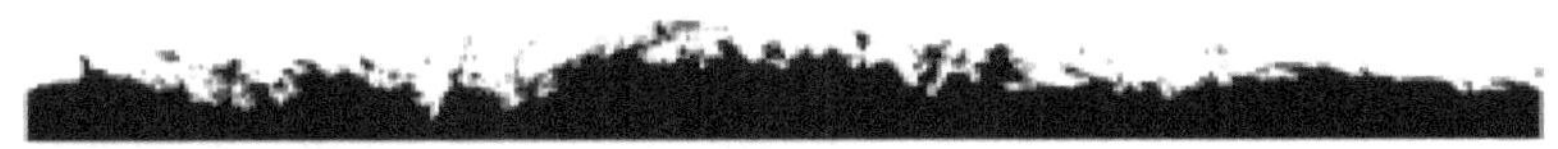

The drive home was a conflicting one. I felt good about the chat with John and his wife. It felt like a part of my heart and soul that had been bruised long ago had finally been given the opportunity to heal over. John didn't hold a grudge, and he defied all odds and came out the other side a much better person. A feat in and of itself that made me feel good. God was definitely watching over him.

The other part of me was still troubled by the sight of Lucy and how he and the doll had crossed paths once again after all these years. I wasn't sure whether that felt better or worse than the idea that he had kept the doll for twenty-five years. The world can be a small place, but not *that* small.

I wish I could've gotten more time with him. More time to dig into the how it came to be. What events took place that led him to the discovery of Lucy at New Hope Orphanage. Had he, Megan, or Eddie had any experiences since coming in contact with the doll? Were things in their home still happy and light? Questions that would have to go unanswered.

As I drove up I-77 North back toward Norton, I prayed for John and his wife.

"Please, God. Please continue to watch over them."

Chapter Thirty-Three

November 7th, 2023
Megan Tinsley

The Ohio Paranormal Summit was a great success. There were some upset fans, and the event organizers weren't thrilled that we had no trailer for them to share, but everyone understood that *"shit happens"* and *"technology is great when it works...but when it doesn't..."*

We promised everyone that we would more than make it up to them. John was the most frantic about it – touting that if we didn't make things right soon, we would lose all credibility, and that the streaming services would move on to other ventures. Immediately following the event, John went back into planning mode.

"We can just do something local. Make it an easier trip, especially on short notice. We can re-visit the orphanage storyline later down the line."

He said he'd found an alternate location. One that was available in a couple of weeks. He called our connections with the streaming services and let them know. He said they were pleased to hear we were going to be able to make such a quick turnaround.

John's wheels were spinning. I was sure steam was going to begin billowing from his ear canals at any moment.

"The Old Harrison County Jail will be perfect, babe!" he said. *"A lot of tragedy struck that jail. It's been reportedly one of the most active haunted locations in the country for over a decade now. I can already picture it."* He gave a grand gesture with his hands. *"Forever Imprisoned: The Harrison County Jail"*

I told him it sounded great, and we should go for it. Immediately, he called the owner to schedule a time to come out and interview him, get more history on the building, as well as to get an idea of the layout.

"November 7th? That sounds perfect." He hung up the phone.

With heavy rain in the forecast, I told John I wasn't feeling it. He was taken aback by my decision but said he and Eddie would manage it just fine.

"We will take care of it. We probably won't be back until late though." He gave me a peck on the lips before heading out the door.

The owner had other prior engagements he was tied to for the day, but John was willing to be flexible to knock this portion of planning and documenting out. The Old Harrison County Jail was a couple of hours away. I looked at the clock. It was already a little after five in the evening. By the time John and Eddie got down there, interviewed the owner, Sam Cooke, and filmed any B-roll – it was going to be close to midnight. A lot of work went into all of it. Finding and assembling the proper lighting, navigating the interview, and finding the photogenic spots to highlight the ominous vibes of the building. They had their work cut out for them.

Things in our lives had admittedly returned to normal following Shawn's cleansing of our home. The nightmares ceased. The blood curdling noises, gone. The sightings of anyone walking around our home, no more.

Everything felt right once again. I breathed easy on the sofa, snuggled up with Bruce as we watched re-runs of *Stranger Things* on Netflix with a cup of hot cider in hand. A heavy pattering of late autumn rain pounded against the house. The perfect weather for staying inside and wrapped up in a blanket. Part of me felt guilty for staying home. The other part felt relieved. I was still recovering from New Hope and all the incidents that occurred following it. I was finally beginning to feel comfortable in our home again – no longer frightened to walk around alone. I wanted to bask in it and leave the paranormal in the rearview for another week or two before diving headfirst back in.

The pounding rhythm of the heavy rain mixed with the comfort of the blanket and our plush sofa began to cause my eyes to feel heavy. Bruce was snoring away down by my feet, occasionally flinging his paw as if he were chasing something in his dream. I swung my feet off the couch, waking him.

"You ready to go to bed, bubba?" I asked.

He stared at me with tired and confused eyes. He looked from me to the area our front door was at, and then back to me. Dogs may not be the most intelligent animals on Earth, but he definitely knew what the word *bed* meant.

"Aw, I know you miss your daddy. He'll be home in a few hours," I said, glancing up at the clock to see it was a little after eleven. "Come lay down with Mama."

I got up from the couch and couldn't help but grin and let out a lighthearted laugh as Bruce remained cemented to the sofa.

"Fine, suit yourself," I said, mostly kidding – but still a little hurt.

After brushing my teeth and changing into my pajamas, I climbed into bed and pulled the comforter over me. I left the bedroom door open on the off chance that Bruce decided he'd had enough of being stubborn while waiting for John to get home. The torrential downpour was still going strong, smacking our roof shingles with hellacious force – causing one of the best sleeping environments. There was nothing like being lulled to sleep by a heavy rain.

Completely content, I opted to not even bother reading. I re-positioned my head on the pillow, laying on my side, and immediately felt myself drifting further and further into a deep and comfortable sleep.

Grrr...

I felt myself begin to stir.

Grrr...

"Bruce..." I said groggily, not even bothering to open my eyes. "That's enough."

Grrr...

"Bruce!" I called out in annoyance. "I said that is enough!"

I lifted my cell phone up to check the time. It was a little after twelve in the morning. I glanced over at the still open bedroom door and slammed my phone down on the nightstand in frustration. Things fell silent.

Click. Click. Click. Click. Click. Click.

After having fallen into another deep sleep, I rustled half-awakened in a daze. It felt like the room was spinning. I looked at my phone. It was almost one in the morning.

Click. Click. Click. Click. Click. Click.

"Bruuuuce! Please lay down!" I begged. The sound of his little paws walking across the hardwood floors incessantly were the equivalent of a dripping faucet from a sink while you were trying to sleep. Enough to drive you mad.

Click. Click. Click. Click. Click. Click.

The steps were getting closer now. Heavier. I sensed that there was movement coming into the bedroom.

"Good boy, Bruce. Come lay down and go to sleep. Daddy will be home in a little bit."

The interruption to my sleep was enough to make me silently curse John under my breath. I laid my head back down on my pillow when the bedroom door slammed shut.

I sat bolt upright in bed, staring into the pitch-black abyss before me. My heart was racing. Things in the room had fallen silent once more. Had John gotten home earlier than expected?

"That wasn't funny, John. Knock it off."

I angrily lay back on my side, grumbling curse words under my breath as I tried to get my blood pressure back to a normal level. John getting home would explain why Bruce had been trotting around the house at this ungodly hour.

A few moments passed, and the silence was still deafening. Normally after this much time, John would've already stripped down to his underwear and climbed into bed.

"John?" I called out.

Silence.

I rolled onto my back, trying to allow my eyes to adjust to the darkness. I swept my eyes across the dark room. I could faintly make out the window curtains to the right, the shape of our walk-in closet door frame, our dresser, and directly above it, our TV that had been mounted to the wall. To the left of the dresser, the farthest from the window was the corner that led out to the main hallway. The corner was darker than any shade of black I'd ever seen.

"John? What the fuck are you doing?" I whispered hoarsely.

The more I stared at the featureless corner, the more it felt like it was growing and beginning to consume the rest of the bedroom. I sat up in bed again, trying to get a closer look.

Jagged, deliberate breaths bellowed from the darkness. Angry breaths.

"John! Quit fucking around and come to bed!" I hissed.

Movement. Slow. Deliberate. Coming straight toward me.

"This shit isn't funny, John!"

Shhhp. Shhhp. Shhhp.

Short, languid steps shuffled directly toward me. The outline of a figure began to form. A silhouette darker than the shadows it moved from, piercing through the darkness. It was so close now. An unforgiving iciness enveloped me. John's attempt at scaring me was working flawlessly.

"You're going to get blinded by a flashlight if you don't cut it out!"

Shhhp. Shhhp. Shhhp.

Closer it came. Agonizingly slowly getting closer. Were my eyes deceiving me? A sudden rush of confusion only served to further amplify the electricity coursing through my veins. The sway near the base of the silhouette told me it was wearing a night gown. The faint wispy shadows of a female's hair dangled beside the shape of the shadowy head. Was it the woman I had seen the night before Shawn came to do his cleansing?

An unearthly snarl thundered from beside the bed. It shook the walls and bedframe I rested upon.

In a moment of panic and confusion, I reached for my phone and flicked the flashlight on, pointing it straight for the source of the noise. My heart stopped dead in its tracks. I couldn't believe my eyes. A scream I didn't know my body possessed, erupted from the depths of my soul. The first thing I noticed was the blue night gown...then came the rest. Standing at the foot of the bed was the mountainous goat man from my nightmare.

Bruce began howling outside the bedroom door.

In the midst of pure fright, I dropped my phone with a loud thud to the floor, the flashlight pointing straight up toward the ceiling, cascading the area beside my bed in a dim white light.

With a quickness I could barely comprehend, the creature surged forward and gripped a charred black hand around my throat.

"I gave you a warning," it hissed.

It tightened its grip around my throat, cutting off all oxygen to my brain. The goat man's eyes flashed a crimson color, swirling like marbles inside its hideous skull. It lifted my shirt up with its free hand, revealing my bare stomach. It placed its other blackened claw down on the lower region of my belly, the long needle-like nails piercing into my flesh with a fiery pain. I wanted to scream. I wanted to cry. I wanted to kick, scratch, and fight my way out of this. I felt paralyzed, unable to move. Unable to do anything except stare into those blood red eyes.

The burning sensation began to swirl around in my stomach before traveling further south. I watched in horror as inky black tendrils weaved their way around my flesh like parasitic worms eating away at my insides. Bruce continued to wail outside the door, clawing at it with violent fervor.

"Did you honestly think lost words of prayer and smoke from an insignificant weed were going to get rid of me?" The creature's voice rattled with an animalistic, guttural roar. Its lips curled into a sinister smirk.

The searing pain was almost blinding. It felt like battery acid was sloshing around my insides. Dots began to line my vision. I was about to die – and I was helpless to stop it. I closed my eyes and tried to find the words to pray.

"God cannot hear you. God does not care about you. You are nothing more than the bastardization of his creation and he left you all here to rot. And rot you shall."

Even my thoughts were no longer safe. I was fighting to survive with everything I had, even if my body wasn't cooperating. My line of vision was beginning to fade. I was a complete and total invalid, begging for air and suffocating under my own saliva. The figure snickered at me. It was enjoying this.

"You are a disposable piece in a fateful path carved out long ago. I gave you a choice and you ignored it. Choices have consequences. You went back on your word. And I just cannot allow that. But I am a giver. So, here's what I am going to do. I will give you one last shot to play your part. If you do not, I will come for you and torture you in ways your mind cannot process. Is that understood?"

The figure loosened its grip on my throat slightly, allowing some air to seep into my starving lungs. I nodded my head, letting out a ferocious cough – spittle and phlegm flying from my mouth.

"Excellent. Hear me and heed my words. You are going to leave your husband behind. No explanation. No warning. If you do not...I will flay the skin from your bones with a rusted butter knife in front of one another – allowing you to stay alive just long enough to bear witness to the bloodshed and horror in each other's eyes. You have three days."

The figure released its grip from my neck and stomach and floated backwards away from me. Its piercing gaze never breaking eye contact.

"But what about my baby?" I croaked. My throat was bone dry. The goat man said nothing as it slid out of sight, disappearing into the abyss. I looked down at my stomach. There were no puncture marks. I thought I might be losing my mind when an explosion went off inside my body like a ticking time bomb.

I rolled out of bed and rushed into the bathroom. I doubled over the toilet and heaved all the contents that had been resting inside my stomach and broke down into hysterics.

I couldn't bear to look at John when he returned from his trip to the Harrison County Jail. I couldn't imagine the whirlwind of emotions he went through when he heard Bruce going ballistic outside our bedroom door, only to find my cell phone lying flat on the ground with the flashlight pointed straight up.

"Megan?" he called out in a frightened timbre.

I hadn't moved from my place on the floor of the bathroom, resting against the bathroom vanity.

"Ba-Babe! Baby! What happened? Are you okay?" He rushed forward and began wiping the tears away from my cheeks. Bruce looked on from behind him, his tail tucked between his legs.

"I-I think I need to go to the hospital," I grunted.

The pain was still intense. I didn't need to be a rocket scientist or a doctor to know what was going on. John continued to rapid fire questions at me. I didn't have the energy to speak. I was on the verge of passing out from the pain. I was exhausted. I was an emotional wreck. And something was going on inside my body. Something was wrong. Very wrong.

"Hospital."

It was all I could mutter.

John helped me to my feet, scooching Bruce out of his way. John scooped me up into his arms and carried me out of the house. I could feel his heart racing and his body trembling as he carried me out to the Jeep. He wasn't asking questions anymore. He was silent. His brain was a proverbial hamster wheel again, thinking up all the possible worst-case scenarios that I knew were going to wind up becoming true.

John buckled me into my seat and raced around to the other side of the Jeep. He quickly put it into reverse and floored it as we made our way out to the main road. I couldn't even begin to process what had happened tonight. My brain was clouded. My body was in excruciating pain. My soul felt bleak and empty – knowing what was coming. I couldn't even stand to look at John when he tried to reassure me that everything was going to be okay as we sped down the highway toward the local hospital.

Chapter Thirty-Four

November 8th, 2023
John Tinsley

Life is such a fickle thing. It can be great. It can be brutal. It can rear its ugly head in an instant. I would be the perfect poster child for that sentiment. I have loved. I have lost. I have scaled to the tippy top of the mighty mountain of shit that life has thrown in my direction. Enjoying the short glimpses at true happiness – overcoming all of my hardships only to slip and fall back down into the bedrock of lows.

Ten hours. That was all it took for my entire life to be flipped onto its head once again.

Don't get too comfortable, John. When life seems to be going too well, you'll get a humble sandwich faster than you can say 'depression.'

Returning home from a successful trip to the old Harrison County Jail made me wish I had never taken the drive out there in the first place. Every man's worst fear is coming home to find their significant other hurt or in danger. Coming home and seeing my wife crumpled on the floor in a heaping ball of a teary mess nearly sent me to my knees. It took the wind right out of me. Disbelief.

Terror. Confusion. You name it, I went through the gambit of emotions. I couldn't get a word out of her, other than she needed to go to the hospital. Questions were scurrying around my brain like a hive of angry hornets. Did someone break into our house and attack her? Did she have another nightmare? Was she experiencing some complication with our baby? She absolutely refused to open up. She stared out the window with a distant gaze for the duration of our trip.

I would go on to get an answer that no prospective parent ever wanted to hear.

The nursing staff, nervous about Megan's demeanor and short responses, rushed her back and began to run an ultra sound. The nurse looked up with a solemn expression.

"I am so sorry."

Those words lingered in the air for an eternity and thrust themselves into my midsection with the force of a lead pipe. I couldn't breathe. The nurse didn't need to say anything else for either of us to understand what she meant. She set the transducer down on the medical table beside her. I stared blankly at the nurse who had a pained expression plastered over her face. I felt numb. My heart ached. I turned to look at Megan who remained deadpan and slack jawed. A single tear trickled down her left cheek.

"I'll give the two of you a moment," the nurse said. She got up from her stool and exited the room, closing the door behind her.

How could this happen? Everything was fine. And in the blink of an eye, the house of cards came crashing down. I wanted to scream. I wanted to cry. I wanted to put my fist through the fucking wall. But I had to remain strong for Megan.

I reached over and placed a hand on top of hers, caressing it with my thumb. With tears welling in the corner of my eyes, I let out a sniffle and said: "I...uh...I'm sorry, baby." My voice cracked. I was on the verge of breaking down right in front of her.

Megan said nothing. She merely stared straight ahead. The silence in the room was deafening. I wished she would speak, but I couldn't bring myself to push it. Megan's body was going through an unexpected and chaotic change that I could never comprehend. While the idea of having a child brought me great joy – being a man, I would never understand the bond a mother builds during the term of their pregnancy with their child. She was losing more than the exciting thoughts that came with having a child. She was losing a physical, spiritual connection that had been growing inside of her.

So much loss. So much grief. If God were real, how could he continue to lead me down a path filled with so much sorrow?

The events that followed felt like a whirlwind. The doctor came in and spoke candidly with us, explaining that based on the nurse's findings, an emergency D&C surgery was going to be needed. Megan seemed unfazed by the words and said nothing, stunning both the doctor and I.

"Emergency surgery? What? Why? What's going on?" I asked.

He motioned with his hand to let me know he was getting to it. "Based on the results of the ultrasound, there appeared to be some internal hemorrhaging. I know this is quite frightening to hear but trust me Mister Tinsley. This will be a simple procedure. Your wife is in good hands."

Moments later, nurses entered the room and helped Megan onto a rolling hospital bed. With an urgent pace, they began wheeling her down the different hallways. I struggled to keep pace until they reached the double doors to the O.R.

One of the nurses placed a cautionary hand on my chest. "Sorry, but you're not allowed in. You will have to wait out here."

"But...But my wife!" I cried out in a frenzy.

"I know this is a difficult time, Mister Tinsley. I can assure you that your wife will receive the best care in the world. Please wait out here. We will let you know when you can see her."

And with that, she joined the other nurses and left me standing in the vacant corridor, staring at the double doors completely dumbfounded. Things had escalated so quickly. I didn't have time to process my thoughts or emotions. I don't know how long I stood in the hall staring at the two doors before me before I finally turned back and sat on an old pink pleather seat cushion with wooden armrests. I thrust my head back, staring at the fluorescent light above me.

No number of doctors assuring me about a *simple* procedure were going to make me feel better. I had to deal with the news of losing my future child and watching my wife get whisked away to an operating room – all within an hour. The spiral continued to unravel itself.

"Why do you continue to torture me, God? Why?"

My blood was boiling. My eyes were watering. I leapt up from my chair and grabbed hold of it with gritted teeth, fully intending on throwing it across the fucking room in a tirade. I hadn't eaten and hadn't slept in almost twenty-four hours. I gripped the armrests tightly, my knuckles turning white.

Deep breaths, John. Deep breaths.

I released my hold on the chair and exhaled deeply. I still couldn't wrap my mind around all this. There was nothing to bite into. No substance. How? It was the only question my brain could fire off.

Seeing the terror and agonizing hurt in Megan's eyes when I first got home would be another haunting memory forever etched into my memory. All of it brought me back to my childhood. The helpless, hopeless feeling. The fear of the unknown. Miscarriages were not an uncommon occurrence in the world. I shouldn't have been surprised. Based on my history, I should've assumed the worst when Megan broke the news about being pregnant.

Could anyone else possibly have had it worse than me? Sure. But for all I had been through and overcome, I felt karma owed me a few dozen times over to tilt the scales in my favor for once. Yet here we were. I sat back on the chair and stared at the floor.

"Please, God. If you have any love in your heart for me or Megan, you will see to it that she and I come out the other side of this stronger."

I'd be the first to admit, events in my life had fractured my faith and made me question my relationship with God on many occasions. But during difficult times, I would still pray, for reasons unbeknownst to me. Perhaps the inconsistencies in my faith were part of the problem. Maybe God *was* punishing me.

I fished my wallet out of my pocket and yanked out Father Rosario's business card. I smacked the card against the palm of my hand – wondering what guidance, if any, he could provide under this particular set of circumstances. I just needed a comforting voice that didn't belong to a nurse or doctor to let me know things were going to be okay. I let out a sigh and slipped the card back into my wallet. It was neither the time, nor the place.

Minute after agonizing minute had turned into several hours. The coffee served as nothing more than an accelerant to my growing panic and anxiety, constantly worrying that there may have been complications. I surfed the internet like a hypochondriac reading about all the worst-case scenarios. Most of the articles I found stated these surgeries only take ten to thirty minutes but could take up to five or six hours. After falling into the rabbit hole of possible complications, I finally set my phone down and tried to take a moment to just breathe. My eyes were heavy – weighed down from lack of sleep and the effects of crying. I glanced up at a picture on the wall of a mother, father, and their baby being pushed in a stroller. The caricature of a model family smiling from ear to ear – elated to be together with their newborn child. A heaviness rested on my chest.

Suddenly, the doors to the O.R. burst open and a doctor and nurse came out and greeted me.

"Your wife is doing great, Mister Tinsley," the doctor said, holding a clipboard in his arm like a football. "The surgery was successful, and we will have you both out of here shortly. I did write her a five-day prescription for hydrocodone. Normally, over the counter acetaminophen is more than adequate. But given the nature of the trauma in this case, a stronger pain reliever is necessary. Make sure she eats something before taking the medication and that she gets a lot of rest over the next few days. I know this is a difficult time, and both of you have my deepest condolences."

"Thank you, Doctor." I shook his hand before he turned and exited back into the O.R. The nurse remained behind.

"I'm so sorry, Mister Tinsley," the nurse said with a sorrowful glance and a pamphlet in hand. "I know this is a very trying time. I wanted to let you know that we do offer memorial services in cases like these to try to help in processing your grief."

Memorial services? My blood began to boil. Just another way for a hospital to capitalize on emotional turmoil to make a buck. Fuck her.

"And do what? Make us a little mini headstone as a constant reminder? I don't need your goddamned memorial services. I just want to see my wife."

Even being exhausted and angry, I was still clear minded enough to sense that the venom behind my words were wrong and stung the nurse. She had only been trying to help.

"I-I'm sorry. I don't know what came over me," I said almost immediately after.

"No, I totally understand. It's a lot to process. I'll tell you what. You can just take the pamphlet. You can feel free to discuss this with your wife when you both are ready. You can both make your decision from there."

She handed me the pamphlet. It was just as morbid as one would expect. Offerings included a dedicated memorial garden on site, a memorial service – similar to a funeral, to commemorate the loss of our baby, or going all the way through to doing a burial or cremation. I was flabbergasted.

"Let's go see your wife," the nurse said, breaking the awkward silence of me staring at the pamphlet.

I nodded my head and followed her as she led me through the labyrinth of halls before we finally reached Megan's recovery room.

"Mrs. Tinsley, there is someone here who wants to see you!" the nurse said in an upbeat tone.

I tried my best to put a smile on as I entered the room. Megan lay on the bed, completely void of any expression. She didn't acknowledge me walking into the room. She merely stared straight ahead at the opposite wall. I rushed forward, tossing the pamphlet aside and leaned in and gave her a gentle hug before planting a kiss on her forehead and telling her how much I loved her. The corner of her mouth curled into a slight smile when our eyes met.

"I love you too," she said with a voice barely above a whisper.

I watched as her eyes darted up to the TV mounted in the corner, her expression changing to fear. I looked up at the screen but didn't see anything.

"Is everything okay?" I asked.

Megan said nothing. Her gaze fell back to the opposite wall once again. A tear trickled out of the corner of her eye.

Chapter Thirty-Five

November 9th, 2023
Megan Tinsley

What do you do when you feel everything is being taken from you? What if you have no choice? I'd been served a constant reminder of the most horrific night of my life at every waking moment. Shadowy silhouettes of the goat man everywhere I went. Hiding in the corner of my hospital recovery room? I saw its reflection in the TV screen. Lying in bed? It stood by the foot of my bed. When I would walk past a doorway? It was there. There was no respite. It was always around. Just watching. Waiting. Whispering horrible things to me. The worst part? I couldn't talk to anyone about it – fearing what may happen if I did. I had to do my best to come to grips with not only losing my child but also losing the love of my life. Losing everything.

Some people would look at this situation and think about how crazy I was. I don't think anyone could have gone through the experiences I did and not believe that something far more insidious was at play in our household.

Whatever this *thing* was. It was powerful enough to paralyze me, take away our child, and make it appear as a natural occurrence.

Something that strong was not something I wanted to attempt to go toe to toe with. I'd tried reconciling in my head that this was something brought into our home from our paranormal adventures, but it didn't matter. All that mattered now was getting away from John. Sparing him from the evil that was lurking. The voices had reassured me he would be fine – all I had to do was listen.

"Hey, baby," I said softly while kicked back on the sofa with my feet on his lap.

"Yeah, babe?" He stopped rubbing my feet and looked at me with puppy dog eyes.

He'd done such an amazing job at comforting me since we got back from the hospital. I loved this man so much. Off in the distance, I saw the shadow figure looming. A swift reminder of the dire situation. I looked back at John and his deep blue eyes again. The pain in my heart was almost unbearable, and up to this point I had done my very best at masking my true emotions. I looked at the time on my phone. It was a little after noon.

"Do you think you could run into town and grab us a pizza from DiNuzzio's?"

John shot me a perplexed look. "Do you think your stomach will be able to handle it?"

I nodded.

"It's literally the busiest time of the day right now."

Both Bruce and I looked over at John with pleading eyes. Bruce knew what the word pizza meant.

"Fine," he said in mock frustration before letting out a laugh. "What do you want on it?"

"Whatever. Anything you want sounds good to me, baby. Thank you."

"I'll be back as soon as possible." He walked across the room to grab his car keys off the counter, Bruce following in close pursuit. "Do you need anything else while I am out?"

"No, just the pizza is fine. Thank you!"

I sat up on the couch as John walked over. "Oh, no! You don't need to get up! Just rest, baby!"

"I'm alright." I squeezed John into a tight hug and pulled him in for a passionate kiss. "I love you."

John pulled back after the kiss, a prideful gleam in his eyes. "I love you too, babe. I will be back as soon as I can. Please get some rest."

"I will."

John gave me one last peck on the lips before turning and walking out of the house. Standing in the foyer, I felt icy tendrils wrap onto my shoulder as a frigid breath blew onto my ear. I peered over my shoulder to find nothing there. Another chilling reminder that I wasn't alone even when I was alone.

"It's time," a faint voice hissed.

I walked over to the window and peeled the curtain back to watch as John pulled his Jeep out of the driveway, stealing one last glance at him. The flood barrier failed, and tears started flowing freely. I turned away from the window with the shadowy silhouette remaining attached to my hip. I walked into the kitchen and grabbed a pen and a piece of paper. With the figure looming over my shoulder, I wrote a note to John remembering its haunting words.

"I want you to cause a gash so deep in his soul that it wilts like a dried-out grape. Leave him. Or I will take your baby...and then I will come for you!"

Up to this point it had owned up to its word tenfold. After my operation, it began to threaten to harm John and I if I didn't follow its words. I placed the pen down onto the piece of yellow scrap paper and began to write a note I wish I never had to.

"You caused all of this," the voice whispered as I scribbled. *"The baby, your love, your life. This was all your doing."*

The spectral words slashed me like daggers. I didn't want to believe what was being said to me, but how could I not? I didn't heed the warning and do as it had said. I bent down and gave Bruce a big hug, scratching his belly which caused him to begin kicking his leg. "Mama loves you, Brucie." I planted a big smooch on Bruce's head and walked up to our bedroom. Bruce followed close behind, but I closed him out of being able to come into our room.

"Will you leave John alone?" I asked to the empty bedroom.

"Yesss."

I walked into the bathroom and looked at my prescription bottle and grabbed a plastic bag out from a vanity drawer. I looked up into the mirror and saw those horrible red eyes staring back from directly behind me. This was the way. The only way to keep John safe. I grabbed the bottle of Hydrocodone. Openly sobbing now, I dumped its contents into my hand and readied the plastic bag.

"Do it now, WHORE!" the voice, no longer a whisper – but now a deep and guttural roar, nearly caused me to spill the tablets down the drain.

"I love you, John Allen Tinsley. Forever and always," I whispered.

Chapter Thirty-Six

November 9ᵗʰ, 2023
John Tinsley

With the smell of pepperoni and fresh garlic swirling around inside my Jeep, my stomach grumbled. DiNuzzio's had been Megan and I's favorite pizza parlor in Medina since moving here. They were the only pizzeria in the area that served thinly sliced fresh garlic on their pies.

I was shocked when Megan seemed so keen on ordering a pizza today, given that she'd just had surgery. I wasn't sure whether the doctors would approve or not, but who was I to argue? She knew how she was feeling better than I did, and maybe one of our favorite comfort foods would help us both in trying to feel a little better, if only for the short term.

Megan had shown true strength. She was quiet and reserved for a while after the surgery. Completely understandable. But occasionally, I would still catch glimpses of my wife coming through the dense and heavy fog. I had done my best to be strong for her. To care for her. I had to put my own needs on the back burner. I would have the time to pick myself back up one day. For now, I wanted to make sure I could do whatever I could to lift Megan back up.

After having to sit in the car with the smell of that pizza for a little over ten minutes, pulling up our driveway was such a welcome sight. My mouth was watering. I quickly gathered up the large pizza box and stormed into the house, closing the front door behind me.

"Babe, I'm back!" I announced, taking my shoes off on the rug just inside the door. There was no response – except for Bruce trotting up to greet me and sniff at the pizza box.

I petted Bruce on the head and walked past the doorway that led to the living room. I didn't see Megan laying down on the couch anymore.

"I got the pizza, babe!"

I walked into the kitchen and placed the box down on the stovetop. The house remained silent. I turned from the stove and noticed a note had been left on the kitchen island. It read:

-John,
I am so sorry I let you down. I know how much it meant to you to become a father. I failed you. I could barely stand to look you in the eyes anymore. I tried. I really did. I am ashamed of myself, and I know you'll be better off without me.

Sincerely,
Megan

I couldn't believe what my eyes were reading. I tossed the paper back down onto the kitchen island and rushed toward the living room and up the staircase. Our bedroom door was closed.

"Megan!" I cried out.

I reached for the doorknob, but it was locked. I called out her name again and got no response.

"Oh, fuck. Oh, fuck. Megan!" I thrust a shoulder into the door, but it didn't budge.

I pulled my phone out and quickly dialed 9-1-1.

"9-1-1... What's your emergency?" the dispatcher asked.

"I-I think my wife is trying to kill herself. She's locked herself in our bedroom!" I cried out, throwing another shoulder into the door with no success.

I gave the dispatcher our address and she said she would send help right away. I didn't have time to wait for them, though. I took a step back and thrust my foot into the door. The wood around the door frame began to splinter. I took a step back and thrust another kick with everything I had, and the door flew open.

I rushed inside and quickly made my way to the bathroom where the sight before me sent me crumbling to my knees in a heaping mess.

Numb. A feeling that can only be properly explained if you've truly experienced it. Somewhere between the anguish, anger, hopelessness – your wires get mixed, and you feel empty. Void. Hollow. In a constant free fall even when you aren't actually falling. You feel nothing. A complete ethereal abyss.

I laid on the sectional sofa in our living room, staring at the ceiling. A single tear trickled down each side of my face. I didn't have the energy to wipe them away. Bruce had attempted to console me several times. I could tell that he felt lost and confused as well. But still, he did his best to lift my spirits. After the medics and law enforcement officers had wrapped up with their duties and investigation, I went up to our bedroom, collapsed onto the floor in a fetal position, and cried so hard my nose bled. I didn't even know that was possible. Bruce came in and kissed my face repeatedly on both sides, his tail wagging gently until I finally rolled onto my side and cracked a thankful smile as I wrapped my arms around him. We laid on the floor of the bedroom together until I could bring myself to get up and head to the couch.

Talking with the detective had been an exhausting experience. His implication that I had any involvement sent me into a borderline fit of agony-filled rage. He said they would check the cameras at DiNuzzio's to substantiate my alibi and I replied with a *"Great. Now get the fuck out of my house."*

I thought back to the detective I spoke with as a child. I couldn't remember his name anymore, but the flashback to the night my father took his own life right before my eyes had weaseled its way out of the vault in my brain and sat on the forefront of my mind, resting heavy on my conscience. *Everything and everyone that I ever love dies.*

What was it about me that caused so much loss? I felt like a walking embodiment of a reaper. A harbinger of death.

Knock. Knock. Knock.

The soft rapping came from my front door. Bruce perked his head up and looked at me, as if to question whether I was going to answer the door. I remained planted. I looked at my phone. It was almost nine o'clock at night. I hadn't even realized how much of the day had passed me by. I saw I had several missed calls and text messages from Eddie.

Knock. Knock. Knock.

The trio of strikes came at the door again – this time with more rapid, pronounced blows. Brucie let out a low growl, his hackles raised, as he stared intently in the direction of the front door.

"It's okay, Bruce," I whispered, giving him a pat on his hip.

I really did not want to see any visitors at the moment. Not after everything that had transpired.

Three more thumps at the door.

"Will you let me in?" I heard a female's soft voice call out from outside. I remained silent. Bruce grumbled in displeasure once again, his body tensing up.

Bang. Bang. Bang.

Three sudden pounds at the door sent a jolt through my heart. I quickly twisted my body off the couch, grumbling obscenities as Bruce trotted directly next to me, his hackles still raised. I stood silently in front of the door for a moment. The wind outside was whipping across the night sky, an autumn cold front blowing in.

"Please. Will you let me in?" the hushed woman's voice asked once again.

My body was on pins and needles. It wasn't a voice I recognized – not with the way the wind was howling outside. I placed a careful eye up to the peephole. It was too dark outside to see anything. I turned away to flip the porch light on. Just as my finger reached the switch...

BANG! BANG! BANG!

The force of the blows shook the locked door in its frame. The suddenness startled me and caused me to jump in fright. Bruce started barking aggressively, his body hunched in a defensive posture.

"W-Will you...let me in?" the voice said, trailed by a girlish giggle.

"Listen, I am not in the fucking mood today! Just leave me the fuck alone!"

I flipped the light switch on and checked the peephole again. No one was out there. I was in no mood for neighborhood pranksters. Medina was a safe town, but there were definitely entitled kids – as with any neighborhood – that still enjoyed pranking families in their neighborhoods. I couldn't blame them and normally would find the harmless prank to be funny but today was not the day. Wrong time. Wrong house.

I went into the mud room closet nearest our front door and grabbed a baseball bat. No intentions on using it – more of a scare tactic. It was more there for Megan to feel comfortable home alone if I was not around.

"Bruce, stay," I commanded.

I ripped the front door open and lunged outside, screaming like a mad man in an attempt to scare anyone away that may have tried hiding out of sight from the peephole. I glanced around at the empty porch. I could only imagine what a psycho I would've looked like if any of my neighbors had been watching from their windows. Very much a *'get off my lawn'* kind of moment.

With the bat still raised, I leaned over the railing and checked down the row of shrubs lining our mulch bed. No one was around. I could hear Bruce still growling inside. I shook my head in confusion and lowered the bat. Feelings reminiscent of my paranoia as a child came floating back to the surface. I looked back to my open front door, where Bruce still stood guard on high alert. I looked back around the porch and at my yard as the wind continued to tear through the neighborhood.

I didn't see any footprints and hadn't seen any kids running off. Confusion was setting in. And what about that voice? I stood on the porch in the freezing cold a moment longer, mulling everything over, before turning back inside and closing the door behind me.

"It's okay buddy. That's a good boy." I put the aluminum bat back in the closet and petted Bruce. His guard began to come back down as he licked my hand.

I walked into the kitchen to grab myself a bottle of water, telling Bruce it was time to go lay down and go to bed. I turned back toward the hallway and saw the untouched pizza box still resting on my stove. I wondered if I would ever be able to go back to DiNuzzio's again.

"Come on buddy, it's bed time," I said, the waterworks attempting to worm their way out of my eyes again.

A troubled mind cannot rest. That thought bounced around my head as I attempted to clear my mind and allow sleep to carry me into the next morning. Between the extreme loss and grief that I experienced earlier and the odd incident tonight, I found it difficult to stop the momentum of the whistling steam engine in my head.

In all honesty, everything in the house already felt like a relic of a past life. I was trapped in a prison with beautiful memories that would now haunt me at every turn. Even the bed I laid on was a stark reminder of the second half of my heart and soul no longer lying next to me.

On more than one occasion, I had flipped over toward Megan's side of the bed. My arm that would normally wrap around her hips as we spooned before sleeping found a depressing void.

With an exasperated sigh, I sat up in bed praying for a reprieve from the weight of the world that had once again been thrust onto my shoulders. I picked up my phone and saw it was now a little after one in the morning. A cluster of unread texts from Eddie still lined my phone. I finally mustered enough energy to text him back and say *"Don't feel like talking right now. I appreciate your concern."*

BANG! BANG! BANG!

The sudden eruption of knocking nearly caused me to topple out of bed. "What in the fuck?" I groaned. Bruce let out another grumble as he lifted his head from his dog bed.

"Bruce, stay."

I got up from my bed and walked to my bedroom door. Bruce instinctively remained attached to my hip. I slid a hand across his back and told him to stay yet again as I opened the bedroom door and closed it behind me. The house was silent, and my nerves were shot. Lack of sleep was beginning to take a firm grip on me and tug at the strands remaining of my sanity. My eyes were burning with exhaustion. I stood silently in the doorway, waiting for the knocking to occur again. Silence.

I took a few more silent steps down the pitch-black corridor, my socks silencing my footfalls. Bruce began whining in the bedroom, occasionally clawing at the door.

"Bruce, be quiet," I hissed.

Another step. Another.

Thump. Creeeak. Thump. Creeeak.

Footsteps on the hardwood downstairs. I froze in place, my heart now thundering away inside my chest. I wanted to call out but realized I would only be talking to myself. *I'm not crazy.* I took another timid step forward. I was only a couple paces away from the staircase. A surge of cold air pricked at my skin as I took another step forward. Then another.

I stood at the top of the stairs, staring into the inky depths below. A stillness, like the calm before a storm, settled in the murky abyss before me.

Down one stair. Then another. Then another. I slowly scaled down the steps, stealthily making my way to the bottom. The main floor of the house was freezing: a cold I had never felt in my home. The air felt as though it were moving. Gusts of bone-chilling and frigid air flowed right through my body as though I were nothing more than a barren autumn tree in the countryside woods. I glanced around the living room once my eyes had a moment to adjust. Empty. Had lack of sleep caused me to begin hearing things now? A heavy gust of arctic chill slammed into my body once again, gooseflesh forming up and down my entire body.

In a moment of heightened fear, concern, and confusion, I made my way toward the main hall. The breeze was growing stronger.

When I turned to my right where the wind was blowing from, I almost doubled over. *What the fuck?*

My front door was wide open. I rushed to the doorway and peered outside before slamming the door shut and twisting the deadbolt back into place. I had locked the door earlier, hadn't I?

With a newfound panic, I paraded around the house, flipping every light switch on as I went – attempting to make as much ruckus as I could to scare any potential intruders. After going through the entire house, I found it to be empty. I was questioning my memory again about whether I had not closed the door all the way when I attempted to catch the neighborhood pranksters. Admittedly, the brain fog I had been dealing with all day had made it a completely possible scenario – and with tonight's windstorm rolling through, it was highly likely that if I hadn't shut the door, the wind would've blown it right open.

But what of the footsteps? I supposed it was possible the sudden battle between the heated home and arctic air rushing in could cause the floorboards to expand and contract. I let out a collective sigh. I needed sleep.

I turned all the lights out and headed back upstairs where Bruce sat precariously close to the bedroom door awaiting my report.

"Everything's okay, buddy. Daddy forgot to close the door. Let's go to sleep."

Bruce had always been trained to lay in his bed ever since his days as a puppy. But when I flopped into bed, I called his name and patted my hand on Megan's side of the bed.

"Come on, Brucie!"

Without hesitation, Bruce leapt up onto the bed like an excited child and burrowed himself into a ball right next to me.

"Good boy," I whispered, petting his ears and finding comfort from my best friend. "Daddy loves you."

Chapter Thirty-Seven

November 20th, 2023
John Tinsley

"How are you holding up?" Eddie asked from across the table.

He had remained steadfast in being a supportive friend, checking in on me ever since word about Megan had spread. News articles, blogs, and social media influencers were all talking about the shocking death of Megan Tinsley. The rumor mill immediately began to swirl with stories. Fame seekers and ridiculous clickbait headlines ranged from my involvement in her death, to me being an abusive husband.

I was doing my best to stay off social media altogether. I knew in my state of mind, I would not fare well with the internet trolls.

"I'm just taking it day by day." I shrugged.

After a very brief investigation, the local detective determined my story to be factual and that Megan had indeed committed suicide. Suicide. The word hung around in the air with a foul stench, painting my face with a pained expression. Megan's parents flew in from Florida for the funeral. They turned a cold shoulder to me, as though I was the cause for Megan's premature exodus from this world. I didn't press the issue. I didn't have it in me. They lost their cherished daughter. They were hurting just like I was. They were angry at the world and dropping their pain in my lap.

I still couldn't wrap my head around *why* Megan had done it. I memorized the note she had written. It didn't make any sense. We were both extremely upset over the loss of our child, but she seemed as fine as could be expected on the day I left to grab our pizza for lunch. Some people viewed suicide as a release from this world. Others viewed it as a selfish and heinous act. I didn't know where I fell on the spectrum, I just knew I was having an extremely difficult time coping with all of the loss over the course of my life.

"I'm just worried about you, brother," Eddie said before taking a bite out of his buffalo wing.

"I know, and I appreciate it. It's just a lot to process and is going to take time."

"Well, I am here for you whenever you need me."

"Thanks, Eddie."

Through the raging waves of depression, I had spent a lot of time isolating myself: becoming a shut in. I didn't want to be bothered. I didn't want to be around anyone. I just wanted to take time for myself and spend it with Bruce, who had also been blue since Megan was no longer with us. But for those fleeting glimpses where the sunlight reached down upon me, I felt thankful for a friend like Eddie. He made a lonely world not feel so alone. Sometimes, I felt like an asshole for the way I would dismiss his offers to hang out to get my mind off things, but deep down I knew he understood my reasoning behind it. It wasn't a him thing. It was a me thing. That level of respect meant a lot, and I'd made mention of it as we wrapped up lunch.

"I know, bro. If you need anything from me, you know I am just a call away," Eddie said before getting into his car.

"I know. I really appreciate you. Thanks again."

What I had failed to mention to Eddie was that I had been having experiences ever since Megan took her own life. I knew he wanted to stay away from opening himself up to spiritual communication as much as possible, so I didn't want to burden him with it. The truth was that things started off small and infrequent. Things that I could shrug off. Like when I forgot to close the front door, noises in the house, the feeling of a presence nearby.

I took it as an odd comfort that it was Megan trying to connect with me to let me know she was okay. I had even gone so far as to dig out our paranormal equipment in an attempt to communicate with her. It was a major no-no rule we had made when we started investigating. *'Never in our own house.'*

I'd had no luck with any of the devices. Not a blip. Nothing lit up. Nothing moved. It was bizarre. Radio silence all around, until last night, when I attempted to use her favorite tools of the trade: her dowsing rods. I was getting enthusiastic responses. The rods answered questions about our life, our marriage, our memories with pristine accuracy. I was one hundred percent bought in.

I wanted to be able to ask more diverse questions, so I grabbed our antique Ouija board and placed it on my desk. I lit some candles and placed them around the room. They were Megan's favorite scent, pine tree. The flames danced and flickered, kissing the room in a faint orange glow. After opening the session, things got weird.

"Are you always with me?"

The planchette remained idle for a moment, and then ever so slowly began to glide across the board to the *"yes"* answer. My brain was flooded with questions that I wanted to ask.

"Can you show yourself to me?"

The planchette slid to *"No."*

"Do you really feel like you let me down?"

"Yes."

I felt a rush of emotions come boiling to the surface. I took a deep breath.

"I promise you that you didn't baby. I'm so sorry you felt that way. Are you in a better place now?"

"No."

The response sent chills down my spine.

"Where are you?"

"H-E-R-E."

I glanced around the room, feeling a tinge of unease coursing through my body. I'd never used a Ouija board by myself before. I wasn't even sure it was going to work, but to feel the static-like electricity around my hands, and the cold tug on my fingertips, directing the planchette where to go left me almost speechless.

"Are you not able to rest?"

The planchette again slid to *"No."*

"What's keeping you here?"

"Y-O-U."

"What do you mean? How am I keeping you here?"

"N-E-E-D."

"Need what, baby?"

"I-N-S-I-D-E."

I felt my face twist in confusion. *"Inside what?"*

"Y-O-U."

A prickle crept up my spine at the mention. I frowned with a thought, trying to be crafty with my next question.

"You're always with me though, remember?"

The planchette remained motionless. I sat in befuddlement. A sharp pain began to course through my back. It felt as though a human was climbing and clinging onto it.

"Is that you I feel?" I grunted in pain.

"Yes."

The pain grew stronger. My back was beginning to spasm and lock up.

"Why are you hurting me?"

The planchette remained motionless. I wasn't sure how much longer I could continue the session.

"Why won't you answer me?"

A wheezy, heavy breathing started buzzing by my right ear. I began to grow weary and regretted digging out the Ouija board. The planchette now began to guide itself across the board without my prompts.

"S-A-H-P-L-A-M"

"S-A-H-P-L-A-M"

"S-A-H-P-L-A-M"

I couldn't make sense of what was being spelled. The planchette began to slide with an added aggression over those same exact letters. The pain in my back was growing to unbearable levels and the breathing next to me began to grow more and more violent.

"Megan, is this really you?"

The planchette came to a dead stop in the center of the board before shooting back and forth with explosive vigor, spelling out *"M-A-Y-B-E"*.

"This isn't funny. Who is this?"

"S-A-H-P-L-A-M."

At that point, I felt as though I was no longer speaking with Megan – and began to question whether I ever truly was. The planchette was racing feverishly across the board, repeating those same letters again. I felt like whoever I was communicating with was playing games with me.

"What do you want from me?"

The planchette froze in place once again. The room fell silent. The pressure on my back had dissipated just as fast as it had come on. I glanced around the dimly lit room in confusion.

"YOUR SOUL!" a monstrous voice growled right next to my face.

A sudden rush of wind tore through the room with gale force, blowing out all the candles I had set up around the room. I was now enveloped in total darkness. I flew out of my chair and crawled across the floor, trying to find safety outside of this room.

"Hahaha."

The cackling of a small child bellowed from behind me. My flesh was crawling. I managed to crawl to the door, quickly got to my feet, and flipped the light switch on. Down on the floor behind me, was Lucy.

I had never felt a wave of nauseating fear quite like that. I grabbed Bruce's leash, and we left the house immediately. I placed him in my Jeep, found a nearby pet-friendly hotel and we stayed the night there until I could get my wits about me.

I had toyed around with the idea of calling Father Rosario on more than one occasion since the Ouija board session last night. Prior to meeting with Eddie for lunch, I brought Bruce home from the hotel and ensured the house felt safe. I pulled the priest's business card out of my wallet and smacked it against the palm of my hand, just like at the hospital, still struggling to bring myself to make the call.

Finally, on my way home from lunch, I gave it more thought. After weighing my options, I punched the numbers in on my phone. I stared at the screen for a moment. This *thing*...whatever it was. It pretended to be Megan. It said it wanted my soul. What other choice did I have?

With my anxiety in overdrive, I sighed and pressed the send call button.

It was ringing.

Chapter Thirty-Eight

November 20th, 2023
Father Rosario

I sat at the desk in my office, staring off at the poster of John, Megan, and Eddie from their first documentary. I'd bought a nice mahogany frame for it and placed it on my wall. Several members of my congregation shared their displeasure at me touting anything paranormal inside the church.

"It's unholy," or *"That is sacrilegious,"* were the common complaints I would hear.

I would often remind them that it is not our place to judge, and that I had once counseled the young man from the poster, reminding them of the dark history that had once consumed the small town of Norton. That was usually more than enough to stifle their qualms, whether they agreed with my view on it or not.

I'd heard through the local news about the sudden passing of John's wife. The news anchor was vague and provided no details. It was tragic. I nearly fell to the floor in anguish for him as soon as I'd heard about it. Another devastating loss for a young man that had already lived through more heartache than what most people would experience in their entire lives.

I wanted to reach out to him and show my support. I considered attending the funeral but didn't want to show up to the service uninvited, especially so soon after attempting to rekindle any sort of relationship we'd once formed all those years ago. I did what I felt would be my best service to John. I prayed for him to receive help and guidance through these dark times. I prayed for Megan to have smooth passage to heaven where she could rest in peace and look down fondly upon her husband.

I was snapped out of my reverie when the cellphone in my pocket began buzzing and ringing loudly. I pulled it out of my pocket and stared at it for a moment. It wasn't a number I recognized. I flipped the phone open and placed it to my ear.

"H-Hello. This is Father Rosario," I answered.

"Hi, Father," the voice on the other end said. It was a familiar voice but eluded me through the phone speaker. "It's John. John Tinsley."

"Oh!" I exclaimed in shock. "So good to hear from you, John. I heard about Megan and want to give you my condolences."

"Thank you."

A drawn-out silence carried on way too long. From the sound of it, he had to have been driving.

"So, uh... How can I help you, John?"

Another moment of silence.

"I-I think I may be dealing with some sort of dark attachment, Father."

"Oh? How so?"

"Well..." he paused. "After Megan passed, strange things started happening."

"What sort of strange things?"

"Look...I think it would be best if I spoke with you in person. Are you at the church?"

"I am, yes."

"Can I stop by? I am out in Fairlawn. Could probably be there in about ten minutes."

"That would be fine, John. I will see you when you get here."

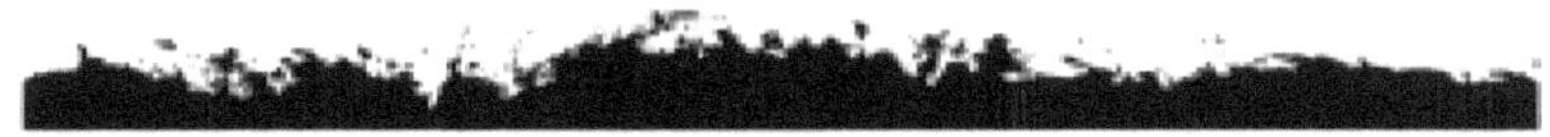

"I think I may be dealing with some sort of dark attachment, Father."

The words launched an assault to my insides. I felt my lungs constrict at the sentence. It took me back to the frightened and confused young boy that came into my office for the first time all those years ago. Now, here we were twenty-five years later, and he was coming back in with more spiritual concerns. Life had always proven to be quite cyclical, but this left me entirely flummoxed.

I made my way out to the front steps of St. Anthony's, awaiting John's arrival. The skies were bleached with cloud cover, a normalcy in Northeast Ohio in the middle of autumn. The leaves had mostly vacated their homes among the trees and left everything in the area feeling more muted – a dull blend of browns and greys. It was one of the many reasons that so many people in the north struggled with seasonal depression. I always saw an uptick in requests for counseling around this time of year. Curiously, I wondered if John – dealing with the traumatic loss of his wife – had begun his battles with mental health that ultimately led him to call me today. I could still remember the terrified expression his grandmother, Edna, had painted on her face when she came back from the Tinsley house that one fretful afternoon. I sighed. Painful times. Painful memories. I was hopeful that with the help of God, I could get John through this difficult time.

A couple of minutes later, I watched a white Jeep pull into the parking lot. John got out of the SUV and headed my way with a brisk pace. He greeted me with a meek smile but maintained a firm handshake.

Through his posture, I could wager he was attempting to put on a brave face. But I saw right through it. Between his unkempt beard and his piercing gaze, I could sense everything I needed to. This man was afraid. The eyes tell a man everything they need to know. They are a gateway to your soul. His eyes were wide in a frightened demeanor, red lightning bolt crackles lining his bloodshot eyes. He hadn't been sleeping. He was broken. He was struggling. But he was still fighting. The fact he came here today was a testament to his strength and willingness to overcome.

I brought him in with a warm hug. I felt his body tremble slightly as I patted him on the back.

"Well, come in. Come in! Weather is a bit nippy today. No sense in hanging around outside."

I ushered him into the church, and we made our way back to my office, attempting to make awkward small talk as we navigated our way past the empty church pews.

"As you can see, not a whole lot has changed over the years."

"Uh huh."

I opened the door to my office and let him pass in front of me before I closed the door behind us. John took his seat in the same tattered leather chair he'd sat in all those years ago. I'd be remiss if I said I didn't feel a slight bit of déjà vu.

I made my way around the desk and took my seat in front of John. His eyes darted back and forth a moment, then they settled on his documentary poster.

"Ah, yes. Your movie poster."

John turned his gaze back at me and nodded but said nothing.

"I just want to say again, how deeply sorry I am for your loss."

"Thanks, Father."

"I understand that you're very well aware, but tragedy like that...it can really take its toll. I know the reason you called me today. But I think it's best if we dig into the root of..."

John waved a dismissive hand. "Father, I appreciate you wanting to delve into the mental health aspect of things. I know you're worried about where my head is at. I miss my wife dearly. And one day, Lord willing, I will be able to accurately put to words the depth of the pain I have been attempting to overcome. But I am here today because I am afraid, Father. I am afraid that I have brought something evil into my home."

I rested back against my chair, chewing on his words a moment. "I understand. And we will get to that. I promise you. Please, I think the context could be very important in offering my help."

John shuffled in his seat. He glanced down at the floor in a way that was eerily reminiscent of his younger self. He opened up about the events that took place leading up to the Ohio Paranormal Summit, and how his friend, Shawn, had come to cleanse his home.

"Things seemed to get better. I went on a trip with Eddie to scout a location while Megan stayed at home. I got back home, and she was on the floor of our bathroom bawling her eyes out and saying she needed to go to the hospital. She seemed scared out of her wits. I rushed her to the hospital. We lost our baby, Father. A miscarriage."

A heaviness befell the room. That was not a detail I had anticipating hearing about.

"The news hit us both very hard. She was rushed into emergency surgery. She seemed very quiet and reserved after the surgery, and understandably so. But then she started to slowly show glimpses of her usual self. We were having a nice and quiet day to ourselves when she told me she wanted pizza. I was caught off guard, but excited by the suggestion. She assured me she would be fine eating it. When I got back, I found her upstairs in the bathroom where she...she..."

John didn't break his gaze from the floor. I cleared my throat. I didn't want him to have to utter the words that had undoubtedly been plaguing his mind ever since. "That had to be so very difficult to witness. I can't imagine the thoughts that were going through your head."

"You don't want to know."

"Trauma like that can be very difficult to work through. How've you been handling it?"

"For the most part, I have been keeping to myself. Staying off social media. Occasionally, I will meet with my friends Eddie or Shawn."

"I see. Anything else?"

"Well..." his voice trailed off. "Strange things started occurring around the house shortly after Megan..."

I nodded. I could already see where this was going. The phenomenon of heightened awareness after the death of a loved one in the hope that they will come to visit you after their passing. Oftentimes, these dreams – these visions, would occur because the mind was so desperate to see their loved ones one last time. The mind is a very powerful thing. You mix in all the stress, anxiety, and insomnia brought on by depressive episodes, and you've got a volatile cocktail that can lead to some very frightening and haunting scenarios.

"Things started off small. Things that I could pretty easily explain away…"

Okay, looking at things from a logical perspective. That helps. I began to jot notes down on the notepad in front of me.

"You know the classic tales of how hauntings begin, Father. All that sorta stuff. But I began to sense a presence. I thought it was Megan…"

Thought?

"I became hopeful. I dug out some of our equipment and began attempting to communicate with her…"

I had to do my best not to sigh in exasperation. I knew where this was headed.

"The results started slow but were encouraging. I still believed I was speaking with Megan. I wanted to take it a step further. I wanted to feel that connection. I dug out our Ouija board…"

I could feel my lips purse together. My job was not to judge – and by all accounts, I was doing my best not to. However, the Ouija board – whether you believed it worked or not – had notoriously been the basis for many stories not ending well. Cliché, if you will. But where there's smoke, there's fire – as my father always told me.

"It started out fine. Just like any other session I've done over the years. Nothing crazy. But the planchette began moving and spelling out that it wanted me to let it in. It started spelling a word I am unfamiliar with."

"What was that word?" I asked.

"Honestly, I'm not even sure how to pronounce it."

"Could you write it out for me?" I flipped to the next page on my notepad and handed it and the pen over to John.

"For sure. I will never forget it."

John proceeded to write the letters *SAHPLAM* before turning the pad of paper back over to me. I glanced down at the page. It certainly wasn't a word I was familiar with. I wouldn't even wager a guess as to what language it could've been – if any. Odds are it was a jumbled mess of letters that amounted to nothing.

"It felt like something was standing on my back and directing the planchette where to go. It was painful. It kept sliding to those same letters on repeat – over and over and over. And then…"

"And then what, John?"

"I asked what the spirit wanted from me out of desperation. The planchette stopped at the center of the board. All the candles blew out, and a voice yelled into my ear that it wants my soul. It rocked me to my core, Father. I scrambled to leave the room. I heard a little girl's giggle. When I flipped the light switch on, I saw my mom's doll, Lucy, laying in the middle of the floor."

My heart beat inside my chest like a grand church bell high up in a giant steeple. My entire rib cage rattled. I placed a pensive hand to my lips, trying to hide any outward concern. While this all could be psychosomatic, the connection back to his mother's doll was a troubling revelation. I reflected back to what John had said at the convention about how they discovered the doll at New Hope. A weird, twisted sort of fate. After their trip there, bad things began happening. Strings of bad luck. Now all of this. I thought back to his childhood and the similarities between the sequences of events. How a frightened Edna had reported to have seen a young girl brushing the hair of the doll when she first went into the Tinsley home. And the night I went to visit her in the hospital – seeing the grim portrait that John drew while waiting in the bedroom. A face he had encountered multiple times, right before things took a turn for the worse.

The dynamics of all this were astounding. Unlike anything I'd ever dealt with. The pieces felt like they fit and the idea of it terrified me. But I also knew I couldn't jump to conclusions without proper due diligence.

The two of us sat in silence a moment.

"What should I do, Father? I am terrified to be in my own home." John stammered, snapping me out of my trance.

I cleared my throat. "That...That's a lot to sift through, John. A very frightening experience for sure. I believe the mind is capable of things we cannot even begin to fully comprehend during times of great stress..."

"You think all this shit is something my brain is causing? No. No. No. I knew it was going to be a mistake coming here." John got up from his chair and stormed towards the door. "A lot of good the church is. When a man needs help and attempts to turn to God, and God's servant turns their back on you. Real fucking helpful."

He slammed my office door shut. I was at a loss for words. John's footfalls could be heard angrily stomping down the main aisle of the church. I wanted to go after him but thought it best that I did not.

Instead, I remained seated at my desk, contemplating my own thoughts and actions. I felt a bit of guilt. The truth was, as startling as John's recounting of the events, there was nothing I could do without concrete proof of that sort of activity happening. All I could do was provide counseling. So, counsel I attempted.

I looked down at the notepad in front of me. My eyes scanned the letters that John had spelled out. I cocked my head when a stunning revelation dawned on me. I wasn't sure and I needed to be certain. I leapt up from my chair as quickly as my body would allow and sauntered over to my bookshelf and began thumbing through the tomes lining the shelves until I came upon one of my old theological textbooks. I yanked it from its place and brought it back to my desk, slamming it down on the oak desk top. I tore through the pages until I came upon the section I vaguely remembered from my studies. I looked down at the book and then up at the notepad, then back to the textbook again. I could feel the hair on the back of my neck stand on end. This revelation changed everything.

Staring me right in the face from the text I'd studied decades ago... *Malphas.*

It suddenly felt as though a veil had been lifted off my head. I began to grow dizzy. I grabbed onto my desk to stabilize myself, even in my seated position. Breathing became difficult.

If this were true. John was in great danger. I felt helpless. The only thing I could do was to try to warn him. I scrambled to my feet, still feeling disoriented as I staggered out of my office and made my way to the front of the church.

By the time I reached the doors and peered out toward the parking lot, his Jeep was gone. With my heart racing, I pulled out my cell phone and went to my recent calls. I tried calling his phone. It went straight to voicemail. I frantically left a message on his phone requesting he call me back and telling him about the discovery I'd just made. I closed my phone and stared off into the distance as a cold chill crept down my spine.

Chapter Thirty-Nine

November 20th, 2023
John Tinsley

I couldn't believe the nerve of Rosario. I peeled out of the church parking lot without looking back. I really put myself out there, hoping for help. Hoping for answers. All Father Rosario had to offer was questioning my mental acuity? Fuck that. I could understand questioning the judgement of a child, but I knew what I saw and experienced. My brain didn't make up candles blowing themselves out and my mother's doll moving itself away from the bookshelf and onto the floor behind me.

I pulled my phone out and in a fit of rage, blocked the old man's number from my recent calls, and tossed my phone down onto my passenger seat. I took a deep breath. Instead of turning left at the intersection like I was supposed to in order to get home, I took a right. There was something I needed to do.

A couple minutes later, I pulled down a familiar street. A place I hadn't been in over two decades. I put my Jeep into park and stared at my childhood home through my window. Sleet began pelting my windshield with light *tick, tick, tick, tick* sounds.

For the most part, the home remained exactly as I remembered it – save a few changes to the landscaping around the house. I never thought I would have the courage to come anywhere near this place again. I stared at it for what felt like hours, listening to the angry voice of my father the night he snapped. I wondered if that had left any sort of residue on the home – if the new homeowners could feel that. Were they aware of the atrocities committed in the home they now rest their heads in?

Ding!

A notification rang out from my phone, snapping me back to the present. I glanced down at it and saw I had a new voicemail.

I picked up my phone and saw I had received a voicemail from Father Rosario. I had blocked his number. How was it possible that I was getting a notification from it? I opened the voicemail and promptly deleted it. I didn't need his apologies.

I began to pull my car around, being sure to take one last glance at the home. A mixed blend of emotions had washed over me – seeing the house was almost cathartic – but it dredged up a hodge podge of both wonderful memories and some of the most haunting ones of my life.

During the drive home, my anxiety was starting to get the better of me. I stopped at a gas station and grabbed a pack of Marlboro Reds and a lighter. I quit smoking cigarettes shortly after Megan and I had started dating. She was repulsed by the habit and that was more than enough motivation for me to quit.

There was nothing to keep me from smoking anymore. My nerves were shot. Minimal sleep, eating like shit, depression, and genuine fear were fueling me through the day now. The second I stepped foot outside the Sheetz, I smacked the pack of cigarettes against the palm of my hand instinctively – shocking myself that that core muscle memory was still there. The brisk wind made it difficult to light.

"Dammit," I muttered under my breath.

Another flick and the flame caught on the end of the narrow stick. I inhaled deeply, my first drag of a cigarette in many years. I half expected it to taste awful and that I would toss it aside angrily after having wasted nearly ten dollars on a pack. But I was wrong. My body welcomed the smoke into my lungs like they were long lost friends. The nicotine instantly sent a shuddering buzz through my body. I glanced down at the cigarette in my hand and smirked. "Whoa."

When I finally arrived back at the house, I stood outside the front porch contemplating everything that had just transpired. I lit up another cigarette, cautiously eyeing up the home.

I stared up at the pallid skies for a moment and let out a sigh. I wasn't sure what I was hoping for, but I found no answers in the clouds and made my way up the stairs and headed into the house.

Bruce immediately alerted to the sound of someone entering his domain, woofing with his deep, bass bark. The moment he came around the corner, his expression quickly shifted to one of excitement as he leapt up with his front paws into my stomach, his tail wagging ferociously.

"Hi, buddy. Daddy sees you." I gave his little ears a good rub. Satisfied, Bruce hopped down and scampered back into the living room.

I stood in the doorway a moment longer. I took a deep breath, made my way downstairs, and went straight for the horror room. I closed the door behind me. Lucy still lay where I left her last night, staring up blankly at the ceiling. I scrambled forward, taking hold of the doll. I stared into its lifeless and haunting eyes.

"Were you the cause of all of this?" I asked.

I thought back to my childhood and this doll. How things really started to crumble and fall apart after my talk with my mom.

"Can I move into Lucy? So that we can always be together. Isn't that what you want?"

"Yes, Mommy. I'd like that."

But that just couldn't be. Could it? A flash flood of all the horrifying memories played in my mind like a reel on fast forward. All the terrible things that occurred in my life after that point ending with the vision of my dead wife. Anger welled up inside me more than I could even register. Before I knew what I was doing, I reared an arm back and threw Lucy with all my might against the opposite wall, her head crashing into it and shattering into tiny shards.

I stared down at the floor, looking at the parts and pieces of the mangled doll. I walked over and stomped it with a heavy foot. I stomped again and again until the porcelain fragments were nothing more than a chalky sediment beneath my shoe. I let out an exhausted breath and stared at my faint reflection in the window. I looked like a crazy person.

I knew, based on my experience in the paranormal, that if the doll was actually haunted, that destroying the doll would not provide any sort of protection, nor relief. It could actually make things worse. I was beyond caring. I wanted to take my anger out on something – and the more I thought about that doll's connection to the most fucked up times in my life – the more I wanted to destroy it. And not just destroy it, but to smash it into a filthy powder that I could blow away with a single breath. Inanimate object or not, I wanted to believe I was hurting something besides myself. Fuck that doll.

"The gloves are off now! You hear me?" I yelled to no one in particular as I spun around the room with my arms outstretched. "I don't give a shit anymore. You don't scare me! Come on out and show yourself!"

I was fed up. Years and years of pent up, unresolved anger were flowing out of my vocal cords now. If I was losing my mind, so be it. But if on the off chance, my mind wasn't turning into a bowl of porridge, I wanted to let *whatever* had been infesting my life all this time to know that enough was enough.

Other than the sound of Bruce scampering around outside the room, the house had fallen silent.

"What? You only mess with people in their sleep? Coward! Why not show your real power? Come on out!"

Silence again.

The anger continued to fester. "No? Well, how about I just...fuckin...destroy...everything?" I asked through gritted teeth as I tugged at the bookshelf nearest me and sent it toppling to the floor.

No response again. I rushed to the opposite side of the room and flailed my arm across my desk, sending the horror action figures flying across the room. I gripped hold of my laptop and smashed it onto the floor. I swiftly turned back toward the desk and threw my fist into the wall several times, puncturing apple-sized holes into the drywall. I doubled over, breathing heavy.

"Still..." I said between breaths. "Nothing?"

I stood upright and surveyed the mess I had just made. Utter destruction. Healthiest way of coping? Most certainly not. But I did feel slightly better, save for the fact that if there was a haunting happening, my provocation went unchecked. As my heart rate began to return to a normal rhythm, I began to feel a pulsing throb in my hand. I lifted my arm and noticed my bloody knuckles where the skin had been peeled right off. I lowered my fist and exhaled.

"John..."

"Joooohn..."

"Johnny..."

A voice hissed to me from the cave opening on the rock side hill before me.

"Can you hear me?"

The voice started to sound familiar. A feminine voice.

"Johnny? Won't you come inside?"

"M-Mom?" I asked, bewildered.

"Yes, my son. Come to me."

I took a step forward toward the gaping maw on the forested hillside. Each footfall sent a crunch of pine needles and stones stabbing into the arches of my feet.

"Why are you inside this cave?"

There was no response. I took a couple more steps, crossing the threshold of the cavernous opening. I was on the brink of passing the point of no return. That nonexistent line where the light met the darkness.

"Come, my son." Her voice began to feel more distant. Further back in the dark depths of the cave.

I took another couple shuffling steps forward and found myself shrouded in obscurity. I turned to look back to the entrance of the cave and found it no longer existed. I was trapped inside an onyx prison surrounded by nothing but jagged stones and damp, dank air.

"Johnny, boy?" my mother's voice called out behind me. I quickly spun around in the black abyss.

"Why are you so afraid? All you have to do is let me in." The voice called out this time in the opposite direction.

I spun around again, this time flailing my arms out in an attempt to get my bearings of the rock walls next to me, but my hands did not find paydirt. A maniacal laughter erupted all around me. I twisted and twirled, aimlessly shambling around and completely disoriented.

"Let me in," a voice hissed right next to my ear.

I swung an arm in the direction of the noise and only hit air.

"Let me in."

"Let me in."

"Let me in."

The voice was rising in timbre and pace now, sounding like a native chant. The words continued to repeat, circling around me. I began to grow dizzy and fell to the hard stone floor and began weeping.

"Let me in!" an animalistic voice growled just as a cold, slimy hand wrapped around my ankle and gave it a sharp tug.

"K'yuhh!" I woke up with a start, taking a violent inhale of air just in time to feel a distinct pressure around my ankle begin to dissipate.

Once I composed myself from the nightmare, I reached over for my phone when I realized I had been dragged down about a foot from my normal resting place in my bed. With my body and brain reeling, I scooted back up and grabbed my phone. I opened the bathroom door and turned the light on, painting the room in a dull yellow hue. On the edge of the light, I could see Bruce's drowsy and confused expression from the opposite side of my bed. I set my phone down on the sink and looked down at my ankle. Purple lines that looked like bruising in the shape of fingers wrapped around the bone.

Panic began setting in. I hadn't remembered falling asleep. I needed to collect myself. I felt like I was about to hyperventilate. I looked down at my phone and saw I had another missed voicemail from Father Rosario. I clicked on the icon and brought my phone up to my ear.

It began with scratchy silence – like that of an old TV that lost signal – and then Father Rosario's voice came through like a distant shout deep down inside a cavernous shaft amidst the static.

*"John?... It's Tom...Rosario... I think...*static*...me in... Let...*static*...in... LET ME IN!"*

The sudden crystal-clear audio of the guttural yell sent shockwaves through my body, and I dropped my phone with a crash onto the floor. Just as I went to bend down and grab it, I froze.

Somewhere in the house, I began to hear the song *Simple Man* by Lynyrd Skynyrd begin playing.

The hairs on the back of my neck stood on end. The haunting tune that had at one point meant so much to me was playing somewhere outside my room. I left the bathroom and told Bruce to stay. He watched on cautiously as I walked through the bedroom door, closing it behind me. The music was beginning to grow louder.

Dressed in nothing more than a pair of skivvies and my socks, I took a few cautious steps toward the staircase. Louder and louder the music began to grow. "Hello?" I called out.

The song immediately stopped playing as if a needle had been lifted from a record player. The melody now replaced by that of a sobbing woman.

Gooseflesh crawled up my body like poison ivy up a rotting tree. I took a couple of trepidatious steps forward. A faint blue hue from surrounding homes' outside lights illuminated the walls of the stairwell. When I turned and glanced down at the bottom of the staircase, I yelled and nearly toppled backward into the wall behind me.

The silhouette of a feminine torso was sitting hunched over at the base of the stairs, its body convulsed as it openly wept. With a wet, crackling sound, the shadowy figure lifted its head up and cackled a deep, throaty laughter. It placed an arm down at an impossible angle on the bottom step with a loud pop. Then the other. Before I could even register what I was seeing, the figure crawled up the stairs like a humanoid arachnid. Its limbs collided with the hardwood stairs like a cavalcade of angry bison.

Thump! Thump! Thump! Thump! Thump!

I quickly turned and bolted back toward my bedroom, the sound of the heavy footfalls gaining on me. I reached the door and attempted to open it, only to find that the door had somehow become locked. I could hear Bruce on the other side of the door, whining frantically. I threw a shoulder into it, but it didn't budge. A ground shaking footfall collided with the floor in the hall behind me.

Thump!

I tried kicking at the door. It still didn't budge. Another stomp in the hallway.

Thump!

"You're sick, Johnny! Sick! Just like your father!" a voice just like my mother's spoke out.

Thump!

I couldn't turn to look back. I refused to. I thrust my body into the door again and began begging and pleading for the door to open.

"You look at me when I am talking to you!" the voice growled. I felt a hand grip firmly onto my shoulder and tug violently at it.

When I spun around, I found myself staring into an empty hallway.

BANG! BANG! BANG!

My bedroom door shook forcefully from the blows, causing me to jump back in fright.

"Hiya, Brucie!" a sinister voice called out. "Who's a gooood boy?"

My heart felt like it was going to explode. I reached for the doorknob one last time, praying to God it would open. I twisted the knob and found it opened right up. I took a couple of steps into the room. Bruce stood directly ahead staring at me with a confused expression, his head cocked. I surveyed the room as best I could and saw nothing. No one. I crouched down and hugged Bruce tightly. "I'm okay buddy. We're okay."

Something was wrong though. I swiped a hand around what should've been Bruce's bristly fur coat and now found it to be smooth. I pulled back from the hug and found myself staring into the mangled face of my mother.

"Oh my god! What the fuck?" I crab walked backwards away from the figure as it crawled agonizingly slowly after me, like a predator knowingly stalking its wounded prey.

She flashed a devilish grin filled with pointed and rotten teeth and let out a spine-chilling laugh, black sputum spilling from her mouth as the nauseating smell of decay wafted in my face.

"What's the matter? Don't you want me to come into your bed and read you bedtime stories?" the thing posing as my mother asked, its neck popping as it cocked its head into an unnatural angle. "I got one for you. It's called Shithead Son Gets His Mother Killed! Sound familiar?"

"Leave me alone! You're not real!" I quickly scrambled to my feet and bolted out of the room. My head was reeling. Was I losing my fucking mind?

I made my way for the staircase and bounded down them two at a time frantically rushing away. When I came to a stop at the base of the stairs, I heard a screeching sound like old rickety metal badly in need of a spritz of oil. I turned to my right to face the living room where I saw the contour of a human rolling toward me in a wheelchair. I stopped dead in my tracks. I couldn't move. I couldn't take my eyes off the figure. I knew in the depths of my soul who this was, and I was frozen in fear. It was my father.

"Boy...you and I have some catchin' up to do!" the figure growled.

It clambered to its feet and took a clumsy step, the sound of joints and bones cracking against one another echoing loudly in the quiet home. His legs bowed out painfully as he slowly staggered in my direction.

"Still nothin' more than a scared little pissant. Look at what you grew into. I am eternally grateful that your mother and I never got an opportunity to see you grow into this sad excuse of a man."

Tears began to sting at the corners of my eyes as the figure crept closer.

"The best memory of my life was making sure you watched me plunge that knife deep into my neck." He laughed a gurgling, wet laugh. "The look on your face as I bled out was the most warmth I ever felt towards you."

"No!" I shouted. "None of this is real! None of it!"

I closed my eyes and tried to picture happy memories when I heard the clanking of pans in the kitchen, followed by erratic, slow shuffling steps coming in my direction. I squeezed my eyes shut tighter, praying to God to wake me up from this hellish nightmare. Things in the home fell silent.

I opened my eyes and found myself staring into an empty living room. Did the prayer work?

On cue, as if my mind was being read, I felt a presence standing behind me. I turned and found myself staring face to face with my grandma. She was holding the severed head of a wild rabbit in her hands.

"Ready for breakfast, Johnny?" she asked, thrusting the arm holding the head in my direction.

I let out a frightened yell, turned the only way I had left, and bounded back up the staircase and into my bedroom, slamming the door and locking it behind me. I slid down to the floor into a fetal position with my back against the door and began to openly sob.

BANG! BANG! BANG!

The bathroom door shook.

"Please! Please just leave me alone!" I wailed.

The bathroom light flicked on, its yellow light kissing the bedroom floor from under the doorway.

BANG! BANG! BANG!

"Please, God! Let me wake up!"

Creeeak.

The bathroom door slowly opened on its own. I closed my eyes and banged my head back against my bedroom door. I knew what this was going to be.

Shhhp. Shhhp.

The sound of shuffling feet exiting the bathroom filled the room. I was trapped. Trapped in my home with all of the horrifying memories life had crammed down my throat and I was completely powerless to stop it.

Shhhp. Shhhp.

"Joooohn," my wife's voice called out, sounding like it were under water. A voice filled with pain and agony.

"No. No. No. I can't do this!" I cried out.

"Look at me, John," she said softly, again her voice muffled.

I shook my head and thrust it back against the door again.

"Look at me!" she shouted angrily this time.

I opened my eyes and instantly regretted it. Standing in the light of the doorway was Megan. She had a plastic bag tied around her head. Every breath she took caused a dimple in the bag to suck in and blow out. She reached up and tore a hole open in the bag and took a step forward.

"Look what you made me do!" she shouted and took another haggard step forward.

"I...I didn't..."

"You did this! You are a cursed soul, John! You brought death upon all of us!" She placed a hand on her belly.

I lost it and began openly weeping and apologizing. Megan took a couple more haphazard steps forward and crouched down. She placed an icy hand on my cheek. I clinched my eyes shut again, trying to block all of this out. It was almost too much pain to bear.

"This would all be so much easier if you would just...let me in."

"No!" I shouted.

When I opened my eyes, I found myself standing in the center of my horror room with no recollection of how I had gotten down here. Had I imagined everything and somehow managed to sleepwalk down here without realizing it?

The dim light of the moon poured in through the ground floor window, painting the room in a dim white glow. The room was still disheveled. As my eyes swept across the space, they discovered a troubling sight that sent a wave of panic through me. Something was propped up and settled under a white bedsheet only a mere couple feet off the ground. I stared at the corner for an indiscriminate amount of time.

BANG! BANG! BANG!

I spun back to the closed door of the room. Was I still dreaming? My brain was scrambled, and I felt myself questioning my sanity.

"You can't hide from me, boy!" my father's voice called out.

BANG!

"Why don't you just open up?"

BANG!

"Open your heart and soul to me!"

BANG!

"And let me in!"

Then...silence. The only noise was my shallow breathing and the pounding of my own heart rattling around inside my rib cage. I let out a heavy exhale.

Suddenly, in the corner of the room, I heard what sounded like the splintering of wood. I slowly turned back to face the spot I previously stared at. What I saw defied all logic. The little figure now towered into the corner of the room, its head nearly touching the ceiling. It was still covered by the bed sheet. My stunned eyes slowly descended from the top of the form to find black furry legs with hoofed feet peeking out from the bottom of the sheet.

It stood silent. Its shoulders bobbing up and down as if it were taking silent labored breaths.

"Wh-What is this?" I whispered.

"It is your time of reckoning. A plan set in motion long ago. And it is time to collect...now do yourself a favor and open yourself up to me!" the figure hissed.

"Please, God. For the love of all things holy. I am calling out to you today for your protection! Please help!"

"Empty wordssss," the cloaked figure hissed. "Just...say...yessss."

It took a step forward. It's hoof colliding with the floor with the force of a sledgehammer, followed by another sending shockwaves straight through me.

I knew what it wanted. It wanted my soul. Things began to click into place for me, as if the veil had finally been lifted from my eyes. A flood of memories came washing in. All the haunting, violent, and traumatizing flashbacks. The taunts, the hateful words, and the loss I experienced.

I will take everything you love from you. And one day you'll be mine.

This…This thing – *it* had taken everything from me. It had been stalking me almost my entire life. Was it responsible for all the bad? Did it cause the accident? Or was that just a happenstance that occurred and it happened to be lurking in the shadows to witness it and capitalize on the heartbreak? My dad. My grandma. Megan. All of them. And now it had its sights set on me. Something I thought Hollywood made up to scare teenagers. A demon.

"No!" I shouted, overcome with rage and sadness.

The beast beneath the sheet let out a monstrous roar and surged forward like a wild bull. The sheet ripped away from its body, revealing the black monstrous creature, but its face had been pieced together with the fragmented remains of Lucy.

Thump. Thump. Thump. Thump. Thump. Thump.

I let out a frightened yell, closed my eyes, and placed defensive arms in front of my face to brace for impact.

Whoosh!

With an electric charge and a hurricane-force wind, a blast of energy passed through me with enough force to send me flying back and colliding into the corner of the desk. A searing pain shot up my spine. When I finally opened my eyes, I found myself laying on the floor. The room was empty, and the house was silent once more.

I hobbled to the door, clutching at my back. I hoped this horrible night was over. I opened the door and found Bruce laying right outside the door. He lifted his head with hopeful eyes, whimpered softly, and gave a little wag of his tail.

"We're going to be okay, buddy," I said quietly. I didn't know whether I believed my own words. "Come on, let's go upstairs and watch some TV. Does that sound good, Brucie?"

Bruce stood up on all fours and continued wagging his tail.

I wasn't sure what the right move was. By destroying Lucy earlier, I'd done nothing but given this...this...demon the power to move around more freely. It was no longer tethered to the doll. I had taken the leash off and enabled it to play its games. Rest assured, I may have stood up to it for the night, but it wouldn't go quietly for long. Knowing sleep was going to evade me anyhow, I came up with the only source of comfort I could think of and that was to snuggle my best friend on the couch and turn on the TV to take my mind off everything – as much as possible, anyhow.

Chapter Forty

November 21^{*st*}*, 2023*
Father Rosario

My attempted calls to John had continued to go unanswered. I was running out of ideas. I tried messaging his social media page with the St. Anthony's page. They went unread. I stared at the grandfather clock in the corner of my office. It was a little after four in the afternoon, and the sun was already beginning to set. All day, I had been anxiously trying to figure out a way to get in contact with John. None of the locals I had spoken with had any ties to him. I wasn't sure where he lived, so I couldn't even call local law enforcement to do a wellness check.

I bit down on my lower lip and tapped my fingers on my desk. I looked down at the desktop monitor I had brought in a couple weeks prior, staring at the social media webpage when a thought crossed my mind.

I typed into the search bar – *Eddie Ingol.*

His personal page had a green dot next to his photo. The local member of my church that had set up my page had explained to me that the green dot meant a person was online. I wasn't sure how to proceed. He was my last option to get someone out to check on

John. I was desperate. I had to work the situation delicately, so I didn't sound like a deranged old man.

Hey Eddie,

This is Father Rosario. I hope all is well. I don't know if you remember me, but I came to visit you all at the Ohio Paranormal Summit. I'm hoping you can help me out.

Have a blessed day,

Tom Rosario

I gave it a couple minutes when I noticed three dots dancing at the bottom of the message screen. He was responding.

Hey! Yeah, I totally remember you. It was so cool that you came to see us! Happy to try and help. What's going on?

I needed to come up with a way to get Eddie out to visit John. I didn't want to lie but also didn't want to scare him off. The evidence was uncanny, but I had no concrete proof that John had been dealing with a demonic presence. I couldn't, in good conscience, place that heavy of a belief in it without proof – even if I truly believed it in my soul. Because if he wasn't truly dealing with an insidious presence, the media and Catholic church would have an absolute field day over it, given John's prominent name.

I am worried about John. He came in to visit with me yesterday. He seemed to be very disturbed. I believe losing Megan is taking a heavier toll on him than he lets on. He wound up leaving the church yesterday in a heightened state of emotion. I tried calling several times and left a voicemail and he has not answered, nor responded. Can you please go do a wellness check on him?

Instantly, the dots started dancing across the bottom of the screen again.

I know what you mean. I'm out in Pittsburgh, visiting family today. But I can head out first thing tomorrow morning and check on him. Thank you for letting me know, Padre.

It wasn't the best-case scenario. But I had to maintain my hope and faith that God was watching over John, would ensure his safety, and keep him right of mind long enough to not make any rash decisions.

Thank you so much, Eddie. Please keep me updated. If you need my help or think I can be of any service, please do not hesitate to reach out to me here or on my cell phone. I will drop everything to head out and help.

God bless!

I sent a separate message with my cell phone number. Eddie read the message and responded with a thumbs up sign. Somewhat satisfied, I closed out of the page.

I pulled open the drawer of my desk and located my small decanter that was filled with a vintage Scotch. I poured a glass of the amber liquid, pulled out an old, crushed pack of cigarettes and lit one up. The sweet nicotine tickled my lungs with a familiar loving embrace.

Horrible habit, but worth the sanity at this moment.

I walked across the room, stared out of my office window, contemplated all of life's mysteries, and hoped that this would all be easily explainable and that John would come out of all of this a better and stronger person. He needed help. I was hopeful that Eddie and I would be able to give it to him. I took a sip from my glass, the beverage burning its way down my throat and into my gullet.

"Dear Heavenly Father, please continue to watch over John. Keep him safe. Keep him grounded. Keep him protected. Amen."

I took a drag on my cigarette, watching the cherry glow in the reflection in the window.

"Stay strong, John. Stay strong."

Chapter Forty-One

November 21st, 2023
John Tinsley

The effects of not sleeping were beginning to take their toll. Throughout the remainder of the night, I kept seeing things moving off in the distance, scuttling about just outside my line of sight. I could no longer discern the difference between my tired brain and true reality. I was beginning to feel my mind slipping from me more and more at every passing minute.

By the time the sun rose above the horizon, I could hardly move. I had placed the TV on mute, hoping the faintest bit of white noise would help usher me into sleep – even a nap. But it never came. The constant thought of everything that had just transpired blended with all the memories from my childhood kept my brain too busy and too loud to allow rest for even one minute.

My eyes burned in such a fashion that I had never experienced. My entire body ached. Anytime I moved, the room would start spinning. I felt drunk and delirious. I couldn't remember the last time I got more than one hour of uninterrupted sleep. I continued to stare blankly at the silent TV as an infomercial played. My nerves had never quite settled, not even now with the sunlight beginning to pour itself over my home.

As the hours passed, I found myself, still glued to the sofa with Bruce – occasionally shutting my eyes, only to snap myself back awake moments later. It was a vicious cycle. Time became more of construct than anything else. It failed to exist. It was just me, my dog, and this giant fucked up house enclosing me within its walls with nothing more than troubled thoughts and a damaged soul. My pain wasn't just on the outside after being thrown into my desk. It was on the inside too.

The only reason I even bothered to get off the couch at all was because Bruce had begun whining and barking at me to go outside.

I opened up the sliding glass door and ushered him out into our fenced in backyard. I watched on as he happily trotted to his potty area that he had always reserved for the deed.

I looked off to my left at the old bar that Megan and I had set up down here after we had first moved in. I'd had a custom sign made for her for Christmas one year that read *"Tinsley Tavern – drinks made with love."*

I sulked my way over to the bar, images of Megan with the plastic bag wrapped around her head leaving a permanent scar.

"Look what you made me do! You did this! You are a cursed soul, John! You brought death upon all of us!"

Was that truly what Megan thought before she took her own life? Did I really bring death upon everyone? Was I cursed?

The thoughts continued to linger and fester away at me. Like a parasite burrowing its way further and further into my mind and latching on – sucking out every last ounce of will I had left to fight. To live.

I walked around the bar and looked at the floor beneath it where a black duffle had been placed. I knew what was in the bag. A way out. Megan and I had several handguns stashed around the house for home protection. This one was no exception. In that bag was a subcompact nine-millimeter Beretta. It was loaded.

I continued to stare at the bag, the haunting thoughts and voices plaguing my brain – urging me to take action. Whispering to me. Calling out to me to take my own life.

I reached down, pulled the bag out, and set it atop the bar. I poured myself a shot of Jameson and downed it. Then another. Then another. I stared at the bag a moment longer and grumbled to myself. I took another shot – tears streaming freely down my cheeks. I wanted to silence the voices – silence the memories. I wanted it all gone. I unzipped the bag and pulled out the gun and placed it on the wooden bar top, continuing to ponder it. I downed one more shot for good measure. The alcohol did nothing to silence the voices or thoughts – only serving to further amplify them.

I could see it now. Picking up that pistol, flipping the safety off, putting the barrel of it into my mouth, and pulling the trigger. I could see the bits of blood, gore, teeth, and chunks of flesh plastered on the wood paneled wall behind me, my body slumping to the floor laying in its own pile of blood. It felt peaceful. It felt right.

Tink. Tink. Tink.

The noise barely registered. I continued to visualize the bloody carnage behind the bar when suddenly Bruce came into the fold. He walked up and sniffed my lifeless body. His tail went between his legs, and he whimpered hopelessly. He looked around the room and nudged his nose against my face and attempted giving kisses.

When my body didn't move, he sat for a moment before lying next to me, never leaving my side.

Tink. Tink.

I was brought back to reality and noticed the pistol I was now holding in my hand. I dropped it onto the countertop with a loud clank and began bawling my eyes out. Visualizing Bruce's heart break right before my eyes was truly gut-wrenching and had managed to snap me out of my suicidal thoughts. I couldn't do it. I couldn't take my own life. I had to continue to fight. Had those thoughts even truly been my own?

Tink. Tink.

I finally realized what the noise was and rushed to the sliding glass door. Bruce was waiting to be let inside. I opened the door, and he came bounding in, ready to play. He ran around in circles with a furious case of the zoomies, and it brought a teary-eyed smile to my face. When he finally burned through enough energy and slowed down, I crumpled to the floor and embraced my dog. He sat next to me and allowed me to openly weep as I pet his face.

"Thank you, Bruce. Thank you for everything, buddy."

The evil thoughts had dissipated. The voices completely silenced. Bruce gave me a knowing kiss, licking away the tears from my eyes before he sprang back into playful action, goading me into a laughing fit as we play wrestled on the floor with one another. This dog was my savior.

I stared at the bottle of melatonin tablets on my kitchen sink. I knew you weren't supposed to mix alcohol and melatonin, but I'd hoped that the mixture would work like an elephant tranquilizer and allow me to get a full night's rest. Something had to give. Even after Bruce cheered me up, I still dealt with exhaustion and felt like I was pouring out of an empty cup with holes poked through it.

I had googled the potential side effects and was satisfied that it wouldn't kill me. It might lead to some dizziness – but I was already dealing with that. I just hoped the sheer fatigue I was feeling would cause me to drop into a deep sleep before any other side effects could even attempt to take hold.

I had been surprised earlier in the day when I saw Eddie tried calling multiple times. I had ignored his calls, so he had texted me asking if everything was okay. I texted him back and said things were fine but just didn't feel like talking. He replied by telling me he understood and may swing up sometime tomorrow to check on me. I left him on read.

Call it pride or call it negligence, but this was my battle. And I felt with a deep night's rest, I would be renewed and ready to fight another day. I just needed that little bit of shut eye to help even the scales a little bit.

I dumped out a five-milligram tablet of melatonin, popped it into my mouth, and washed it down with a glass of water. I left the bathroom light on to ease my anxiety before I stumbled to my bed, where Bruce had already nestled himself into a ball on his side of the mattress. I plopped down with a bounce and tucked myself in under the blanket. I rolled onto my side and pet Bruce for a moment before turning away. I looked over and realized I had left the bedroom door open. Part of me wanted to go close the door for peace of mind, but the effects of the prostration mixed with the melatonin and alcohol were already beginning to gnaw away at my consciousness. My eyes began to grow heavy and tight as a warm relaxation began to wash over me. Before I knew it, my eyes had fallen shut.

Scratch. Scratch. Scratch.

Scratch. Scratch.

I felt my body begin to stir.

Scratch. Scratch. Scratch. Scratch.

I felt my eyes flick open, snapping me out of the stupor of my sleep. The room was spinning.

Scratch. Scratch. Scratch.

What the fuck is that?

I took a deep breath and rolled onto my back, attempting to discern the source of the sound. The clawing continued on repeat. The sound of nails scraping along a hardwood floor at a frantic pace – like an animal clawing into the earth to create a home for itself to rest in.

Scratch. Scratch. Scratch. Scratch.

I slowly rolled over and sat up on my side of the bed, my feet dangling over the edge. I hopped down and had to take a moment to brace myself. My equilibrium was completely shot. The gnashing and clawing on wood continued to echo through the house. I staggered out of my room and toward the staircase. The fervent scraping noises began to grow louder. More aggressive.

I grabbed hold of the railing and slowly took each step down until I reached the landing. I looked to my right into the living room.

"What the fuck?" I whispered hoarsely.

A figure was bent over on its hands and knees busily clawing away at the floor. I took a couple of discombobulated steps toward it.

"Who are you?" I yelled out deliriously.

The shadowy silhouette stopped scratching and sat in its fixed position, completely still. I took a couple more steps toward the silhouette as my eyes began to adjust in the darkness. The motionless figure slowly started to turn its head toward me, its neck popping in a disgusting manner. My eyes nearly bulged out of my head when I realized the thing I was staring at was my wife, Megan.

I shook my head vehemently, trying to clear the cobwebs. Megan spun around onto her rear to face me and sat with her arms behind her holding her up. She was fully nude and on display as she flexed her legs wide open to reveal her most intimate areas. She smiled, her eyes glowing.

"Hi, baby," she cooed, a voice similar to hers, yet not quite identical.

I stood planted firmly in place, my scrambled brain unable to process what I was seeing. Her fingers were covered in wet blood.

"Don't you like what you see? Don't you miss me?"

"M-Megan. Y-You're dead. None of this is real."

"Oh, I can assure you it is very real," her voice responded coldly, a slight inflection of anger nipping at the heels of every word.

"Look," I said, attempting to keep my composure. "I don't know what all of this is. I don't know if you are a spirit...a demon...or a figment of my imagination, but I can tell you right here right now, I will *not* continue to get sucked into this."

Megan's face twisted into an ugly sneer. "Oh? Tsk. Tsk. Tsk. You think you have any choice in the matter, baby?" Her voice began to alter and develop a bit of a rasp.

She began to trace a bloody finger along her inner thighs before bringing it tantalizingly close to her vagina.

"You are not my wife," I responded sternly.

The Megan-like thing let out a boisterous cackle that sent chills down my spine.

"What makes you so sure?" she asked, the voice changing between her own and a monstrous copycat version of it. "Is this not the pussy you liked to fuck?"

I remained silent.

"You always were a bit of a weak dick," a raspy voice escaped her mouth as she chuckled. "You never could satisfy me. You were never much of a man at all. All your crying and sobbing like a baby? It caused me to dry up faster than a sponge in the desert."

Anger, embarrassment, and hurt tugged at my insides. "Stop it."

Megan laughed. "What's the matter? Can't handle a little bit of harsh truth? How about this one? Your weak sperm is why our child died. Just a spineless, weak dick, half-assed excuse of a man. You were never meant to be a father!"

The thing pretending to be my wife fell into a fit of laughter and continued its mockery. Her skin began to grow discolored, crackling and decaying before my very eyes – a faint crimson glow behind them. Needle-like black teeth perforated her smile as her wet, matted hair swayed along with her movements.

"Just shut the fuck up!" I screamed.

The Megan-thing continued on its tirade, throwing its head back tittering gleefully – the laugh becoming deeper with every breath.

"This was God's way of telling you no." It smirked. "Even He didn't find you worthy to bring forth a new creation into this world. What does that say about you? Huh?"

I couldn't shake away the sting of the words. Even when I knew this wasn't Megan, the words still struck me with heavy blows, and they were landing with precise impacts.

"Stop it. Just stop it! None of this is true! It happens to a lot of families!"

The Megan-like thing recoiled at my brash comments. It cocked its head at an angle, the smile never leaving her face.

"Keep telling yourself that. Your impotence led to some weak swimmers attempting to swim their way to safety – only to fail. Just like you!"

"That is enough!" I howled.

The thing splayed out before me let out a raving snicker and then threw its head back. It began grunting an awful noise as blood began to seep out of its vagina, pooling out onto the floor mixed with coagulated black matter.

"Just to give you a little taste of what you lost!" the thing sneered and started laughing all over again.

"Fuck you!" I growled and ran forward full bore and wrapped my hands around the thing pretending to be Megan's throat.

I began yelling obscenities at it as I slammed its head down onto the hardwood floor, wrapping my hands tighter around its throat with a vise-like grip. It began to make whimpering and choking noises, snarling like a beast as it swiped a claw across my face, opening the flesh on my cheek.

"Just leave me the fuck alone! You will never be inside me! Do you hear me?" I howled.

I squeezed even tighter when I felt the figure begin to grow still. The house fell silent once again. I closed my eyes, feeling a little better as I scooted away and sat on my butt in the middle of the living room on the floor. I let out an exasperated sigh and opened my eyes. My stomach dropped at the sight before me.

"No." I said frantically. "No! No! No! No! No!"

I scrambled forward and could literally feel my heart shatter. Laying on the floor was my motionless dog, Bruce.

I don't know how long I openly sobbed over Bruce's body. Every last ounce of fight I had remaining in my body was taken from me in the drop of a hat. I couldn't believe it. How had that been possible?

My last reason for caring about anything on this Earth anymore was just taken from me, and I couldn't help but feel the confusion that Bruce must've felt in his final moments. The helplessness. It absolutely broke me.

Sometime later, I heard a voice call out from behind me.

"I'm sorry it had to come to this."

It was my mother's voice. I didn't have to turn and look. I continued laying on the floor with Bruce, still sobbing. The demon had won. Evil had won. It broke my very will to live anymore.

"If you want all this pain to disappear...all you have to do is say...yes."

A heavy moment of silence fell in my living room. The pain inside me was too much to bear. I was beyond mentally, physically, and spiritually exhausted. I was at the end of my rope.

"Yes."

Chapter Forty-Two

November 22ⁿᵈ, 2023
John Tinsley

The phone sitting next to me began going off. The time was a little after ten in the morning. As though I were floating behind my own eyes watching, I glanced down at the name on the caller ID. It was Eddie. I swiped a finger across the screen.

"Hello?" I answered.

"Hey, bro! I'm glad to hear your voice. I've been worried about you. How are you holding up?"

"I'm sorry I haven't been super responsive. Just been battling my demon."

There was a slight pause. "I think you mean your inner demons." Eddie chuckled. "But I get what you're saying. I'm on my way back from Pittsburgh and was hoping I could swing by and pick you up. Maybe we could grab lunch?"

My lip curled into a smirk.

"I think that would be fine."

"Cool. Want to hit up the new sports pub in town? I think it's called Barker's?"

"Let's do that."

"Okay! Awesome, man! I will see you in about an hour!"

"See you soon."

I clicked the end call button and tossed the phone aside. I got up from my seat at the kitchen island and looked around. It was the most bizarre feeling in the world. I could see and feel everything happening but could not control my own thoughts or actions. It was as though I was floating through an eternal black hole inside my own body. I was screaming at the top of my lungs on the inside, knowing what plan the demon was concocting.

I walked around the island and began rummaging through the drawers. I grabbed hold of a meat mallet tenderizer and pulled the weighty steel hammer out and dropped it with a *thunk* on the countertop.

I felt my mouth form into a grin again.

Knock. Knock. Knock.

I walked over and opened the door. Eddie stood outside dressed in a denim jacket, blue jeans and sneakers. He bore a goofy smirk on his face. He opened his arms wide ready for a hug.

"Come on in," I said, throwing one arm around him lackadaisically and patting him on the back.

"Man, can you believe how chilly it is out there today? Fuckin' high of 18 degrees."

"Heh, yeah. I know, right?"

"You about ready to head out?" he asked.

"Yeah, I need to grab my jacket from the kitchen. Just give me a moment."

"Alright, bro."

Eddie stepped into the foyer and shivered, trying to shake off the cold.

"Where's Bruce at?" he called out as I made my way out of sight.

I didn't answer. Inside my head I was screaming though. I watched as I grabbed hold of the meat tenderizer again. My hand held it out as I eyed up the spiked edge of it.

"Oh! Oh my god! What happened?" I heard Eddie call out from the living room.

He'd found what had happened last night. I maneuvered into a corner around the doorway and waited patiently, the lust for blood growing stronger by the second. The ultimate sin. Eddie's heavy footfalls began to scramble at a frenetic pace towards the kitchen.

"John! What the fuck happened man?" he asked as he passed into the threshold.

THWUCK!

I swung the mallet straight down into the base of Eddie's skull, sending him toppling down to the floor with a loud crash as he groaned in pain.

"J-John...wh-what the fuck is happening?" he mumbled.

His body rolled and writhed on the floor. I was screaming inside my own head, only able to helplessly bear witness to what my own hands were doing. I knelt down next to Eddie and raised the mallet back up and sent it careening down off the side of his skull, the spiky surface digging chunks into the side of his head as his skull crunched and spurts of blood and fragments of skin came peeling off with the mallet. Eddie was no longer moving, but you could hear his gurgled breathing.

I raised the mallet up once again and slammed it back down with a sickening crunch. Eddie was now completely silent and still. But I didn't stop. Again and again, I raised the meat tenderizer up and brutally swung it down until nothing was left of Eddie's face but a muddled mess. Blood, bits of flesh, bone, and gray matter lay exposed on my kitchen floor. I tossed the hammer aside, sending it clanking across the hardwood floor. I took a step back to admire my handiwork.

But the plan was not over yet. With a hand that was sticky with blood and bone fragments, I pulled out my cell phone. I found Father Rosario's number and pressed the call button. After a couple of rings, he answered.

I wanted so badly to command my body to toss the phone aside. To scream from the depths of my soul at Father Rosario to hang up the phone. All I could do was watch.

"Hello?" Father Rosario answered.

"H-Hey, Father. Sorry I haven't been returning your calls. I just needed some time."

"I understand completely." There was a hesitance in his voice. "How are you, John? Is everything alright?"

"Never been better. If it's okay with you, I'd like to come back to the church and finish our talk."

"Y-Yeah. That would be great, John. When can I expect you?"

"I'll start heading out that way in a few. Should be there soon."

I ended the call and tossed the phone onto the floor with a loud thump. I gathered what was needed and turned to exit the house.

Chapter Forty-Three

November 22nd, 2023
Father Rosario

The call had completely taken me by surprise. Had Eddie made it over to John's before the call came in? Did he bail on going to visit him? I walked over to my desk and signed into my social media account. I looked at Eddie's messages. It didn't have the icon to show he was currently signed in. The last time it showed he had logged on had been last night.

I let out a frustrated sigh. Hopefully John calling was a good sign. He'd displayed some worrisome signs when he left St. Anthony's, but maybe he truly did just need some alone time to sort through his thoughts.

"FAAAATHER!" a booming voice bellowed from the nave of the church outside my office.

The suddenness of it took me by surprise and sent my heart into a frenzy. I clutched at my chest and clambered to my feet. Was that...was that John?

I slowly crept to my office door and pulled it open. I peered out into my church and found a hooded figure with their head bowed sitting in the middle of the church pews on the left side. I couldn't make out who it was.

"H-Hello?" I called out with uncertainty dripping from my voice.

The figure did not move and did not speak. I slowly and cautiously started to walk toward the person.

"John?"

No response. No movement. I made it to the row the man was seated in and stepped closer to him. I placed a hand on his shoulder which prompted a swift reaction from the figure, grabbing hold of my wrist and giving it a violent twist. I felt something in my arm pop.

"Get your damn dirty, child molesting hands off of me, Priest!" the person howled in a rage filled voice.

I let out a pained yelp as burning hot pain shot up my entire arm. The person kept a firm grip on my wrist but used their free hand to pull down their hood. It was John, and I was dumbfounded.

"J-John. Wh-What are you doing?" I grimaced.

With a sickening crack, he put more torque on my arm before he took his free hand and shoved it palm first into my chest, sending me flying back out into the main hall of the church, landing in a heap. My entire body was now on fire.

"No one here by that name," he growled.

With dots lining my vision, I was sure I was about to pass out. I watched as John grabbed a length of rope. It had a noose tied around the end of it.

"So, here I am, in the house of God," he said in a voice not of his own. He spun around in a grand gesture. "Just waiting for Him to strike me down."

I spit out a glob of blood that had pooled in my mouth as I tried and failed to get myself pushed off the floor and to my feet. John began to saunter closer now, the rope dangling freely from his hand.

"So, I ask of the...almighty God! Smite me now in your house of oh holy worship!"

John paused and let out a monstrous snicker. I glanced up and saw a smile that stretched impossibly wide. John's lips were cracked and dry, his skin began showing abrasions and lesions and boils. He looked down at me with hate-filled eyes and crouched down. He gathered fistfuls of my hair and pulled my face up to look at him.

"Look at me, Priest! Pray to Him. I want you, in your final moments, to understand that God is not going to save you. You've spent your whole life giving faith to a figure that couldn't care less about his own creations. He's no longer taking messages. But you go ahead! Pray to Him!"

I said nothing and winced in pain as he gave another sharp tug on my scalp. I spit in his face and watched the spatter of blood splash across his hideous maw. He laughed and slammed my head face first into the concrete floor with a sickening crack. I was dazed from the blow, my head feeling as though an explosion had gone off inside it. My nose was undoubtedly broken. I could feel teeth that had been knocked loose swirling around in the blood filling my mouth.

"You know what, Priest? You and the rest of your kind deserve to watch the world burn. Fear and apprehension about backlash from the sheep of the world controls such a powerful organization. You couldn't help John because of rules set forth to protect the church...instead of using your power to actually protect your flock.

But I know, Tom. I can smell it inside you. Deep down in the pits of your soul, you *knew* this was coming...and you did nothing."

I groaned in pain and rolled onto my back, coughing up blood. I couldn't speak. I felt like I was dying as my whole body burned and throbbed.

"Don't worry, Tommy," John's voice changed to mimic my mother's. "After this we will go grab ice cream, okay?" He flashed a sinister grin.

"It...can't be..."

My mind was set ablaze. This couldn't be possible. John had no idea what my mother sounded like, nor about my history with ice cream.

"It is, Tommy boy," the voice had shifted back to a deep, scathing growl once more. "And you had every opportunity to prevent this. You abandoned the boy out of your own fear and selfishness with the hope that things would improve without you in his life. You couldn't stand the thought of raising a child of your own – because inside that pedophilic mind of yours, you couldn't do right being a father. Because of you and the Catholic church's blind ignorance, so much blood has been shed, and I want you to watch as the final chapter of the story you could have prevented plays out."

John reached down, gripped me by my collar, and dragged me to the stairs leading to the main altar. He yanked me up and promptly tossed me down hard onto the floor with another thud. I could feel myself getting ready to lose consciousness. I was going to die here today in my own church. Inside, I began to pray for God to watch over me and John and to help out however He could.

I looked on through squinted and tear-filled eyes as John took the length of rope and threw the end with a noose over top of the cross high above the backdrop of the altar. He took the free end of the rope and wrapped it around the nearby organ, slowly inching the noose higher and higher before tying it into a knot. He pulled on the rope to test its strength and nodded.

"Are you ready, Priest?" he cackled.

I closed my eyes. This was it. John began to make his way toward me before veering right.

He swiftly moved toward the decorative shelves behind the altar that held religious artifacts and candles. He swept the holy items off and climbed up until he could reach the noose. He slid it over his neck and tightened it.

"No!" I croaked, more blood spilling from my mouth.

John tightened the noose.

"Malphas!" I bellowed with all my might.

I watched as John's eyes flashed a scarlet glint for a brief moment. John said nothing – then winked and smirked.

Before I could say anything else, I helplessly watched on in horror as he leapt from high above the altar. My eyes finally closed.

Chapter Forty-Four

November 22nd, 2023
John Tinsley

I'm falling and falling. Fade to black.

Epilogue

March 28th, 2024

The harsh winter was finally coming to a close. A recent warm day had caused the ground to begin to thaw. I stared down at the headstone before me, reading the inscription:

> *John Allen Tinsley*
> *Born May 2nd, 1990*
> *Died November 22nd, 2023*
> *'Forever in our hearts'*

I thought back to that fateful day. Social media, news outlets, and everything in between were reporting on John Tinsley – "The man who lost it all and finally snapped". It had been a feeding frenzy over the story when it broke. Articles outlining his tragic life and reaching his breaking point before murdering his dog, his friend, and taking his own life inside St. Anthony's Church.

I cleared my throat, tears welling up out of the corners of my eyes. I tugged at my collar and bent down to place a baseball at the base of the headstone.

I would never forget the final interaction I had with John. The interaction that left me questioning everything in my life. A real-life abomination in the flesh had walked into my church and had picked clean the bones of a man's life that deserved nothing but the best.

I remembered a quote I had read. It was by a man named Charles Baudelaire that said, "The greatest trick the Devil ever pulled was convincing the world he didn't exist."

And it was true. The Devil and His minions were out there creating havoc and committing atrocities all over the world, right under our noses. Spreading disease, plagues, violence, and any other unholy act meant to tear apart the very fabric of God's greatest creation – humanity.

Life is much easier to go through when pretending that that sort of underlying evil isn't out there. That it isn't pulling on strings like some demented puppet master. Or being a twig that locks up the cogs of a machine. Once that stick pulls free, a series of unfortunate and heinous events take place. Demons are those sticks, and we must remain vigilant in our fight against evil. We must remain strong in our faith.

In the moment meant to cause me to lose my belief, watching John take the leap that would end his life, I wound up finding all of my faith all over again. I was sure I had died. I closed my eyes and found myself shrouded in darkness when a beaming light of warmth came over me. I found myself waking up in the hospital several days later.

After a couple of surgeries and much physical therapy, I was back to my congregation and preaching the word of God. The town of Norton was so relieved to see my return and my first sermon had been an emotional one. I felt our church grow in faith on that very day as the warmth in my heart continued to expand. God saved me from death's clutches on that fateful day in November.

I looked at the tombstone next to John's and saw Megan's name scrawled on it. They were both resting together, and I hoped they were in a better place.

Off in the distance, I heard the sound of a young boy giggling. I peered to my left and saw him and his mother walking down the gravel path together. She wore a black dress and a wide brimmed black sunhat while the boy wore a plaid button-down shirt and khaki pants.

I saw the boy's eyes light up when he saw me. He made a mad dash across the grassy graveyard, leaving his shocked mother behind. She began to give chase after the young boy.

"Mason!" I heard the mother call out. "Mason!"

The young boy zigged and zagged between the headstones before standing idly by at my side. I glanced down at the young boy, giving a friendly smile. The boy looked up to me with hopeful eyes, smiled, and said, "Father, do you believe in ghosts?"

Acknowledgements

I just want to take a moment to thank all of the people that helped make this story happen. Without your help, words of encouragement, and advice, I might have still found myself helplessly log jammed with certain points of this story.

I want to give a big thank you to both of my parents, John and Sharon Ward. They are two of my biggest supporters and believers in what I am doing.

For the people that helped make this novel's engine rumble – I want to give personal thank you to fellow friends and authors:

Jyl Glenn – for alpha reading my first chapter and giving me the hope that this had the potential to be a big-time story.

Ben Young – for alpha reading the first few chapters of this novel early on and always being someone that I can turn to for advice or log jams during my creative and writing processes. Thank you for always being available to help. You are a rock star.

Lauren Young – for alpha reading all of Part One and making me feel like I was on the right path with the story and always giving words of encouragement. You are truly a light in the horror author community.

Nolan Emerson – for also alpha reading all of Part One. You have been one of my closest friends and confidants that I turn to with questions involving plot holes I see, talking through log jams, and helping me connect the dots when I am stuck. You're going to go places, my friend!

Alix Kampen – for alpha reading the first few chapters and always being a willing helper.

Alexandrea Christianson – for being a resource with regards to questions involving healthcare and making sure the information I was writing with was accurate. And also, for helping to give an in-depth answer to a question I had that Google would not allow me to search for! Ha!

Nick Roberts – for being a great friend and even when busy, still finding the time to answer questions I have, and for helping me believe in myself. Thank you.

Also, I want to thank each and every one of you that took the time to read my past work – with the Scareville series, and for continuing to make a guy feel special, even when he doesn't see it in himself. Thank you to everyone for taking the time to read this book and support my work. You are all the life blood that horror authors need to keep creating these terrifying tales. I hope you all enjoyed this dark slice of my mind.

A Note From The Author

This story was truly a labor of love. I ate, slept, wept, and sometimes bled (or so it felt) for this novel. There were many real-life experiences that I went through that served as major inspirations for parts of this novel. There were times where I truly started to believe this novel was cursed. From its conception to finished product, I ran into more hardships and difficult times that set me back from completing this story than I care to talk about. You can truly say I put my heart and soul into this novel.

Taking real life experiences and flipping it into a heartbreaking novel was a very difficult thing to do for me. It forced me to focus on some very painful times in my life and re-live some of those difficult and also horrifying times. Through those challenges that were thrown my way, I started to think along the lines of 'If this happened, what would've been the after effect?' or 'If things had gone like this, how would this have turned out?' – and through that line of questioning, I was able to craft this story in its entirety.

To give context, most of Part One was completely fictitious, save my love for baseball and Goosebumps as a youngster. My family is great and healthy – Thankfully! One thing that I incorporated outside of that, was the song *Simple Man* by Lynyrd Skynyrd. The story of Johnny's mother holding that song in a special place in their hearts because she would dance with him as a baby when he was fighting sleep to that song – that was something my real-life mother did. So, that song will always hold an absolutely special place in my heart and really had a strong impact on me in adding it to the scope of the story!

I won't get super into specifics in Part Two in terms of experiences I went through. The part about filming paranormal documentaries – though on a much smaller scale of success – was factual. I love my paranormal family and have had many great and also frightening experiences with them over the years.

The addition of Lucy to the story was based on a trio of dolls that I had purchased online. The seller never proclaimed them to be haunted, just that he wanted them gone. I had been an avid collector of all things creepy and unusual prior to this and felt they would fit nicely in my collection. The dolls originated from an abandoned orphanage in Australia – hence my use of an orphanage in this story to re-unite John with Lucy. When I took possession of the trio of dolls, things in my life immediately began to crumble around me. I began to watch my life dissolve until my mom had mentioned to me "It's probably all that creepy shit you collect – they're probably haunted and causing all of this." I countered quickly that, no, I had had all the items there well before things started falling apart. Then, the sudden realization hit me, and it felt like the veil had been lifted from my eyes. I had just brought those dolls into my home about a month prior.

I immediately drove back home, snapped a photo of the dolls, and offered them up to a fellow friend in the paranormal community named Eddie Pence. He had similar experiences with his life beginning to fall apart as well. Unexplainable bad luck and terrifying incidents in the home. The dolls now reside within

'The Dark Room' at a haunted museum in West Virginia called "Archive of the Afterlife" that has now since closed but does have plans to potentially re-open one day.

Through this time in my life, I did have a lot of terrifying paranormal occurrences and nightmares that I went through as well. There was also a lot of loss that I went through at that time too. I can't go into too much detail, but if you have questions, you can always reach out to me over social media as well! With all that being said, I want to touch on one of the more emotional aspects of this story, regarding the dog Bruce. I know this is a sensitive topic. I tried to write it in a way that would not be graphic, nor grotesque to read, but still would pull at your heartstrings. Bruce's real-life inspiration is from my dog, Bo. He's still alive and kicking and he is still my best friend. Back when a lot of the chaos was happening in my life, I was battling some real-life mental health issues and the daydream scenario at the bar in John's house was a real thing I daydreamed and contemplated about. It raised the question in my mind – if those dolls were still in my life, and were demonic – what would that demon do to crush my soul? And that was where that emotional part of the story was birthed from. It took a huge chunk of me to write that portion and physically pained me to do so. But at the end, I wanted people to feel the full weight of just how evil this demon truly was, and the lengths it would go to in order to achieve its ultimate goal.

I know this was an extremely bleak story, but I hope you found enjoyment in it. My goal was to write a horror story that would run people through all of the emotions before they were through with it. Hopefully, I achieved that for some of you.

I know this is a complete polar opposite of the middle grade horror series I have become known for. Scareville will continue on, as will my writing of adult horror stories, so stay tuned!

Join John Ward on Patreon:

Trigger Warnings

Look a little further down...

A little more...

- Self-Harm

- Miscarriage

- Graphic Violence

- Suicide

- Violence against animals (non-descript violence – still safe to read)

THE END?

Not if you want to dive into more of Crystal Lake Publishing's Tales from the Darkest Depths!

Check out our amazing website and online store or download our latest catalog here.

We always have great new projects and content on the website to dive into, as well as a newsletter, behind the scenes options, social media platforms, our own dark fiction shared-world series and our very own webstore. Our webstore even has categories specifically for KU books, non-fiction, anthologies, and of course more novels and novellas.

Readers...

Thank you for reading *A Blackened Heart, A Blackened Soul*. We hope you enjoyed this novel.

If you have a moment, please review *A Blackened Heart, A Blackened Soul* at the store where you bought it.

Help other readers by telling them why you enjoyed this book. No need to write an in-depth discussion. Even a single sentence will be greatly appreciated. Reviews go a long way to helping a book sell, and is great for an author's career. It'll also help us to continue publishing quality books.

Thank you again for taking the time to journey with Crystal Lake Publishing.

You will find links to all our social media platforms on our Linktree page.
https://linktr.ee/CrystalLakePublishing

Follow us on Amazon:

MISSION STATEMENT

Since its founding in August 2012, Crystal Lake has quickly become one of the world's leading publishers of Dark Fiction and Horror books. In 2023, Crystal Lake officially transitioned into an entertainment company, joining several other divisions, genres, and imprints, including Torrid Waters, Sinister Smile Press, Crystal Lake Comics, Crystal Lake Games, Crystal Cove Press, Crystal Lake Kids, Memento Mori Ink, and The House of Shadows & Ink on YouTube.

While we strive to present only the highest quality fiction and entertainment, we also endeavor to support authors along their writing journey. We offer our time and experience in non-fiction projects, as well as author mentoring and services, at competitive prices.

With several Bram Stoker Award wins and many other wins and nominations (including the HWA's Specialty Press Award), Crystal Lake puts integrity, honor, and respect at the forefront of our publishing operations.

We strive for each book and outreach program we spearhead to not only entertain and touch or comment on issues that affect our readers, but also to strengthen and support the Dark Fiction field and its authors.

Not only do we find and publish authors we believe are destined for greatness, but we strive to work with men and women who endeavor to be decent human beings who care more for others than themselves, while still being hard-working, driven, and passionate artists and storytellers.

Crystal Lake is and will always be a beacon of what passion and dedication, combined with overwhelming teamwork and respect, can accomplish. We endeavor to know each and every one of our readers, while building personal relationships with our authors, reviewers, bloggers, podcasters, bookstores, and libraries.

We will be as trustworthy, forthright, and transparent as any business can be, while also keeping most of the headaches away from our authors, since it's our job to solve the problems so they can stay in a creative mind. Which of course also means paying our authors.

We do not just publish books, we present to you worlds within your world, doors within your mind, from talented authors who sacrifice so much for a moment of your time.

There are some amazing small presses out there, and through collaboration and open forums we will continue to support other presses in the goal of helping authors and showing the world what quality small presses are capable of accomplishing. No one wins when a small press goes down, so we will always be there to support hardworking, legitimate presses and their authors. We don't see Crystal Lake as the best press out there, but we will always strive to be the best, strive to be the most interactive and grateful, and even blessed press around. No matter what happens over time, we will also take our mission very seriously while appreciating where we are and enjoying the journey.

What do we offer our authors that they can't do for themselves through self-publishing?

We are big supporters of self-publishing (especially hybrid publishing), if done with care, patience, and planning. However, not every author has the time or inclination to do market research, advertise, and set up book launch strategies. Although a lot of authors are successful in doing it all, strong small presses will always be there for the authors who just want to do what they do best: write.

What we offer is experience, industry knowledge, contacts and trust built up over years. And due to our strong brand and trusting fanbase, every Crystal Lake book comes with weight of respect. In time our fans begin to trust our judgment and will try a new author purely based on our support of said author.

To date we've published around 300 books, and with each launch we strive to fine-tune our approach, learn from our mistakes, and increase our reach. We continue to assure our authors that we're here for them and that we'll carry the weight of the launch and deal with third parties while they focus on their strengths—be it writing, interviews, blogs, signings, etc.

We also offer several mentoring packages to authors that include knowledge and skills they can use in both traditional and self-publishing endeavors. This includes Shadows & Ink Creators on our The House of Shadows & Ink YouTube channel and our Crystal Lake Academy.

We look forward to launching many new careers.

This is what we believe in. What we stand for. This will be our legacy.

Welcome to Crystal Lake Publishing—Where Stories Come Alive!

9 781968 532321